"You shouldn't say such things," she murmured. "Not unless you mean them."

"I agree."

Miss Sparrow stared at him in silence, then leaned forward as if to stand. Rafe began to move back, but she slid her arms around his neck. Her eyes widened, as if she was as surprised by the movement as he was, but then they darkened, burning with the same desire pulsing through him.

He raised an eyebrow. "Why, Miss Sparrow, are you trying to compromise my virtue?"

Her gaze searched his as her rapid inhalations filled his ears. "Only a little."

"Well, then," he said with a grin as he wrapped his arm around her waist. "I suppose I can allow that." He untangled his hand from her hair and slowly stroked down her jawline, tilting her chin up. "Just be gentle with me."

She moved closer until their mouths were a hairbreadth away. "I'll try."

THE REBEL
AND THE RAKE

ALSO BY EMILY SULLIVAN

A Rogue to Remember

THE REBEL
AND THE RAKE

A League of Scoundrels Novel

EMILY SULLIVAN

FOREVER

New York   Boston

Forever
Hachette Book Group
1290 Avenue of the Americas, New York, NY 10104
read-forever.com
twitter.com/readforeverpub

First Edition: December 2021

Forever is an imprint of Grand Central Publishing. The Forever name and logo are trademarks of Hachette Book Group, Inc.

The publisher is not responsible for websites (or their content) that are not owned by the publisher.

The Hachette Speakers Bureau provides a wide range of authors for speaking events. To find out more, go to www.hachettespeakersbureau.com or call (866) 376-6591.

ISBNs: 978-1-5387-3734-7 (mass market); 978-1-5387-3732-3 (ebook)

Printed in the United States of America

CW

10 9 8 7 6 5 4 3 2 1

To C. Thanks for the company.
And to J. Thank you for everything.

ACKNOWLEDGMENTS

Many thanks to Junessa Viloria for her enthusiasm for this story and her guidance. Thanks also to Amanda Jain for helping me figure out how to set it in Scotland. As I spent much of 2020 working on this book, my online friendships were more valuable than ever before. Thanks to Rebelle Island and the Slogging thread in particular for cheering me on and keeping me motivated. Thanks also to the Romancing the 20's group for their support and encouragement. Thanks to Elizabeth Everett for being so generous with her time and for her kind words about this book. And thank you to the many readers, reviewers, and bookstagrammers who took a chance on *A Rogue to Remember*. Debuting during a pandemic just a few months after giving birth was overwhelming at times, but I was so touched by the enthusiasm for that book. Thank you to my friends and family for having always been so supportive of my writing. It means more than I can say. And to my husband. Thank you for everything. Always.

CHAPTER ONE

~

October 1897
A village near Glasgow, Scotland

Sylvia Sparrow bolted from her work space, which was tucked away in a corner of Castle Blackwood's cavernous library, and rushed down one of its many hallowed halls toward the upstairs drawing room. If she didn't hurry, she would be late. Though it seemed unnecessary that someone as inconsequential as a lady's companion should be present for tea, her host, Mr. Wardale, had insisted after she had been absent the last few days—and even Sylvia wasn't bold enough to question one of the wealthiest men in England. As her serviceable leather boots thudded against the fine carpet, she prayed no one else caught her in such a state.

She had spent the last several hours transcribing her notes from this morning's session with her employer, Mrs. Crawford, which had covered a rather fascinating stint in Paris during the Second Empire, and had quite lost herself in the older woman's recollections. The septuagenarian had lived a life marked by romance, intrigue, and heartbreak and had finally decided to publish her exploits after a well-known publisher expressed interest, along with a hefty advance. It wasn't the usual set of duties for a companion, but Sylvia had first honed her secretarial skills while helping her late father with his academic work and was happy to provide assistance. She had also become an excellent typist during a brief stint working for a barrister in London after finishing her studies at Somerville College and had further developed her writing abilities while contributing a column to a weekly suffragist newspaper—but Sylvia had left out *those* little details during the interview process.

As far as Mrs. Crawford knew, she had hired the well-educated but genteelly impoverished daughter of a deceased country scholar. Not a woman who had once enjoyed a very independent London life complete with a room in a ladies' boardinghouse, fascinating friends, and a scandalous romance of her own.

And Sylvia was determined to keep it that way.

As she drew closer to the drawing room, Sylvia paused before a large gilt-framed mirror to smooth back a few loose strands of her unremarkable brown hair and straighten her navy tie. There. Now she looked perfectly respectable. No need to advertise that she was the kind of woman who raced down hallways in grand castles. That wasn't the sort of thing one should announce about oneself. Sylvia took a deep breath and continued on, taking care not to move *too* quickly.

Mr. Wardale preferred to host afternoon tea in a large, light-filled room that was part of the castle's newest wing, built sometime during the Regency. Sylvia had never met the eccentric millionaire before this trip, but he was a common fixture in both the business and gossip sections of the papers. Based on what she had observed thus far, he lived up to his reputation as a man with a healthy appetite for both work and play.

Sylvia entered and immediately searched for Lady Georgiana

Arlington, who was Mrs. Crawford's niece by marriage and her childhood friend. It was thanks to Georgiana that Sylvia was here at all and not living under her brother's thumb. Or worse.

Her friend was conversing with two other ladies on the opposite side of the room. All three were elegantly clad in airy afternoon gowns, but Georgiana, who possessed both a discerning eye and a comely figure, looked like a fashion plate come to life. Sylvia's dull tweed skirt and matching vest made her feel uncommonly dowdy by comparison. She stopped a few feet away and clasped her hands, which were becoming clammier by the second. The other ladies didn't give her any notice, but Georgiana caught her eye and nodded slightly.

While she waited, Sylvia pretended to be interested in a painting of a single brown horse in a field mounted on a nearby wall, just one of many at the castle.

"Terrible, isn't it?"

She turned swiftly to find Mr. Wardale by her shoulder. "No, sir. It has an...an...Arcadian charm."

"Don't spare my feelings, Miss Sparrow." He chuckled. "I had no hand in decorating this room. All credit should be given to the previous owner. In fact, I must insist upon it." Mr. Wardale's smooth voice bore no trace of the accent he must have had growing up. He was widely considered to be one of London's most charming bachelors—if a tad eccentric— who had successfully evaded the marriage trap, though many a debutante had set her cap for him over the years. Even now in late middle age with his blond hair thickly streaked with silver, he still exuded an innate vitality that made him seem years younger—and an intensity that was, at times, unnerving.

"And here I thought you simply had an inordinate interest

in bulldogs and brown horses," she replied, attempting a wry smile.

Amusement flickered in the man's dark gaze as he leaned closer. "If I had any interest in art, I assure you my tastes would be a tad more...*eclectic.*"

Sylvia couldn't help but shrink a little under his attention, along with the suggestive note in his voice. Why on earth had he bothered to approach her, of all people? This room was filled with the very cream of society, if one was impressed by that sort of thing.

"How is your work with Mrs. Crawford progressing?"

"Very well, sir."

"A fascinating woman. I'm quite looking forward to reading her memoirs." He grinned, and it brought to mind a powerful jungle cat toying with its prey. "If you need anything— pens, paper, more typewriter ribbons—please don't hesitate to ask."

Sylvia nodded. "Thank you. That is too kind."

"Good afternoon, Mr. Wardale." Georgiana's greeting put her immediately at ease.

"My lady," the man said with a courtly bow. "I understand you were among the party that walked to the falls this morning."

"We started to but then turned back at the threat of thunderclouds." She cast a contemptuous glance toward the window, which was now filled with blue sky and sunshine. "The weather is so changeable here. I'm hoping to mount another attempt tomorrow."

In addition to her philanthropic work, Georgiana was known for her seemingly boundless energy, which she applied to everything from planning a lavish charity ball to a simple

4

afternoon picnic. It was a trait Sylvia didn't share with her friend. She would much rather curl up alone with a good book and a cup of tea than traipse around the forest or attend a ball, not that Sylvia had ever been invited to one.

"A fine idea."

They exchanged a few more empty pleasantries before their host moved on.

Sylvia let out a breath once he was out of earshot. "You certainly took your time."

"Once Lady Delacorte starts talking, it's difficult to get a word in. But I wouldn't think conversing with Mr. Wardale is exactly a hardship."

"No, but I can't imagine why he bothered with me."

Georgiana gave her an amused look before changing the subject. "I think Aunt Violet noticed your late arrival. You got lost in your work, didn't you?"

"I was reviewing the notes I made this morning," Sylvia admitted. "Your aunt was telling me how she met her second husband. The one who knew Manet."

"Oh, yes." Georgiana laughed. "The Comte who was actually a civil servant's son. I love that story."

"I think he was her favorite of the lot."

"Well, all *he* did was make up an identity to impress her. The other three husbands were far more destructive."

The late Mr. Crawford, her last—and, she often stressed, *final* husband, had made a number of poor investments before having the decency to die, which had further induced Mrs. Crawford to publish her memoirs.

"Yet another point for eternal spinsterhood," Sylvia quipped.

Georgiana ignored the remark and subtly gestured to Sylvia's hands. "You forgot your gloves again."

Sylvia's cheeks heated as she rubbed at the ink stain on her finger. "So I did." It had been ages since she'd had any reason to bother with the conventions of polite society. Back home at Hawthorne Cottage, she had never worn gloves, as they were hardly practical when completing the many household chores that needed to be done. Tomorrow she must bring the blasted things with her.

What does it matter? No one here would mistake you for a lady.

She was nothing more than a glorified secretary. And lucky for that.

"Here comes the grande dame now," Georgiana muttered. Sylvia quickly put her hands behind her back and turned to greet her employer.

"There you are, Miss Sparrow," the older woman bellowed as she shuffled toward them. She leaned heavily on her cane, likely weighed down by the massive necklace, earrings, and bracelets she insisted on wearing no matter the occasion, but anyone who thought her enfeebled quickly learned otherwise. "I trust you finished this morning's notes?"

"Very nearly, Mrs. Crawford. I had to stop in order to come here."

The woman let out a disappointed huff. "Well, see that you have something for me to review by this evening."

Sylvia bowed her head. "Of course, madam."

Mrs. Crawford gave a sniff of approval. "Come along, then," she ordered, before turning away to accost another guest.

"I think someone wants a little bedtime reading," Georgiana whispered.

Sylvia stifled a laugh. "Who can blame her? You should have seen the glint in her eyes when she talked about the 'not-Comte.' She made a particular point to tell me he had the largest *hands* she had ever seen."

Georgiana barely had time to smother a most unladylike snort into her handkerchief. "Oh, bless the old dragon. I'm actually starting to be glad I came," she added under her breath.

Mrs. Crawford had insisted Georgiana accompany them to Scotland, arguing that the viscountess had been spreading herself too thin between her charitable endeavors. Georgiana reluctantly agreed, mostly for Sylvia's benefit.

Before Sylvia could respond, she was interrupted by the entrance of several maids pushing tea carts. Georgiana nimbly stepped away. "Oh, you must try the jam tarts."

As they moved to join Mrs. Crawford, a group of men who had been sitting by the massive stone fireplace rose. She barely spared them a glance at first. It would be the same mix of pallid, weak-chinned aristocrats as the day before. Mr. Wardale wasn't exactly eclectic when it came to the company he kept. But as the group approached the tea carts, Sylvia noticed a man she had privately dubbed "Lord Lecher" after his tendency to openly stare at ladies' chests conversing with someone and cheerfully slapping him on the back. The recipient had stooped to meet Lord Lecher's middling height, but now he laughed and fully straightened, displaying every impressive inch of his lean, long-muscled form.

How on earth had *he* escaped her notice?

They had been at Castle Blackwood for a number of days, and in that time, Sylvia had not come across any tall, broad-shouldered, and strong-jawed men. But then there had been so much battling for her attentions—settling Mrs. Crawford, repeating everything anyone said to her thrice, and finding the time and space to complete her duties.

It wasn't until the man gave her a perfectly polite smile and extended his arm to let her pass ahead of him that she realized she had been quite obviously staring. Because not only was he tall, broad-shouldered, and strong-jawed—he was absolutely *devastating*.

And well he knew it.

"What is keeping you, child?" Mrs. Crawford bellowed over her shoulder.

To her profound embarrassment, Sylvia had come to a very abrupt and very noticeable stop.

The older woman may have had trouble hearing, but she had eyes that rivaled a bird of prey. Now she turned her sharp gaze directly on Sylvia. "Don't tell me you never encountered a handsome rogue or two in your little village."

Oh, dear Lord.

Sylvia's neck grew impossibly hot. It wasn't that Mrs. Crawford intended to embarrass her. The woman was simply beyond such trivial concerns at this stage of life. A group of bloodthirsty highwaymen could enter the room at this exact moment and she would probably ask which one was the best shot. Now she waved her bejeweled wrist in the man's direction. "You will have ample opportunity to gape at Mr. Davies during tea, like the rest of us, but for now I need to *sit down*."

Sylvia inhaled deeply before she dared to speak. "Of course, Mrs. Crawford. My apologies." She immediately moved aside to let her employer pass and cast a cautious glance at Mr. Davies. His polite smile now held the barest hint of a smirk, the faint lines around his mouth suggesting he did so often, and their eyes met for one excruciating moment. Long enough to note his were the exact shade of melted chocolate. Then his gaze swiftly moved to Georgiana. Sylvia got the distinct impression that she had been assessed, found wanting, and roundly dismissed.

"Lady Arlington, good afternoon," he said in a rich baritone that trailed lazily down Sylvia's spine. "You look as lovely as ever."

"Why, thank you," she said, accepting the compliment with her usual grace. "Wonderful to see you again, Mr. Davies."

"The sentiment is mutual, my lady." He then arched a dark brow and leaned toward her. "But don't let your aunt think I'll forget that 'rogue' comment."

Georgiana gave him one of her famous serene smiles. "Oh dear. I suppose it's pistols at dawn, then," she quipped. "Miss Sparrow, will you be my second?"

"It would be an honor," she mumbled after an awkward pause. As if it weren't already humiliating enough to have her rather obvious ogling pointed out, she couldn't just stand there while the man proceeded to flirt with Georgiana.

Without another word, Sylvia strode ahead, dutifully took the teacup a maid handed to her, and sat down beside Mrs. Crawford. Several other guests were already seated, none of whom bothered to acknowledge her. It was just as well. Ladies' companions weren't supposed to garner attention from anyone except their employers. As Sylvia took in the finely decorated room, Georgiana approached them, now on the arm of Mr. Davies. He smoothly pulled out the chair beside Sylvia, and Georgiana sat down. No man had ever done such a thing for Sylvia before—not that she had ever wanted one to. She was independent. She could sit in a blasted *chair* by herself. And yet that slight tightening in her chest was most certainly from envy. Sylvia cast another subtle glance at him through the veil of her lashes and noted sharp cheekbones and a strong, straight nose. She was tempted to call him beautiful, if not for the distinct air of superiority that seemed to emanate from him. Just then the afternoon light glinted off his glossy hair, a shade lighter than his eyes and perfectly styled. There. A flaw. She couldn't possibly be attracted to a man who paid such exacting attention to his own appearance, even if the results were sublime.

Georgiana flashed him another smile. Her bronze tresses looked even more radiant than usual. "Thank you, sir." He returned her smile and stepped away.

Sylvia released a breath. Now Mr. Davies would take his unexpected handsomeness and be on his way. Then she could go back to several minutes ago, when she had been entirely unaware of his existence. Unfortunately, the man took a seat directly across from her instead. Their eyes immediately met, and Sylvia barely had time to conceal her surprise as a hot flush fanned out across her cheeks. Of course the fiend noticed. Just as one corner of his full mouth began to turn up, Sylvia pretended to take great interest in the richly patterned carpet. It looked old and expensive, just like everything else in the castle.

"Mr. Davies," Georgiana began in her cut-glass voice, "allow me to introduce Miss Sparrow, my aunt's companion."

Sylvia swallowed her sigh and reluctantly lifted her gaze. Now she'd have to look at him again. And for longer this time.

"Delighted to meet you," he said, his eyes practically twinkling. "I understand you've taken up residence in the library."

All Sylvia could manage was a nod, as her throat had apparently decided to stop working. He waited a moment, no doubt expecting her to make some kind of vocal response, as was generally expected in social situations, but instead she buried the screaming impulse to keep his attention and looked away. *No.* Let him think she was an absolute dullard. At that moment a maid appeared with a tray of warm cinnamon-scented buns. Sylvia had never been so thankful for the appearance of pastry. Anything to distract her.

But just as she brought it to her lips, Georgiana leaned over and whispered by her ear, "Mr. Davies is the younger son of the late Earl of Fairfield."

Sylvia glanced over. He was now talking with Lady Taylor-Smyth, a glamorous widow who hadn't deigned to acknowledge Sylvia's presence. She focused on the faint pang of disappointment that lanced through her chest. Of course. Another aristocrat. All the more reason for her to ignore him.

"But his mother was a notorious actress, and the marriage caused a rift with the earl's older children."

That was slightly more interesting.

"Rumor has it he joined the Royal Navy under a false name as a boy years ago. Though after his father's death he developed a predilection for more *idle* entertainments. Since then he's been living mostly abroad, but he returned to London last spring. He's made quite an impression already."

Just then the woman beside Mr. Davies let out a giddy laugh, and he flashed her a raffish grin. Sylvia had a fine idea of how he managed that.

"I'm not sure why you're telling me any of this," she hissed as softly as possible.

Even Georgiana's shrug was impossibly elegant. "I thought you'd like to know."

Sylvia's mouth tightened. "Well, I *don't*," she insisted.

Georgiana looked unconvinced. "Suit yourself."

"What are you young ladies whispering about?" Mrs. Crawford barked, startling them both. Sylvia began coughing as she nearly choked on her bite of bun, and Mrs. Crawford gave her a look of concern that a stranger could easily confuse for extreme irritation. "You aren't feeling *ill*, are you?"

Sylvia coughed a few more times and managed to shake her head. "No, Mrs. Crawford. But thank you for asking." Out of the corner of her eye, she saw Mr. Davies turn toward her.

"Are you certain? Now you're turning rather red." Then she leaned closer and lowered her voice to a mere yell. "Do you need to be sick?"

The older woman was constantly worried about the health of everyone around her but never her own. Sylvia took a breath before answering. "I assure you, I am quite well," she said, taking care to enunciate each word. Loudly. Across from her, Mr. Davies's shoulders trembled slightly.

Mrs. Crawford eyed her for a moment. She didn't look the least bit convinced. "All right, then. But don't stand on ceremony here. If you feel overcome, you have my permission to leave. *Immediately*." She then resumed her conversation with the ancient man to her left.

"Thank you, madam," Sylvia said with all the dignity she could muster under the current circumstances.

Whatever was ailing Mr. Davies worsened. She cast a sidelong glance at him, but it appeared he was *laughing*. He flashed her a conspiratorial smile free of artifice, and for a very brief moment the room faded away. No more richly bejeweled ladies, gentlemen in country tweeds, or bustling maids trying to hide their exhaustion. It was just the two of them, staring at each other as if they were sharing some delightful secret, some kind of elemental recognition, of like finding like. A feeling of warmth that came very close to comfort began to sweep over her as his gaze seemed to move beyond the perfectly modest, carefully bland exterior Sylvia had created, exposing her true form.

She inhaled sharply at the thought and belatedly realized she had been on the verge of smiling back, like a fool. Like a woman who actually *wanted* to be noticed by the gorgeous son of an earl. The teacup she had been gripping clattered against the saucer, thoroughly breaking whatever spell had just come over her.

"I—I think I will go after all." She had meant to address Mrs. Crawford, but her eyes were still entangled with Mr. Davies's. His smile began to fade as she forced herself to turn away.

Mrs. Crawford distractedly waved a hand, too fixated on the man to her left, but Georgiana squeezed her wrist. "Do you want me to come with you?"

Her sympathy made Sylvia feel even more ridiculous. "No. Please. Stay here. Enjoy yourself."

Georgiana opened her mouth, likely to argue, but then glanced toward Mr. Davies and gave a reluctant nod. "I'll check on you before supper."

Sylvia whispered her thanks and stood. Mr. Davies immediately rose, followed a beat later by the other gentlemen, several of whom grumbled under their breath at the momentary inconvenience. She managed a nod as she excused herself, taking care not to look directly at him. But as she carefully picked her way through the room, she felt a heavy gaze tracking her every step, burning the back of her neck until she disappeared through the doorway.

CHAPTER TWO

❧

"M r. Davies?"

Rafe tore his gaze from the doorway and turned to Lady Taylor-Smyth, who had apparently just asked him a question he hadn't heard a word of.

Damn. That wasn't like him.

"Terribly sorry," he said, flashing her his most rakish smile. "Could you repeat that?"

Good thing Rafe had a reputation for not being particularly sharp. The woman looked amused rather than irritated. "I asked if you had ever been to Scotland before," she crooned, not at all noticing the source of his distraction.

He shook his head. "I've visited nearly every part of the Continent, but I had never been north of York until today."

"How exciting for you." The alluring baroness's dark eyes stared intently into his own. "I've been coming to this area since I was a girl. My granny was a Glaswegian. I'd be happy to show you around, if you'd like." Then she lowered her voice. "Just the two of us."

The suggestive note in her words made it very clear what sorts of things they could get up to alone. Only five minutes

14

in her company and she was already propositioning him. That was certainly a first.

As she continued to describe the many charms of the Scottish Lowlands, Rafe tilted his head to at least appear like he was listening to the woman this time, but his mind was still occupied by the one who had practically fled his company.

Yet another first, but a much less welcome one.

Miss Sparrow was pretty enough to catch the eye, with a mass of light brown hair trying valiantly to escape its pins and fine, almost elfin features, yet most people wouldn't pay her much notice while she stood next to the outrageous Mrs. Crawford or the voluptuous Lady Arlington, whom he had met before in London.

But then, Rafe wasn't most people.

On first glance Miss Sparrow appeared to be little more than a timid lady's companion finding her feet with an overbearing employer, but her ink-stained fingers and slightly rumpled clothing gave her away. She reminded him of those confounding New Women types he saw in London sometimes, riding bicycles, working in offices, and meeting in groups to discuss plans to win the vote. Was this Miss Sparrow one of them?

The idea was rather intriguing.

There was a hidden sharpness vibrating in her just below the surface, if one only bothered to look. Rafe strongly suspected that she possessed a bone-dry sense of humor she likely took great pains to conceal in front of her employer, except the poor girl had a pair of enormous gray eyes that betrayed even her most fleeting emotion. It was the hint of challenge in her gaze that had so thoroughly arrested him mere moments ago, before it turned sour.

Rafe had never minded acting like a useless aristocrat before, as his work on behalf of the Crown required him to play up his blue-blooded roots, but the sort of people he usually caroused with were cut from the same cloth. Seeing that brief little flit of disapproval pass over Miss Sparrow's features had unexpectedly stung.

Lady Arlington also watched Miss Sparrow's exit with a look of concern very different from the tranquil expression she normally wore. She glanced toward him and immediately turned away, her face now carefully blank. Rafe brought his teacup to his lips and took a long, considering sip despite the warning note echoing through his head.

He didn't have time to be distracted by an awkward young woman suffering from a bout of nerves. He had arrived at the castle only hours ago at the behest of his host, who suspected one of his guests was behind a series of anonymous threats. But Rafe couldn't ignore the prickling sensation at the back of his neck. The one that began when his eyes met Miss Sparrow's from across the room. The one that he suspected she felt too, until she bolted from her chair. She may have found him distasteful, may think of him as nothing more than a callow rogue, but something else had crossed that lovely little face of hers before she left. Something like fear.

Rafe shook his head and recalled his purpose. Wardale thought this would be an excellent chance for him to meet the other guests, most of whom he already knew. It was the usual mix of aristocrats and nouveau riche. Rafe shoved all thoughts of Miss Sparrow aside and focused on performing the role of charming dilettante. But in between his jokes and bon mots, his attention was drawn more and more to Lady Arlington, who had grown steadily quieter since Miss Sparrow left. Renowned for her gold-spun beauty and highly respected for her charitable efforts, she was married to a viscount who was nearly twenty years her senior. Rafe didn't object to the age gap, as his own parents were similarly paired, but Viscount Arlington's vicious streak was legendary. He was particularly harsh on the many female workers who populated the garment factories he had been given as an inducement to marry well below his station. There were also whispers that the viscount was furious that his marriage of nearly a decade still hadn't resulted in an heir.

How could such an effervescent woman find any kind of happiness with a man like that? Perhaps this Miss Sparrow had proved to be a valuable source of friendship. From what little Rafe had observed, the two women seemed remarkably at ease with one another. Like friends. Like *old* friends.

Rafe moved closer to Mrs. Crawford. He had to practically shout before she acknowledged him. "May I ask how long Miss Sparrow has been your companion?"

The great lady frowned in consideration. "Oh, about two months, I'd say. She's helping me write my memoirs, you know. She's a sharp girl and takes excellent notes. I'm planning to take her on a tour of Egypt after Christmas. At my age I simply *refuse* to endure another English winter."

"How generous of you."

"Yes, it is. She's never gone anywhere, poor thing. Spent nearly all her life in some miserable little village near Oxford. Hollychortle or Chortlewood. Something silly like that."

"Where did you ever find her?"

"That was all Georgiana. She's involved in some women's employment society. Teaches them skills so they can earn a living and then places them in positions. That sort of thing."

Rafe nodded. Interesting. "And I take it Miss Sparrow had undergone training at this society?"

"No. She's had some formal schooling. But she did write to them asking for help finding a position in London after her father died, some middling scholar I've never heard of." She considered this for a moment and then airily waved a hand. "I can't recall the particulars exactly, but it is no matter. Her references were excellent, and her work has been far superior to my last secretary, a gentleman down from Cambridge who believed he was *much too important* to be working on the memoirs of an old lady."

"He sounds like a fool."

"Indeed, sir," Mrs. Crawford heartily agreed.

He then waited a moment before turning to Lady Arlington, who was watching him closely. "So, then, you did not know Miss Sparrow before that?" he asked lightly, with a distinct edge of polite boredom.

The viscountess continued to sip her tea, but her fingers tightened ever so slightly around the delicate porcelain handle. "No, Mr. Davies." Then she met his gaze with a piercing blue stare. "I did not."

He smiled at the lie. So that was how she flourished in a marriage to the viscount—swathed in silk with a backbone made of steel.

"How fortunate for you both," Rafe said. "I confess I thought she had been with you much longer."

Lady Arlington returned his smile. "We are very lucky to have found Miss Sparrow."

And this time he believed every word.

* * *

After tea ended, some guests adjourned to the billiard room while others took advantage of the sunshine to tour Castle Blackwood's legendary labyrinth, which had been a point of interest in the area for nearly two hundred years. Wardale met Rafe's eyes and gave him a subtle nod before he left with a lady on each arm. There had been time for only a brief introduction after Rafe's arrival before the guests had started congregating for tea, so they'd planned to rendezvous afterward in Wardale's study.

Rafe slowly made his way upstairs, taking in the timeworn interior's vaulted stone ceiling, while a mixture of questionable art, faded tapestries, and other baronial memorabilia hung from the walls. He had been in his fair share of stately residences over the years, but nothing that came close to the pure majesty of a damned *castle*. One could practically feel time passing through with every breath.

"And now it's in the hands of a man born in an East End slum," Rafe murmured.

John Wardale was a man of obscene wealth and even more influence, having pulled himself out of grinding poverty to eventually become one of the most successful land developers in the country. These days he had a finger in nearly every promising business in England, whether as an investor or member of the board or outright owner. The blue bloods held their noses at his East End roots as they attempted to curry his favor for their own endeavors, while the working class saw him as something of a modern-day folk hero.

A generation ago such an ascent would have been unimaginable. Today it was extraordinary.

Rafe couldn't help but respect the man. He had made something of himself instead of simply being born lucky. As he turned down the hallway that led to the study, Rafe was surprised to find the door open and Wardale already sitting behind a massive rosewood desk. Based on the furious scribbling he was currently engaged in, he had been there for a while.

Wardale glanced up. "Ah, Davies. Come in. And close the door, will you?"

"I didn't mean to keep you waiting."

The rest of the room was decorated in dark colors and heavy furniture, while tobacco scented the air, lest anyone was foolish enough to mistake this as anything other than a supremely masculine lair.

Wardale set aside his work. "One of the first things I did when I came here was explore all the back stairwells and secret passageways. This place has more twists and turns than a rookery," he said with a laugh. "Now I know it like the back of my hand." Rafe was pleased to see that Wardale didn't try to hide his roots, unlike other self-made men he had met. "Have a seat. I understand you met with your brother this morning?"

Rafe nodded. He had returned from a delightful evening spent in the bed of an elegant older widow to find Gerard Davies, his older half brother, current earl, and all-around twat in his sitting room. Rafe could count the number of times they had met on one hand, but Gerard had recently been given a prominent position in the Home Office, thanks to his support of the current government, and wasted no time all but ordering Rafe to take the next train to Glasgow. Though Rafe technically worked for the Foreign Office, men with his particular set of skills were few and far between, so it was common for Crown agents to carry out missions for different branches of government when called upon. Still, Scotland seemed an odd place to send him given the growing worries about German militarization and rising tensions with the French regarding control of Egypt—not to mention a likely conflict with the Boers on the horizon. But while Rafe would have loved to experience the thrill of denying Gerard something, the truth was he had begun to grow tired of London, especially after having spent much of the last few months mingling with society to ensure he was the last man *anyone* would suspect of working for the Crown. In this case, the desire to leave town and meet the legendary John Wardale proved to be stronger than his contempt for Gerard.

"Yes, but he wasn't very forthcoming with the details, sir," Rafe began as he sank into a sumptuous leather armchair. "He mentioned that you had recently purchased the castle and suspected a group of Scottish separatists in the area were stirring up trouble."

Gerard had also made it clear that, seeing as Mr. Wardale was a "great friend" to the prime minister, Rafe's assistance would not go unnoticed.

"The previous owners descended from a branch of the Chisolms," Wardale began. "They were well liked for the most part, even though the first baron betrayed the Jacobins in exchange for more land and a title from the Crown. Robert Chisolm, the last baron, was typical of large landowners of his time. Kept things going along as best he could while making as few changes as possible. He married an heiress, which helped keep the castle from falling into too much disrepair, but they never had any children. She's left for the Riviera, while his heir was a distant cousin living in America without the means or inclination to own a Scottish castle. They were quite happy to have me take the place off their hands." Wardale's feline smile indicated that it had been a very good deal indeed.

"But this unrest, as you described it, was unexpected," Rafe supplied.

The smile vanished. "To put it mildly. I've made it widely known that I plan to bring Castle Blackwood and the surrounding land into the modern era: electricity, running water, and new roofs for the tenants, a new schoolhouse for the village— and I have the capital to do it. Yet a small, very vocal faction can't get past my place of birth. These Scots have been emboldened by the calls for Irish Home Rule and have gotten it in their heads to demand the same thing." He then reached into a drawer and threw a packet onto the desktop. "These are just a fraction of the letters I've received since the sale of the castle a few months ago. I offered to keep the original staff on and gave pensions to those who wished to retire, but that wasn't enough to appease everyone."

Rafe leafed through the small stack of paper. They were all short and to the point, and written in the same childlike scrawl, though the writer bothered to switch hands for a few:

Leave ye English RAT.
Banish the SNAKES from Scotland.
The only good Englishman is a DEAD one.

"Might it not be better to contact Special Branch?" Rafe asked as he set down the papers. "They certainly have more experience in these matters than I do."

Wardale scoffed at the suggestion. "They're no better than a pack of street thugs. I need discretion. That's why you're here. Besides, it isn't only the threats I'm concerned about."

"Yes, I understand some documents had gone missing."

Wardale nodded. "They were taken from the desk in my bedroom. The perpetrator must have known I was receiving sensitive information. That sort of thing isn't usually announced on the envelope, you see."

"And usually not sent to civilians," Rafe couldn't help adding.

Wardale raised an eyebrow. "I know you must think me a fool, Davies. I suppose I can't blame you, given the circumstances, but I am exactly the sort of man this government needs. One who knows how to get things done. Not another mindless bureaucrat determined to needlessly tie everything up in red tape." It was on the tip of Rafe's tongue to point out that adherence to that so-called red tape helped ensure the rule of law, but he remained silent as Wardale went on.

"I asked your brother to contact you specifically. The PM is aware of the work you have done involving that nasty business with Sir Alfred. He thinks you have great promise. And know how to keep things quiet."

Rafe narrowed his eyes. After spending most of the last decade abroad, he had returned to London specifically to deal with the mess the late legendary spymaster had created. His goal hadn't been to cover up the misdeeds of Sir Alfred but rather to prevent such an occurrence from ever happening again. "Then you must also be aware of my feelings about powerful men who are left unchecked."

Wardale chuckled. "You're awfully self-righteous for someone who makes his living lying to people."

Rafe paused before he answered, choosing his words with the utmost care. "I believe that my work can save lives by avoiding unnecessary escalations that lead to conflict."

"Then you can see why this mole must be found and this

group of rabble-rousers snuffed out before it goes any further."
Wardale leaned forward, his dark eyes glinting with purpose.
"You and I both know an independent Scotland will never
happen, yet these men are willing to destroy anyone and anything in their path. Help me stop them."

Rafe didn't exactly object to the idea of an independent
Scotland. And he knew better than most that the Crown would
never relinquish one of its jewels unless forced to, but he
avoided answering by posing a question. "Why do you suspect
one of your guests is involved?"

Wardale snorted. "The timing is a little too convenient,
wouldn't you say? The documents went missing only *after* the
house party began."

"Perhaps this is unrelated to the threats you have received."

"It bloody well may not be related, but in the meantime, I
want all avenues explored."

"I suppose you won't tell me what the documents contained?"

"No," Wardale ground out. "Those papers carry sensitive
information that would be of *great* interest to Her Majesty's
enemies and threaten Crown rule. If you do succeed in finding
them, it is in your best interest not to read any of it."

Either these documents really did contain highly sensitive
information that even someone like Rafe couldn't be privy to,
or they discussed something deliciously tawdry. He tried to
conceal his curiosity.

"Noted. Have any of the guests been in your bedroom?"

Wardale's gaze immediately shuttered. "I don't suspect any
of the ladies."

"That isn't what I asked," Rafe said as politely as he could
manage.

"But that's all you'll get," Wardale snapped. "Focus on the men. Start with those with Scottish ancestry."

The tension that had been slowly gathering in Rafe's shoulders twisted sharply. "May I remind you that I'm here as a favor—"

"Come now, Davies," Wardale began, taking on a syrupy tone that turned Rafe's stomach. "Haven't you ever engaged in a little quid pro quo? What will it take to keep you happy?"

The voice in Rafe's head screamed, *Get up. Get up and leave right now.* He refused to be beholden to anyone, especially this man. But a mission like this was an unusually delicate matter. Possibly a dangerous one.

Before Rafe could answer, Wardale pressed on. "I know you live and breathe your work, just like I do. And I also know what it means to be constantly proving yourself to men who look down their well-bred noses at you," he added with surprising emotion. "Think of what I could do for your career. For your future. In no time you could have more power than any man downstairs. Even more than your brother."

Rafe steepled his fingers. He had been recruited years ago by Sir Alfred to carry out special assignments for the government. The spymaster's death had exposed a number of security breaches, and Rafe had spent most of the summer and fall cleaning up the mess left behind while simultaneously forming a plan for a new, more secure organization with strict protocols that didn't revolve around the whims of a single man.

"Distrust between branches of government created a situation that was exploited by Sir Alfred," Rafe began. "There needs to be one solely dedicated to intelligence gathering and carrying out missions with highly trained staff. Britain has been lagging behind her adversaries since Napoleon. We don't even have a codebreakers department anymore."

When he had brought this up to Gerard, his brother had wrinkled his nose and called it *ungentlemanly*. It was a refrain Rafe had heard many times before from men who were all too happy to use the information he procured while turning their noses up at the process. Gerard had begrudgingly agreed to pass on his proposal, but Rafe didn't entirely trust him. However, Wardale looked intrigued, and the prime minister in particular had an avid interest in foreign affairs. Surely *they* would see the advantages of his proposition.

"If I uncover the mole, I want the funds to form and manage an elite group of agents."

Wardale leaned back in his chair and stared at Rafe for a long moment. "I can ensure that the PM is informed of your proposal and give him my full support," he finally announced. "What say you?"

For years the work had been more than enough to sustain Rafe, but perhaps he had been a fool to stop at the little corner he had carved out for himself while other, more privileged men bungled the opportunities handed to them on silver platters. Like Wardale, Rafe couldn't make the blood that ran in his veins any bluer, but he could rise up the ladder of power, if given a proper chance.

Even he couldn't deny it was a tempting prospect.

"All right," he said. "Who do you suggest I start with, then?"

Wardale's smile returned. "There's a good chap. I made a list for you," he said as he passed over a slip of paper. "I want to know everything you uncover, even if it doesn't seem relevant. We can't be too careful. My majordomo has been instructed to give you whatever you require. And here." He held out a ring with several keys. "These should open all the guest rooms in the house."

Rafe hesitated a moment. He had undertaken similar tasks dozens of times—and hadn't once felt any qualms about it. It was rather an inconvenient time to develop a conscience, but this seemed excessive even to him. So far he had observed nothing that suggested this theory Wardale had pieced together. But men like him saw enemies in all corners, usually with good reason. And if one of the guests did take the letter for nefarious purposes, Rafe could uncover it easily enough. No one suspected anything was amiss so far, and even Rafe's sudden appearance at the castle was readily accepted without much comment. Over the last few months he made sure he was known as just the sort of fellow to turn up somewhere unannounced and uninvited. If the guilty party was among them, they were extremely confident. And Rafe would give them no reason to suspect otherwise.

"We *are* in agreement. Aren't we, Davies?" Wardale raised an eyebrow, still holding out the key ring.

Think of your career. Of all that you could accomplish. All you could be known for.

Rafe clasped the ring between his fingers, ignoring the unsettling chill that raced up his arm. "Yes, sir. Completely."

CHAPTER THREE

❧

S ylvia returned to the blessedly empty suite she shared with
Mrs. Crawford and Georgiana. She would ask to have a
dinner tray brought up instead of attending supper later. Then
she should have the evening to herself until Mrs. Crawford
came in demanding to be read to. The woman possessed several strange habits, but Sylvia had come to enjoy this little
nighttime ritual. They were halfway through a rather sensational—and absurd—Gothic novel, as her employer had an
absolutely burning passion for penny dreadfuls.

Her room, slightly bigger than a closet, was just off the
communal sitting room. She entered and went to the washstand
in the corner. Though her stomach had indeed begun to roil, it
was hardly the reason behind her abrupt exit. Sylvia splashed
water over her face and then pressed a soft cotton towel to
her cheeks.

It was a ridiculous feeling, of course. A momentary panic
brought on by her overwrought nerves. Whatever she thought
she saw in his gaze, Mr. Davies couldn't read her mind and
certainly couldn't see into her heart.

He doesn't know a thing.

Sylvia closed the door behind her and sank to her knees in front of her travel trunk.

No one does.

She ran her trembling fingers over the smooth edge and lifted the lid, then began removing each item until the bottom of the trunk was exposed.

Not even Georgiana.

Sylvia pulled out the false bottom and gave a huff of relief. The plain brown envelope was still there. Still untouched. Just as it had been days ago when she first packed it away after retrieving it from Mr. Wardale's bedroom. After noting the movements of both the upstairs maids and her host's valet, she entered during a time the room would be empty and found the envelope in a bedside table drawer, just as her blackmailer had predicted. Her hands had shaken for nearly an hour afterward as she'd waited for someone to call out her misdeed and banish her from the property. But the day had continued on as usual, as if the theft hadn't occurred. As if she were a perfectly ordinary lady's companion.

Sylvia's blackmailer had warned her against opening the envelope, claiming that the information inside was *highly sensitive* and could put her at risk. She snorted as she recalled the warning, just as she had on the afternoon a nondescript letter had appeared sans return address a mere day before they left for Scotland. It still seemed like a wildly far-fetched description meant to put her off, but she obeyed anyway. Whatever the envelope contained, whether it was of a personal nature or involving one of Mr. Wardale's many business ventures, she wanted as little to do with it as possible, and the more ignorant she remained, the better.

Her mysterious blackmailer had laid everything else out

quite plainly: the writer knew about her past as an advocate for social reform, the scandal that had resulted, and that Georgiana had deceived her husband and aunt so Sylvia would be hired as a lady's companion. They had even included one of her more radical columns from *The Defender*, the newspaper she had once written for, in which she argued in favor of equal wages for women to support their economic independence rather than relying on marriage. The truth would be revealed if she didn't provide the information they demanded, beginning with the envelope she had taken from Mr. Wardale's room.

Sylvia simply couldn't let that happen.

She stared at the envelope until her eyes began to water, until her fingernails bit into the paper's rough grain. She had already lost so much these last few years: her home, her family, her future. She couldn't lose Georgiana, too. Her dear friend faced everything life had thrown at her with a serene pragmatism, but the mask Georgiana wore for the world was for her own protection. And she would be roundly punished by the viscount for anything that marred the faultless image he demanded.

So get on with it, then.

That, at least, was something Sylvia could do. As she placed the envelope back in the false bottom of the trunk and repacked her things, the fear that had propelled her to her room was slowly replaced by the guilt that had been burning through her for days. But there was nothing she could do now. The chance to come clean had passed when she'd placed that envelope in the bottom of her trunk instead of taking it directly to Georgiana. Her friend had been full of understanding when Sylvia had been abruptly turned out of her childhood home thanks to her brother's reckless spending, but there were some things even Sylvia could not share. Some secrets she needed to keep safe. And shouldering this burden alone would have to be the price.

* * *

Later that evening Rafe returned to his room ready to tumble into bed fully clothed. And he probably would have, if not for Tully, his rather piratical valet. Rafe had engaged the brooding Irishman, a former navy man like himself, shortly after his arrival in the capital city, when it became clear his visit would be a long one. The nature of his work for the Crown also necessitated both extreme privacy and adaptability, so Rafe was accustomed to making do on his own. But that was before he experienced the unique pleasure of one of Tully's signature shaves. He was a bit rough around the edges for a valet, and perhaps his hair was too long, but he mixed the best shaving soap Rafe had ever used and was an absolute wizard with a needle and thread. Rafe had been thoroughly spoiled these last few months, and if he did decide to leave London, he wasn't sure he could do without Tully now.

"Christ. Being charismatic is exhausting," he moaned as he loosened his necktie. Tully tied the damned things so intricately he could barely manage to get them off on his own now.

Supper had been a prolonged affair. Afterward, he had spent several hours carousing with a few other gentlemen, living up to his reputation as a thoroughly dissolute rake.

"I can imagine, sir."

Rafe's lips quirked at the idea of his humorless, hulking valet working a room. He shrugged out of his dinner jacket and handed it to Tully. "I trust you had a pleasant evening?"

31

Rafe noticed a new book on the chair. The man had a ferocious appetite for detective stories.

Tully nodded. "The library is open to anyone—and well stocked."

"Yes, I believe the former baroness was a voracious reader," Rafe murmured as he removed his cuff links. "Perhaps I'll take a look tomorrow."

Whenever he was feeling particularly blocked, reading helped relax his mind. It was on the tip of his tongue to ask if Tully had seen Miss Sparrow, but he wouldn't indulge in this ridiculous curiosity. Since her awkward exit that afternoon, Rafe hadn't seen the mysterious lady's companion again. And yet, to his growing annoyance, he had thought of her more often than he liked.

"A fine idea, sir." Tully took the cuff links, jacket, and necktie and slipped into the other room.

Rafe walked over toward the window. There was nothing to see at this hour but black, black night and a blanket of glittering stars above.

Since his arrival, he had made a point of conversing with each guest. It was incredibly tedious, and he resolved to *never* have another conversation about horseflesh for the rest of his life—but it helped him narrow down potential suspects.

Unless there isn't even a damned mole among them.

Regardless, tomorrow he would begin searching rooms. Rafe slowly rolled his shoulders to release the knot between them. It didn't work. He had received a cable from Gerard already, asking about his progress, but he was in no hurry to respond. Let his brother sweat a little. Rafe had never seen the earl in anything other than a foul mood, but that morning he seemed even more agitated than usual. When Rafe had briefly intimated that he might not take the case at all, Gerard had gone as white as a sheet.

But this is what you do. *This is what you're trained for. You've no wife, no family, and no other responsibilities to speak of. You can drop everything and go traipsing off to God knows where whenever you damned well want, and no one will even blink an eye.*

Witnessing Gerard's rattled expression paired with the note of envy in his voice had not been as satisfying as Rafe would have liked. It was true. All of it. That was the problem. For years Rafe had made decisions designed to ensure he remained as untethered as possible. Was beholden to no one other than his superiors. But now it didn't sound quite so appealing as it once had.

No wife.

No family.

No other responsibilities.

He felt the sharp pinch of regret in his chest while the voice in his head once again warned that it had been a mistake to come here. And Rafe wasn't used to making mistakes. Gerard would always have more money, more power, more respect simply because he had the good fortune to be born first. But Rafe had his work. Work that he had always excelled at. Failure was never the goal, but to fail in front of Gerard was simply unacceptable. There was no other way. Rafe rolled his shoulders and neck again, harder, longer, until his dress shirt clung to the faint sheen of sweat coating his heated skin, but those tight knots finally gave way to his will. He braced his hands against the back of a chair, panting from the force of his exertions, waiting long minutes until the pounding of his heart subsided. Then he performed a few more basic exercises and stretches to keep his lean muscles loose before washing up and changing. Sleep would come heavily tonight.

And tomorrow he would begin again.

* * *

The cool fall air stung Sylvia's nose as she walked toward the folly on the castle grounds with Georgiana and Mrs. Crawford, but she still took another sharp, biting lungful. After spending so much time in the library these last few days, it was a relief to breathe in air that wasn't tinged with the scent of moldering books, to have the blue Scottish sky overhead, and to feel the breeze off the nearby loch kissing her cheeks.

"I've been working too hard. That's all," she explained to Georgiana earlier over breakfast in the viscountess's room. Her friend was still concerned over Sylvia's abrupt departure the previous afternoon, along with her decision to take a dinner tray alone. "I'll be more careful from now on. No need to worry."

Georgiana's brow remained puckered, and she lowered her voice, though no one was in the room besides the two of them. "Sylvie, it's been ages since I *haven't* worried over you." Sylvia felt a flush that began at her hairline. She had nearly forgotten that long-ago nickname. "But you would tell me if something else was bothering you, yes? More than work, I mean."

Tell her, a quiet voice urged. *Tell her everything.*

Instead, Sylvia forced her mouth into the biggest smile she could manage. "What have I to worry about now? I'm here with you, and we're staying in a castle!" She added a genuine burst of laughter, because it really was extraordinary.

A year ago she had been nursing her father through the last

few months of his life, hadn't seen Georgiana in person since she had been forced to leave London, and was still clinging to the hope that her brother would honor their agreement to let her stay in Hawthorne Cottage for the remainder of her life.

She should be happy—*was* happy.

If not for that blasted envelope.

Soon she would receive instructions on where to deliver it. The thought filled her with dread, but there was nothing to be done about it. She would slip away for an hour or two, perform her task, and then get on with her new life.

While Mrs. Crawford and Georgiana stopped to chat with another group of guests, Sylvia politely stepped away and continued on toward the folly, as she wasn't of interest to anyone here. She glanced back and waved at Georgiana, then gestured to the structure, which was built to resemble a crumbling stone tower and said to offer a marvelous view of the loch. Sylvia entered and walked up the staircase. It led to an open platform ringed with a stone wall that came up to her chest. She walked over and placed her hands against the wall's pebbled edge. The loch was about a mile off. There had been talk of taking a boat out today, but even from this distance Sylvia could make out the white-capped waves. Her stomach was already turning. As she stared at the murky, churning surface, Georgiana's laugh carried on the breeze. She sounded so much happier here, out of her husband's reach. It was a welcome reminder of why Sylvia had taken such a risk in the first place and why she would do whatever it took to keep her dear friend safe.

"Do you suppose anyone will ever explore the bottom?"

The question pulled Sylvia from her thoughts. She hadn't even heard anyone approach. Mr. Davies of all people stood beside her, also looking out at the loch.

"Pardon?" she rasped, taking in his strong profile.

He gestured to the water with his chin. "The locals claim there isn't one. That it just goes on forever, to the other side of the world. Fascinating prospect, don't you think?"

A chill went through Sylvia as she imagined being swallowed beneath those churning waves and enveloped in darkness. "It sounds a bit terrifying, actually. Sinking indefinitely."

He huffed a laugh. "Ah, well. I suppose that does sound terrifying. I was imagining it would be more like something out of a Jules Verne story. I wanted to be Captain Nemo when I was a boy, exploring the ocean depths in my very own Nautilus," he said, turning toward her. "And fighting a giant squid."

The corner of Sylvia's mouth tilted up to mirror his smirk as she practically sank into his warm brown eyes. Women must come so easily to him.

"Is that why you joined the navy?" The question tumbled out before she could stop herself.

His eyes widened slightly before he looked back toward the loch, frowning in consideration. "I joined for many reasons," he murmured after a moment. "To annoy my parents, for one. And to see the world, like all restless young boys."

"And girls," she couldn't help adding.

"Of course." He cast her a sly smile. "But I'm sure my enduring admiration for Captain Nemo was also an influence."

Then he touched the brim of his hat before moving on to smoothly greet a group of guests that had joined them, where he was enthusiastically received. Sylvia watched as Mr. Davies adeptly wielded his considerable charm, making lighthearted comments and compliments to each of the ladies. But she couldn't forget the vulnerability that had briefly flashed in his eyes when he spoke of his boyhood dream. It called to something within her. A need buried so deeply she had nearly forgotten it existed.

Sylvia turned away. A burst of laughter rose behind her, as if to punctuate the absurdity of the thought. No. She must have imagined it. Of course she had. Perhaps he had spent time in Her Majesty's service, but he was clearly a man without worries. A man that had benefited immensely from unearned privilege. A man that seemed perfectly content to bask in the admiration of others. Sylvia's fingers tightened against the rough stone wall. She had been deceived by such men before. And had lost herself in the process.

No one can take away your education, Sylvia.

Her mother had been dead for over a decade, but it still hurt to think of her on her deathbed. Worse than her father's much more recent demise.

No matter what your father says, you make sure he sends you to university. He owes you that. He owes us both.

It was the only time her mother had ever hinted at her discontent, suggested that she had wanted more from her life than to be a wife and mother. Sylvia had thoroughly failed to heed her warning once before, when she threw herself into a relationship with Bernard Hughes, an aspiring politician she had met at a lecture when she first moved to London. Sylvia had been so flattered by his interest, especially once he learned who her father was, that she ignored everything else that didn't fit.

She would not make that mistake again.

* * *

Rafe turned a corner onto the landing that led to his room. He leaned against the wall and released a breath. What the devil had come over him back there? The sons of earls were expected to converse with members of their own class. To rib gentlemen, romance debutantes, and flirt with merry widows. They did *not* seek out inconsequential ladies' companions, let alone share such maudlin thoughts. That was the kind of behavior that drew notice. That led to questions he couldn't afford to answer. But Miss Sparrow had cut such a lonely figure walking away from the other guests toward the folly that it seemed only natural to try to cheer her up. The trouble was he hadn't been acting like the Honorable Rafe Davies, shallow yet charismatic bon vivant. Just himself. And for a moment she had seen it.

Seen *him*.

A throat cleared by the entranceway, and Rafe immediately straightened. It was a footman. How long had he been there? Rafe hid his unease behind a smile as the footman held out a small silver platter bearing an envelope. "This came for you, sir."

Rafe gave his thanks and took the missive. Good God. Couldn't Gerard go a *day* without contacting him? He retreated to the privacy of his room and took a deep breath before opening it. As he read, relief washed over him. It was from Captain Henry Harris, an old friend Rafe had cabled before he left London. The captain was currently recuperating after an incident in Turkey. The official story was that he had been in Istanbul on a personal holiday when he was wrongly imprisoned after trying to intervene while two other British tourists were being robbed. In actuality, it had been an intelligence-gathering mission gone horribly awry, which had led to a minor diplomatic incident.

The brief message contained wishes for a safe journey and an invitation to visit him in Glasgow, where he was staying with his sister and her husband. For the first time in days, Rafe had something to look forward to. He had met Henry his first year in the Royal Navy. They were two young officers barely out of boyhood. But while Henry had come from a family with a long and distinguished history of naval service, Rafe had simply been trying to escape his own.

He served a lengthy stint at sea before his father conceded that Rafe had made his point and pleaded with him to take a relatively safer but infinitely more boring job he had secured for him in the War Office, contingent upon completion of his studies. Rafe had refused the offer for well over a year, until his father's sudden death. Earning his degree and taking the job had then felt like paying penance for his youthful impudence, and his grieving mother was comforted that he was no longer so far away. But new dangers awaited when his gumption caught the attention of Sir Alfred, who had lots of uses for a restless young man like him. Meanwhile, Henry stayed in the service and gradually ascended through the ranks. But in the last few years he had done some intelligence work of his own, and they met whenever the opportunity arose.

Rafe hadn't seen him since the skirmish in Turkey last year that landed him in jail, where he had languished for weeks until he managed to orchestrate a daring escape for his fellow prisoners. Like everyone else in the Empire, Rafe had learned the details of his friend's heroism in the scores of breathless newspaper articles devoted to his actions. Not that that was surprising. Aside from his former colleague Alec Gresham, who had resigned from the service last spring, Henry was one of the most honorable and modest men Rafe knew. Which meant that the captain would be haunted by the lives lost, not the ones saved.

Most of Rafe's Crown service involved following people, reporting information, or coordinating with other agents. He had been in his fair share of scrapes to be sure, but nothing like the violent imprisonment Henry had endured. Rafe had seen firsthand the lasting mark such experiences could leave upon a man. All the more reason why he needed to form a new organization, so that men like his brother could not send others off to be killed or maimed in situations they didn't fully understand.

Gerard's words echoed in his mind, and he saw his brother's lip curling in disgust:

It isn't gentlemanly.

As if empire-building ever could be.

The nagging suspicion that had begun last spring surfaced again. The suspicion that perhaps he wasn't on the right side anymore. That perhaps there had never been one at all. Just men like Gerard locked away in their fancy clubs, carving up the world with gilded knives.

Rafe shook the dark thought away. Even if that was true, he had a plan to change things. For the better. He just needed the chance. Rafe pulled out his father's gold-plated lighter, which had been a wedding gift from his new bride. Rafe didn't smoke, but since his father's death he always kept this on him. He ran his thumb over the inscription: *The course of true love never did run smooth.* Rafe's mother had been performing as Titania, queen of the fairies, in *A Midsummer Night's Dream* when they met.

Then he lit the message and threw it into the hearth, watching as the paper's blackened edges slowly curled inward and turned to ash.

CHAPTER FOUR

❧

S ylvia poked at the under-seasoned quail before her. Earlier, Mrs. Crawford had insisted that she accompany her to supper this evening, and the knot in her stomach had grown steadily tighter ever since.

"Tonight won't be very formal, if that's what you're worried about," her employer had explained. "No one will mind your lack of fashion, my dear."

The thought hadn't even occurred to Sylvia. After spending the previous evening alone, she had actually been looking forward to the prospect of eating with company. It had absolutely nothing to do with Mr. Davies, though. Not at all. Now Sylvia was acutely aware of her "lack of fashion," but unless Mrs. Crawford decided to increase her wages, there was little to be done about it.

Another loud burst of laughter came from a few seats away, where the man himself was busy enchanting the guests around him. Despite Sylvia's best efforts, he had hardly strayed from her thoughts since their encounter that morning. Whenever Lady Armstrong leaned over to take a sip of wine, she had a clear view of Mr. Davies. It should be a crime to look that dashing in a dinner jacket. He was listening attentively to the older woman seated beside him, who was practically glowing—not that Sylvia could blame her. Being the focus of his formidable attention, even for a moment, was a heady experience. She glanced over in his direction for the umpteenth time, but he paid her absolutely no notice. Sylvia couldn't shake the feeling that this was some kind of snub. An overcorrection for his friendliness in the folly.

Or perhaps she had simply forgotten how dangerous charismatic people could be.

"I say, where is your *head*, Miss Sparrow!"

That Sylvia managed not to hear Mrs. Crawford's question the first time she asked was a testament to her distraction.

"I'm very sorry, Mrs. Crawford. You were saying?"

Her employer raised an eyebrow. "I was telling Mrs. Barnes about our plans for Egypt, and she asked if you had ever been abroad before."

Sylvia turned to Mrs. Barnes, a refined woman in late middle age, and gave her an apologetic smile. "No. This is my first time outside England, ma'am."

"And soon you will go all the way to Egypt! What an adventure that will be for you."

"Miss Sparrow spent nearly her whole life in her little village," Mrs. Crawford added, unknowingly parroting the lie Sylvia and Georgiana had fed to her. "Can you imagine?"

Mrs. Barnes shrugged, unimpressed. "I barely traveled farther than Richmond until after my poor Walter passed." Then she addressed Sylvia directly. "Once you see a bit of the world, you won't want to go back to your old life, my dear."

"Yes, ma'am," she replied, catching Georgiana's eye across the table.

It was also no longer a possibility.

Sylvia resumed her dissection of her quail, but after a moment her skin prickled with awareness. She glanced up and found Mr. Davies staring at her with the same closemouthed smile that had so enchanted his dinner partner, but there was a playfulness in his eyes now. As if he had been listening to their conversation. And Sylvia got the distinct impression that he had been slyly doing so the entire evening. Just as her cheeks began to burn under his inspection, she shot him a scowl and turned back to her plate. What did this man *want*? Yet her body continued to flush, as if those eyes of his were slowly raking across her skin, but she refused to look up again. Refused to give any sign that could be interpreted as encouragement.

Sylvia passed the rest of the meal by pointedly looking anywhere but in his direction. If Mr. Davies expected her to fawn over him like everyone else, he was sadly mistaken. Yes, she had been momentarily blindsided by his unexpected hand-someness—*entirely* understandable—but she wasn't interested in alleviating his boredom during a house party.

Not in the least.

She didn't spare him a glance as she followed Mrs. Crawford and Georgiana out of the dining room, nor barely a thought as she played a few hands of whist in the drawing room with the other ladies until Mrs. Crawford demanded they retire, or as she spent the remainder of the evening reading aloud. When Sylvia closed the book with a satisfied thud, it was well after midnight, and Mrs. Crawford was fast asleep and snoring away. There. Three whole hours with not a single thought of Mr. Davies, his fathomless brown eyes, or his impressive shoulders. Really, she was quite proud of herself.

As Sylvia stretched her legs, Georgiana stirred awake.

She had dozed off in her chair somewhere around chapter twelve.

"Oh dear," she said, trying unsuccessfully to hide a massive yawn. "What did I miss?"

"The monk was actually the villain. He tried to ravish the heroine, but she stabbed him and fled the monastery with the help of the mysterious coachman, who turned out to be the duke's long-lost heir. And handsome to boot."

"Good for her." Georgiana gave a nod of satisfaction as she stood up. "Aren't you coming to bed?"

Sylvia shook her head, too restless to sleep. "Not yet. I'm going to the library to pick a new book to start tomorrow."

"All right. Maybe one with a little more romance this time?"

Sylvia grinned. "Excellent idea."

"Make sure to take a candle," Georgiana reminded her. "It's horribly dim out there."

Mr. Wardale had plans to add electric light to the castle eventually, but until then it was candlesticks and oil lamps. They said their good nights, and Sylvia exited the suite. Georgiana was right. The low flicker of wall sconces provided some light but not much. Sylvia held her candleholder up as she walked down the hall, feeling rather like a Gothic heroine in one of Mrs. Crawford's novels. A chill ran down her spine as the floor suddenly groaned beneath her feet. She had heard guests whisper about the castle being haunted. It was the usual tale about a lonely young woman, the beautiful eldest daughter of a long-dead baron, who had been abandoned by her lover, a Scottish ruffian, and now roamed the grounds for all eternity, searching for him.

In other words, absolute drivel.

But as she continued down the hall, the chill turned into

a different sensation. Almost as if she were being watched. Sylvia paused and glanced down the hallway that led to the other guest rooms. Including the one occupied by Mr. Davies. The hour wasn't so late for a man like him. He might not be abed yet.

Or he might not be alone.

Sylvia's jaw tightened, and she hurried in the opposite direction. The uneasy feeling dissipated the farther away she moved, and by the time she reached the library, her head was swimming with unwanted questions about a certain guest's nocturnal activities. She took a moment to gather herself before pushing open the door and stepping into the room.

Then she got her answer.

"Well, good evening, Miss Sparrow," said the man himself, who was lounging in a chair and—most shocking of all—wearing a pair of adorably unfashionable wire-rimmed spectacles. "Fancy meeting you here."

* * *

Miss Sparrow flushed quite prettily at his greeting, which shouldn't have pleased Rafe so much. Then her wide gray eyes assessed the situation before her. Continue into the room or turn back? A cautious young lady would turn around without a word, but Rafe had a feeling about Miss Sparrow.

She then lifted her chin and stepped toward him. "Yes. Hello, Mr. Davies."

Rafe's smile grew despite her flat tone. By God, she was game. As he removed his spectacles and tucked them in his breast pocket, he could have sworn a strange look of disappointment flashed across her face. But it must have been a trick of the light. Then he closed the book he had been reading and set it on the chair as he stood. Her eyes immediately skimmed over the cover.

"*The History of the Decline and Fall of the Roman Empire*?"

She didn't even try to hide her surprise. Rafe raised an eyebrow. "Even rogues like to know a bit of history."

She blushed again. "My apologies. And please, don't let me interrupt your reading."

"Nonsense," he said. "I welcome the intrusion."

She didn't respond and instead moved toward a shelf that took up nearly the whole length of the room and began to diligently scan a row of book spines. Rafe stepped closer until the faint smell of lavender soap filled the air between them. "Looking for something in particular?"

"Mrs. Crawford enjoys penny dreadfuls," she replied, still keeping her eyes firmly on the shelves. "The more macabre, the better. I've been reading *The Mystery of the Red Monk* to her."

Rafe chuckled. "A classic of the genre." And, from what he remembered, rather salacious. He liked the old lioness even more. "You probably won't find anything over here, though, unless you want to read about the natural sciences."

Miss Sparrow paused in her inspection and frowned. "Oh. Right."

"Come." Rafe gestured for her to follow as he led her deeper into the cavernous library. There was a long silence before he could hear her light steps as she moved to catch up. Rafe turned on his heel and swept a hand toward a much larger section of books. "I believe this is where the popular literature is kept."

Miss Sparrow cast him a glance as she walked past him. "Thank you," she said primly.

Rafe stood a few steps behind her and watched as she resumed her search. He should return to his book. She hadn't asked for his help, or pretended to be confused by something commonplace, or used any of the other brazenly transparent reasons women typically employed to keep his attention. No, Miss Sparrow studiously ignored him. And Rafe liked her all the more for it.

"Have you read this?"

As he reached over her left shoulder, Miss Sparrow's sharp inhalation threaded through him. He bit his inner cheek and pulled a book out from the shelf right above her head.

She looked down at the cover as he held it out to her, giving him an excellent view of her profile. "No."

The top of her head barely reached his shoulders, making her a little shorter than average, but nothing else about her was. For one, her eyelashes were *ridiculously* long. Then there was the delicate slope of her nose, the finely pointed chin, and the lushly curved mouth. She wasn't classically beautiful like Lady Arlington, but it was a face he could imagine staring at for a long time and never growing tired of. For years, even.

His entire body tensed. Where had *that* thought come from?

"Here," he prompted, handing her the first Inspector Du-Monde book. "My valet swears by this series. There's murder, intrigue, and a bit with a dog."

She took the book from his hands, and Rafe stepped back until he couldn't smell lavender. Until he couldn't feel the heat that blossomed so easily between them. But as their eyes met, her steel-gray gaze felt like an unexpected punch to the gut, and his abdomen automatically tightened. The ingrained response was usually reserved for bodily threats, not sharp-tongued spinsters. And to think he had been waiting all evening for her to look over at him.

"And romance?" she asked after a moment. Her eyes had gone rather limpid, but she stood firmly in place, her body as rigid as his own.

The question slowly penetrated his woolly brain. "Pardon?"

Her tongue darted out as she wet her lower lip. Was the movement involuntary, or an invitation? "Lady Arlington," she rasped. "She sits with us sometimes in the evening and asked for something with a bit of romance."

"Oh." She had been asking about the book. Not *him*. "I believe there is a plucky assistant and a mysterious heiress who vie for his affections throughout in the series."

Miss Sparrow gave a dismissive sniff and rolled her eyes. "Of course they do," she muttered.

Her visible annoyance over a tired cliché was adorable. Rafe had to suppress the smile tugging at his lips. She then addressed him with perfect politeness. "Thank you. I think they'll both enjoy this."

"My pleasure," he said, the words coming out more roughly than he intended. Rafe cleared his throat. He should take his leave. Say good night and make sure to keep his distance. But his mind would not give up just yet. "And what about you?"

She tilted her head at the question. "Me?"

"Do you share Mrs. Crawford's bloodlust?"

Miss Sparrow finally smiled a little. "Somewhat." She looked back at the shelves and began to run a finger lazily over the spines. "Do you think Mr. Wardale stocked this room, or did these come with the house?"

Rafe swallowed and shifted on his feet as he imagined that finger drawing a path down him instead. "My understanding is that the previous owner's wife was an avid reader."

She made a murmur of approval. "And an eclectic one." She paused at one book and turned back to him. "Have you read *The Gadfly*?"

Rafe frowned at the mention of the sensational and, in his opinion, melodramatic novel that had been published by Ethel Voynich only several months ago. "She's a Communist, you know."

Miss Sparrow smiled again, undaunted by the censure in his voice. "The author? Yes, I do. But it's about a romance."

"And a revolution."

Her gaze flickered, as if she had only just recalled where she was and who she was with. Her arm fell away from the shelf, and she hugged the book tightly to her chest. "Is that such a bad thing?"

"People can get hurt."

People like her.

She glanced down, not bothering to hide the disappointment on her face. "I suppose someone like you is invested in maintaining the status quo, no matter the cost."

It took him a moment to realize she was referring to his family. Not his work.

"I'm not opposed to change, Miss Sparrow," he said tartly. "But I don't think marching in the streets is the best way to achieve it."

"Sometimes that's the only way to be heard."

Of all the things he thought might occur when she stepped into this room, debating the merits of public protest was decidedly *not* among them.

"That is what parliament is for. So the laws can be debated and changed accordingly." Christ, he sounded so much like Gerard, he wanted to kick himself.

Her eyes rightly flashed with anger. "Well over half the population isn't even allowed the *vote*, Mr. Davies."

Oh, but he had walked right into that one. He understood her outrage, even agreed with it, but the Honorable Rafe Davies couldn't possibly.

"And for good reason." He forced the words past his lips. If his mother could hear him now, she would box his ears.

Miss Sparrow's gaze turned deadly, and she stepped forward with impressive gravitas given her short stature. "I suppose you're going to spout that drivel about women's brains not being able to manage such complex thought. Meanwhile, you have to pay someone to knot your own *necktie* because you can't be bothered to do it yourself."

"No," he said quickly. "I don't believe that." Even he had his limits. "But in these matters I…I only think most ladies are best served by guidance from their husbands. Or fathers. And other male relatives. Because they have more varied experience of the world." There. It was the least insulting reasoning he could think of. But it did not have the intended effect.

Miss Sparrow seemed momentarily stunned by this admission, and her eyes hardened. "Then you have far more faith in the inherent goodness of men than I do. *Sir*."

Rafe blinked and stepped aside to let her pass. The door shut soundly behind her, and the resulting silence was deafening. He stood in place for a few more minutes, waiting for the smell of lavender soap to fully fade as he turned the scene over in his mind.

Guilt swept through him, hot, harsh, and biting.

Someone had disappointed her once. Someone she trusted.

And now he had just done the same.

CHAPTER FIVE

D id you sleep poorly last night?"
Georgiana's question roused Sylvia from her tangled thoughts. Their eyes met across the table, now scattered with the remnants of breakfast. After her encounter with Mr. Davies, she had spent hours tossing and turning. Leave it to Georgiana to notice.

"It's nothing," she demurred.

But the viscountess shook her head. "If it was nothing, you wouldn't have those circles under your eyes." Then she glanced around the breakfast room. Mrs. Crawford had gone off with a group of ladies, and they had so few moments alone together. "I know something is bothering you. Please tell me."

Sylvia stared at her. They had shared everything once, when they were two lonely girls away at school. Sylvia had missed her mother, who had died too young, and Georgiana was learning how to live without her gaggle of younger siblings. That was years before Sylvia went off to university and Georgiana had celebrated her first Season. Before either of them had any secrets worth keeping. An uncomfortable encounter with a man she barely knew did not deserve to be ranked among them.

Sylvia released a breath. "Mr. Davies was in the library last night. He was the one who recommended the Inspector DuMonde mystery."

Georgiana raised one of her bronze eyebrows. "Is that so?"

Sylvia frowned at her suggestive tone. "I left within five minutes." Then she slumped a little in her chair. "He doesn't think women should have the vote." Disappointment laced through her every word. But of course he believed such things. Just because the man was a notorious rake didn't make him a radical.

Georgiana looked amused. "An interesting topic of conversation to have on so short an acquaintance. I suppose you told him exactly how you felt?"

"Well, I couldn't just let him stand there being *wrong.*"

"No, certainly not." Georgiana laughed. "And how did he take it?"

Sylvia shrugged and looked away, recalling the odd expression that had crossed his face. "He didn't seem offended." That was a reaction she was quite familiar with. "But almost... resigned." She turned back to Georgiana, whose gaze was now thoughtful.

"Then perhaps you've given him something to think about. Gentlemen like him rarely move outside their own circles. You may be the first woman he's ever encountered to voice such beliefs."

"But the suffrage movement has been active for decades now."

"Yes," Georgiana said gently. "But I would imagine that reading about it occasionally in the paper or walking past women handing out pamphlets is an altogether different experience from engaging with an advocate. Especially one like you."

Sylvia bristled. "What is that supposed to mean?"

Georgiana tilted her head and smiled. "Only that you can be a force of nature. When you allow yourself to be."

Sylvia glanced down at her lap. They had been over this before. Georgiana thought Sylvia was too cautious, too pessimistic. But she simply didn't understand. Sylvia had been fearless once, determined to change things for the better. No matter the cost. Sometimes it felt as if Sylvia had dreamed up that younger version of herself. Who she had once been was so far removed from the woman she now was—except she still bore the very real consequences of her actions.

"Yes, well. Look how that worked out," she grumbled, twisting the napkin in her lap. Then alarm shot through her, and she looked up. "Oh God. What if he says something to Mrs. Crawford? What if he tells her I support the vote?"

"I'm sure he won't."

"But he *could*." Sylvia pressed a hand to her forehead. "I've been so careless."

Georgiana slid her hand across the table in a calming gesture. "Sylvia, don't do this to yourself. Everything is fine. You have nothing to fear now. My aunt adores you. Really. And even if Mr. Davies did say something to her, I'm not sure she would much care."

"Your husband would, though," Sylvia murmured, then immediately wished she could take back the words. Georgiana's mouth tightened, and her complexion paled, as was usually the case when anyone mentioned the viscount. "I'm sorry. Forget I said anything."

But Georgiana had already pulled back her chair and was moving to stand. "No, you're right," she said, flicking Sylvia a cool glance. "We should both be more careful." Without another word, she turned and glided out of the room, leaving Sylvia to her misery.

She stirred her lukewarm tea in a spot of sunshine. Sylvia had once told Georgiana what the jail had been like. Filthy, cold, and so dark. How the smell of stale, moldy air and unwashed bodies had been so thick it seemed to choke her. How the damp had sunk into her bones so deeply that it was months before she could move with any kind of lightness.

And to think she had been lucky. Sylvia had been there for only a couple of days before her brother, Lionel, came and took her home to Hawthorne Cottage. To a house that was safe and clean, even if she did have to endure her father's silent disappointment and Lionel's outright disgust.

Everyone warned Father not to send you to university, that it would only fill your head with more nonsense. Then he let you go off to London and look how you've repaid him. He is a laughingstock now. We both are.

But it had been hard to sympathize with her brother. The other women she had been arrested with had no one to post their bail, would have been unceremoniously turned out of the boardinghouses where they rented rooms, and likely lost their jobs. They had all been brought in on charges of solicitation, when really Sylvia had been trying to convince them to attend a meeting on the rights of working women. At the station she had been interrogated by a detective who claimed a police informant insisted she was part of an anarchist collective conspiring with known prostitutes to target their clients. It was a ridiculous claim, one she suspected had been orchestrated by Bernard's father, a haughty, status-hungry man who had made his disapproval of her no secret. Sylvia had spent hours trying to convince the detective that what she primarily wanted was voting rights for women—*all* women—not to bring down the entire government. But he refused to listen until Lionel had appeared and thrown around a few names—and banknotes. Sylvia had also insisted that Lionel post bail for the other women, a debt he still held against her, but she had never once tried to find out what happened to any of them afterward. She had been far too scared.

A coward.

But even though she had been able to leave the jail, her ordeal had only begun. Once the newspapers got ahold of the story, those who knew of her work for *The Defender* distorted the truth further and further until Sylvia was portrayed as some kind of anarchist mastermind recruiting people from the lower classes to do her bidding and join her revolution. By the next week, the papers had moved on to a new scandal, but the damage to her reputation had been swift and permanent.

She had been too humiliated to fight back, to even attempt to defend herself. She had been fired from her typist job, her editor at *The Defender* claimed that she could no longer publish anything under her byline, she was turned out of the boardinghouse where she rented a room, and all the friends she had made in London deserted her. Even the ones who had been staunch supporters of reform were not willing to risk their own reputations by associating with her.

I'm sure none of it is true, but of course you understand.

Of course, she said again and again as each door was firmly shut in her face.

She set down her teaspoon as that old familiar shame washed over her. She let it soak through every limb. Cover every inch of skin until she practically burned. It was no less than she deserved. No less than she had asked for.

But if she failed to meet the demands of her blackmailer, she knew things could get much, much worse.

* * *

Rafe trudged toward his room. After a long morning spent prowling through guest rooms like a common burglar, he had absolutely nothing to show for it except a nasty crick in his neck from craning over and under any visible crevice. Tully would need to fix one of his poultices, a practice he had learned from his Irish grandmother. A woman he proudly referred to as "a batty old witch." The smell was positively eye-watering, but they worked wonders on aching muscles.

At that very same moment, Lady Arlington was coming down the hall in the opposite direction, looking uncharacteristically troubled. When she spotted him, the furrow in her brow immediately disappeared. One had to admire her commitment to upholding her public image.

"Good morning, my lady," he said with a polite nod.

She returned the greeting, but just as he moved to continue on his way, she held up her hand. "Do you have a moment, sir?"

"For you, I have more than a moment."

But she did not return his roguish smile. "It's Miss Sparrow. I understand you met in the library last night."

So, she had confided in the viscountess. That aligned with his theory that their connection was long-standing.

"I know she can be rather spirited in her beliefs and that she voiced some unconventional opinions to you," Lady Arlington said, obviously choosing her words with great care. "But I trust you won't say anything to my aunt about your encounter.

56

Despite her colorful past, she has some firm ideas about what constitutes proper behavior."

Rafe's eyebrows rose. "No, my lady," he swore. "The thought never once occurred to me."

It was the truth. But he could understand her caution. Rafe had been so focused on his own guilt over upsetting Miss Sparrow that he hadn't stopped to consider the risk she had taken in revealing such opinions to him, a veritable stranger.

Her features relaxed. "I'm happy to hear it. But, Mr. Davies, you seem to have forgotten how to behave around unmarried ladies. The proper form is to *remove* yourself from the room."

Rafe glanced down bashfully. "I confess I was reluctant to divest myself of Miss Sparrow's company." When he looked up, the viscountess was giving him what appeared to be a reluctant look of approval.

"I understand, but do take care from now on. I am honor bound to protect her reputation, and I don't take my responsibilities lightly."

"Nor should you." The viscountess tilted her head and moved to leave, but now it was Rafe's turn. "My lady, last night Miss Sparrow said something troubling. She suggested someone had...hurt her once. And I admit the thought has stayed with me ever since."

Lady Arlington's eyes softened. "She told you that?"

"Well, not directly," he admitted.

Disappointment flitted across her face, but she quickly recovered. "I am not at liberty to reveal any confidences she has shared with me, but I will say that Miss Sparrow is one of the most stalwart women I have ever met. Even still, I have found that those who appear to be made of stone often have the softest edges." Understanding vibrated inside him. "Have a care with her, Mr. Davies," she added.

"You have my word." Rafe gave her a short bow, and this time she went on her way.

He took a few steps toward his room, then immediately turned around and headed for the library. As a Crown agent, he was duty bound to maintain his cover at all costs. Apologizing to Miss Sparrow was decidedly out of character for the dissolute scoundrel he was supposed to be. And yet he did nothing to suppress the urgency propelling him forward. For years Rafe had reveled in his role, revealing his true self to only a select few. But in some places the lines between who he was and who he pretended to be were so finely drawn that sometimes he couldn't tell where he ended and his cover began. The few moments he had spent with Miss Sparrow had made those lines stand out, harsh and unmovable. He didn't want to be that man. He wasn't.

Now he burned with a visceral need to be understood. By her. And for the first time in his career, it seemed worth the risk.

* * *

Rafe had far greater luck tracking Miss Sparrow down than the ever-elusive mole. After a half hour of diligent searching, he found her sitting on the terrace along with Mrs. Crawford and several other ladies. The air still held the morning's chill, but for the moment it was sunny and bright out. Rafe wished them all a good morning and chatted with the older women for a few minutes to keep up appearances.

Just then Lady Taylor-Smyth approached him while lazily twirling her parasol. The woman never missed an opportunity to draw attention to herself. "Mr. Davies, how lovely to see you at this hour. I was planning on taking a walk through the labyrinth. Care to join?"

Rafe gave her a tight smile.

"Another time, perhaps."

"I will take you up on that," she murmured suggestively before sashaying away.

He snuck a glance at Miss Sparrow, who sat near the end of the row, but her eyes were still fixed on the page, a Baedeker guidebook for Egypt. After he finished his greetings, Rafe strolled over and took the empty chair beside her. Miss Sparrow pointedly ignored him and buried herself even deeper into her woolen shawl until the wrapping nearly swallowed her up.

"Are you cold, Miss Sparrow?" he asked loudly enough to draw attention. "I'm happy to find you a blanket."

Mrs. Crawford immediately leaned forward. "Is that true, child? Careful now. You don't want to catch a chill."

Miss Sparrow cast him a dark look before she sat up a little straighter and adjusted her shawl. "No, I'm perfectly fine," she assured her employer. Then she turned to him with the kind of beatific smile that would send hearts fluttering—if one didn't notice the flint in her eyes. "Mr. Davies is mistaken." She lowered her voice so only he could hear. "No doubt a *frequent* occurrence for him."

Rafe let out a full-bodied laugh that was much too loud, but he couldn't remember the last time a woman had been so blatantly immune to his charms. It was delightful. Miss Sparrow was not so amused. She grumbled something that sounded an awful lot like *Impossible man* and resumed her reading.

"I understand Mrs. Crawford is taking you on your first trip abroad," he began. "I've been to Egypt several times. I'd be happy to share my experiences with you or answer any questions you have."

She did not look up from the page. "That is what this guidebook is for, Mr. Davies," she said crisply.

By God, she would not make this easy. He suppressed the urge to tug on his collar. "Yes, of course. I won't take up any more of your time, then. But before I go," he began, lowering his voice. "Please let me extend my most sincere apologies for last night. I offended you. It was not my intention, but that is rather beside the point, isn't it?" She turned to him slowly, one eyebrow raised in shock. "I've been doing some thinking about what you said," he continued. "And I'd like to know more about your opinions."

"You would?" He nodded. "But I spoke so rudely to you."

Rafe shrugged. "I deserved it."

She was still incredulous. "I—I suggested that you couldn't knot your own necktie. To your face."

"And you weren't wrong." He chuckled. "My valet ties the blasted things in more intricate knots than even I can manage."

Her mouth curved in the faintest hint of a smile. "That must be embarrassing, considering you were once a sailor."

"Oh, terribly so." He grinned, then leaned in a little closer. "Please don't tell anyone. I *do* have a reputation to maintain."

She finally laughed, and it felt as if someone had shot his veins full of sunshine. Rafe had tried all manner of illicit substances over the years, all in the name of experimentation, of course, but nothing had ever come close to *this*.

It was dangerously addictive. He wanted more. Immediately.

Miss Sparrow continued smiling at him. "Not to worry. Your secret is safe with me, sir."

He glanced over and noticed Mrs. Crawford watching them with great interest. Time to move on.

"I hope we have a chance to talk again," he said as he rose. "Enjoy the sunshine, ladies. I will see you at luncheon." Then he held Miss Sparrow's gaze for a beat longer than necessary before he turned and left.

Your secret is safe with me.

If only.

Rafe decided long ago that he would never burden anyone else with his escapades. Thanks to her theatrical training, his mother had often assisted her husband in his work for the Crown. Though the late earl was officially a diplomat, at times a bit of espionage was called for. His mother rarely spoke about these missions, but from what Rafe had discerned from her cryptic comments, it had put a heavy strain on their marriage at times. If he continued this acquaintance—and that was *all* it would be—with Miss Sparrow, she could only ever see him as a feckless rogue. The thought sank through him like a stone. His cover had always provided a kind of shelter. A way to move through the world that protected him from all the things beyond his control.

The Honorable Rafe Davies didn't give a fig about receiving the cut direct from his pompous older brother at the theater.

The Honorable Rafe Davies enjoyed more romances than his mother ever had, and he flaunted them proudly.

The Honorable Rafe Davies spent more at his tailor than most men made in a week merely because he could.

None of it was true, but all that mattered was that people believed it. That they never bothered to look past the image he had carefully crafted, lest they catch a glimpse of the man underneath. But it was different with Miss Sparrow. A part of him *wanted* her to strip him of every last lie until he was laid bare before her. Until all that remained was himself. Just Rafe.

He silenced the thought, which had brought him to a full stop. What if the feckless rogue became reformed? That was believable, if a tad predictable.

But *believability* wasn't the issue here. This woman was a distraction. And he certainly didn't need anything else on his plate. Rafe shook his head and continued down the hall, making sure he appeared as relaxed as possible. Like a man who thought of little more than his next meal or tumble. But it wasn't quite as easy as it had been before, and even he couldn't ignore the slight drag in his step.

CHAPTER SIX

❧

Sylvia did not see Georgiana again until she breezed into their suite an hour before tea. When Mrs. Crawford left the sitting room to dress, Sylvia took the chance to apologize.

The viscountess accepted it with her usual grace. "I overreacted. I know you meant no harm. And I understand your caution. I only wish..." She trailed off. Sylvia waited on tenterhooks, hoping that just this once Georgiana would give voice to her thoughts, and concerns, about her marriage, but she only shook her head. "It is no matter. What's done is done." Then she perked up and swiftly changed course. "I did see Mr. Davies in the hall earlier. We spoke about your little encounter. Don't worry. He won't say a thing to anyone." Then she gave Sylvia a sly look. "I think you may have charmed the man."

"Ridiculous," Sylvia insisted, even as her cheeks began to heat. "I'm sure it's just as you said. I'm something of a novelty to him."

"I never said anything of the kind," Georgiana protested. "Though I admit this is an unexpected development." She tapped a finger to her lips in consideration.

"Do you know him well?" Sylvia forced the gnawing

question out even while it felt too much like giving in to hope. A hope she couldn't afford.

"I only met him once in London, but *everyone* has heard about him, of course." She punctuated this with an airy wave of her hand.

"Heard what? What do they say?"

Georgiana raised an eyebrow at her urgent tone. "Well, as I said before, his mother was an actress. It would hardly be the first time an aristocrat made an imprudent marriage, but she was the earl's second wife. As I understand it, Mr. Davies was their only child. And the current earl and his sisters still refuse to recognize him. There was gossip last spring about Mr. Davies being snubbed at the theater by his own brother. I'm not sure they've ever even spoken."

"That's awful." Sylvia burned with the secondhand embarrassment such an act would create. Mr. Davies seemed impervious to discomfort, but to be ignored so publicly by one's own family must have stung. "He certainly couldn't control the circumstances of his birth. Why would his siblings punish *him* for it?"

Georgiana shrugged. "By all accounts the old earl was very much in love with his new bride until his death. I'm sure his first marriage was one born of duty. Perhaps his children acted out of loyalty to their mother. It must have been terribly difficult for them."

"Still, it isn't right to act as if he doesn't *exist*." Sylvia shook her head. "He might not have anyone now."

Georgiana looked at her intently. "I know you are thinking of the many ways in which your own miserable excuse for a brother has been a great disappointment, but you must allow that Mr. Davies hasn't exactly helped his situation. One does not become a known profligate by accident. And his brother is not the kind of man to tolerate such behavior. If he is at all interested in having a relationship with his family, then there is a good deal he could do to facilitate that. Starting with his *own* behavior."

Sylvia nodded reluctantly. Georgiana was only trying to protect her. And rightfully so. The viscountess rose and declared she needed to change before tea. Sylvia took the opportunity to freshen up, as her wardrobe was decidedly less extensive than Georgiana's. But she used the chance to add the tiniest bit of rose-tinted salve to her cheeks and lips. Then she sat down on the small couch in the suite's sitting room and waited for the other ladies to finish. By then a maid had lit a small fire in the hearth, and Sylvia let her mind wander while she stared at the dancing flames.

Mr. Davies may have been shut out of his own family, but he had still been born with every advantage. Advantages that, in her opinion, should not exist. And yet she couldn't help imagining the scene at the theater. What must it have felt like when his elder brother turned his back in front of so many? She strongly suspected Mr. Davies would have hidden his true feelings behind a cool smirk. But those dark eyes would have remained intent, taking in every detail with a steady, unflinching gaze. Others might dismiss him as little more than a charming wastrel——Sylvia had certainly done so initially. But the more time she spent with him, the more she noticed that he exuded a sharpness that belied a keen intelligence. One only had to bother to look.

I'd like to know more about your opinions.

His words slowly weaved through her, past the warning in her heart and the tightness in her chest. Past all the reminders of why she shouldn't trust him. Why she couldn't trust anyone. Until they nestled deep in her belly beside all the other secret words she held on to over the years. The ones that spoke of who she had once been and who she still wished to be.

"All right," Mrs. Crawford bellowed as she exited her room. "Let's get on with it. Where is Georgiana?"

"Here," she answered, entering dressed in a pale blue confection with gauzy puffed sleeves that accentuated her generous curves and brought out her eyes.

"Oh, my lady," Sylvia breathed. "You look lovely."

Georgiana gave a delightful little turn at her urging, but Mrs. Crawford seemed far more concerned with *her* wardrobe.

"Miss Sparrow." She raked her disapproving gaze over Sylvia's comparatively dull form. "I have yet to see you in anything other than gray, brown, and that particularly hideous gown that resembled animal droppings."

"That was fawn, madam," Sylvia calmly explained.

"The name isn't the issue. You need a little more *color* in your life."

"I agree," Georgiana said pointedly, drowning out Sylvia's weak protest. "Perhaps we can find something for you in Glasgow. You will need a new wardrobe before you leave for your trip."

Mrs. Crawford's eyes sharpened. "A splendid idea, Georgie. Now, lend Miss Sparrow one of your shawls. The sapphire one will do wonders for her complexion, don't you think?"

"Oh yes." Georgiana's smile rivaled the Cheshire cat, and she immediately disappeared into her room and called for her maid, Bea.

"Really, Mrs. Crawford," Sylvia pleaded. "This isn't—"

The older woman held up a hand. "I'm not interested in

your excuses, nor your thanks. I am merely doing my duty. You are a young woman who has lived much of her life away from society, but that doesn't mean you need to dress like a schoolmarm."

Sylvia lowered her eyes and bit her lip. "Yes, madam. I appreciate you thinking of me."

Georgiana returned with the shawl and drew it smartly around Sylvia's shoulders. "There," she said with an air of satisfaction. "It suits you perfectly. I'm afraid you'll just have to keep it."

Sylvia ran her fingers over the delicate paisley-patterned silk that covered her shoulders. This was far finer than anything she had ever dreamed of owning. She glanced up and met Georgiana's eyes. "Thank you."

The viscountess gave her a soft smile. "My pleasure."

"Very good," Mrs. Crawford grumbled. "Now let's move along. I won't sit anywhere near that dashed Mr. Thompson again. The man lumbers along like an ox. And smells even worse!"

* * *

A little while later, Mr. Davies appeared in the upstairs parlor resplendent in forest-green tweeds. Sylvia suddenly felt rather shy, as if he could tell just by looking at her that she had spent the better part of the day thinking of him. If the man noticed, he didn't give any indication. He took a seat diagonally across from her and greeted everyone with the same warm cordiality he always did. Sylvia let out a little breath of relief and began buttering her scone. After a moment Mr. Davies spoke.

"That is a lovely shawl, Miss Sparrow."

Sylvia looked up so sharply it was a wonder her head didn't fly off. "Oh. Thank you, Mr. Davies."

Mrs. Crawford not-so-subtly leaned over to catch Sylvia's eye and gave her a significant look. The words *See? Didn't I tell you?* may as well have been written above her head for all to read. Sylvia had to take an enormous bite of dry scone just to keep from laughing, but Georgiana, who was sitting between them, was less successful. Mr. Davies took notice of the viscountess's quaking shoulders and flashed her an amused look. "Is there something I'm missing?"

"Not at all, sir." The reply would have been slightly more convincing if she wasn't simultaneously wiping away a tear.

Sylvia chewed solemnly and stared up at the room's vaulted stone ceiling until it felt safe to proceed. But as soon as Georgiana glanced at her, the two burst out into a rather raucous fit of laughter. For the space of a few moments they were girls again, running through the meadows that surrounded their school, spying on the strapping village boys while they swam naked in the local swimming pond, and giggling in a back pew during church service. She had forgotten that lightness.

When Sylvia was well and truly recovered, everyone was shooting them veiled looks of disapproval—as no one would *dare* to outright frown at the viscountess—everyone except Mr. Davies. He was smiling at the pair of them with a fondness that made her heart turn over. This man may well be a rake, but there was something more there. More than he would ever reveal without a little prompting and probably a great deal of trust. As their eyes met, an unfamiliar kind of desire kindled within her. A kind that wasn't born of aching passion or burning lust, but a desire to understand and be understood. The joie de vivre that seemed to cling to Mr. Davies slowly faded to reveal an unfamiliar intensity. How could anyone look upon this man and see nothing more than a raffish scoundrel?

As if he had heard the very thought, Mr. Davies swallowed hard and looked away. Leaving Sylvia with the distinct feeling that she had done something wrong. And had been dismissed once again.

* * *

Rafe tore his gaze away from Miss Sparrow's and made sure to look in her general direction as little as possible for the rest of tea. Every time he did, Mrs. Crawford vibrated like a damned tuning fork. But no one could accuse him of anything more than politeness—if only because they couldn't hear his thoughts.

The meal finally came to a merciful end. A short program of piano music performed by some of the guests was the afternoon's entertainment. Rafe hadn't planned on attending, but the thought of fruitlessly rifling through another drawer of underclothes held little appeal. When Miss Sparrow shot him a curious glance before dutifully following her employer, the decision was made. But Rafe held himself back. What happened next needed to look like a coincidence. If people noticed him paying her any particular attention, tongues would begin to wag, and it would be Miss Sparrow's reputation that suffered.

He waited a moment, then fell in step with an older gentleman, Mr. Leonard, and his son Bert. Mr. Leonard had once been Wardale's lawyer and had recently sold his very successful law practice, but it seemed unlikely that his son would follow in his father's footsteps. Bert was one of the few male guests around Rafe's age, but the callow young man could barely tie his shoelaces, never mind engage in subterfuge.

Rafe exchanged a few friendly words with the stoic old barrister. The man had a quiet, unassuming air, but Bert couldn't have been more different. As soon as he had the chance, the fop sidled up to Rafe as if they were old friends. Rafe had to force himself not to step away, as this was exactly the type of man he was *supposed* to be friends with.

"That Miss Sparrow is rather pretty, don't you think? I thought she was quite plain at first. Hard not to when the viscountess is present," he said with a suggestive wink. Rafe's jaw tightened in outrage over the lad's shameless shallowness, but hadn't he had the very same thought? How much had changed in only a matter of days...

"I'll have to pay her more attention," Bert continued. "Maybe even ask her to take a walk through the labyrinth with me. Plenty of privacy in there."

And he was handsome enough for her to be tempted by the offer. The image of Bert snatching a kiss from Miss Sparrow in one of the labyrinth's dead ends flashed through his mind.

"Miss Sparrow is a companion. Her duty is to Mrs. Crawford, not to forward young men."

But Bert didn't appear to notice Rafe's clipped tone, or the insult. He was too busy running a practiced hand gingerly through his blond locks. Rafe would bet good money the man slept in curling papers. "Then perhaps you can put in a word? I saw you talking to her this morning. You looked rather chummy."

Rafe's hands were in his trouser pockets. Otherwise Bert might have noticed the fists he was currently making. "I make no promises," he said tightly.

Bert shrugged. "Even if you can't, I'll find a way. Not much else to do in the middle of the damned forest. She's probably bored out of her skull listening to that old bat morning till night anyway. Why would anyone want to spend their time being a companion?"

"I imagine the pay is a rather strong incentive," Rafe said dryly.

"Say, tell me again how you know Wardale? This doesn't seem like your scene, if you don't mind me saying."

Rafe's mouth tightened. He absolutely *did* mind, not that he could say so. "We do business together on occasion."

"No kidding?" Bert's bright blue eyes flickered with interest. "What kind of business?"

Rafe only smiled at the invasive question. "Oh, a little of this, a little of that. It's all rather boring, I'm afraid."

Bert grunted. "I was invited to spend the fall traveling the Continent with some old schoolmates, but Father wouldn't hear of it." His handsome face twisted into a petulant scowl. "I got into some trouble in town. Nothing so terrible. Just the usual fun. But the old man insisted I come along."

He clearly expected to find a sympathetic ear, but Rafe knew what "the usual fun" meant: gambling, drink, women. He had engaged in a menu of similar activities these last few months, but thinking of it now only elicited a feeling of extreme exhaustion.

"Don't be too cross with him," Rafe said, surprising himself. "He wants to spend time with you while he still can. My father and I always wanted to go to America. We spent most of my youth planning a route that would take us from New York to San Francisco. He died before we got the chance to go."

As Rafe had been far too busy putting as much distance between them as possible.

Bert was quiet for an uncharacteristically long moment. "Well, isn't that rotten luck," he finally murmured. "I'm sorry about your father." He looked properly chastened.

Rafe waved a hand, displaying a casualness he did not feel. "It was years ago, but thank you, anyway."

Once they entered the music room, Bert loped off in search of the refreshments while Mr. Leonard came beside him.

"I apologize if my son caused any offense. He is a high-spirited young man. Though I suppose that's my fault. His mother died when he was a little boy, and I worked so much that I didn't have the heart to discipline him as much as he needed. Is that true about your father?"

Rafe nodded reluctantly and tried to ignore the metallic tang of regret bubbling in the back of his throat.

Mr. Leonard's inquisitive eyes, the same shade of blue as his son's, softened. "That is a terrible shame. I met him once, you know."

Rafe cocked his head in interest. Since his father had spent so much time outside England, it was rare that he encountered such people—fewer still who wished to share their remembrances with him. "Is that so?"

"Many years ago in London." A glimmer came into the old man's expression as he recalled the night so long ago. "He was that rare combination of an honorable aristocrat. And your mother, my goodness!" Mr. Leonard pressed a hand reverently to his heart. "The rumors of her beauty didn't do her justice."

Rafe laughed. "She would appreciate that, I promise you."

"Ah, she is still living, then?"

"Yes. I plan to see her soon. She lives in Monaco now." With a French-Moroccan hotelier who treated her like the queen she was.

Mr. Leonard gave an understanding nod. "Society was intolerably cruel to her. She must have suffered terribly after your father died. They seemed quite taken with one another. It is a rare thing, to experience that kind of love. That was why I decided never to marry again after Bert's mother died. I knew I would forever be comparing her to my Maude, and it seemed cruel to put an innocent woman in that position."

"Yes," Rafe murmured. He had caught sight of Sylvia sitting in the front row with Mrs. Crawford. The seat beside her was empty.

"Are you open to a little friendly advice from an old man, Mr. Davies?"

That got Rafe's attention. "Sir?"

Mr. Leonard leaned closer and lowered his voice. "Don't you *dare* let my son take that seat."

Rafe stared at him in surprise until the man nodded. "Hurry now. Bert won't dawdle for long."

Rafe did as he was told and strolled over to the row of chairs. Mrs. Crawford immediately noticed his approach, but Miss Sparrow was distracted. "Is this seat taken?"

She glanced up at the question and broke into a smile. Rafe had addressed her, but Mrs. Crawford answered: "Sit, sit, Mr. Davies," she urged with a wave of her fan.

Rafe hadn't realized he was holding his breath. He slid into the chair and immediately inhaled that wonderful scent of lavender and fresh linen. "Do you enjoy the piano, Miss Sparrow?"

She nodded, then seemed to consider something. "I took

lessons when I was younger," she said after a moment. "My father hired a rather exacting German man to teach me, though he never deemed my talent anything more than 'tolerable.'"

"Then you were far more successful than me. I spent most of my music lessons playing pranks on my teacher. The poor chap finally quit after I hid a frog in his satchel."

"Oh, that is awful." She laughed. "I was *terrified* of Herr Becker. I used to tremble during the first few minutes of every lesson."

"Do you still play?"

"Only when I am called upon. But nothing more advanced than Beethoven's middle period. I do love the Impressionist composers though."

Rafe nodded in agreement. "I saw a wonderful program that included a piece by Mr. Debussy at the Proms in London this summer. Have you ever been?"

She hesitated again, the movement so tiny that he almost didn't catch it, but then she shook her head. "No. I've never had the privilege. I've only been to London briefly, once I was hired by Mrs. Crawford. And we left for Scotland shortly after."

"I have great plans for her once we return, though," Mrs. Crawford cut in, giving Rafe a significant look. He could have sworn she was hard of hearing, but it was a good reminder that she was sharper-eyed than most. "I think my young companion will be particularly interested in the British Museum's Egyptian collections, especially before our trip. Wouldn't you agree?"

Rafe nodded. "Unfortunately, much of the country's greatest treasures are housed there."

Miss Sparrow raised an eyebrow. "You disapprove of the practice?"

"Well, yes. Those items are invaluable cultural artifacts stolen by tomb raiders. If someone had come to England and taken off with the crown jewels, there would be a war."

"Oh, but it is hardly the same!" Mrs. Crawford insisted. "If it were not for the valiant efforts of men like Sir Petrie, much of those artifacts would be lost to the desert."

"Those efforts were aided by the native Egyptians, madam," Rafe gently reminded her. "Most of whom were deceived by those very same explorers. I don't call that valiant."

Mrs. Crawford looked like she had a great deal more to say about that, but Lady Arlington, who had been busy discussing the program with the other performers, took her seat at the piano, and the audience went quiet. The old woman huffed and sat back in her chair, but Miss Sparrow was looking at him with a delightful little smile of approval. Rafe gave her a wink, just in case she (or he) forgot his libertine ways, and turned toward the front.

CHAPTER SEVEN

Sylvia had had very few opportunities over the last few years to hear live music, aside from Sunday church service. Unfortunately, Herr Becker would have declared the organist in her little village intolerable, as old Mrs. Morrow's repertoire seemed to consist of the same three hymns. One could hear "Nearer, My God, to Thee" only so many times without screaming. When Sylvia had first arrived in London, she had taken every available opportunity to see concerts, including a particularly memorable outing with Bernard to the Queen's Hall. She had been so dazzled by both the concert and his attentions that she'd ended the evening in his bed for the first time.

But after she'd returned home to Hawthorne Cottage, she had been restricted to the piddling entertainments available in the village and church on Sundays.

Listening to Georgiana, however, was an even rarer treat. At school she had been widely regarded as an excellent musician who played with an undeniable joyfulness. But all that had ended after her marriage, as the viscount didn't approve of his wife performing for an audience. Usually Georgiana never questioned him, but he was hundreds of miles away now. And they were all the better for it.

As soon as Georgiana pressed her hands to the gleaming white keys and released the opening notes of a Chopin nocturne, Sylvia was transported. The music seemed to pulse through her body, racing across every inch, every limb until she was filled with nothing but pure sound. How she had forgotten what it felt like to get lost in something that went beyond herself. To revel in one of life's true pleasures. Sylvia would never understand why Georgiana had given up so much of herself for a husband, and during her first Season. The longer she played, the more she seemed to emit a glow. With every note her blue eyes grew more vibrant, while the furrow between her brows deepened in a look of single-minded focus. Where had this Georgiana gone to? A bittersweet ache moved harshly through Sylvia, and she closed her eyes. A Mozart sonata followed, along with a newer piece Sylvia didn't recognize. But every note was full of Georgiana's passion, her talent, her determination. The things she tried so very hard to hide behind her serene smile and cool exterior. All too soon the music ended, and the pulsing sensation slowly faded into the echoing silence.

When she opened her eyes, Georgiana was perfectly calm and collected once again. All traces of her impassioned display had been carefully smoothed away, as if they had never surfaced—though she looked slightly embarrassed by the audience's enthusiastic applause. Sylvia felt a sudden, sharp pang of regret. She wished she knew how to help her dear friend, but Georgiana refused to even admit anything was wrong. Refused to see just how much she had given up. And

Sylvia wasn't in any position to push her further. They were both trapped by their lies. Mr. Davies wordlessly handed her his handkerchief. To Sylvia's utter embarrassment, a tear had slipped down her cheek.

"Thank you," she said softly, but she couldn't bring herself to look at him just yet. She felt too raw to be seen by anyone at the moment, as if the very notes themselves had stripped her bare.

"Of course," he murmured with a gentleness that washed over her like a warm embrace, and she turned to him then, drawn by something even stronger than her embarrassment. But his voice was nothing compared to the kindness in his eyes, and Sylvia's heart twisted so hard that for a moment she couldn't breathe.

Mr. Davies noticed her distress and grew alarmed. "Are you all right?"

She inhaled deeply as the precious organ skittered, searching for the right beat. "Yes," she breathed. "Yes, I'm fine."

"You were affected. By the music," he offered as his gaze darkened. The penetrating look sank even more deeply than the music had.

Sylvia turned away, unable to articulate her true feelings. It wasn't only the music that had affected her. "I haven't heard anything so beautiful in a very long time," she admitted, then shook her head and tried to give him back his handkerchief. "I'm sorry. I feel so silly—"

"Please don't," he urged in a rough voice. "It was quite... moving."

He closed her fingers firmly over his handkerchief, then pulled away. They touched for only a brief moment, but Sylvia felt the loss acutely, as if her own hand had been taken from her. Before she could say anything more, he stood and bowed as Georgiana joined him.

"My lady, you were extraordinary. I hope to have a chance to listen to you play again very soon."

Georgiana blushed. "Really, it was nothing," she demurred.

"Hardly," he said with a smile before addressing Sylvia and Mrs. Crawford. "Thank you for allowing me to keep you company, ladies. Enjoy the rest of your afternoon."

Before either could respond, he swiftly turned and exited their row. Sylvia stared dumbfounded at his abrupt departure, still clutching his handkerchief.

Mrs. Crawford's eyes followed him with a barely veiled moue of disapproval. "That man is incredibly *odd*," she pronounced.

Georgiana also kept her gaze on Mr. Davies. "Take pity on him, Aunt. I think the fellow is a bit out of sorts today." Then she caught Sylvia's eye and lowered her voice. "And I think I know the reason."

Sylvia blushed and looked down at the handkerchief. She ran a finger over the finely embroidered *R X D* at the edge done in a simple, classic scrollwork. She had seen gentlemen far lower in station with vastly more elaborate handkerchiefs and accouterments. The linen itself was of superior quality but soft from wear. Mr. Davies may be many things, but boastful and frivolous were not among them. This brought a smile to her lips as she folded the handkerchief and tucked it into her sleeve, where the brush of the linen against her wrist set her pulse throbbing anew.

* * *

After nearly kissing the tear from Miss Sparrow's cheek in front of the entire room, Rafe resolved to keep his distance as much as possible. It was insupportable for a reprobate of the highest order to be affected by such a maudlin display of feminine emotion. And yet the thought of licking her salt from his lips had left him breathless. It was one thing to be pleasantly distracted by a pretty face, but the sheer force of his desire was alarming. He didn't simply want to bed her, but to talk to her. To reveal things he spoke of to no one else. But hearing her speak about her childhood was a harsh reminder of the depths of his own deception. And the ache that followed had driven him from her company.

He still saw her briefly during the day, dutifully walking with her employer or emerging from the library with the dazed look of someone completely absorbed in their work. Then his ravenous eyes would devour her delicate features from across the room, while his ears stretched to listen to the few words that escaped those rosebud lips. On more than one occasion she caught him outright staring, but Rafe always made sure he was the first to turn away even as his body cried out in protest.

Instead he forced himself to indulge in the growing attentions of Lady Taylor-Smyth, who, like him, was an outrageous flirt. She was exactly the type of woman he should want. A meaningless dalliance while they were both at the castle would be entirely in keeping with his reputation—and frankly, it would be strange if he didn't indulge. Rafe had often found such encounters acted as a much-needed release from the pressures of his work. And yet, even as he smiled at her bon mots and winked when her hand lingered just a touch too long on his arm, he could not muster any interest in pursuing things behind closed doors.

The rest of the time he focused on the search, making use of those fleeting hours when the guests were busy with entertainments and outings, leaving their rooms empty. But after three days he had uncovered nothing. Rafe needed to consider the possibility that he would not succeed.

Missions had gone belly up before, but to have Gerard know of his failure particularly grated. Rafe had so wanted to throw this success in his brother's face and see that smug mouth thank him for his service. And there was a hell of a lot of things he was still willing to do to make that happen. Rafe hardly ever experienced jealousy or anger, emotions he considered largely useless. He had never minded when his lovers weren't faithful or if someone excelled at a task he found difficult or even impossible. When his friends earned promotions or found love or uncovered secret inheritances, Rafe was always the first to offer his congratulations and always with genuine happiness.

But whenever he thought of Gerard, something ugly and rotten burned inside him. And every time he snuffed out the flame, it came back twice as hot. Rafe knew he should be above this. Knew he should work harder to control such emotions. And yet he could not summon the desire. It hadn't always been that way. When he was a boy, there had been a fine portrait of his half siblings in his father's study. Rafe used to spend hours playing under it, imagining all the adventures they would have once they were together. He was particularly dazzled by the very idea of his older brother, an interest that bordered on obsession. But, as his father explained over and over with a patience that still made Rafe's heart ache years later, Gerard was away at school, then university, then traveling abroad. His father visited his other children occasionally, when estate business or governmental duties required him to return to England, but none of them ever came to see him at any of his diplomatic posts. Eventually Rafe realized that the long-wished-for reunion would never come and that the children he had imagined during those long lonely afternoons didn't actually exist. It was some years hence before he fully understood why or learned how very deeply his half siblings' loathing for him went.

Rafe began taking bracing walks late at night on the terrace that ran along the castle's ground level. It was the only thing that helped clear his jumbled thoughts and kept his growing panic at bay. And it was during those turns breathing in the peaty fall air that he worked to unravel the case before him, as well as his growing attraction for Miss Sparrow. He had been bowled over by lust before and had succumbed to inconvenient desires, but this was a different kind of want. A different kind of need. Something that went beyond the physical. He had experienced a similar ache last spring when he met the woman who would become Alec Gresham's wife. He had at first mistaken the former Lottie Carlisle for a delightfully fiery courtesan, but she had quickly set him straight with a solid slap he most certainly deserved. Lottie was only a young woman hopelessly in love with his idiot friend. But Rafe had greatly admired her spirit, even when he suspected her of having mercenary motives. Perhaps even more then.

There was the same kind of quiet indomitableness about Miss Sparrow, as if she could conquer far-off lands before sitting down to breakfast. But she could also be exceedingly wary. Reluctant to share even the most inconsequential details about herself. Rafe could usually spot a liar, but reticence was a different sort of challenge. As far as he knew, the only solution was to develop trust over time.

And then what? You will tell her about yourself?

Rafe stopped in his tracks and pressed his palms against a low stone wall, staring off into blackness. For nearly ten years he had lived behind an image he had created all in service to queen and country. But what had that left him with? The longer he stayed in this position, the more his old friendships had withered as his contemporaries got on with the business of real life. But Rafe didn't have a real life anymore. He had traded it for the chance to be a different version of himself, and for many years that had been enough. More than enough. Now, though...now he couldn't shake the feeling that he had been caught up in a very long game of pretend, just like when he was a boy.

From a dozen yards away came the sound of a door opening. In the dim light emitted from the castle, Rafe could make out a figure stepping onto the terrace from the library. After several moments the faint glow of a match flared as the figure lit something and the smell of burnt tobacco wafted toward him. His heart warmed from long-ago memories of his father, who had ended every meal with a pipe. Rafe walked slowly toward the figure, taking care to muffle his footsteps as much as possible until he could determine who it was. Then decide if he felt like making his presence known.

The figure let out a soft sigh and moved into a streak of light from the library. Rafe's breath caught. There was only one guest in the entire castle who would be caught dressed in something as sensible as a plain white shirtwaist and dark skirt or allow her hair to become even slightly disheveled.

Miss Sparrow.

Before he had time to think twice, Rafe approached her, his tread growing louder with each step. But she seemed entirely lost in thought. Rafe wasn't daft enough to think he was on her mind, but that didn't stop the little flicker of hope in his chest. She leaned back and blew an impressive ring of smoke into the air. It hovered for a moment like a halo before dispersing into the night.

"Hasn't anyone told you that's a filthy habit?"

Sylvia let out a short shout and nearly dropped what Rafe could now see was a small pipe. "Mr. Davies," she gasped, pressing a hand to her chest before shooting him a glare. "Don't you know it's not *polite* to sneak up on a person?"

Rafe held up his hands. "So sorry. I should have announced myself immediately. But I wanted to see who you were first."

Sylvia stared at him for an achingly long moment before the glare faded. Then she crossed her free arm just below her breasts, lifting them slightly. Rafe made sure to keep his eyes on her face. She may not possess the eye-catching curves of Lady Arlington, but there was still much to admire in her figure.

"I suppose I should be flattered, then," she said flatly before she took another puff and blew the smoke out from the corner of her mouth. "I only smoke when I'm working, you know. I find it helps when I get stuck, or so I tell myself."

"I've not seen many women smoke a pipe. At least, not in England."

Sylvia held the instrument out and looked at it with something like fondness. "It was my father's. It was the only thing of his I kept after he died."

"I'm sorry for your loss. When was that?"

Sylvia gazed out into the night. "Last year. He had been

sick for a long time, so people said it was a blessing. I never understood that. The true blessing would have been him never falling ill in the first place."

"I heard the same sentiments when my own father died," Rafe said as he moved closer. "Many find comfort in reciting platitudes to the grieving. Loss is viewed as a universal experience, but in so many ways it is deeply personal. Any suggestion otherwise feels like an insult."

Miss Sparrow raised an eyebrow. "Yes," she agreed.

"But then I try to remember that people mean well, that death can be an uncomfortable subject to discuss, and that most are ignorant of the offense they cause." He ignored Miss Sparrow's surprised expression and gestured to the pipe. "Mine smoked one as well."

She blinked at the change of subject. "I think it's the smell I like best," she explained, still watching him with a new kind of wariness, as if she hadn't encountered a creature of his ilk before. "It makes me think of childhood. Comfort. Cozy evenings by the fire." Rafe smiled. It was as if she were narrating his thoughts. She turned away again. "Sometimes I wonder if it's possible to ever feel safe like that again." The words were spoken in a near whisper, as if they were half thought. Miss Sparrow then shook her head, her entire body tensing. "Never mind. I don't know what I'm saying," she said. "I've spent too much time alone with words today." She took another puff of the pipe and turned to him. "Why are you out here?"

"The night air helps clear my head." Was that a snicker he heard? "So, you're having a bit of trouble finding words tonight?"

Miss Sparrow held out a hand. "Don't even say it. You'll curse me. No, I just needed a break from writing about Mrs.

Crawford's adventures. It's fascinating. She's done so much, and all without apology. I...I envy her." Based on the surprise in her voice, Rafe guessed this was a new realization.

"You're hardly ancient, Miss Sparrow." He chuckled. "There is plenty of time to have adventures of your own." Rafe ignored the voice in his head offering himself up as one of them. "And you will be traveling abroad this winter."

"If I'm still employed by then," she muttered.

"Why on earth wouldn't you be?"

Miss Sparrow shook her head even harder and looked down. "No reason. Sorry, I'm afraid I'm something of a pessimist." Then she turned toward him. "I should go. It's quite late...and I don't want to keep you."

"Keep me from what?" Rafe couldn't keep the incredulity from his voice. Until he suddenly caught on to what she was suggesting—or rather *whom*.

Lady Taylor-Smyth means nothing to me. It is all for show. But not this.

Rafe pressed his lips together to keep the words from spilling out. She had moved out of the light, and he couldn't see her face clearly now, but he could feel her eyes upon him. Watching. Wondering.

"Nothing. No one," she said quickly. "Good night, Mr. Davies." Then, before he could wish her the same, Miss Sparrow turned and retreated back to the library. Rafe waited until the smell of tobacco smoke faded away into the cool night air before returning to his room, alone.

CHAPTER EIGHT

◦

Sylvia and Georgiana had whiled away the afternoon quite pleasantly in the library in a pair of high-backed chairs by the massive stone fireplace. Sylvia had spent much of the time transcribing her notes from another revelatory conversation with Mrs. Crawford, while Georgiana gobbled up another Inspector DuMonde novel. Aside from the bits about her second husband, Mrs. Crawford was not the least bit interested in Sylvia's progress as long as she had enough completed pages by the time they returned to London. When she had written for *The Defender* Sylvia had worked well under deadlines— *thrived* on them, in fact—and this gave her something to think about other than Mr. Davies.

When he had approached her last night, she had been busy picking out Cassiopeia. It was a clear night, and the stars were scattered like diamonds above them. She assumed he had been waiting to meet Lady Taylor-Smyth. Whispers about the pair had been growing stronger by the day. It seemed like the perfect setting for a romantic rendezvous, and he certainly hadn't been skulking about in the darkness waiting for *her*. Ever since they shared that lovely moment during the musical performance, he had been quite obviously avoiding her. Adding to her confusion were the few times she had caught him outright staring at her from across the room. But rather than stay in the shadows, he had made his presence known.

She could just make out his tall frame, smell his shaving soap, and feel the warmth coming off his body, barely inches from her own. Though she hadn't been able to see his face, she could sense every expression. It had been easier to speak with him like that in the near darkness, like being in a confessional. Once again he surprised her with his not-so-hidden depths, and she marveled at how this man appeared to have two very different sides to him.

Or perhaps he is simply bored and toying with you.

Sylvia was no stranger to deception. She knew all too well that a man could show one face in private and a very different one to the rest of the world. And she had been caught on the wrong side of the coin before. Though Mr. Davies had seemed perfectly happy to continue their conversation, Sylvia had no desire to be there when his paramour arrived. Besides, she had little use for a man who could only be vulnerable under the cover of darkness.

Just as a fresh wave of disappointment began to crest, her pencil came to a scratching halt. Sylvia glanced down and realized she had been scrawling absolutely nothing these last moments. She clucked her tongue in annoyance.

Damn that man.

She arched her back in a much-needed stretch and looked over at Georgiana. "My goodness, you're nearly done!"

"Yes," Georgiana replied while keeping her eyes firmly on the page. "I don't think I'll be able to stop until the end."

"Well, I've reached the end of my pencil. I'm going to

nip back to the suite for another. Do you need anything while I'm gone?"

The viscountess responded with a distracted grunt that Sylvia interpreted as "No, thank you."

She returned a short time later with a freshly sharpened pencil to find Georgiana laughing with someone who had taken her seat. The occupant boasted a head of perfectly styled dark hair that immediately set her teeth on edge.

Him.

She glowered at his back, something she hadn't the nerve to do to his front the past few days. But why bother with niceties she didn't feel? The house party would end next week, and she would never have to see him again. She ignored the bite of regret that followed the thought.

Georgiana tilted her head back to laugh again and caught sight of Sylvia. "Oh, there is Miss Sparrow now!"

Sylvia let out a little sigh. It was too late to make an escape. She approached them stiffly, determined to stay only a moment to retrieve her things and treat Mr. Davies with the same cool politeness he bestowed upon her in public.

"Good afternoon, Miss Sparrow."

Her resolve faltered slightly at his silky tone and easy smile, but Sylvia tipped her chin up. "Sir," she said with only a touch of asperity. It would go against her purposes if he knew just how deeply he had gotten under her skin. Then she held out her hand, palm up. "If you'll be so kind as to pass me my things, I will leave you to your visit."

Her imperious tone seemed to take him by surprise, but Mr. Davies quickly gathered her notebook from the side table. "Here you are."

His fingers brushed hers briefly, and Sylvia had to fight

the tremble that rippled down her arm. It had not escaped her notice how well-formed his hands were. "Thank you," she said with exacting politeness, then glanced over at Georgiana. The viscountess's mouth was hanging open in such a decidedly unladylike display that Sylvia had to look away before she burst out laughing and ruined everything.

Once she had exited the room and made it halfway down the hallway, her shoulders sagged with relief. There. That had gone remarkably well. If she *had* to see him again, she could easily treat him in the same distant manner—

"Miss Sparrow!"

Sylvia froze. It was Mr. Davies. And he looked rather aggrieved.

She had not planned for this.

He approached her and swiftly bowed. "I can't help but think you left on my account. Not that I don't deserve it," he added sheepishly.

Sylvia rolled her eyes. This false modesty was really too much.

"Don't trouble yourself with such delusions, sir." He let out a little huff, but before he could speak further, Sylvia continued. "I know this must be a difficult concept for you to understand, but I am not flattered by your fickle attentions."

Instead of being offended, he merely tilted his head and studied her. "Is that so?"

The lazy drawl of his voice paired with the gleam in his eyes caused the most distracting flutter in a rather inconvenient part of her body. "What is it you *want*?" she demanded.

"Right this moment or in general?" Sylvia scoffed and began to turn away, but he caught her elbow. "Wait! I'm sorry. I came to ask if you were going to the entertainment this evening."

The warmth from his large, firm fingers seeped through the sleeve of her blouse, and the inconvenient fluttering turned into a rather fierce pulse. His eyes were now dark and serious. "You—you mean the dancing?" Mr. Wardale had arranged for a quartet to come to the house and play for the guests. He nodded and pulled his hand back slowly, letting the tips of his fingers drag down her arm just a little. Sylvia cleared her throat and straightened. "I am Mrs. Crawford's companion, Mr. Davies. What use would I have for dancing?"

"I imagine the same as everyone. For fun."

She gave him a determined frown, desperately trying to recapture her disdain. "I have work to do."

"Surely Mrs. Crawford's memoirs can be neglected for an evening," he teased as his full mouth stretched in a slow, tantalizing smile.

Sylvia cleared her throat and shrugged. It was the only response she could manage at the moment.

Mr. Davies's smile turned into a grin, and he bowed again. "Until then, Miss Sparrow."

He turned around, tucked his hands in his pockets, and began whistling a tune she didn't recognize. Sylvia watched him stroll down the entire length of hallway back to the library before she came to her senses and stormed off in the opposite direction.

* * *

Georgiana returned to the suite a little while later wearing a knowing smile, but she said nothing of Mr. Davies, and Sylvia refused to *ask*. But when it was time to dress for dinner, Georgiana pulled her into her room and thrust an evening gown into her arms.

"You need to wear that later. I know we aren't quite the same size, but Bea said she could easily take it in for the night."

Sylvia held up the gown, which had been tailored to fit over Georgiana's enviable curves. It was a gorgeous burgundy velvet overlaid with intricate black beadwork at the bodice and quarter-length puffed sleeves. "Absolutely not," she immediately said. "Why on earth did you even bring it? I've never seen you wear this color."

"I thought it might be useful," she said with a wink. "Aren't the sleeves adorable?"

Sylvia shot her a half-hearted glare before running her fingers over the impossibly fine fabric. "Thank you, but I have an evening gown already."

"All of your gowns make you look like a drab little spinster."

"I *am* a drab little spinster."

Georgiana fixed her with a look. "But you needn't be, Sylvie. I know Mr. Davies sees what I see."

"Georgiana—"

"And this is a wonderful chance for you," she continued.

The hope burning in the viscountess's bright blue eyes was nearly as vexing as her words.

"A chance for what?" Sylvia burst out. Then she craned her neck toward the open door and lowered her voice. "The man is clearly interested in Lady Taylor-Smyth. Everyone says so." Georgiana began to dismiss this, but Sylvia pressed on. "And what happens when he finds out the truth?" she hissed. "What happens when he learns that Sylvia Sparrow doesn't exist, and all I am is Sylvia Wilcox. Harlot. Anarchist. *Conspirator.*"

Not to mention accomplice to a blackmailer.

"You aren't those things," Georgiana insisted.

92

"Don't try to deny it. My views were printed in enough columns to prove otherwise."

To say nothing of the so-called news articles that twisted the facts surrounding her arrest to create the most salacious story possible.

Georgiana let out an exasperated huff. "You made thoughtful critiques about a system that works for only a select few and gave voice to the thoughts many have had. But thanks to that *coward* Bernard and his horrible father, you were wrongly arrested while trying to help other women. Then you made sure they were all released, even at a personal cost to yourself. It was an act of bravery."

"Not everyone would call it that," Sylvia said darkly.

Georgiana wrung her hands and turned away. "Yes, I know. And I hate that we had to lie to my aunt, but I couldn't take the chance that his lordship would find out about your past."

Sylvia sighed. Even before the arrest, she hadn't been deemed appropriate company for Georgiana. The viscount rarely let his wife mix with anyone outside their vaunted social circle, as he didn't want any reminders that he had been compelled to marry outside the aristocracy.

"Besides," Georgiana continued. "You wouldn't accept my money, remember?"

Sylvia bristled. When she first told Georgiana that her brother had reneged on their agreement in order to let Hawthorne Cottage and offered her a one-way ticket to Australia, an increasingly popular destination for single women, the viscountess immediately sent an outrageous check that she refused to cash. She didn't want charity. She needed a future. "No. I asked for help finding a position."

"And it's all worked out. You're perfect for my aunt. And

it's been so *nice* seeing you again." Georgiana's voice wavered slightly, and Sylvia's throat tightened.

"It has," she agreed. "And I will never be able to repay your kindness, but this...this thing with Mr. Davies can go no further. Besides, even without my past, I'm still nothing more than the daughter of a middling country scholar. Men like him don't marry below their station without—"

"Without an economic incentive, you mean," Georgiana finished.

"Well, yes," Sylvia agreed distractedly. "But it's hardly the main reason. I know you think finding a husband will make me happy, but that isn't what I want. It never was. There is too much to give up."

Georgiana stared at her for a long moment. "I would be the very last woman in the world to ever think such a thing," she said softly, but there was a brittle edge in her voice that grew more pronounced as she spoke. "This was a suggestion specific to Mr. Davies. A suggestion to talk to the man. Because I have seen the way you look at each other. Because I know what that means. And I don't want you to make the same mistake I did."

Georgiana's eyes widened as she realized what she had just admitted. Then she looked away and pressed a trembling hand across her brow. Sylvia watched, stunned, as Georgiana's face crumpled for a moment before she mastered it. When was the last time she had allowed herself to exhibit such a loss of control? Sylvia couldn't remember.

"Oh, Georgiana. I'm such an idiot," she said, moving to embrace her. "I didn't mean to insult you. I only meant that I've never believed such things were for me."

After a moment Georgiana returned the hug. "Of course.

I'm sorry. I don't know what came over me," she explained, her tone now carefully composed. "And I suppose I understand the source of your reservations."

Sylvia pulled back and raised an eyebrow. "That he is the son of an earl and I was once accused of harboring anarchistic sympathies?"

"Well, when you put it that way," Georgiana said sheepishly. "But I still think you should wear the gown. For yourself. In fact, I am making it a condition of my forgiveness."

Sylvia laughed and hugged her tighter. "In that case, I accept."

* * *

Castle Blackwood's ballroom, which hadn't been used in well over a decade, was still being readied for the fancy dress ball to celebrate Halloween that would be held in a few days' time, so tonight's activities were taking place in the music room. As it was a touch smaller than needed, the room was positively packed with guests, and the space left for dancing was tight. Rafe spotted a few harassed-looking musicians in the corner being instructed by Lady Delacorte. She was one of the biggest snobs in London but now took up the role of de facto hostess whenever the opportunity arose. Mr. Wardale was standing nearby, watching the commanding young woman go through potential songs with the violinist with a steadily growing smile. They had agreed to meet briefly at the top of the hour, as fewer people would notice their absence once the dancing got underway. Rafe wondered if the man planned to offer for his burgeoning hostess—or maybe he simply enjoyed having the daughter of a lord try so very hard to win his approval. With

Wardale it could be either, both, or a third option Rafe would rather not imagine.

Even after spending the last week in his home, Rafe still didn't have a firm grasp of his host's character. This was unusual, but then so was Wardale. Rafe was further ruminating on the man's mercurial nature when the room's air seemed to thicken. He turned around just in time to see Miss Sparrow make her entrance a step behind Mrs. Crawford and Lady Arlington. She was resplendent in a deep red gown that hugged her nimble waist, while the low-cut bodice shimmered in the soft light, drawing even more attention to the tops of her small but shapely breasts. It was hardly the most revealing gown in the room, but Rafe had yet to see her wear anything that didn't button at her throat. Her light brown hair had been pulled back into a simple knot at the nape of her neck, while a few artfully placed curls perfectly framed her face. She wore her usual expression of watchful wariness, but without her typical somber attire as an accompaniment, one could mistake her for a naive innocent. A debutante at her first dance. A kind of predatory awareness streaked through him. No one would overlook her tonight.

The glass of the county's finest single malt Rafe had taken in his room beforehand had not numbed him nearly enough, and he shoved his hands into his trouser pockets. It was obscene how she drew his truest self to the surface with nothing more than a few words or a glance. And yet, even as the logical part of his mind demanded he retreat, the rest craved more. He weaved through the crowded room to meet the trio by the refreshments table, but Bert Leonard got there first. Rafe stopped in his tracks and glowered at the young man's back. He was making grand overtures to Mrs. Crawford and

Lady Arlington, but they were not his true target. Rafe caught the viscountess's eye, and she gave him a helpless little shrug. According to the dictates of polite society, he should wait his turn and greet Miss Sparrow's betters first. Luckily, no one expected him to bother with such civilities. If there was something the Honorable Rafe Davies wanted, he simply took it.

He moved to step around them and inadvertently came directly into the path of Lady Taylor-Smyth—though he guessed it had not been quite so accidental on her end.

"Good evening, my lady," he said politely.

"You are looking well, Mr. Davies. I certainly hope your dance card isn't full yet," she teased as her eyes slid down his form in an appreciation so blatant, even Rafe felt a little uncomfortable. He darted a subtle glance at Miss Sparrow, who stood only a mere foot away, then looked back at Lady Taylor-Smyth, but her eyes narrowed. He was losing his touch. "Don't let me keep you," she scoffed. "I confess, I was given to understand your tastes were decidedly more sophisticated. But I won't be *any* man's second choice. Especially one who lacks such discernment."

Before Rafe could reply, she snapped open her fan and heaved off on a dismissive flutter. He glanced again at Miss Sparrow just as she turned away.

Damn. She must have heard everything.

Rafe's face flushed. His reputation was hardly a secret, but having it alluded to so baldly, and in front of Miss Sparrow, was surprisingly embarrassing.

Turn around and make your apologies to Lady Taylor-Smyth. Show her exactly *how discerning you can be.*

But something that ran miles deeper than his embarrassment took hold, propelling him forward. To hell with Lady

Taylor-Smyth and her snobbery. He came up behind Miss Sparrow's shoulder, and though she had just been pretending not to eavesdrop, she turned her head slightly toward him.

"Good evening, Miss Sparrow."

She nodded. "Mr. Davies."

He cut a glance toward Bert. Luckily, the boy was still lavishing praise on Mrs. Crawford and hadn't yet taken notice of him. "I want the waltz." The rough command tumbled out before he had time to think, and regret immediately followed. Who was he to make such a demand of her? Rafe held his breath, waiting for the inevitable rejection.

But her full lips pursed, as if she were suppressing a smile. "All right."

Rafe blinked. "Truly?"

She began to laugh and then caught herself. "Yes. If it's so important to you."

Rafe leaned in as close as he dared, until he could catch a whiff of lavender and fresh linen. "I'm afraid it is," he murmured by her ear.

She shivered a little and swayed toward him, the movement so subtle she probably wasn't conscious of it, but Rafe stepped away and allowed the crowd to swallow him. Only a moment later Bert addressed Miss Sparrow. Then he asked a question, and Miss Sparrow tilted her head, her body language the perfect picture of regret. Bert scanned the room, and when his eyes fell on Rafe, his face screwed up in a childish frown. Rafe raised his hands in a show of penitence they both knew he didn't mean. The boy's scowl deepened briefly, but then he turned back to Miss Sparrow and gave a gracious bow. He would take another dance instead.

As the musicians started up a lively polka, Rafe slowly made his way around the perimeter waiting for his turn, ignoring the not-so-subtle pouts Lady Taylor-Smyth kept casting in his direction. He had searched the rooms of nearly every male guest here and uncovered far more than he wanted and nothing that he needed. The older man leaning heavily on an elaborately carved cane was battling a laudanum addiction, an attractive widow on the hunt was flirting with a man who worked very hard to give the appearance of wealth while having barely a penny to his name, while the two middle-aged gentlemen standing near the refreshments table were not only friends of long-standing but lovers.

There were agents who relished having these little glimpses into the lives of others, but intruding on the privacy of innocent people unknowingly entangled in a mission had always repulsed Rafe. Let them have their secrets; Lord knew he had plenty of his own, and his conscience did not need the extra weight. He rolled his shoulders and shook his head, ridding his mind of those heavy thoughts. Wardale wanted to meet soon. But Rafe hadn't found anything relevant to his purposes, and it was fair to assume that a man like him didn't like being disappointed.

Rafe found an empty corner of the room and leaned against the wall with an apathy he did not feel. Miss Sparrow was now dancing with someone else and moved through the intricate steps with a graceful competence. She may harbor some more radical opinions, but it was clear she had received some education in the feminine arts. No doubt that would have been a trying experience. Rafe's lips quirked at the thought of her not-so-subtly rolling her eyes through a deportment lesson. As the song ended, Miss Sparrow curtsied to her partner, then exchanged a smile with Lady Arlington. Perhaps they had met at some fancy finishing school for young ladies or had grown up together. Both were perfectly innocuous explanations, and yet they had taken great pains to conceal their history...

Rafe bit back a sigh and pushed away from the wall. He would ruminate on that later. Now it was time to claim his waltz. Miss Sparrow appeared to sense his approach even from across the room and turned toward him. Those large gray eyes flashed with a heat that sank into his bones, while a part of him raged in frustration. He didn't have *time* for this. He should leave now. Wait for Wardale and discuss his next move. But Rafe did none of those things. He continued walking until he stood before Miss Sparrow. Until he could count the beats of the pulse thrumming at the base of her exposed throat. Until he could fill his lungs with her delicate scent, which was now so achingly familiar. Then he bowed and took her gloved hand in his. When the first notes of the waltz commenced, he pulled her close and gripped her waist with greedy fingers. Miss Sparrow inhaled sharply, as if a clap of thunder had cracked just above their heads, and Rafe felt an answering charge bolt down his arm, causing him to stumble through the first few steps.

"Terribly sorry."

Miss Sparrow raised an eyebrow, obviously surprised that a gentleman of his standing couldn't manage a simple box step. He renewed his focus and managed to successfully maneuver them through the first turn. After that inauspicious start, they found their rhythm.

Rafe considered himself to be a reasonably good dancer, and none of his partners had ever complained, but dancing with Miss Sparrow was an entirely new experience. Their bodies were so highly attuned that they could anticipate each other and react accordingly. Rafe was tempted to close his eyes just to see what would happen, but then he would not have the pleasure of staring at her face.

"Are you always this silent when you dance?" Miss Sparrow asked in a deceptively sweet voice. "And do you always glower at your partners?"

Rafe immediately relaxed his brow. "I am not glowering. I was simply looking at you."

"Well, then, do you always look at your partners with such focus?" She kept her tone light, giving him a chance to save face.

"No," he admitted as he held her gaze. "I most assuredly do not."

A faint blush stained her cheeks, and she glanced away. Rafe's fingers flexed against the small of her back. They had only a few more moments together. And if there was something their host wanted, Rafe would have no choice but to deal with it immediately.

But she was a mystery he desperately wanted to solve.

"Meet me in an hour," he murmured. "In the library."

She continued to keep her eyes trained on a spot just over his shoulder. "For what purpose?"

It was a fair question. Rafe didn't have a clear answer. He simply wasn't ready to part with her yet.

"I want your opinion on a novel." Her lips quirked at the joke. "And this is hardly the place. I have something I need to attend to now, but I will go directly there afterward."

She remained silent, and he could see the hesitation in her gray-eyed gaze. If only she could hear how loudly his heart pounded.

The waltz then came to an end without her answer, and Rafe brushed his lips to the back of her hand. "I hope this is not good night, Miss Sparrow."

CHAPTER NINE

S ylvia crept down the darkened hallway toward the library.
She had complained of a headache to Mrs. Crawford, who
insisted she go to bed *immediately* lest it developed into something more serious. Now the music and laughter from the
gathering slowly faded until only the swishing of her skirts, the
tinkling of beads, and the rapid beating of her heart filled her
ears. Sylvia paused to look over her shoulder. The hallway was
completely empty. No one had followed her, and yet she
couldn't quite shake the feeling that she was again being
watched.

She picked up her skirts to move faster. It was only a bout
of nerves, likely spurred by the sheer madness of what she
was doing: meeting a man she hardly knew by herself—not
to mention a man with his reputation. But it was hard to
remember all her well-thought-out reservations when he was
standing before her, staring as if she were the only woman
in the world. Why, he had invoked the legendary ire of Lady
Taylor-Smyth—a dangerous prospect, indeed—by asking *her*
to dance. Sylvia should have said no. A lady's companion
wasn't supposed to draw attention to herself. And waltzing

with handsome men in the most expensive piece of clothing she had ever worn had the exact opposite effect. But the trouble was Mr. Davies didn't feel like a stranger at all, and she had felt more like herself in his company these last few days than she had in years.

While they were dancing, he had held her a touch closer than appropriate in his powerful arms as the heat of his body and the scent of his bergamot shaving soap mingled together to create a rather potent narcotic. Even when he had been glowering down at her, Sylvia had felt safe, as if he would fight whole armies before letting any harm come her way. She wasn't used to that. Normally, she shouldered her burdens alone and solved other peoples' problems. But Mr. Davies seemed to want to solve hers instead, if she let him. Not that she ever would.

Good Lord, you don't even know his first name.

A minor detail that could be easily righted.

And if you are discovered together, you will be ruined. Again.

That was not so easily brushed aside.

Sylvia paused a few feet from the entrance to the library. She could still turn back. No one would have even noticed her absence yet. The part of her that had urged caution these last years, the part that burned with constant shame, with regret, the part of her that ached to go back in time and make different choices cried out in the low light of the hall.

You have not come this far to throw it all away on another man.

She most certainly had not. But then how many of those choices had been of her own making? And how much more had she been forced to sacrifice because of the choices *other* people had made? Even now she carried a burden foisted on her by someone else.

You're a force of nature. When you allow yourself to be.

How she ached for Georgiana's words to be true again. She was so tired of shrinking down to a more manageable version of herself. But whatever Mr. Davies wanted from her, whatever awaited on the other side of that door, would be her choice to make.

Sylvia straightened her shoulders and strode toward the library with renewed purpose. Excitement thrummed through her every muscle, every nerve, propelling her forward until she could barely breathe. She pushed open the heavy wooden door and stepped into the silent room, greeted by the now familiar scent of aging books and wood polish. Her eyes darted around, searching for his tall form. But as she walked in a slow, wide circle, taking in every unoccupied chair and darkened corner, a dim realization took hold, snuffing out the faint hope that had just begun to take shape.

The room was empty.

He hadn't come after all.

And she was an utter fool.

* * *

"Dammit, Davies, this is not what I wanted to hear." Wardale punctuated his disappointment by pounding a fist against his desk.

Rafe couldn't blame the man for his agitation, but that didn't change the facts.

"I will continue to search the rooms of the remaining guests, with your approval, of course."

"I want to know what you found."

Rafe's jaw tightened. "As I explained before, I did not find your missing letter, nor anything to suggest your guests are mixed up with Scottish separatists. They are as they appear."

A group of lazy, self-involved aristocrats.

"That isn't good enough. My butler could do the same job. I wanted *you* because I expected you would be able to tell me things that wouldn't be immediately obvious to a layman." In other words, Wardale wanted his guests' secrets. Rafe could understand his reasoning, but that didn't mean he agreed with it. "Otherwise," Wardale continued, "I will be unable to uphold my end of our bargain. Have I made myself clear?"

The back of Rafe's neck grew hot. Without Wardale's support, there was little chance his proposal would be accepted. He could see the blasted smirk curling Gerard's lips right now. "Perfectly," he growled.

He would turn this entire blasted castle inside out to prevent that.

"Good. I want a report of everything you find. And search *everyone* now. Perhaps you were right about that," Wardale grumbled. "Any of these ladies could be involved."

"Yes, sir."

Rafe turned to leave, but Wardale held up his hand. "What is your interest in Miss Sparrow?"

"Sir?"

Wardale frowned at his innocent tone. "I saw you dancing with her."

"My interest is obvious. She is a good-looking woman. And I am a rake."

"Rakes don't usually bother with ladies' companions. Not when there is far better fare to be had. You're in danger of causing talk, Davies. Lady Taylor-Smyth is not someone you want as an enemy. For that matter, neither is Mrs. Crawford."

"I assure you," Rafe said through his tightening throat, "nothing has happened."

Wardale's eyes took on a flinty edge. "Keep it that way and we won't have a problem."

Rafe's hand flexed against his thigh, but he said absolutely nothing. Let Wardale think he had all the power here. Rafe was then dismissed with a wave of his host's hand, and he immediately headed toward the library, doubts and worries nipping at his heels. But Miss Sparrow loomed larger. A blessed relief from the mess that trailed in his wake. Wardale had a point. A woman like her wasn't suitable, but he was selfish. Perhaps more than he realized. And he was abominably late. If she had bothered to come at all, there was little chance she was still there. His heart clenched at the thought of her waiting alone, wondering what sort of cruel joke he had played with her, and he moved even faster. He burst into the room, chest heaving, and whirled around. There she was, curled up deep in a chair in a shadowy corner. She looked up at his entrance, and Rafe's heart loosened with relief.

She had waited for him.

But as he strode over, the firelight caught a glimmer on her cheeks. Rafe fell to his knees before her. "You've been crying," he said dumbly.

The Honorable Rafe Davies was not the sort of man ladies cried over. He had expected anger, regret, or irritation but certainly not *tears*.

"Don't be absurd." She sniffed, wiping her face as she sat up. "I would never do such a thing."

But her breath caught as he reached out and brushed a thumb against her damp cheek. Her skin was even softer than he had imagined. "I'm sorry. My errand took longer than expected, but that is still no excuse for keeping you waiting."

She avoided his gaze. "I don't even know what I'm doing here. Meeting with a known scoundrel. This is madness."

"A *scoundrel*?" Rafe pressed a hand to his chest. "Miss Sparrow, I'm offended."

She cut him a glance. "No, you're not."

Rafe grinned. It would have been easier to claim that his impulsive suggestion was born of nothing more than simple desire. They were both adults. She knew his reputation. Why not enjoy a little fun together? But Rafe was so damned tired of pretending. Just this once he wanted to be himself with someone.

No. With her.

"You came for the same reason I did," he began. "Because there is something drawing us together. Something neither of us can explain—or ignore."

At that she faced him. Her gray eyes sparkled in the low light. "I've been attracted to men before, I assure you. And I have no doubt this isn't exactly a novelty to you." She tried to sound detached, but the soft note of hope in her voice tore through him, and the words spilled out faster than he could think.

"You're wrong." He moved his hand to caress the soft curls gathered at the back of her neck, and she pressed into his touch. "I've been avoiding you these last few days. I told myself it was for your protection. That it wouldn't do you any good if people thought I was paying you particular attention. But I was also protecting myself," he added softly.

"From *me*?" She looked as bewildered as he felt.

Rafe nodded. "You make me want things. Things I never dreamed of having."

She shook her head slowly. "The house party ends next week, and our tour will leave the following month. And I'm sure you have plans of your own."

All fair points, but the protest in her voice was weak.

"Yes." He continued to move his fingers gently through her hair, and she melted a little more. "I promised my mother I would spend the holidays with her."

She let out a breath. "Oh, she is still alive, then."

Rafe tilted his head. "You thought otherwise?"

"I had wondered," she admitted, and bowed her head shyly. "The viscountess told me a little about your past."

"Ah. Well, I guess that saves me the trouble, then," he said with a lightness he didn't feel. Now she would let him down gently. Explain why a raconteur like him wasn't for her.

"I'm sorry," she said, meeting his gaze. "It's rude to gossip about people."

Rafe shrugged. "I'd be more surprised if you hadn't. It's a terribly old story anyway," he said with a wave of his hand.

"That shouldn't matter," she insisted. "It is your *life*. I'm glad to know you have her."

His breath caught at her tender words. The scandal of his parents' marriage had always followed him. People felt entitled to comment on it. Rafe had never once considered whether they shouldn't.

"And I'm sorry if this is too forward," she continued. "But I think it is absolutely abominable the way your siblings have treated you."

Rafe blinked as he absorbed her words. Aside from his closest friends, no one had ever said such a thing before. Most of society understood Gerard's actions because they would have done the same in his position. Whether it was right or fair was entirely inconsequential.

"Thank you," he murmured.

What would the dowager countess make of this sharp-eyed country girl harboring subversive opinions? Who freely defended her only son? The corner of his mouth lifted. She would probably *adore* Miss Sparrow. He owed her a letter anyway, and now knew the subject.

"So, this is all we have, then," she said glumly.

Rafe longed to say otherwise, but he didn't belong entirely to himself at the moment. Duty came first.

"For now. But I could write to you, while we're both away," he suggested. "I'm an excellent correspondent."

By the time she returned, this business with Wardale would be settled. He might even have a new position, if he found this damned mole.

You could have more power than any man downstairs. More than your own brother.

And then he could tell her the truth. That he wasn't just a feckless rogue with a scandalous reputation but a man who could offer her a real future.

"You shouldn't say such things," she murmured. "Not unless you mean them."

"I agree."

Miss Sparrow stared at him in silence, then leaned forward as if to stand. Rafe began to move back, but she slid her arms around his neck. Her eyes widened, as if she were as surprised by the movement as he was, but then they darkened, burning with the same desire pulsing through him.

He raised an eyebrow. "Why, Miss Sparrow, are you trying to compromise my virtue?"

Her gaze searched his as her rapid inhalations filled his ears. "Only a little."

"Well, then," he said with a grin as he wrapped his arm around her waist. "I suppose I can allow that." He untangled his hand from her hair and slowly stroked down her jawline, tilting her chin up. "Just be gentle with me."

She moved closer until their mouths were a hairbreadth away. "I'll try." Then, without another word, she eagerly pressed her lips to his. The scalding kiss held the weight of every look, every word, and every touch that had passed between them these last weeks. Then her plump lips parted, and the soft velvet of her tongue slid against his. Her enthusiasm was a particularly delicious surprise, and it took Rafe a moment to realize that low moan was coming from him. He pulled away abruptly, but the daring glint burning in Miss Sparrow's eyes only inflamed him more.

"My God," he muttered. Rafe pressed his palm to the side of her head and ran his thumb over her bottom lip, red and swollen as a ripe berry. A fresh wave of hunger broke over him, and he pressed his mouth to hers again, entirely at the mercy of his own desire. This time she thrust both hands in his hair, pulling him even closer, until all space between them was extinguished, until he could feel the soft curves hidden beneath her fine gown and count the beats of her racing heart. Rafe groaned in frustration and grazed his mouth down along the smooth column of her neck until he could rake his teeth against the delicate skin of her collarbone as a sudden, wild urge came over him. He would give anything to strip her bare right then, to drag his tongue over every exposed inch of skin, but now was hardly the time. After a few more agonizingly slow, deep kisses, he wrenched himself away again.

Miss Sparrow blinked up at him. "You stopped," she panted.

Rafe pursed his lips. He would have to be the responsible one this time. "This is me trying to be a better man," he said with all the gravitas he could muster. "It isn't safe for you. If someone were to come in..."

His words seemed to bring her to her senses, and she immediately stiffened. "Right. Yes, of course. I—I quite forgot myself." Her cheeks blazed as she began to pull away, but Rafe caught her hand.

"Please don't think I want to be anywhere other than here. With you."

She watched him closely for another agonizing moment, but her gray eyes betrayed nothing. "All right," she said flatly, as if they hadn't just been a few heated kisses away from tearing each other's clothes off. Rafe then stood and helped her to her feet. Miss Sparrow patted her hair.

"I must look a mess."

"You look lovely." Rafe turned her around and made quick work fixing the pins that had come loose. "There," he said. "Now no one will know you were being naughty in front of the books."

She gave him a faint smile. "You're never serious for very long, are you?"

"Only when the situation requires it."

This time she didn't return his smile. "I think you hide an awful lot behind that smirk." Rafe's eyebrows rose at this uncomfortably astute observation. But then, she looked at him more closely than most. "Good night, Mr. Davies." She turned to leave, but Rafe caught her hand.

"This may come as a surprise to you, but I don't often kiss women without at least learning their first names."

There was still a wariness in her gaze. "It's Sylvia."

"Sylvia Sparrow." His lips curved as he spoke. "Delightful name. 'What light is light, if Sylvia be not seen?'"

"Yes." She dipped her chin, and a devastating ache bloomed in Rafe's chest. "My mother loved her Shakespeare," she added softly.

Rafe noted the past tense. "Then she had excellent taste," he quipped, attempting to clear the heaviness that had filled the air while filing this precious detail about her background away. "My name is Rafe, by the way. In case you wished to know," he said lightly, trying to hide the desperation that had suddenly come over him at the thought that she might not care at all, actually.

But then her mouth quirked. "Rafe," she said slowly.

The sound of his name on her lips was unexpectedly erotic. He leaned over and brushed a fairly chaste peck to her cheek. "Until tomorrow, Sylvia Sparrow."

She gave him one last parting glance, then left the room. Once he was alone, Rafe mulled over this new information. Mrs. Crawford had said her father had been a scholar, and it sounded as though her mother had received a decent education. Yet now Sylvia worked as a companion, which indicated she had fallen on hard times after her parents' deaths. But there were still a few mysteries that remained, like the source of her friendship with the viscountess. Some of her wariness around him could be attributed to his reputation, but Rafe suspected there was something else she was hiding.

He worried his bottom lip, savoring what little of her taste was still left, and wondered where the hell she had learned to kiss like that.

CHAPTER TEN

Rafe spent the next morning searching the rooms of Lady Armstrong and Mrs. Barnes, while carefully noting anything that would be remotely of interest: an excess supply of laudanum, an unsent letter demanding repayment of an old debt, a diary entry that made reference to an unnamed paramour. At least Wardale would see that he was being thorough. He then delivered his findings to his host, who seemed uncharacteristically pleased by the information.

"I still don't suspect either of these ladies," Rafe cautioned. "As you can see, I found nothing to suggest otherwise."

Wardale nodded swiftly. "Yes, of course. It's a comfort to me all the same, though. Well done, Davies. Can you search a few more rooms today?"

"I'm afraid I have an engagement in Glasgow. I won't be back until supper."

Wardale's expression darkened until Rafe mentioned who he was visiting.

"Captain Harris? Do you think he would come to the castle? My guests would be fascinated."

Considering that Henry had barely left his sister's house in months, Rafe highly doubted it. "I will pass the message along, sir," he said diplomatically. "And not to worry. I will make use of the empty rooms tomorrow evening while everyone is downstairs enjoying the festivities. I plan to slip away early."

"Excellent, excellent," Wardale murmured, still preoccupied with the thought of the illustrious Captain Harris crossing his threshold.

Rafe left him to his musings. He had a train to catch.

* * *

Sylvia stared out the window above her desk, watching rain streak down the paned glass. After days of good weather, dark clouds had rolled in just after breakfast. It made no difference to her, as she had pages of notes to type up, but she couldn't seem to concentrate for more than a few minutes before her thoughts returned to last night.

Sylvia idly tapped the end of her pencil against the glass. She hadn't seen Mr. Davies since their encounter in the library but overheard someone mention he had gone into Glasgow to visit a friend. Since then she had been burning with curiosity. He hadn't said anything to her. Not that he needed to, of course. She had no claim on him.

I could write to you, while we're both away.

As flattered as she had been by the suggestion, it sounded even more absurd in the light of day. But then, neither of them had been thinking very clearly last night. Their scorching kisses had nearly turned her brain to mush. Perhaps Mr. Davies—*Rafe*—had been similarly affected. But he was still right on one account: a fierce attraction drew them to one another. Just the memory of his lean, muscular form pressing against hers set off a fierce burst of heat that tore through her body. Sylvia sat back in her chair and her restless hands began to shuffle the papers before her, but the effort was useless. Her mind remained stubbornly fixated on Rafe. It had been years since she'd had any type of virtue worth saving, but perhaps she could enjoy a little tryst. He wouldn't want anything more than that. No doubt the man knew how to be discreet. And she could keep her secrets.

What had Lady Taylor-Smyth alluded to yesterday? Sylvia had barely been able to make out the words over the din of the crowd, but the woman had obviously made some suggestive remark about him. Rafe had looked quite aggrieved afterward, and Sylvia burned with anger on his behalf even while a part of her insisted that it was ridiculous to feel sympathy for a man like him. He couldn't help the circumstances of his birth, but as far as she could tell he was busy indulging in the worst sort of excesses of his class. *That* should matter. *That* should make her immune to his advances. And yet she knew just what it felt like to have people make ghastly assumptions based on your sexual history. As if you lacked all agency. As if there were nothing more to you besides what you did in bed. It had been an incredibly demeaning experience. Why should Rafe feel any differently?

Though he hid it well, Sylvia suspected he was remarkably sensitive. She couldn't forget the tenderness in his gaze or the emotion in his voice when he spoke of his past. And he had seemed genuinely shocked when she apologized for gossiping about him and denounced his siblings. Had no one ever said such things to him before?

Another wave of heat rolled through her at the thought of his lips on hers, so smooth and commanding. It had been undeniably thrilling to see how affected he was by her. To know that this madness was not hers alone. But it was also not born of mere physical desire. This was something that ran deeper. Something that seemed to surprise him as much as it did her. And something that could prove dangerous for them both, if left unchecked.

After whiling away the rest of the morning at the keys, Sylvia let out a sigh and gathered her papers. She had accomplished enough for today, and Mrs. Crawford would want to hear of her progress. As she made her way back to her room, her thoughts were so lost in Rafe's kisses that she almost didn't notice the envelope on the floor. Someone had slipped it under her door while she had been out. At first Sylvia was merely confused. Letters were delivered by the footmen to their suite once a day, and the only person who sent her mail was Georgiana. But as she bent down to pick it up, fear seized her. She turned the envelope over in her trembling hands. The front and back were both blank. Sylvia swallowed and put her papers down. Then checked to make sure the suite was still empty before closing her bedroom door. She moved toward the window and took a breath, then opened the envelope:

> *I have received word that you completed the first part of your task. Now you must deliver it to me. If my instructions are not followed, a telegram will be sent to the Viscount Arlington detailing everything mentioned in my first letter. Once again, I urge you NOT to read the contents of the envelope. It contains sensitive government information that could make you liable for treason. Simply deliver it to the*

*coordinates below by tomorrow night. I will have
further use for you once you return to London and
can report on the viscount's business dealings.*

The blood pounded in Sylvia's ears. Tomorrow night a fancy
dress ball was being held at the castle. Guests would be attending from miles around. Whoever was blackmailing her clearly
had eyes here. Sylvia's stomach turned. It could be anyone. She
read the letter again and memorized the coordinates. She would
have to return to the library. There were maps of the property
there. Hopefully this place wasn't too far away. Another thought
suddenly gripped her: What if her mysterious blackmailer was
there waiting for her? And what if Bernard was behind it?

*No, you fool. He would never have anything to do with you.
Especially now.*

The highly respectable and undoubtably ambitious Bernard
Hughes was in the middle of his first term as MP, likely already
planning his reelection campaign, and his wife was with child.
It was the life his father had expected from him. The one he
had taken extraordinary measures to ensure. The one that could
not include Sylvia, a woman who lacked the dowry or social
standing needed to make up for her unconventional views. But
whoever was behind these letters knew things about her that
very few could. And her former love was among them.

Sylvia let out a sigh as a heavy weight seemed to press
on her shoulders. She ripped up the letter and tossed it in the
hearth, watching as the flames licked the edge of the papers,
slowly curling them inward before they burned. If only her
past could be reduced to ash so easily.

* * *

Rafe arrived at a handsome town house in the respectable Hillhead neighborhood of Glasgow shortly after noon. Henry's sister, Agatha, had married a doctor last year, and Rafe knew it had taken a great weight off his shoulders. For years Henry had been the sole provider of both his mother and sister after his father, also a captain in the Royal Navy, died young.

A fresh-faced maid with bright copper hair answered the door and showed him into a small but charming parlor. "Can I get you anything while you wait, sir?" the girl asked shyly.

"No, thank you."

Her green eyes lingered on him until Rafe raised an eyebrow. She flushed and then bobbed a quick curtsy before fleeing the room. Rafe smiled to himself as he began to look around. It was a cozy, well-lit space, filled with furnishings clearly picked out by the lady of the house. Agatha seemed to have a particular interest in porcelain figurines of farm animals and chubby-cheeked angels.

A rustling came from down the hall, and Rafe turned to see Agatha herself enter. She shared Henry's brown eyes and dark blond hair.

"Mr. Davies." She smiled warmly. "It is so nice to see you again."

"Please, Agatha. I know you're a properly married woman now, but call me Rafe."

She gave him an indulgent smile. "Rafe, of course." She shut the door softly behind her and gestured to the sofa.

Rafe sat down while she took an armchair. "Allow me to offer my belated congratulations. I assume your husband is busy saving lives and helping to usher Glasgow into the modern era."

For years Dr. Burnett had been one of the loudest voices calling for improved sanitation conditions across the city.

A delicate flush stained Agatha's pale cheeks and she lowered her eyes demurely. "Yes. He is a remarkable man. I'm a very lucky woman."

A thick spike of envy pierced Rafe's chest. What must it feel like to have the admiration of another person? Of one you loved? "I've no doubt he considers himself lucky as well."

"You always did know how to flatter a woman." Agatha smiled. "Henry will be down in a moment, but I wanted to speak to you first." She glanced at the door again and lowered her voice. "To prepare you."

Rafe grew concerned. "What is it?" he asked gently.

Agatha shook her head and turned back to him. "I know the papers have talked about my brother's heroic actions, but you will find him much changed. It won't be something a man like you will be used to."

Rafe tensed as he caught her meaning. Agatha knew Rafe had served with Henry in the navy for a time, but like so many others, she assumed his working days were far behind him. In her eyes he was a playboy far removed from the daily hardships of life—to say nothing of the horror Henry had gone through.

"I see," Rafe said slowly. The desire to tell her the truth suddenly bubbled up through him. He wasn't a useless rake. And he understood all too well the lasting impact intelligence work could have on a man—the constant stress, the flashbacks that came after a violent encounter, the knowledge that a simple reconnaissance mission could be your last. And he had worked with men who had been imprisoned before, albeit more briefly than the weeks Henry had endured. But Rafe was confident that he could help his friend, or at the very least provide some comfort. Dammit, he was good for *something*.

Agatha's slight inhalation brought him back to the moment. Rafe followed her downward gaze, where the hand at his knee had turned into a tight fist. He immediately flexed it open.

"Thank you for telling me. I know it's been years since I... I made myself useful," he began, surprised to find his voice faltering over the last word. "But I want to support him. In any way I can."

Agatha's eyes softened as she placed her hand over his. "I know he'll appreciate that. But be warned, he may not show it." Rafe nodded. He was prepared for a brusque welcome. "I'm just glad our poor mother wasn't alive to see what happened to him. She would have been beside herself with worry," she added.

An ominous thudding heralded Henry's approach.

"He's coming," Agatha said as she rose. Rafe stood as well. "I'll leave you fellows alone and see that some tea is brought up." She opened the door just as Henry had moved to do the same. "Ah, there you are," she said with marked cheerfulness and held it open for him.

"I think I can manage a damned door, Agatha," Henry snapped as he entered the room, gripping a silver-topped cane in his right hand. The newspapers had mentioned a leg injury, a detail that had only increased esteem for his actions. His sister closed her eyes in a brief wince at the curse. "Sorry," he mumbled. "My knee is worse today. It's the coming storm."

Though Henry wasn't quite as tall as Rafe he had always carried more bulk. But he had lost weight in the year since their last meeting, and there were painful shadows under his eyes. And no doubt there was a bevy of invisible scars as well.

Agatha nodded but didn't look at Henry. "I'll send Mary in with the tea," she said before leaving, but Rafe didn't miss the pain that flashed across her face.

Henry walked over to Rafe and held out his hand. "Hello. You're looking well," he said flatly. Henry had always been a bit serious due to his responsibilities, but there was a new darkness in his haggard gaze.

Rafe took his hand and pulled him in for an embrace. "It's good to see you, old friend." Henry's body tensed at Rafe's words. "I'm a miserable old bastard these days," he mumbled.

Rafe laughed and pulled back. "I hate to tell you this, but you were always a miserable old bastard. At least now you have an excuse."

Henry's lips quirked as he gestured to a pair of paisley printed armchairs by the fireplace. "Have a seat."

Rafe did as he bade and watched as Henry set the cane aside and gingerly eased himself into the chair. Rafe longed to ask about the injury but sensed that Henry would share what he wanted when he was ready.

"Some days are better than others," he explained as he began to rub his left knee. "I'm afraid you've caught me on a bad one."

"I understand."

Henry met his eyes and seemed to accept the words as genuine. Then he leaned back in his chair and folded his arms across his chest. "So, what brings you to bonny Scotland? Your message said you were staying at Castle Blackwood."

"Yes. A bit of business."

Henry raised an eyebrow. He knew just the kind Rafe meant. "Is Mr. Wardale as eccentric as they say?"

Rafe shrugged. "No more than any man with his resources." He then explained the purpose of his mission, beginning with Gerard's sudden appearance in his sitting room.

Henry's frown grew more pronounced with every new detail. By the time Rafe finished, it was a full-on glower. "I don't like this," he announced. "You've always had a weak spot for your brother. And Gerard knows it. He's manipulating you."

Rafe straightened. "Don't be absurd."

But Henry ignored him. His mind was already turning over the problem before him. "He's in league with Wardale—that much is obvious—but how? And why?"

Henry had never been one to mince words, but this was a shocking accusation. "Because they are political allies," Rafe said hotly. "This isn't a conspiracy against *me*. It's one wealthy, influential man helping another. Even the PM is involved." The lack of sleep suddenly crashed over him. Wardale's paranoia was already enough to bear; he couldn't endure Henry's, too.

"As if that matters," Henry grumbled. "You've been in this business long enough to know how dirty it can be. I hate that things went sideways in Turkey, but at the very least it gave me an out."

Rafe was stunned. Henry had always approached his duties with such single-minded focus it bordered on obsession. "I had no idea you felt this way."

"Of course not. It wouldn't align with my status as a *national hero*," Henry said contemptuously before letting out a dark laugh. "There was nothing to do in that jail cell but reflect on how, exactly, I got there. And why. You would do well to do the same." Rafe let his glare speak for him. "Come now. You can't really believe there's a band of *separatists* out to get him," Henry scoffed. "That's utter rubbish."

"I saw the messages. They appear legitimate," Rafe said

tightly. "And what cause would Wardale have for making it up? The man already has everything."

"Perhaps." Henry rubbed his chin, which was covered in thick brown stubble. "But I still find it difficult to believe. There is some unrest, of course, but this isn't Ireland. And I can't see why Wardale would be targeted."

"He has assumed ownership of one of Scotland's most historic properties."

Henry didn't look convinced. "Let me help. I can make some inquiries. The locals might be more willing to talk to me than a dandy like yourself."

Rafe hesitated. "Is that wise?" He couldn't help glancing at the cane.

"Don't put me out to pasture just yet." Henry narrowed his eyes. "I still have a few uses."

"Sorry. I didn't mean to suggest—"

Henry waved a hand. "I know. I'll be careful. Besides, it would be good for me to get out of this blasted house. Agatha hovers over me like a nursemaid. I can't take much more of it."

"I'm grateful for any assistance."

Now seemed like a prime opportunity to ask how Henry was feeling, but before Rafe could get the words out, the door swung open. It was the maid with the tea tray. He hid his disappointment behind a genial smile. Mary cast him a not-so-subtle glance as she set down the tray. "Would ye like me to pour, sir?" she asked Henry, her voice practically quaking in the face of his forbidding glare.

Henry shook his head. "No. We're fine. Thank you, Mary."

The girl gave Rafe another parting glance before she fled the room.

As Henry moved to fill Rafe's teacup, one corner of his mouth curved up. "Still catching the eye of every woman with a pulse, I see."

Rafe chuckled, recalling his first encounter with Sylvia when she had seemed incredibly perturbed to have even noticed him and worked hard to pretend otherwise.

That was the moment.

People always talked about the moment they "knew." When they met eyes across a crowded ballroom or bent to pick up a dropped handkerchief. How the smallest gesture had changed the entire course of their lives. Even his father had claimed such a moment in the way Rafe's mother, born in one of the poorest sections of London, had held out her hand to him when they first met, as proud and regal as a queen.

I knew right then that no one else would do ever again.

The words shivered up his spine with new understanding.

"Actually," he began, surprised to find his throat tightening with emotion. "I've met someone."

Henry had moved to pass Rafe his cup and now froze, his face gone blank. "Pardon," he said after a moment. "Did I hear that right?"

"Yes," he said, taking his cup. "You don't need to look quite so shocked."

"No, sorry." Henry gave himself a shake. "I'm just… surprised. You always said you couldn't be bothered. The work came first."

"I know," Rafe cut in, recalling his youthful arrogance. "I was an idiot."

"Well, who is she?"

He suddenly regretted having said anything. This was still so new, so vulnerable. Like a butterfly unfurling its wings for the first time, wet and trembling with fresh life. When the slightest wrong movement could kill. He poured too much cream into his tea and stirred the beige liquid. "I met her at the castle. She's a lady's companion to one of the guests."

"Really? How very interesting."

Rafe wanted to wipe that smug smile right off Henry's face. "Yes. Her name is Sylvia."

"Lovely. And does she know how you feel?"

"More or less."

Henry snorted. "You know, I assumed when you were finally felled by Cupid's arrow, you would be positively rapturous."

"Don't be absurd," Rafe bristled. "I'm not some damned poet."

"Absolutely not, but you've always carried an air of the romantic about you."

Rafe stared at him a moment. "Did Mary slip something into your cup?"

Henry let out a hearty laugh. Rafe would have been happier about it if he wasn't the cause. "Not at all. It was just an observation I've made over the years."

That explanation was not comforting in the least. Henry had been recruited for intelligence work in part because of his extraordinary memory. He could easily recall entire conversations from years past or describe rooms he had walked through down to the last insignificant detail. The man was a living, breathing memory vault. Which made him an incredibly valuable asset. Henry might be done with Crown service, but that didn't mean the Crown was done with him.

Rafe decided a subject change was needed. "She's helping Mrs. Violet Crawford write her memoirs. The woman's led a rather colorful life."

Henry stilled. "Isn't she related to Lord Arlington?"

"Yes," Rafe answered, noting that his friend's jaw had tightened considerably. "The viscount is her nephew. His wife is also staying at the castle."

Henry then set down his teacup so abruptly Rafe was certain the porcelain had cracked. Tea spilled over the edge and onto the table. Henry growled his annoyance and began to mop up the mess with a napkin.

"I take it you've met the viscountess?"

Henry's brow furrowed, but he continued to focus on the spill. "It was years ago. Before she married."

In all their years of friendship, Henry had never mentioned any involvement with a woman. Rafe didn't know if his inclinations lay elsewhere or if he was simply the most reserved man alive. Based on the flush currently working up his neck, Rafe guessed it was the latter.

"How very interesting," Rafe mimicked, trying his best to keep the glee out of his voice.

"Not really." Henry sat back with a sigh. "It was during the Season in London. She was incredibly popular. I wasn't."

"What on earth were *you* doing in London during the Season?"

"I thought to find myself a wealthy wife." Henry shrugged. "It was a short-lived exercise. Intelligence work found me instead."

Then it really had been ages ago. Rafe would have already been taking on missions himself. He tried to think that far back, but he lacked Henry's memory. His friend had been comparatively more lighthearted in years past. Before the work had taken its heaviest toll. But perhaps it hadn't only been the work that affected him so.

"Well, I'd say it's time for a reunion. Wardale extended an invitation to—"

"No." Henry met Rafe's eyes. There was no anger there now, no irritation. Only resignation. Defeat. "Just…no." The hollowness in his words was somehow more forbidding than his growl. Something had happened between him and Lady Arlington. Something devastating.

The conversation plodded along for another few minutes, but the haunted look never left Henry's face. Rafe agreed to send him a message every day, if only to placate Henry's suspicions.

Henry rose and held out his hand. "Take care of yourself."

"You too." Rafe took it and pulled him in for another hug. "It will get better. And if there's anything I can do—"

Henry held up a hand. "I know." He then gave him a weak smile. "Best of luck wooing your lady's companion. Not that you'll need it." Rafe laughed off the comment, but Henry's gaze turned serious. "You've always known exactly what you wanted and how to get it. I suppose I've envied that about you."

Rafe's smile faded. "Don't. I may know what I want, but I haven't a clue what I need."

"Have a little faith, Davies. You may know more than you realize."

As Rafe left, Sylvia's gray eyes twinkling with warmth came to him. The unique understanding he found there called to something that had long lain dormant within him, in a place so deep few bothered to make the journey, including himself.

CHAPTER ELEVEN

❧

After finding a map of Castle Blackwood and the surrounding property in the library, Sylvia had a fairly good idea of where her mysterious blackmailer wanted her to deliver the envelope. She sketched out a small version on a piece of paper to carry with her and tucked it in her pocket. Luckily, Mrs. Crawford had already granted Sylvia permission to spend the rest of the day to herself since she and the other guests were busy preparing their costumes for tomorrow evening's ball. Georgiana had been sorely disappointed when Sylvia explained she had no interest in attending. It would provide the perfect opportunity for her to deliver the envelope, and she couldn't let it pass by. Now the castle buzzed with even more excitement than usual as servants scurried back and forth with scraps of fabric and other bric-a-brac. Mrs. Crawford was planning to go as Empress Maria Theresa and was in desperate need of a wig. Meanwhile, Georgiana was trying to locate a shield for her interpretation of Athena, goddess of war.

Sylvia was grateful to slip away from the madness for a bit. As she made her way down the back terrace that led to the stables, she inhaled the crisp air that still smelled of that morning's rain. Scotland truly was beautiful, especially this time of year, but the surroundings offered only momentary relief from the gnawing dread that had been following her since the envelope had appeared under her door. Everyone she met was now suspect. Sylvia couldn't live forever looking over her shoulder. But what choice did she have?

Her heart sank. She had hoped this business would end once she delivered the envelope, but that had been a naive wish. As long as the viscount lived and Georgiana was under his power, Sylvia would never be free. Her blackmailer could surface again, demanding information whenever it was desired. Perhaps she should leave after this was over. She would have to tell Georgiana what had happened, but the viscountess had forged one set of recommendations for her. Surely she could do another.

And then what? You will have to leave London—possibly England—to truly get away.

So be it, then. She could go to America. Make a real fresh start. There were newspapers there, and a robust women's movement. Sylvia had enough experience to find work in an office. It wasn't an impossible idea. But even as she pieced together her plan, her heart sank further. She was so tired of being forced to leave, forced to give up the things and people she loved. And for what? Because she had dared to have an opinion? Dared to lend her voice to the voiceless? She knew men who had freely advocated for violence, encouraged uprisings, and even called for the end of the monarchy, but they were heralded as free thinkers, feted for the boldness of their views, no matter the personal cost others would have to bear.

Meanwhile, Sylvia was excoriated for suggesting that women have a say in government alongside men. And not just married, property-owning women. For it was the factory workers, the laundry washers, the nursemaids, schoolteachers, and mothers who helped the rest of society function. And yet their contributions were only valued in relation to the men they supported. Or worse, they were condemned for luring men down the path of vice. Sylvia could not count the number of times a member of the Aurelias Club, a political debate society she had belonged to with Bernard, had dismissed women's suffrage because, God forbid, what if a common *prostitute* was allowed a vote?

It was hearing that very same point trotted out yet again during one meeting that had pushed Sylvia to her limit:

"Then by the same token, men who visit brothels should be stripped of their rights. These women don't exist in a vacuum, sir. Someone is paying for their services. And yet no one ever suggests punishing their clients, many of whom are wealthy, powerful men. Dare I say, some are even sitting in this room."

Being able to get a word in during meetings had always been a trial, as most of the men barely seemed to notice whenever any of the female members tried to speak, but Sylvia had been so angry that she'd stood up and interrupted. At that moment she hadn't cared about being liked or perceived as polite, tactics the other women members maintained were important so that they were taken seriously. Sylvia only wanted to be heard. And on that point she had succeeded. Her statement had caused such an uproar that the meeting was dismissed early. Sylvia could still feel the thrill that had run through her, born of both rage and righteousness. While she had always found it difficult to speak up for herself, advocating for others had given her a purpose. But then she had looked to Bernard sitting next to her and saw the embarrassment in his eyes. It was then she truly understood that it didn't matter how sound her argument was. These men, for all their posturing as thinkers driven by logic, still refused to see the humanity in every person who didn't look exactly like they did. For then they would be forced to truly accept them as equals, and that would be a direct threat to their own superiority.

But Sylvia too had been driven by emotion over logic, for she still rendezvoused with Bernard later that night, had still believed they had a future together, and had still expected his arrival a week later when she sat in that stinking jail cell.

"Careful, miss!"

The sudden shout pulled Sylvia from her memories, and she turned abruptly to the speaker. A man was pointing toward a gnarled patch of brambles not a foot in front of her. Sylvia hadn't realized she had diverged off the path. She let out a short laugh at the absurd scene she must have created and shook her head.

"I'm so sorry. I—I don't know what came over me."

The man removed his cap, revealing a head full of chestnut hair, and approached her. Based on the dirt spots on his knees and the shovel he gripped in one hand, Sylvia guessed he was some kind of gardener. And a handsome one at that.

"Ah, it looked like you were deep in thought," he offered in a rich brogue that washed over her.

"Yes, I was. Still no excuse for nearly walking into a bush."

The corners of his eyes crinkled as he smiled, and he seemed like the kind of man who did so often. There was an easiness about him that reminded her of Rafe. As someone who had never felt entirely comfortable in her own skin, it was always fascinating to encounter others who were. She wondered if she would ever learn the secret.

"Perhaps you could help me," she began, managing what she hoped was a coquettish smile. "I was told there was a path near here that ran through the woods."

"Aye. It begins a little ways back there," he said, pointing toward the tree line. Then he raised an eyebrow. "You aren't planning to walk it alone, are ye?"

"Well, yes. Is it not safe?"

Sylvia couldn't explain that she had walked all over London, often by herself. Mostly without incident. She was perfectly capable of an afternoon jaunt through the woods.

He shrugged and leaned against the shovel's handle. His shirtsleeves were rolled up to the elbow, exposing his exceptionally well-muscled forearms. "If you were my lass I wouldn't say so. All kinds of creatures could be roaming these woods, man and beast alike."

Despite herself, Sylvia's cheeks heated. "I'll be careful," she insisted.

He stuck the shovel into the ground and came closer, until she could smell the fresh earth upon him mixed with sweat. "Here." He withdrew something from his pocket. "For my own peace of mind." In his open palm was a small pocketknife.

Sylvia shook her head. "I can't take that from you."

"Return it before you leave, then. I can miss it for a few days."

"I wouldn't even know how to use it."

"Just jab at the soft parts," he said with a wink. "That should be enough."

Sylvia let out a startled laugh. "Yes, I'd imagine so."

He held out the knife. "Please."

Sylvia's resolve weakened at his soft tone and the plaintive look in his green eyes. It had been ages since anyone aside from Georgiana had exhibited such concern for her well-being.

"If you insist," she said as she took the knife. In London she had carried a hatpin to ward off any unwanted advances, but this was much bulkier. And could do far more damage. He then showed her how to release the blade, his thick, rough fingers brushing against hers more than once. Afterward, he stepped back and donned his cap.

"You must tell me your name," Sylvia said, breaking the tension that had suddenly thickened between them.

"I go by Brodie."

"Brodie," Sylvia repeated.

"And you're Miss Sparrow, the lady secretary."

The blunt description made her laugh. "I suppose it is a rather odd position for a woman."

"No, I think it's admirable. You're making your own way in the world."

He held her eyes for another moment. His really were a remarkable shade of green.

"Miss Sparrow."

Rafe's commanding voice cut through the air. Sylvia turned around and blinked as he swiftly approached them. What was he doing here? Rafe shot an impressive glare at Brodie, who touched the brim of his cap to her and slunk away without another word. Sylvia discreetly folded the knife and put it in the pocket of her skirt as Rafe came beside her, but his eyes were still fixed on Brodie, and he made no effort to hide his disapproval.

"That was unnecessary."

Rafe finally looked down at her. "Do you always engage in such deep conversation with the help?"

Sylvia stiffened. How long had he been watching them? "You forget, sir, that *I* am the help. Don't be a snob. He's a person."

The suspicion in his eyes softened to chagrin. "You're right. I apologize. But still, you don't know anything about that man."

Sylvia tilted her head. "Are you suggesting I have something to fear from the *gardener*?"

"He's a man. You're a woman alone. That is enough," Rafe insisted.

Indignation began to flare within her, but the concern in his tone gave her pause. Sylvia reached out and placed her hand on his arm. "I'm fine. Truly. I'm not that naive."

Rafe glanced at her hand, then back to her face. The moment stretched between them as heat filled his dark eyes. Sylvia was all too aware that now *they* were quite alone. In another instant, he tugged her along with him until they were behind the stables, in a spot hidden from view by more shrubs. Sylvia's heart pounded in her chest as Rafe gently pressed her back to the cool brick of the stable's outer wall and placed one large palm against the curve of her waist, while his other hand brushed a fallen curl behind her ear. The now familiar smell of his aftershave tickled her nose, and she inhaled deeply.

"I know you aren't." He sighed. "But I...I don't trust anyone around you." The admission appeared to surprise him as much as her.

Sylvia pressed her hand over his. If only he weren't wearing gloves. "That's absurd."

"Yes." Rafe nodded. His eyes then dipped to her mouth and glazed over. "It is."

How on earth had she captured this worldly man's attention?

Sylvia truly didn't understand what he saw in her, but that wouldn't stop her from enjoying it.

Rafe slowly leaned down, and Sylvia, impatient, rose onto her toes. This brought a smirk to his lips, which immediately dissolved into a flurry of sparks as their mouths touched. He grunted softly as his arm snaked around her waist, drawing her up against his hard chest, while his other hand tangled in her hair.

He continued to surprise her. He felt nothing like an experienced lover used to quick trysts in shadowy corners. While Sylvia was all urgency, Rafe kissed her as if they had all the time in the world. As if the threat of discovery didn't hang over their heads. He kissed her like a man who planned to do this forever. His lips were warm and gentle as they gradually teased her mouth open and forced her to slow down, to enjoy the growing heat between them. When he tugged her bottom lip open with the pressure of his tongue, Sylvia couldn't hold back a soft moan and pressed harder against him. It was as if this man was composed entirely of features designed to make her melt. She had never been so fully engulfed by desire before. And in that moment she would have given him everything. Gladly. Rafe seemed able to read her thoughts.

"God, Sylvia," he gasped, breaking the kiss. Her heart warmed as he pressed his forehead to hers, running his large palms along her torso. "Sylvia Sparrow. My little bird."

Sylvia's breath caught at the endearment. This was too much, too soon. And yet it didn't feel that way at all. She had ignored so many things with Bernard. But as she gazed into Rafe's eyes, she saw no flash of wariness. No sign of reticence. Of coming regret.

That will come later, once he knows the truth.

But before she could dismiss the nasty thought, Rafe abruptly cleared his throat and pulled back. He stooped down and began picking up the pins that had fallen out of her hair. Sylvia slouched against the wall, still trying to catch her breath. He then stood up and held out his palm. Sylvia glanced at it before meeting his eyes.

"I suppose this sort of thing is expected at house parties," she said reluctantly, giving him the opportunity to dismiss this. And her.

"I suppose it is." Rafe held her gaze. "But not for me. Never like this."

Sylvia closed her eyes against the force behind the words. Even though she very much wanted to interrogate him on what, exactly, "this" meant to him, his certainty only increased her guilt.

"I know what you must be thinking," he continued, his voice taking on a surprisingly bitter tenor. "My reputation has no doubt preceded me. I can't change that. But if I—"

"You don't know anything about me," she interrupted, unable to hide her rising anxiety as the visceral ache of regret surged through her. She couldn't let him think her reticence was his fault.

He paused and tilted his head in consideration. "Then tell me what I need to know."

"I'm not—I'm not what you think I am."

Rafe studied her for a moment. "I think you're a lovely and intelligent young woman who has worked very hard to be where she is. What about that isn't true?"

Sylvia looked down. How badly she wished that was all she was. "There are things about my past that would make anything between us difficult—no. *Impossible*." She forced her head up to meet his gaze head-on.

Rafe raised a dark brow. "How intriguing."

Sylvia frowned. "This isn't a joke."

"Very well." He leaned his shoulder against the wall beside her and crossed his arms. "Please, tell me what makes this so impossible. And keep in mind that I have absolutely no right to cast judgment on anyone else."

Sylvia stared at him. She had never been so tempted to tell someone else before. Even Georgiana only knew the basic details. But now the weight of it all pressed against her throat, begging to be released.

Rafe might understand the wrongful arrest if she explained it well enough, but what about the rest of it? This was a man used to swanning around London. Not dealing with public slander, blackmail, and *theft*. No, she needed to protect him. If he was dragged into this too, she would never forgive herself. But she had to tell him something. Something a man like him could understand.

"I...I lied to you before. I did live in London for a time. After university."

Rafe looked impressed. "You went to university?"

"Yes. At Somerville College." She slanted him a glance. "So which did you attend? Oxford or Cambridge?"

"Neither," he said mildly. "I took correspondence courses."

Well, that was unexpected. But before she could ask more, Rafe steered the conversation back to her. "What did you do in London?"

"I worked as a typist for a family friend and took a room in a women's boardinghouse."

"I'm surprised your parents allowed that."

Sylvia shrugged. "My mother died when I was fourteen, but I think she would have approved. It had always been her dream to attend university. Then she met my father." Now wasn't the time to add that her father had been her mother's tutor, until she fell pregnant. "He became a scholar who taught the moral sciences at Oxford for a time. Absolutely brilliant, but his work always came first, you see. Everyone said he was too indulgent of my intellectual pursuits, but the truth was he simply couldn't be bothered to mind me after my mother died. It was easier to let me do as I wished. When I left he mourned the loss of my secretarial skills, but he barely noticed my absence, whether I was at school or in London."

Or back at home. She could still picture the door of his study, firmly shut as always unless she was taking notes or typing for him. After Mother died, he only came out for supper. And usually only on Sundays. All other meals were taken alone. It was only later, when he was dying, that they spent any real time together away from his work. But the shadow of her scandal had always hung over them. Unspoken but never forgotten.

"But that isn't the important bit. When I was in London, I met a man," she said hastily, then squeezed her eyes shut waiting for his censure. But after a moment, Sylvia opened them. Rafe hardly looked scandalized.

"Well, what happened?" he asked with genuine curiosity. As if the answer weren't painfully obvious.

"His father didn't approve of me and threatened to cut off his allowance. He made his choice."

There. That was close enough to the truth.

Rafe's jaw hardened and he pushed away from the stable wall. "The bastard."

Sylvia knew she shouldn't say any more. That was the best

reaction she could hope for. But the trouble was now that she had started, she found it was rather difficult to stop.

"We were friends first," she continued, as the words she had held back for so long rushed out of her. "We met at a lecture given by the Aurelias Society."

"The political group?"

Sylvia nodded. "Bernard was interested in their ideas. Well, we both were. Eventually we became involved and began planning our future." Rafe could hardly want to hear all of this, but Sylvia had kept it to herself for so long, she couldn't seem to stop. "We wanted to find a house near Hampstead Heath with a small barn in the backyard where we could hold meetings and host reading groups of our own. He was so terribly excited by the idea," she added softly, taking a moment to marvel at how very different her life had turned out. And how very little she had meant to him in the end.

"I don't understand," Rafe began. "He did all that, but then he wouldn't marry you?"

She stiffened at the incredulous note in his voice and gave him a withering look. "You know, for a man with your reputation, you're awfully traditional. I didn't care about being his *wife*. I wanted to be his partner. And a wife isn't an equal in the eyes of the law, so I was in no great hurry to wed."

Not that Bernard had ever offered.

His dark eyes flared with anger. "And yet you thought to live together openly in this little intellectual paradise with absolutely no repercussions?"

She bowed her head. "I suppose I was naive about that. I didn't realize he was so beholden to his family." Or their money.

"Yes. But he was also a coward," Rafe growled. "He

shouldn't have agreed to such a ridiculous idea in the first place. He should have protected you—"

"I am a grown woman." Sylvia punctuated the words with a heavy stomp of her foot. "I did not need his protection, and *I* insisted on our arrangement."

"Perhaps, but you were the one taking on all the risk, Sylvia. Can't you see that?" Rafe put his hands on his hips. "I know the world is changing. I know that women are taking to the streets, demanding their fair share, and I hope to God they get it, but he still had a responsibility to look out for you. And not because he's a man," he said over her objection. "But because that is what you do when you *care* for someone."

A part of Sylvia knew that what he said made perfect sense. Hadn't she had the very same thoughts? But all she felt now was that old, raw shame, exposed for him to see. And to judge. Just as everyone else had. She could still recall the disappointment in the faces of so many people. People she had considered friends. Allies. Mentors. But worst of all was the blank space when she thought of Bernard. She didn't know what his reaction to her arrest had been because he had never bothered to formally end things between them. He simply hadn't appeared when she needed him most. But his absence spoke for him. Loudly.

"Fine. He didn't love me enough. Is that what you want me to say? Is it so important for you to be right about this? I wasn't worth the risk," she insisted, her body tensing more and more with every word. "I wasn't worth losing his father's approval, or his inheritance, or his bloody social standing."

Rafe's face paled. "Christ. I didn't mean—"

"And yes, you're absolutely right that I was taking on all the risk. Trust me, I paid for it dearly. I lost everything I had earned myself. My stupid little London life that I had been so proud of all fell apart because of him."

Rafe stood there in silence. He looked like someone had slapped him.

"But that's not the worst of it," she continued. "He still bought that house, you know. He still hosts gatherings and publishes articles using the words *I* wrote. The ideas *we* discussed. He is living the life we planned with someone else. Someone with an acceptable pedigree who was content to be his wife and have his babies and didn't demand to be a part of his work. To be his equal." Sylvia then paused before voicing the one thing no one, not even Georgiana, knew. "And do you know what the worst part of it is? I think he's happier," she whispered. "Happier without me."

To her utter horror, her eyes had filled with tears. She angrily began to wipe them away until Rafe gently smoothed his thumbs against her cheeks, collecting the moisture that had gathered there. Through her haze Sylvia managed to register the feel of his bare hands. At some point he had removed his gloves. They were rougher than she imagined. Nearly as rough as Brodie's. But how? He was a pampered gentleman. She was so distracted by this discovery that she nearly missed his words.

"He isn't."

"What?"

Rafe tilted her chin up. "He may feel safer or more in control, but he isn't happier. Most likely he's bored, or soon will be."

She tried to shake her head. Tried to deny his words. "You've never even met him. You can't possibly know that."

But Rafe held fast. "No, but I've met you. And I know

men. So I feel quite certain when I say that there is no damned *chance* he is happier without you." She inhaled sharply at the unexpected thrill of his curse, but he didn't stop. "You threatened some part of him, Sylvia. Some part that he won't let go of. And that must have scared the hell out of him. As I said before, he's a coward, so he took the coward's way out. I'm sure his wife is perfectly fine, but she isn't you."

Somehow Sylvia was breathing even harder than before. Never, never could she imagine someone else saying such things to her. And with such conviction.

"Don't ever think for one second that you aren't worth the risk," he continued. "You deserve someone who not only takes it, but someone who loves you all the more for it."

Her heart stopped. Had he actually *said* that? It should be ridiculous. And yet it felt...true.

Understanding seemed to dawn on Rafe at the same moment and he stepped back. "I'm sorry. I don't know what came over me." He let out a surprised laugh and pulled a hand through his hair, disturbing the usually perfect strands.

Oh God. I've said far too much. We both have.

Rafe glanced at her, and the regret must have been etched on her face. "No, please don't look like that." He pressed his palms against her arms. "I think you're incredibly brave."

Sylvia wasn't sure she could take any more of his admiration. She wasn't brave. She had been an idiot. "But you understand my—my concerns. Regarding us."

"Actually, I'm more concerned that if I ever meet this fellow I won't be able to keep from thrashing him in the street." He gave her a small smile. "Thank you for being so honest. I only wish...I wish I could do the same."

Sylvia frowned. "That isn't necessary." She certainly didn't want to hear about his no doubt *extensive* affairs.

Rafe looked at her sadly. "Maybe not at the moment, no."

She ignored the cryptic comment. Let him keep his secrets. "I've revealed a great deal to you today. I appreciate your understanding, and your discretion. The viscountess knows all of this, but not Mrs. Crawford. And you may feel differently about me once you've thought it over."

Rafe shook his head. "I'm sorry that man ever gave you a reason to doubt yourself. But I'm not like him. I can promise you that, at least. And I won't ever say a word to Mrs. Crawford. Your personal life is not anyone's business."

The invisible wall inside her crumbled a little more. "Thank you."

He then set a gentle kiss against her lips. The sweetness of it curled around Sylvia's heart, and she drew her arms around his neck. This man seemed to have a hundred different sides to him.

And, Lord help her, she wanted to know every one.

CHAPTER TWELVE

❧

A t Rafe's urging, Sylvia left soon afterward with vague
plans to talk again after the ball. The longer they were
together, the greater the chance they would be caught. That
she had a past lover wasn't entirely surprising, but to hear of
how she had been treated, and how she saw herself as a result, had inspired an unholy rage within him. For a man who
prided himself on his ability to shake off the more trivial an-
noyances of life, it had been a touch concerning just how
swiftly, and deeply, this anger had come on. But then, this
was Sylvia. He had feelings for her. Feelings that were still a
bit baffling to him—not that she could inspire them in the
first place but that he had become so quickly, and completely,
enamored.

Rafe never really expected to fall in love. His parents' union
had been such a rare and precious thing that it seemed impossible he could ever be as devoted to someone as his father
had been to his mother. And even their happy marriage had
not been free of scandal, sacrifice, and pain. His career choice
had also acted as a rather large deterrent for any possible
relationship. And he had never minded in the slightest. But

now, for the first time in his thirty-one years, Rafe was actually interested in trying. With her.

I wasn't worth the risk.

His chest grew tight once again at the mere memory of her words. It was the surety in her voice that had most angered him. Rafe thought he hid it from her fairly well, but the truth was as soon as he got back to London, he would track down this Bernard bastard and ruin his life. Though he was glad to learn more of her past, he sensed she was still holding some things back from him, like the length of her friendship with the viscountess, but he could find out more in time if need be, with or without her.

Because you are a bloody spy.

Rafe pinched the bridge of his nose. If he did intend to have a future with this woman, he would have to tell her *something* about the nature of his work. Though he wasn't sure how much he could reveal, or how she would react. But leaving Crown service simply wasn't an option. Not when he was on the cusp of something that could transform British intelligence for the better and lead to greater things for them both. Surely even Sylvia would see the value in that. Eventually. Rafe then laughed to himself. He had fallen for a damned radical. Well, she couldn't be that zealous if she could overlook the fact that he was the son of an earl.

Rafe straightened and renewed his focus. Sylvia was a safe enough distance away now that he could be seen in the area without drawing unnecessary attention. Besides, he had a gardener to interrogate. Rafe quickly located the man Sylvia called "Brodie." He was inspecting a herbaceous border nearby that had seen better days. He wasn't solely motivated by the urge to protect Sylvia from all vaguely suspicious persons.

This man was likely a local and could potentially provide him with valuable information. But all rationality vanished as soon as the man turned around.

"What were you doing talking to Miss Sparrow?" Rafe demanded.

Brodie appeared unsurprised by both his appearance and his ire. "Good afternoon, sir. Mr. Davies, is it?"

Rafe narrowed his eyes. "Stop stalling and answer the question."

The corner of Brodie's mouth lifted. "She was in great danger of walking into a thorn bush. I provided some assistance."

A *thorn* bush? Rafe bit back the urge to tell Brodie to stay the hell away from her. He didn't want to act like an overbearing brute, and Sylvia did seem quite able to manage herself. "All right. If that's all it was," he muttered. "How long have you worked at the castle?" He forced the slightest hint of congeniality into his voice, which only amused Brodie further.

The man pushed up the brim of his cap. "Since I was a lad. All the Brodie men have worked the gardens here, going back over a hundred years."

Rafe grunted. "And you enjoy working for Mr. Wardale?"

Brodie continued to watch him with an open gaze. "He's a good master, aye."

"It must have been difficult, though. Having worked for the Chisolm family all your life."

Brodie shrugged his impressive shoulders. "The old baron was a fine man, but toward the end of his life he could not keep up the property the way it was needed. And his heir did not have the funds. Selling the castle was the best option. I can understand that."

"But not everyone does, I hear."

Brodie's gaze turned thoughtful. "There are some who find the changes harder. They see Mr. Wardale with his money, and fast friends, and motorcars, and feel threatened. But that's the way of the world now. It won't stop for any of us."

Rafe didn't hide his surprise. "Well said." Were all gardeners so philosophical, or just the Scottish ones? "I don't suppose you've heard anything specific, from those unhappy with the changes Mr. Wardale is suggesting?"

Brodie shook his head. "I canna see why anyone would be angry over plans to improve the village. But there are some who have grumbled about an Englishman coming in, 'tis true. And I can't say for sure whether it's only talk. But Mr. Wardale isn't one of those nobs. He's made his own fortune." Brodie's eyes then widened. "Oh, sorry, sir."

Rafe laughed. "No apology needed. I, too, admire Mr. Wardale's drive."

Brodie nodded his approval. "Soon enough the world will be run by men like him, and we'll be all the better for it."

Rafe didn't exactly share Brodie's optimism, but he certainly agreed that the future seemed to belong to men like Wardale, not his brother. He then stepped closer and lowered his voice. "If you do hear of anyone grumbling about your master more than usual, would you be so kind as to inform me? Anyone at all. Even one of the guests."

Brodie raised an eyebrow. But it was good that he was suspicious. The most valuable informants tended to be the reluctant ones. "I suppose. If it will help Mr. Wardale..."

Rafe nodded. "It will."

After a few more minutes of conversation designed to further solidify Brodie's trust in him, Rafe headed back to the castle. Between the gardener, Henry, and himself, something was bound to be uncovered that would put Wardale's mind at ease. Then Rafe could count on his support for his proposal and carry on with the rest of his life. And for the first time, he had something other than work in his future. Yes, it looked quite promising indeed.

* * *

"It isn't my best effort, but I suppose it will do," Georgiana said as she gazed at her reflection in the mirror, the very image of a commanding Athena down to her ankle-length tunic, golden sandals, and glinting shield fashioned from a repurposed silver platter.

Sylvia smiled to herself. Georgiana had always been a bit of a perfectionist, and fancy dress parties were no exception. "Well, I think you look absolutely splendid. And Bea did a truly wonderful job on your hair."

Georgiana lightly touched the thick, coiled tresses braided and pinned into an elaborate bun at the back of her head. "She used a curtain cord from my room. Very clever." Georgiana then met Sylvia's eyes in the mirror. "I wish you were coming. Athena could use a nymph."

Sylvia let out a snort at the idea. "I am many things, my friend. But a nymph is not one of them."

"Perhaps a sorceress, then. What about Circe, who turned Odysseus's men into swine?"

"That's more like it." They shared a laugh. "No. I'll be fine here," Sylvia insisted. "I have some more work to do anyway. But I want to hear every detail tomorrow."

Georgiana smoothed her hands down the front of her tunic.

"I'm sure it will be like every other party." Sadness flashed in her eyes so quickly Sylvia nearly missed it.

She pressed her lips together, resisting the urge to do a little prodding. She was certainly in no position to ask for honesty, when she herself was sitting on a mountain of her own secrets. She glanced at the clock on the mantel. Guests from neighboring estates would be arriving within the hour. Sylvia should have no trouble slipping away in the ensuing crush to deliver the envelope. She had traveled the route just this afternoon (this time without any interruptions from Rafe) and found a nondescript metal box nestled at the base of a tree in the exact location mentioned in the letter, near what appeared to be an abandoned cottage. It should be an easy marker for her to find in the coming dark. Coincidentally, she had run into Brodie again on her way back to the castle. He explained that the structure was once the gamekeeper's cottage, but it hadn't been used in years.

Sylvia still didn't like the idea of walking the path at night and couldn't forget the gardener's warning from yesterday:

All kinds of creatures could be roaming these woods, man and beast alike.

Georgiana's usual look of serene cheerfulness had returned. "I think this goddess is ready to enter the fray."

Sylvia gave her a soft smile as she slipped her hand into her dress pocket to stroke the cool metal of Brodie's pocketknife. She, too, was prepared for whatever trials lay ahead.

A short while later, Georgiana and Mrs. Crawford, dressed as a regal Maria Theresa, left the suite. A steady parade of carriages had been making their way up the long drive for some minutes, and the sounds of guests arriving had begun to filter upstairs. Sylvia then wished Bea good night and retired to her room. Bea intended to nap in preparation for her mistress's late return, and Sylvia wasted no time taking advantage. She scurried into her room, closed the door, and opened her trunk. She had a costume of her own to don.

* * *

"I look bloody ridiculous," Rafe grumbled as he adjusted the lace cuffs at the sleeves of his blue velvet frock coat.

Tully didn't even try to hide his irritation. "Then we should have brought something from London."

"I didn't know I was going to need a damned costume." Gerard had left that bit out. Now Rafe was stuck in the best outfit Tully had managed to scrounge up on short notice. All in all, it was a fine effort, but Rafe was less than pleased by the subject. "Must I wear the hat *and* the wig?"

"Yes. Otherwise you'll look like a pirate. And I'm told there will already be several pirates in attendance."

"Well, heaven knows we can't have that," Rafe said as he snatched the ridiculous black wig from his valet's hands. The blasted thing barely fit over his hair. Tully then fussed with the curls and fluffed it until Rafe finally had to brush him away.

"Now the mustache."

"*No.* That is where I draw the line." Tully didn't say a word. He merely raised one dark brow. After a tense moment, Rafe heaved a sigh. "Fine. But hurry up, dammit."

Pure glee filled Tully's eyes as he moved to apply the glue and false whiskers. When he was finished, he stepped back and made a great show of ushering Rafe over to the mirror. "Behold: King Charles the second."

A very flamboyant pirate stared back at Rafe, but he held his tongue for Tully's sake. The man had never looked so proud in his life. "Beautiful job, Tully."

His valet's face immediately fell. "You hate it."

Rafe considered his reflection. Between the wig and the mustache, he didn't look like himself at all, which could have its benefits. He had never employed disguises in his work and suspected that they could prove very useful. "I don't. Truly. I won't be wearing it to the theater, mind you, but your resourcefulness is unparalleled."

Even Tully wasn't immune to flattery. He blushed a little and bowed. "Thank you, sir. I hope you enjoy yourself."

There was little chance of that happening, but he graciously accepted the sentiment anyway.

Rafe straightened the sizable brim of his hat and made his way downstairs into the scrum below. Wardale was greeting guests dressed as the emperor Caesar, while Lady Delacorte had taken the bold step of dressing as Calpurnia, Caesar's last wife. Rafe couldn't help scanning the crowd, hoping that perhaps Sylvia had changed her mind and decided to attend.

An image of her dressed in a much more revealing tunic lounging on a chaise holding a succulent grapevine at the ready suddenly flashed in his mind. Thanks to his continued search and her duties, they had only been able to exchange a few heated and brief words since yesterday afternoon, but she had rarely left his thoughts. Rafe had to fight through the impulse to turn around and march right back up the staircase in search of her. Then again, perhaps it was better that she didn't see him dressed like this. Tonight Rafe planned to engage in a little light subterfuge with some of the guests, as the convivial atmosphere of a fancy dress ball tended to loosen peoples' tongues, not to mention the copious amounts of spirits. Wardale had been particularly adamant that Rafe target Lord Essex over a rumor he had a penchant for women's underthings. Rafe didn't see what that had to do with the threats Wardale had been receiving, but the man insisted that such a deviant couldn't be trusted. Rafe privately decided to clear Lord Essex of any suspicion. It was no concern of his if the man enjoyed wearing women's stockings, and certainly not Wardale's.

Rafe had just located the gentleman in question when someone accidentally jostled his elbow.

"Oh, pardon me. Terribly sorry."

Rafe sketched a grand bow. "Lady Arlington, good evening." He then took in her costume. "Or should I say, the goddess of war?"

Lady Arlington squinted at him for a long moment. Either she had already sampled the punch, or she simply didn't recognize him. "It is Mr. Davies," he finally said.

A delighted grin, much wider than her usual aloof smile, crossed her face. "Mr. *Davies!*" she squealed.

Definitely the punch, then.

She took a step back and looked him over, head to toe. The squint returned. "But who are you supposed to be?"

"King Charles II," he huffed.

Lady Arlington then burst out laughing. "Oh dear," she said after a moment. "You're serious."

"Quite." Rafe then offered her his arm. "May I escort you to the refreshments?"

It was growing crowded in this section of the room, and Rafe was becoming uncomfortably warm.

Lady Arlington threaded her arm through his. "Please. I've been meaning to speak to you."

He raised an eyebrow. "Oh? I'm all ears."

"It's about Sylvia—I mean, Miss Sparrow." Rafe wondered if she felt his arm tense beneath hers. "I hope you don't think me too forward. I only wanted to say how important she is to me—and my aunt, of course."

He kept his focus forward. "Naturally."

"And that we have grown to appreciate her greatly in a very short time."

"Understandable." Rafe longed to press her on this lie to gain more information about Sylvia, but now was hardly the time. She was protecting her friend. He respected that.

"And that I don't think we are the only ones who have developed a...a...*fondness* for her."

Even in its subtlety, this was a bold statement for her to make. Rafe decided to give credit to the punch once again.

"You are not wrong, my lady," he began. "I have indeed noticed that Miss Sparrow has many fine qualities."

"I knew it. You *like* her."

Rafe couldn't help but laugh at the delight in her voice. "Yes, I'm afraid you've caught me."

A rather smug smile came over Lady Arlington before she abruptly stopped and turned to him. "I've decided to trust your intentions here, Mr. Davies. I'm sure you must realize how significant this is."

Rafe began to blush, and this time he couldn't blame it on the heat of the room. "Yes," he said softly.

"But if you give me the slightest reason to doubt you, I will not hesitate to destroy you. Understand?"

All Rafe could do was nod in the face of a stare so commanding it would make even Athena cower. Her eyes appeared to search his, but she seemed to like what she found there, and after a moment the lightness returned. "Wonderful.

Now, would you be so kind as to fetch me a glass of that delightful punch?"

Rafe returned her smile and bowed. "Of course, dear goddess. It would be my pleasure."

* * *

An hour later Rafe escaped onto the back terrace. The ballroom had grown even more stifling, and he needed a break from the crush. Rafe had spoken with nearly all the guests staying at the castle but once again found nothing of substance. He descended the stairs and headed toward an empty space of lawn. A few couples strolled arm in arm on the grounds lit by dramatic, medieval-looking torches, but the cool weather kept most of the guests inside. He needed to seriously consider the likelihood that he would not uncover anything at all, that he would not win Wardale's favor, and he would have to return to London a failure.

The one thing Rafe had spent years diligently avoiding now seemed inevitable. His chest tightened at the thought of meeting Gerard and explaining what had happened. It wasn't his fault, but that would hardly matter. His brother would gloat in his usual way, and Rafe had no recourse to challenge him. Nothing that declared "See, I *am* worth something."

There would be no group of agents to train, no improvements to oversee, no chance to make his own mark on the world— a world inherited by men like his father and brother and built by men like Wardale. Instead, all he would be left with was the reputation he had carefully crafted to make him seem as useless and dissolute as possible. What a marvelous joke.

Rafe turned around. The castle glowed with light from the

ballroom, while a few windows on the upper floors emitted faintly flickering lights. Sylvia's room was part of a suite shared by Lady Arlington and Mrs. Crawford, located on the same floor as his own, though on the other side. Rafe had put off searching it in a desperate bid to retain some degree of morality, but he wouldn't be able to avoid doing so much longer. Not if Wardale demanded it. His shoulders sagged as he let out a weighty breath. Was she still awake, sitting beside one of those windows with the lonely lights? Was she thinking of him? And would she still want him if this was all he could ever be?

He glanced back at the ballroom. It was still early. No one would be retiring for several more hours, including Mrs. Crawford, who was busy holding court when he left.

Go to her.

They had promised to meet tomorrow after the ball, but that felt years away.

Now.

His blood began buzzing, and before his mind could reason otherwise, his feet took him across the lawn, toward a side door he knew led to a servants' staircase. Not a soul could see him go to her room. Even without Lady Arlington's dire warning, Rafe would not do anything to cause Sylvia harm. She had already been through enough, and he refused to treat her like the other men in her life. Whatever happened between them needed to be her choice. But dammit, he hoped she would not turn him away.

Rafe was near the entrance when there was a rustling on the path that led to the stables. A figure appeared a few feet away. At this distance, Rafe could only make out the outline of a young man, possibly a boy. He spotted Rafe and froze in his tracks.

Rafe took a step forward. "Who is that?" But instead of simply making himself known, the boy turned and darted away. Rafe paused for a moment before instinct took over and he ran off after him. Every single castle servant was busy with the party. And none would run away from a guest into the night. Whoever this was didn't work at the castle. And that made him very interesting. "Stop!"

But Rafe's command only had the opposite effect. The boy was quick, but he was faster. And thankfully the moon was bright enough to provide some light. He lost his hat somewhere near the stables, but he would come back for it later. They reached the tree line, and the lad darted onto a walking path that led through the forest. Rafe followed the sound of snapping twigs. He could just make out the boy's outline a few feet ahead of him. Another hard push and Rafe could grab his collar. He reached out, his fingers grazing the rough linen, but then the boy took a sharp turn and disappeared. Rafe slammed to a halt. A cool wind whipped through the trees, and the ancient forest let out an ominous groan. It appeared the long-anticipated storm was finally on its way. Rafe squinted into the dark woods. The trees were thicker here. The boy couldn't be far. He then spotted a structure just off the path. Rafe took a few tentative steps toward it and was able to determine it was some sort of cottage. He could just make out a shadowed figure stealing inside. It had to be the boy.

Rafe considered calling out to arrange a truce, but the element of surprise had always served him better. He watched the house for several minutes and detected no more signs of movement. The wind whipped up even stronger, and telltale drops of rain sprinkled his cheeks. Thunder rumbled in the distance. Time to seek shelter. Rafe crept around the back of the cottage and found a door nearly rotting off the hinges. It opened easily, and he slunk through the doorway. What he wouldn't give for his electric torch right now. It then occurred to him that he had absolutely no weapons—and this boy might be armed. Rafe made a fist. He regularly kept up with his physical training at a fitness club in London, but it had been years since he actually had to fight someone bent on harming him. Rafe abhorred physical violence. He could defend himself when necessary, but his weapons of choice were words. Manipulations. Even threats. And he was damned good at it. One didn't grow up with a celebrated dramatist without learning how to put on a show. So that was what he would do.

Rafe had entered a storeroom at the back of the cottage and headed toward the doorway, which he guessed opened into the main living space. Years of dust and stale air filled his nostrils, and he suppressed the urge to sneeze.

Outside the wind howled and the thunder grew louder, which conveniently muffled his footsteps. Just as he entered the main room, lightning flashed, filling every corner with a burst of brilliant white light. In that second, Rafe was taken by surprise, and the boy, who had been waiting for him by the doorway, seized his chance. All it took was a quick, well-placed hit on the head, and Rafe pitched forward into the darkness.

CHAPTER THIRTEEN

Rafe stumbled blindly until a pair of hands pressed him down onto a chair. He could hear someone shuffling around him, and when he finally regained his alertness, his wrists were bound behind his back while his head throbbed. Rafe immediately flexed his hands and ran his fingers as best he could along the rope. Damn. It was double knotted. This boy had proven to be a worthy opponent. Rafe could get out of it, of course, but it would take some time, and the boy might notice his fidgeting. He slowly opened his eyes, which felt sensitive even in the room's low light. A decent fire crackled in the hearth, and the boy crouched before it, staring at the flames. Rain battered the cottage's windows, and cool gusts of wind escaped from under the rickety door. Most of the room's few pieces of furniture were covered in dust sheets. Rafe noticed his wig on the floor beside him. The false mustache had also fallen off. Or perhaps it had been removed.

"I have to hand it to you," he began with all the geniality he could muster under the circumstances. "It isn't very often that someone takes me by surprise. So a point to you there."

The boy rose, and Rafe blinked. His eyesight must be worse off than he realized, or it was simply a trick of the light. Otherwise...

The figure turned around. "I suppose that makes two of us, then."

Rafe could think of very few, if any, occasions when he had been rendered completely speechless. But as Sylvia Sparrow stood before him in a pair of trousers, he found himself at an utter loss for words. One side of her face was illuminated by the firelight, and a few dark strands had escaped from under her cap. He could only stare, agog, as she tossed her cap aside and ran a hand over her pinned hair.

Rafe's gaze then immediately fell on her trousers, which fit rather snugly around her waist and hips. It had been the way the fabric clung to her perfectly heart-shaped bottom as she crouched by the fire that gave him the first indication that perhaps the boy was not a boy at all. But he never would have guessed it was *Sylvia*.

"What are you doing here?" he snapped, suddenly feeling unmoored, as if the floor were tilting underneath him.

Sylvia crossed her arms and ignored the question as her eyes traveled down the length of his form. "What are you supposed to be? A pirate?"

Rafe lifted his chin. "Charles the second, actually. And don't change the subject."

Her eyes flickered back to his face. "Does your head hurt? Is that why you're so irritable?"

"My irritation is in no way related to my head injury, I assure you." But Sylvia moved toward him and gently ran her fingers through his hair. God, that felt good.

"There's a bit of a lump but no blood. Luckily, you have a

hard head. You bent the pot I used." She gestured to the object in question, which indeed was now concave.

Rafe snorted. His mother had often said as much during his notably rambunctious childhood. Sylvia then moved before him again.

"Now that that's settled, perhaps you could be so kind as to untie me."

She eyed him warily. "I'd rather not."

"This is absurd," he protested, pulling against the rope. "Sylvia—"

"Why were you following me?"

Rafe heard the fear underlying her sharp tone. He needed to tread carefully here. He had already underestimated her once. "I didn't know it was you. I saw someone acting suspiciously. I followed them."

Sylvia narrowed her eyes. "But *why*? Why wouldn't you get someone else to do it?"

Frustration flared within him. The Honorable Rafe Davies may be a charming rogue, but he certainly wasn't a coward. He had served in the navy, for God's sake. Did she truly still think so little of him? "There wasn't time," he said through gritted teeth.

She leaned closer, and he saw the sadness in her gaze. "I wish you hadn't," she nearly whispered.

Rafe began to slowly twist his wrists. "Sylvia, please," he said as gently as he could manage. "Tell me what's going on. Why were you out there?"

But she turned around and walked back toward the fire. "It's better you don't know."

Dammit, was she trying to protect *him*?

"I can help you," he insisted, but she only shook her head.

Rafe sighed. Not once had he ever been so tempted to reveal his cover. But if it persuaded her to be honest with him, to let him help her get out of whatever mess she was in...

No. He simply couldn't. Not until he had a better understanding of what was going on.

"Will you at least tell me where you got your trousers?"

Sylvia glanced over her shoulder but didn't respond.

"This is a rather good knot," he tried again. "And a decent fire. I'm beginning to think your skills extend far beyond secretarial work." That elicited a snort. "Few know this," he continued, "but a competent woman is one of my weaknesses."

That got her. Sylvia whipped around. "Are you actually *flirting* with me right now?"

Rafe managed what he thought was a rather rakish shrug. "Is it working?" She rolled her eyes in answer, and he let his gaze linger on her form. "You know, I imagine there are a lot of men who would pay quite handsomely to be tied up by a woman wearing trousers. And here I am, getting it for free."

She put her hands on her hips and glared. It was absurdly attractive. "If you want to shock me, you'll need to do better than that."

"All right. Come closer."

"You're ridiculous," she huffed, but even in the low light he could see the flush cresting her cheeks.

"I'm tied to a chair in a glorified pirate's outfit and you're dressed as a boy. There are several things about this situation that are ridiculous."

The corners of her mouth twitched as she tried not to smile. "I suppose that's true."

Rafe pulled harder against the rope. "You can't keep me tied up like this forever, Sylvia. A man has needs, you know."

The concern returned to her eyes, and she moved toward him once again. "Are you saying you need a wee?"

Christ, that made him sound like a child. "Well, not now. But it's damned uncomfortable." That wasn't *entirely* true. Sylvia stepped closer, and Rafe's cock began to stiffen.

"I'm not untying you, Rafe."

Why did his name always sound so wicked coming from her lips? It sent a delightful shiver down his spine.

"Well, then," he drawled, slowly dragging his gaze up to her face. "I suppose you'll just have to do something else to make me more comfortable."

* * *

Even while indisposed, the man was positively incorrigible.

Sylvia had only realized the identity of her pursuer once she had deposited him in the nearest chair and removed that ridiculous wig. She hadn't been scared in the least, as the adrenaline from their chase was still coursing through her veins, just incredibly angry. Everything had all been going according to plan. And she had been so close to putting this awful night behind her. But when she tore off the wig, she had gasped aloud in the quiet room, so deep was her shock.

She needed time to figure out what this all meant. Why *Rafe* had followed her into the woods. It was nearly a half hour later, and she still wasn't any closer to unraveling the mystery before her. Was he simply trying to be heroic? Did he think she intended to harm someone at the castle? Or was he somehow connected to her blackmailer? The last thought was why she was reluctant to untie him just yet.

It also seemed much safer for them both if his movements were limited. Unlike their previous meetings, there was no chance of anyone finding them here. No worry that they could be caught at any moment. They were deep in the woods. And entirely alone. Her eyes began to drift toward the narrow bed in the corner, but she immediately halted their progress and returned her focus to Rafe. The corner of his mouth lifted. Of course he had noticed.

She came closer, even while her mind screamed out with every step. He wore a blue velvet coat with gold embroidery and she smoothed her palm across one of his well-formed shoulders. His breath caught at her touch. She pulled her hand back, wishing she wasn't quite so flattered by his reaction. "Your coat is damp. Are you cold?"

Rafe's eyes burned into her own. "At the moment I feel rather overwarm."

Sylvia blushed again. She, too, was growing warmer, and it wasn't from the measly fire she had built.

"Sylvia," Rafe murmured, a faint note of urgency in his voice. He strained against his bonds and shifted in his seat. "Is it really so impossible to imagine that I would go after someone acting suspiciously?"

"Yes," she answered quickly, and Rafe grimaced. "No. I don't know," she amended and let out a breath. "Sometimes it feels as if...as if you're two different people."

He stiffened slightly before he tilted his head and gave her the look that always managed to make her feel both uncomfortable and enthralled. It was horribly confusing.

"I could say the same for you. We all have faces we show the world and those we keep more private."

Sylvia looked away from his too-perceptive gaze and fiddled with a button on her shirt. "I suppose that's true."

"But you're right." He sighed. "The Honorable Rafe Davies isn't the sort of man who goes racing off into the night to play the hero."

She smirked. "Did you just refer to yourself in the third person?"

"It's how I think of myself sometimes," he admitted. "The public face, anyway."

"Why?" she asked, surprised by this admission. "Why act that way at all, I mean?"

Rafe shrugged. "It makes things easier." But he didn't elaborate on what, exactly. Sylvia guessed it was connected to his family. The one that still refused to recognize him. Perhaps acting like a shallow rake was a way to shield himself from hurt. Sylvia could understand that.

"So who are you being now?"

The corner of Rafe's mouth lifted. "That depends." He lowered his voice. "Who do you want me to be?"

Sylvia's mouth went dry at the unexpectedly arousing question. The fire crackled in the bracing silence that followed as she tried to form an answer. Sylvia was certainly no innocent. She and Bernard had managed to arrange more than a few clandestine encounters, but their intimacies had always been rather perfunctory. Despite his supposed contempt for the status quo, Bernard had been utterly conventional in bed. But regardless of what was real or just for show, Rafe was still the most wickedly handsome man she had ever met, and his reputation as being even more wicked behind closed doors was not of his own invention. Standing here before him while he was tied to a chair went well beyond her experience. Beyond her imagination. And yet, despite the possible danger, there wasn't anywhere she would rather be.

"What do you want, Sylvia?" he asked again. The question practically burned with dark promise.

"I . . . I don't know," she finally offered, but Rafe saw through her evasive response.

"Yes, you do," he said in a voice smooth enough to tempt the devil. "I've never met a woman who seems to know her own mind so decidedly as you."

Sylvia couldn't find the words. He saw her so much better than she saw herself.

Rafe seemed to take pity and gave her an affectionate smile. "Would you like to touch me?" At her hesitant nod, his smile turned into a grin. "Well, that's a start. Do it," he urged. "Touch me, Sylvia. Anywhere you please."

She had just caressed his shoulder. Surely she could manage *that* again. Sylvia swallowed hard and reached out, intending to repeat the movement, but found her hand running through his hair instead. It was just as thick as she had imagined, and the strands were as soft as silk. Rafe let out a little groan and pressed up against her palm, as if he craved her touch. Was desperate for it. She moved closer until she stood between his legs. He wore breeches for his costume, and it hadn't escaped her notice how they seemed practically painted on his long, muscular thighs.

The heat radiating off his body mingled with the scent of fresh air, mossy rain, and the rich bergamot tang of his shaving soap. Sylvia inhaled deeply as the space between them grew even smaller. Rafe's entire body seemed to tense as she leaned closer. She was already well aware of his height and breadth, but standing so closely made him seem even larger. Her heart beat a little faster. It was the danger of it, she realized. Of having a powerful man at her fingertips.

He remained silent as she continued to gently stroke his hair, but his breaths grew increasingly ragged. Sylvia became emboldened enough to place her other hand against the side of his throat. She rubbed her thumb along his skin, marveling at how warm and smooth it was to the touch. He must have shaved right before the ball.

"Sylvia," he said roughly. "This is torturous."

She tilted his face up to meet her gaze and gave him a shy smile. "Is it?"

"Most definitely."

He had never looked so serious before, and her heart ached a little. How had she ever thought she would be immune to this man? Sylvia leaned down and pressed a soft kiss to his lips. But after a moment that ever-present spark between them flared anew, burning her from the inside out, and she let herself be wholly consumed by the flame. The kiss grew harder, hotter, and more intense, driven by an unspoken urgency. He parted her lips with his and welcomed the entrance of her tongue. Somehow, even in this position, Rafe seemed to be guiding her. Driving her toward what she most wanted before she even realized it.

She moved to straddle his thighs and wrapped her arms around his neck, extinguishing all space between them. Rafe tilted his hips up, and she broke the kiss on a gasp as she felt the full weight and length of him. She instinctively writhed against him, chasing more of that delicious sensation. Her forehead fell to his shoulder as a wave of pleasure moved through her. But it was just the beginning.

"That's it, my darling," Rafe growled by her ear. "Don't stop. Ride me. Ride me till you come." The command was thrilling. He rocked his hips again, urging her further. Dazed by the sensation building within her, Sylvia was compelled to comply. She sat back and met his eyes. They had grown darker and more intense. He really did look like some mad pirate king, which only heightened her desire. Sylvia's nipples tightened under his heated gaze, and her hands flew to the buttons of her shirt. Now everything felt too tight, too restricted. He watched, riveted, as she began to unbutton each one. She continued until her shirt gaped open, exposing the tops of her breasts and chemise. She thanked her past self for having the sense to loosen her corset more than usual, as she was now having trouble breathing. The cool air hit her overheated skin, but it did nothing to quell her desperation. Rafe stared at her chest as if he had just uncovered a horde of gold coins. It was incredibly gratifying, given that her breasts weren't of an exceptionally large size. But that didn't seem to matter at all.

"My God," he whispered.

Now she was breathing just as roughly as he was, and his eyes followed the bobbing of her breasts with every inhalation. He leaned forward and began to nuzzle her cleavage. She gasped at the feel of his lips and breath against her sensitive skin and roughly pulled down her chemise. Her breasts spilled over the neckline, fully exposed for him, and Rafe immediately pulled one nipple into his mouth. He ran the tip of his tongue in slow, torturous circles before giving her a gentle bite. The sensation was so powerful that she cried out. He continued licking and sucking as Sylvia arched up and leaned back, giving him more of her. Rafe then moved to the other, and she began writhing harder against him. Hot desire pulsed between her legs so hard it hurt. She felt her release coming fast, faster than it ever did when she touched herself—and never had with Bernard.

She suddenly cried out and buried her face into his neck as the pleasure overtook her in wave after shattering wave. He pressed the side of his face against hers and began murmuring into her ear about how lovely she was and how good she felt against him. Brightness seemed to burst through her, traveling along every limb. It took a moment for her to recognize the feeling—utter joy.

As her release began to fade, she sagged against him, waiting for her heartbeat to slowly returned to normal. After a minute she pulled back. Rafe met her gaze, clear and steady. She felt no trace of shame, no embarrassment at what he had just witnessed. This wild abandon he seemed to inspire in her felt more real and true than anything she could remember. For a long moment they simply stared at each other. Rafe was still panting. And still hard beneath her. She shifted and moved to touch him, suddenly feeling very selfish.

"No, darling." He chuckled. "Don't worry about me. Watching you was more than enough."

Sylvia looked up at him and, without a word, pressed another lush kiss to his lips. One that was full of thanks. When she pulled back, Rafe let out a gasp.

"But you'll need to stop kissing me like that, I'm afraid. One can only endure so much torture."

Sylvia gave him an apologetic smile. "I'm sorry. I couldn't help it." She pushed off him and stood up.

"I don't suppose you'll untie me *now*."

Sylvia bit her lip. It did seem awful to keep him tied up after that. And perhaps she was being a little too paranoid. Why would *Rafe Davies* have anything to do with her blackmailer? She gave him an assessing look as she began to button up her shirt. Rafe's eyes tracked her every movement.

Then again, untying him would be like letting a tiger loose in his cage while she was still trapped inside. She was on the verge of telling him no when a loud rustling drew her attention. She turned around just in time to watch as a rather large hole in the roof near the hearth opened up. Rainwater came rushing in, nearly dousing the fire. Sylvia cried out and immediately moved to stop the leak. She picked up the bits of roof that had fallen on the floor and tried to shove them back into place, but the tiles were slippery and she wasn't tall enough to reach.

Rafe called out from his chair, demanding she let him assist her. Sylvia turned back and stared at him as rainwater poured down her arms.

What choice did she have?

CHAPTER FOURTEEN

❧

R afe could see the exact moment when Sylvia gave in. The wariness that had filled her eyes finally gave way as the reality of the situation dawned on her. She needed his help. Rafe had already been working to free his bonds, so by the time Sylvia dashed over, it took only a few pulls to release him. He sprang out of the chair, threw off his ridiculous coat, and immediately set about plugging the leak. Luckily, the rush of water had already begun to slow to a trickle, as it must have been collecting on the roof for some time. Rafe retrieved the fallen debris and examined the hole.

"Bring the chair," he called to Sylvia, who had been standing there watching him in disbelief, but she quickly sprang into action. He suppressed the urge to roll his eyes and privately vowed that she would not leave this cottage without acknowledging that he did have *some* practical uses.

Rafe then instructed her to hold the chair steady as he stepped onto the seat. The light was so dim he could barely see what he was doing, but Rafe felt along until he determined the contours of the hole and pressed the roof shingles back into place. He looked down and pointed to some piles of refuse that had fallen along with the shingles.

"Here, hand me that."

Sylvia did his bidding, and he shoved the debris into every available crevice to further secure the shingles. After a moment the leak stopped entirely. Rafe wiped his hands and surveyed his work. "There," he said with an air of satisfaction as he stepped off the chair. He wouldn't be starting a career mending roofs anytime soon, but it would do for now.

Sylvia's eyes were fixed on his chest. "Your shirt is soaked."

Rafe looked down and found that the front had turned translucent. Sylvia's sleeves were just as wet. He built up the fire until it was roaring once again, then began unbuttoning his shirt. Many would consider Rafe's expansive sexual history rather depraved, but the truth was nothing he had experienced had been as erotically charged as this encounter with Sylvia. And he only craved more. Rafe dragged the chair closer to the fire and peeled off the soaked linen before draping it across the back.

He held out his hand to Sylvia. "Now yours."

"I beg your pardon?"

Rafe laughed at the scandalized look that took over her face. "It's a little late for modesty, don't you think?"

Sylvia shot him a disapproving frown but took off the shirt in composed, measured movements. It was the exact opposite of the heated, wildly seductive performance she had put on only minutes ago, when it was as if she needed to tear the very fabric from her skin. Both were arousing in their own way.

She held the shirt out to him and pressed her other arm across her chest. Rafe did his best to avert his eyes, which was a trial, as she possessed the loveliest pair of breasts he had ever seen. Round and full and firm. He guessed one would fill his hand completely. And if she ever gave him the chance, he would damn well take it.

Sylvia shook the shirt by his face, and he snapped to attention. "Here."

Rafe took the garment before carefully draping it over the chair in the spot closest to the fire. When he turned back, Sylvia was clutching her jacket around her shoulders. A shiver racked her frame, and Rafe longed to gather her in his arms. But he must wait for her invitation. He turned more fully toward her and was pleased to see her eyes roving over his body.

"Is that a mermaid on your arm?"

Rafe flexed the biceps in question, so she could better see.

One corner of her mouth curved up. "A navy man with a mermaid tattoo. How original."

God, he loved when she teased him. "I've others that are more eclectic. Would you care to see?"

In truth, none of his tattoos were particularly original. They had been a way to prove his mettle and build camaraderie during his time at sea. An important feat for a young lad with his privileged background.

Sylvia continued to stare at him with that devilish little smile, as if she was actually considering it. "Please," she finally said. That single, husky word burned through his brain as she stepped closer.

"The mermaid is named Margarita. She was my third and hurt the most by far. I'm not ashamed to admit I shed a few tears. But this," he began as he showed her his other arm, "was my first."

"An anchor?"

Rafe shrugged. "Most sailors get that during their first

voyage. I woke up in a Grecian port with the worst hangover of my life and that on my shoulder."

"Oh dear." Sylvia laughed.

"And this was my second." He grazed his right pectoral muscle. Dark chest hair obscured it a little, so Sylvia had to lean closer.

Rafe's breath caught as she reached out and brushed the letters with the tips of her fingers. "Mother."

Their eyes met. Rafe had to clear his throat before he could speak. "I got it before my first visit home. She absolutely hates it."

Sylvia gave him that adorable little side smile again. "I would too."

Rafe took her hand by the wrist, brought it to his mouth, then gently kissed her fingertips. All while never breaking his gaze.

His cock jerked at the sound of her sharp inhalation. But then she quickly pulled her hand away and stepped back, now taking great interest in the battered wall to her right. "Was she upset when you joined the navy?"

So. It was tenderness that scared her most.

"Livid. I was supposed to be back at Eton. By the time my parents realized what I had done, I was already on my way to the Mediterranean."

Sylvia whirled around. "My God. How old were you?"

"Fifteen." Rafe continued in the face of her wide-eyed stare. "I absolutely hated school, you see. My father had taken a diplomatic post after he married my mother, and we traveled quite a bit when I was young. Turkey, Malta, Persia. My mother tried to put off boarding school as long as possible, maintaining that I was having a world-class education staying with them, and my father indulged her until I was twelve." A shudder came over him at the memory, even now. His mother sniffling into a handkerchief, his gentle father trying his best to look severe, talking about duty and honor and how it was important for him to meet other boys of his class. But Rafe knew, even then, that he hadn't a chance of fitting in.

"Then what happened?" Sylvia prompted, bringing him back to the present.

"I was sent away, in accordance with my birthright, and it was an utter disaster. I don't think a day went by that first term without someone trying to fight me. I had been a scrappy boy, used to playing with the children who lived in and around the embassies. But these English boys were different. They were cruel in ways I couldn't even imagine." That was when he had first learned to use words as a weapon. His fists soon followed out of necessity. "My father assumed the scandal would have died down by the time I went to school, but my mother knew better. She knew those boys would eat me alive. And they very nearly did."

Sylvia gave him a confused look. "The scandal? You mean, your parents' marriage?"

Rafe nodded. "I assume you know my mother was an actress, but she was also born into poverty. The theater was her escape. She started as an assistant to a dresser when she was little more than a girl, until one day someone noticed she had become a beauty and put her in the chorus. But she took the craft seriously, working her way up to bigger and bigger roles. It was all she had, really. Her own mother worked herself to an early death as a laundress, and she never met her father, as he disappeared soon after her mother realized she was with child."

"And those...those boys knew all that?"

Rafe nodded. "From their parents. They knew details even I didn't," he said with a bitter laugh. "A notorious actress from a lower-class background married a man who eventually inherited one of the oldest earldoms in the country. It was the scandal of the decade. They had to leave England."

Sylvia's eyebrows rose in shock. "How awful."

"They were happier living abroad anyway," he said with a shrug. "Not everyone is as obsessed with class and bloodlines as the English. For my father, the dutiful second son, it was the adventure he had always wanted. He married the woman his father told him to when he was barely twenty and had children immediately. The old earl didn't have much faith in his heir, and rightly so. My father's brother never did get around to getting married. He was too busy gambling and pickling his liver. My father, on the other hand, did as he was told. He gave my grandfather the heir he needed, after having three extraneous daughters. He was married to his first wife for nearly twenty years before she died. So he decided to live for himself for once in his life."

"And then he met your mother."

Rafe met her gaze. There was no judgment in her eyes, only sympathy. Understanding. Why had he never told anyone all this before?

Because no one had ever asked.

"Yes. When his brother died unexpectedly, my parents were already married."

"And yet, after all they had endured, he still sent you to school in England?"

Rafe smiled at her defense of him. "He thought he was helping prepare me. And I was angry with him for sending me away for a long, long time. But he wasn't exactly wrong. I did need to understand how those boys operated in order to interact with them."

In many ways it was still the most valuable education he had ever received.

Sylvia nodded and stepped toward him. "I suppose he had a point. But still, it must have been awful. My brother went to Rugby. Before that we were friends. We used to go on long tramps around the countryside. He taught me to fish and build a fire. But after he went to that school…" She shook her head, sadness in her eyes. "It turned him into someone I didn't recognize."

Rafe kept his face carefully blank. She had revealed so little about herself, he didn't want to scare her off with his interest. "I'm sorry for that. You are no longer close?"

Sylvia let out a snort. "No. And we disagree on nearly everything."

"Sounds like me and my brother. What does he do?"

"Something in banking. Supposedly." Sylvia rolled her eyes. "I'm certain he has gambling debts, but he'll never admit it. He had to let our family home last year, after my father died. He offered to send me to Australia, but I refused. That was how I—" She hesitated and cast him a wary glance. "How I met Lady Arlington. Through an employment agency in London."

Rafe swallowed hard and continued to keep calm despite the anger growing inside him. That fiend. Apparently this Bernard fellow wouldn't be the only man Rafe needed to track down.

"Was your father ill for very long?"

Sylvia hugged the jacket closer. "About a year. After everything that happened with Bernard, I went home to care for him.

My brother was not willing to give up his career in the city, or pay for a nurse, so there wasn't anyone else."

"That was still good of you."

She shrugged. "A daughter's duty, I suppose. We came to an agreement. In exchange for caring for Father, I could live in the house for as long as I wanted. But, afterward, he said he simply couldn't. He needed the rent money."

"And you were at his mercy, because he inherited everything."

Her brief, disappointed nod caused a sharp pain to flare in his chest.

"I have a small inheritance from my mother, but it wasn't anywhere near enough to buy the house from him."

"No wonder your position is so important to you."

And why any association with him short of marriage could absolutely ruin her, and Sylvia had already said she had no desire to wed. It seemed incredibly important that she remain entirely her own woman.

"It's all I have now," she murmured, meeting his eyes.

He moved closer and took her hands. "Good God, you're freezing." He began to rub them between his own. "I want you to know that nothing that has happened between us will jeopardize you in any way. I simply won't allow it."

There. That sounded like something a nob would say. It wasn't as if he could reveal his methods.

Sylvia gave him an indulgent smile. "I'm sure your discretion is enough."

She was placating him and still hiding whatever business had driven her into the woods. Either she didn't trust him or didn't think he could help her. But Rafe was determined to show her otherwise. Without revealing his true identity, of course.

Hypocrite.

Rafe ignored the voice in his head. He couldn't just stand by and let her get hurt. Not when he could do something about it. And Rafe refused to be another name on the list of men who had disappointed her. But there was no doubt this complicated things. And if she was somehow connected to the threats made against Wardale...

No.

He brushed away the half-formed thought. This was something else. Something personal to her. He knew well enough all the varied secrets a person could keep. Based on what she had already told him, it was most likely related to money. Perhaps he could find a way to help her secretly, as he highly doubted she would accept any he offered. Proud little Sparrow.

He tugged her closer, still trying to warm her hands with his own. Rafe turned them over and rubbed his thumb along the ink stain that marked one finger.

"Oh, don't look at my hands. They're awful." Sylvia tried to pull away, but he held fast.

"They most certainly are not."

She shook her head. "They're not the hands of a lady."

"The body they are attached to suggests otherwise."

Her brow puckered in frustration. "Ladies don't *work*."

Rafe continued to smooth his hands over hers. "It's nothing to be ashamed of. Truly."

The wary look returned to her eyes, and she hesitated just as a shiver racked through her. Rafe bit back a sigh. She wasn't interested in his tenderness but seemed to have no qualms about giving in to desire. If he had to mask his affection in fleshly pleasure for her to accept it, so be it.

"Let me keep you warm, my little bird," he murmured.

"I'm f-fine."

Rafe raised an eyebrow. "Your lips are turning blue."

Before Sylvia could protest further, Rafe flung the jacket from her shoulders, picked her up, and deposited her onto the bed. He then climbed in next to her and wrapped the sorry excuse for a blanket around them both.

"Really," she huffed. "This isn't necessary."

Rafe smiled against her hair. "Then why are you cuddling me?"

"I am not *cuddling* you," Sylvia insisted even as she wriggled her back against his chest. "You're merely a convenient source of heat."

Rafe wrapped one arm around her waist and pulled her closer until all space was extinguished. The soft skin of her arms slid against his, and his muscles instantly flexed at the sensation. He felt her sigh, but it didn't sound like a sigh of relief.

"We'll leave as soon as the rain stops."

Outside, the worst of the storm had passed, but raindrops still drummed against the windows.

"I'm not worried about that," she said softly. "It will be many hours before anyone notices my absence."

Rafe nodded his agreement. Most of the guests wouldn't wake until late afternoon. They were safe until then. "Then what is it?"

Sylvia turned in his arms until their noses were practically touching. "What happens tomorrow?"

"Well, you see, the sun will rise, as usual. You'll have breakfast first. Here that means eggs and something vile the Scotch call haggis—"

Sylvia clamped a hand over his mouth. She was trying

179

not to smile, but her eyes danced with amusement. "I mean between us."

Rafe kissed her palm before pulling her hand away. "Whatever you want."

Sylvia watched him closely, no doubt looking for the lie. But she would find none. He meant it. Whatever she wanted from this encounter, he would give it to her.

"I want you to leave me alone after this. No more accidental meetings in libraries, or waltzes, or sitting across from me during tea." Rafe opened his mouth to object, but she talked over him anyway. "No. You are utterly transparent. Lady Arlington has already noticed, and soon others will, too. I want you to treat me like a man of your class usually would."

Rafe pressed his lips into a hard line. There were several ways "a man of his class" would treat a woman like her, but he knew what she meant. "You're saying you want me to ignore you." He didn't even try to hide the sulky tone.

Sylvia nodded. "It's for the best." She then lowered her eyes. One fingertip began to gently trace the letters of his chest tattoo. "Besides, you'll go back to London soon. I'm sure you have a hundred different things to attend to. And there will be so many distractions, you'll forget all about me."

On any other woman this display of self-pity would have registered as an irritation not worth acknowledging. Instead, he wanted to tell her how tired he was of London. How nothing in that monstrous metropolis was anywhere near as compelling as she was. *Forget her?* Impossible.

But Rafe said none of those things. Because he knew she was trying to convince herself more than him.

"And I'll be leaving for my trip with Mrs. Crawford soon. So, you see, it will be easier this way. For both of us."

A strange emptiness opened inside his chest at the thought of her thousands of miles away.

"Yes," he managed after a moment. "Quite right."

He would abide by her wishes, for now. But he wouldn't stop trying to uncover her mystery, either. And for that he wouldn't ask permission.

Her fingertips then drew a lazy path up his chest, toward his clavicle. Rafe held his breath, the better to feel every ridge and whorl from her fingerprints as they marked his skin. "But until then..."

She met his gaze. Her eyes burned with dark lust. He could nearly see himself reflected in the obsidian surface and slid one hand behind her head to cup the back of her neck. Rafe slowly tilted her face toward his, watching as her pupils came dangerously close to swallowing her irises. He had never felt so gratified by a woman's admiration. It was a gift to be wanted by her.

"Until then," he continued, pausing just before their lips touched to listen to her sharp, delicate breaths. "I'm yours."

CHAPTER FIFTEEN

❦

As Rafe set his lips so surely to hers, Sylvia had to remind herself to breathe. This man, who looked at and held her with such tenderness, was also in possession of a most wicked mouth. Sylvia arched against his muscular front, giving in to the heat already building between them once again. She appeared to have lost all composure. All sense of control.

It is only for tonight.

But for this one night, she would allow herself to be at his mercy. Completely.

Rafe let out a low moan of approval, as if he had heard the thought, then gently rolled on top of Sylvia. He pressed his forearms firmly into the mattress, bracketing her between them. The kiss turned hungrier as their tongues tangled together, both seeming to wrestle for control. Rafe began to laugh and pulled back.

"Do you ever let anyone lead you?"

"Not usually, no."

Rafe grinned down at her and ran his fingers through her disheveled hair. "Good."

He then leaned in and gave her a fierce, deep kiss that left

Sylvia breathless. She wrapped her arms around his neck and pulled him closer, until her senses were full of his heat, his scent, his weight. She never wanted this to end. She wanted to feel him against her forever. Rafe moved to adjust himself to keep from crushing her, and Sylvia let out a whimper. Without a word, Rafe flipped them over. Now Sylvia sat astride him.

"There," he panted. "I've always preferred this position anyway. Marvelous view."

Sylvia managed an amused smile even while she tried not to think of the women who came before her. Then privately vowed that after tonight, they would all be a very distant memory. She had never been interested in competing over a man before. But now, with Rafe, she felt strangely possessive. Jealous, even. It went against so many of her own principles, and yet, as she stared down at his flushed cheeks and drew her hands along the lean muscles of his chest, a single word echoed in her mind in time with her heartbeat:

Mine. Mine. Mine.

Thank God he couldn't tell, and she would have vehemently denied it, if asked. Sylvia slowly caressed his pectorals and down along the hard planes of his stomach. Rafe's breath caught when she paused to linger at his defined obliques.

"You're built like a statue. Remarkable."

Her fingers slipped lower, and the groan Rafe emitted was extremely satisfying. She glanced up. He was riveted, watching her every movement.

The corner of her mouth lifted. "I think these are no longer needed," she said as she ran a finger along the waistband of his breeches.

Rafe raised an eyebrow. "Well, then, we'll just have to do something about that."

Sylvia looked down and smiled. His hands moved toward the placard at the front of his breeches and made quick work of the buttons. Sylvia reluctantly moved aside so he could pull the garment off, and gasped. He was completely bare underneath.

Rafe turned to her. "They didn't fit correctly with my drawers on," he explained, though it really wasn't necessary. "All right. Now you."

Sylvia tore her eyes away from the impressive specimen resting between his legs. "Me?" she squeaked.

Rafe slowly nodded. "I'm afraid trousers of any kind are no longer welcome here."

Sylvia rose to her knees and began the process of unbuttoning. When she glanced over, Rafe had leaned back and laced his hands behind his head, which did fantastic things to his arms. His chest was rising more rapidly, and his gaze was fixed on her hands. Then he looked up. His eyes burned nearly black.

"Keep going."

His deep murmur set off a thundering pulse in her core. Sylvia gave herself a shake and finished the last few buttons. She pushed the wool fabric along with her drawers down over her hips and pulled them off her legs with as much grace as she could manage.

"I never dreamed watching someone remove their trousers could be so...diverting," he drawled. Sylvia then began to unlace her corset, but Rafe sat up and turned her around. "Allow me. It will go faster."

"You have somewhere else you need to be?" she teased, trying to fight down the nerves that had suddenly taken hold.

Rafe placed a lazy kiss against the back of her shoulder. "No. All I need is right here."

The quip shouldn't have made her feel so good. It was simply more of their usual banter.

It meant nothing.

It must.

The corset gaped open, and Rafe helped her pull it over her head, then tossed it aside. She reluctantly turned around. It made no sense, this sudden shyness, given all he had just witnessed. Rafe must have sensed this, for when she finally faced him, his gaze was soft and gentle.

"Have I told you how very lovely you are?" He reached out and cupped his hand against her jaw, stroking his thumb along her cheek. Sylvia fought against the urge to look away and shook her head. "You aren't used to hearing such sentiments," Rafe suggested.

She lifted one shoulder. "I never cared whether or not a man found me attractive." Bernard believed it was shallow nonsense to speak of such things, and at the time Sylvia proudly agreed. Though perhaps she had been kidding herself, given the warmth that had spread through her at Rafe's words. "I wanted to be appreciated for my mind," she insisted. "Not my body."

Rafe stared at her for a long moment while still brushing his thumb against her cheek. "I believe it is entirely possible to appreciate someone's physical attributes while also respecting their mental acuity."

Sylvia bit her lip and smiled down at him. He was entirely right, of course. Bernard was an ass. "Beauty *and* brains. What a combination you are."

Rafe threw his head back and laughed. Then he tugged

her closer. "That smart mouth of yours needs to be kissed. Immediately."

Sylvia allowed herself to be pulled down on top of him, taking the chance to run her palms over his shoulders as he kissed her thoroughly. Like a man who meant to do far more. Soon enough their kisses turned rough, and Rafe's hands slid from her waist to the hem of her chemise, which had been tucked into her drawers and now rode up to the tops of her thighs. Sylvia leaned back to allow him to push the fabric up more easily. His eyes darkened even more as his breath quickened. Feeling bold once again, Sylvia pushed his hands away and tore the chemise over her head.

Rafe stared in silence for an endless moment as his heated gaze seemed to take in every inch of her. Then he suddenly sat up, one arm snaking around her waist, and began kissing her neck. Sylvia gasped as his teeth scraped against the sensitive spot where her neck met her shoulder. His other hand cupped her nape, and they stared at each other, his breath fanning her lips. Then, with great deliberation, he pressed his mouth against hers, practically devouring her in an aggressive open-mouthed kiss. The feel of his tongue drove Sylvia's desire even higher, and soon she was writhing against his hardened length in rough movements. Rafe's hand moved from around her waist and angled his impressive erection deeper between her thighs.

"Is this what you want, my little bird?"

"Yes," she panted. "God, yes."

Rafe gave her a naughty grin. "Then take what is yours."

Sylvia reached down between them and took hold of him, nearly gasping at the heat and weight. How strong and solid he felt. After a few moments of trial and error, Sylvia fit him against her entrance. She met Rafe's eyes, and he seemed to read the anxiety in them.

"We'll go slow," he promised as he stroked her lower back.

"I can't get pregnant," she blurted out.

"I know. And I'll be careful. But there's always a chance..."

Her courses were due in two days, but he was still right. She should proceed with caution. Instead, Sylvia stared at him for an excruciating moment before answering. "I'll take it."

His lips curved in what appeared to be a smile of relief, and Sylvia relaxed a little more. Rafe tilted his hips as she rose onto her knees. Then she slowly sank down, taking his length inch by glorious inch. When he was fully sheathed inside her, Sylvia let out a ragged moan and pitched forward, pressing her face into the crook of his neck. It had *never* felt like this before. He filled her completely. Perfectly.

She must have said as much because Rafe chuckled and pulled a hand through her tangled hair. He then ever so gently began to move his hips. Sylvia sat up, which only increased the pressure within her. It was so intense that for a moment she thought she would pass out from the pleasure. Rafe continued to watch her closely. He seemed able to read every minute emotion as it fluttered across her face. He reached down and rubbed his thumb against the sensitive nub, and Sylvia could not stop the cry that came out of her.

That devilish grin took over his face once again. "Lean back, Sylvia."

She did as he said and was able to take even more of him deeper inside her. Rafe continued to manipulate her sex with one hand while his grip on her waist grew increasingly tight. Though he seemed entirely in control of his actions, there were signs that he was beginning to unravel. And she wanted more of it. She wanted to watch this notorious rake fall apart between her thighs. She began to match his thrusts with her own, and Rafe suddenly squeezed his eyes shut and tilted his head back.

"Mother of God. That feels..."

The words died on his lips as Sylvia did the motion again. Rafe opened his eyes and raised an eyebrow. She grinned back at him. He had underestimated her yet again. In response, Rafe pressed his thumb harder against her and raised his knees. Now it was Sylvia's turn to gasp. When she managed to open her eyes, Rafe's intense stare only increased the fire smoldering within her. Sylvia could feel another release already cresting, and she could do nothing to hold it at bay.

She groaned his name as a powerful climax rushed through every part of her body in an endless, crashing wave. Rafe held on to her tightly, never stopping his own increasingly ragged pumps. Through it all his gaze had lost none of its intensity. Sylvia leaned closer until her lips touched the soft skin of his ear.

"Come for me," she breathed.

And that was all it took.

Rafe smoothly flipped them over until Sylvia was on her back. He then took two more deep thrusts before he wrenched himself from her. She watched in fascination as he took hold of his shaft and pumped it until he spent in the sheets beside them, letting out a dark curse as he did so before collapsing into her waiting arms.

A few silent moments passed until Rafe groggily whispered by her ear: "Sylvia, you're perfect."

She smiled and nuzzled against his neck. "You've much to recommend you as well."

When his answering chuckle didn't come, she turned toward him.

He was already fast asleep.

* * *

Rafe slowly woke from the most refreshing sleep he'd had in ages. The rain had stopped at some point during the night, and the faint blue light of dawn was slowly filling the cottage. His arms were tangled in Sylvia, while her backside was nestled perfectly against his front, as if they had been forged in the same flame. Rafe nuzzled her hair and inhaled. He had never slept beside a woman all night before, and now he wouldn't be able to smell lavender again without thinking of her. His heart twinged, remembering their conversation from last night and his promise to leave her alone. He hugged her more tightly against him, but he could not change things. Not yet, in any case. He wouldn't ask her for more than he was willing to give himself.

Sylvia stirred. "Rafe, you're squeezing me."

"Oh, sorry." He forced his arms to loosen.

She slowly sat up, taking in the dawn. For once Rafe wished he had Henry's extraordinary memory. Then he could remember just how the light fell on her face, illuminating the curve of her lips, the gentle slope of her nose, and her rounded cheeks with their faint dusting of freckles. He really could stare at her forever.

She looked at him over her shoulder. "Did you hear me?" Rafe's dazed expression answered for him. "It's time to leave."

They both dressed in silence, lost in their own thoughts. Rafe had just finished buttoning his coat when Sylvia produced the horrendous wig, which had somehow found its way under the bed and was now coated in dust. Rafe was sorely tempted to leave the blasted thing behind, but there could be no evidence that he had been here.

"I've no idea where my valet scrounged this up, but I suppose he'll have my hide if I don't give it back."

She smiled weakly, but there was no hiding the sadness in her eyes. Rafe longed to reach for her, to demand she tell him what had driven her into the forest last night, but with the return of their clothes came the return of the wall between them. They each had their secrets to keep, and Rafe would respect that for now, but he also privately vowed that no harm would come to her as long as she was at Castle Blackwood.

They tidied the cottage as best they could and made their way out into the cool dawn. Rafe guessed it had once been used by a gamekeeper. As far as he knew, no one currently held the position, which explained why it stood empty. The trees were filled with chirping birds, and the smell of fresh rain enveloped them as they walked along the path back to the castle. An otherworldly mist blanketed the forest floor.

By this time the last remaining revelers would have been drunkenly carted off home in their carriages or carried to their beds. If anyone asked after his whereabouts, Rafe planned to say he had felt ill and retired early, though he guessed most of his fellow guests' memories of the last few hours were rather hazy.

He cut a glance to Sylvia, dressed once again in her disguise, and smiled. She must have felt his gaze on her, for she turned toward him and raised an eyebrow.

"I was just marveling at your costume. You make a fine lad."

She let out a snort. "Whatever you say, guv."

Rafe laughed at her cockney accent. "There. Now no one will suspect a thing."

Her smile faded, and she looked ahead. The castle was visible through the trees. "Remember what we discussed," she said. "You're to ignore me from now on."

Rafe stared at her profile. She had tucked her beautiful hair into the cap, but a few strands had fallen loose. What he would give to twirl one around his finger now.

"I don't think I will ever be able to ignore you completely, Sylvia. But I will keep my distance. I promise you that."

She said nothing to this, just continued to walk ahead, as if she hadn't even heard the words. When they reached the tree line near the stables, Rafe came to a halt. Sylvia looked back at him. "Go," he said. "We don't want to risk the chance of being seen together." Sylvia stood there for another moment, a pained look on her face. Finally, Rafe could take no more. He glanced away. "Hurry."

When he turned back, she was gone.

* * *

"Are we both going to pretend that you were in your room all night?"

Sylvia whirled around in her chair to find Georgiana peering over her shoulder.

"Goodness, you *scared* me."

Georgiana stepped back. "Sorry. I forget how wrapped up you get in your work."

Sylvia sat back and pinched the bridge of her nose. After a short nap in her room, she had come to the library to do work.

Anything to keep her from reliving every detail from last night. Instead, she had been staring at her pages of notes for hours, with little to show for it.

"Is your aunt still abed?"

"Yes. It was a late night for her. And don't try to change the subject. I noticed Mr. Davies disappeared before midnight." Georgiana raised an eyebrow. "He's claiming it was a headache," she said, drawing out the last word in a suggestive lilt.

"Don't." The word came out more sharply than Sylvia intended, but she couldn't pretend that this was some tawdry country house escapade. Last night meant something precious. To them both. She was sure of it. Sylvia turned to face Georgiana, but her friend's worried look only irritated her further.

"You've been acting strangely ever since we arrived. Please don't deny it." She held up a hand just as Sylvia had been poised to protest. "And perhaps whatever is going on between you and that man has escaped others' notice, but not mine. I *know* you, Sylvia. And you...you're shutting me out." Georgiana lowered her eyes, the hurt etched on her beautiful face.

If Sylvia had had a proper night's sleep, or if she hadn't had to constantly look over her shoulder, worrying about which servant or guest was reporting on her every move to her mysterious blackmailer, or if she wasn't driven to distraction by a funny, handsome, and irritatingly tender man she could *never* allow herself to be with, then perhaps she would have been able to master her temper, but at that moment her threadbare control failed.

"Then you now have some inkling of what I have felt for over seven years."

Georgiana's head snapped up. "What?" The word was uttered so quietly that Sylvia could barely hear it.

"You claim to know me? Well, do not forget that I know *you*, Georgiana Fox." The viscountess's eyes widened at the sound of her maiden name, but Sylvia could not stop the words she had held back for so long from pouring forth. "I know you are miserable in your marriage. I know that Arlington is absolutely horrible to you. And I know that you take *great* pains to pretend otherwise so that you are the envy of society. And yes, you have some people fooled, but not me." If she had simply stopped there, then perhaps things could have been easily mended between them. Instead, she pressed ahead, giving voice to the very worst of her suspicions.

"But what I still don't understand—what I have *never* understood—is why you ever married that awful man in the first place. Only days ago you called it a mistake."

"I didn't mean it," she said firmly.

Sylvia blew out a frustrated breath. "You can't lie to me the way you do everyone else, Georgiana. You could have had anyone. *Anyone.* And yet you cast aside your own personal happiness for what? A *title*? Are you truly that shallow that you would subject yourself to a lifetime of misery for some antiquated social marker?"

Two pink marks stained Georgiana's cheeks, and she lowered her eyes. "That is what you think of me?" she finally asked, twisting her delicate hands together.

"I don't know what to think because you share nothing," Sylvia insisted as she tried to fight against the guilt rising within her. Voicing the questions that had run through her mind for years hadn't made her feel better.

Georgiana nodded. "I see." When she raised her head, Sylvia was shocked to see tears in her eyes. It felt as if someone had hollowed out her insides. "Not all of us were born to be radicals, Sylvia. Perhaps it was easy for you to throw away everything you were born with as some sort of grand protest against convention, but look where that got you. I will not apologize for having a sense of self-preservation, along with responsibilities you clearly don't understand." As she spoke, her voice grew stronger, and she blinked away the tears until they vanished entirely. It was an impressive display of control. Georgiana straightened her spine and lifted her chin. "I never explained my reasons for marrying the viscount because I didn't think I needed to. Obviously I was mistaken. I entered into my marriage with absolutely no illusions, and I was given what I was promised: a secure future for my family. Did that come at a cost? Of course. But I *refuse* to give in to self-pity. And I would make the same choice again and again. Can you say the same of your relationship with Bernard?" At Sylvia's silence, Georgiana narrowed her eyes. "I didn't think so." Without another word, she turned with a grand flick of her skirts.

Sylvia scrambled to her feet, sending a stack of papers sliding to the floor. "Georgiana—"

"No." The viscountess shot her a glare over her shoulder. "I want to have the last word. Just once."

Sylvia pressed her hands against her stomach to keep herself from moving and nodded. Georgiana eyed her for a moment before she gave a dismissive sniff and swept out of the room. The slam of the door echoed loudly in the cavernous library. Every reverberation seemed to further emphasize how very alone Sylvia was. And how very much she deserved to be.

* * *

Sylvia spent another hour trying to focus on work but eventually conceded and headed back to her room. It was nearing dinnertime, so Georgiana would be busy dressing now. It was a cowardly move, but Sylvia couldn't face her just yet. Not until she could tell her the truth, or something close to it. She was so lost in her thoughts that she nearly walked past Mr. Wardale in the hall.

"Another afternoon spent hard at work?"

Sylvia bobbed a curtsy. "Oh, yes, sir."

"Mrs. Crawford has spoken very highly of your talents, Miss Sparrow. It was quite the stroke of luck that you two found each other."

The man's words were perfectly polite, but there was something in his eyes and the turn of his mouth that caused the hairs at the back of her neck to stand up. It was as if he knew a secret about her. And was enjoying it.

"Yes," she answered carefully.

He stepped closer, and Sylvia couldn't keep from glancing down the hallway. Mr. Wardale chuckled. "Not to worry, my dear. Everyone is either tucked away in bed or primping for the evening meal. Though there is hardly anything scandalous about conversing with your host, no?"

"Of course not," she answered. His attention always made her feel uncomfortable. It was something about the way he looked at her.

He stepped even closer until she could smell his expensive sandalwood aftershave. Sylvia held her breath. A paid companion couldn't count on being treated with the same respect as a woman of his own class. She reached into her pocket and gripped the cool steel of Mr. Brodie's pocketknife.

Mr. Wardale met her eyes and took note of her tightened jaw.

He huffed a laugh. "I pity the man who underestimates you, Miss Sparrow," he said as he stepped back. "Though I suppose that doesn't happen very often. These days."

"It does not," she answered through gritted teeth.

He flashed her a bedeviling smile before sauntering off in the other direction. "Enjoy your evening."

Sylvia stood frozen in place, listening to his soft footfalls. It was another moment before she was able to move. As she hurried down the hallway, she couldn't shake the feeling that something of great importance had occurred. Something he wanted her to know. But it wasn't until she had returned to her room, shut the door, and collapsed onto her bed that it came to her.

Though I suppose that doesn't happen very often. These days. These days.

Sylvia sat up. He knew. Wardale *knew* who she was. That she had stolen the envelope from him.

And he seemed delighted by it.

A bizarre thought suddenly gripped her. Could *he* be blackmailing her? It didn't make much sense, but she couldn't dismiss it outright, either. The blackmailer had wanted information on the viscount. Information Sylvia was in a prime position to find. She didn't know much about Mr. Wardale's business interests, but men like him were always hungry for more. More power. More money. More influence. And what better way to get it than by knowing your rivals' secrets?

A sickening dread suddenly washed over her, forcing Sylvia to lie back down.

First she needed proof. A part of her longed to be proven wrong, but the more she went over their exchange, the more her suspicion grew.

Wardale must want her to know the truth. Why else would he approach her and say such things? He had been so careful this whole time, playing her like a blasted fiddle. Sylvia clenched the blankets beneath her. The dread receded as her anger grew. She refused to be manipulated by that man—by anyone—anymore. He thought his money gave him license to do as he pleased? Well, he would learn otherwise.

Wardale would learn just what happened to men who underestimated Sylvia Sparrow.

CHAPTER SIXTEEN

❦

Rafe paced in his room. A message from Henry sat un-opened on his desk beside another note from Gerard demanding an update. But he couldn't be bothered with either at the moment. He had chosen to take a tray instead of joining the rest of the party for dinner, which helped legitimize his claim of a headache. But the truth was he was barely fit for company. Since returning to the castle early that morning, he had been in a horrendous mood. Now even ever-faithful Tully was avoiding him.

Every time Rafe tried to sit or read or converse with another person, he was driven to distraction by memories of last night: Sylvia's eyes twinkling as she teased him, her mouth curving into a sly smile, and those same lips parting in the pleasure they had made together. Not for the first time, Rafe damned himself for promising to keep his distance. Barely twelve hours later and he was ready to climb up the walls. Ready to crawl out of his skin. The only thing holding him back was the worry that Sylvia, so full of quiet strength, was absolutely fine. And why wouldn't she be? Hadn't she rejected his multiple offers of help? Hadn't she made it exceedingly clear that she didn't need him in her life beyond one night of passion? By her own account, she had lost everything she had once cared about, and yet she didn't seem tempted in the least by what he could offer. Not his money, not his status, his assistance, nothing. When they parted that morning, she hadn't even given him a backward glance, already too busy looking ahead.

Goddammit. Why had that *bothered* him so much?

Because you went and fell in love with her, you unbelievable moron.

Rafe pressed the heels of his hands against his eyes until the image was banished from his mind.

He had to get out of this room. A walk outside in the chill night air would help. Rafe proceeded down the darkened hallway cautiously. He would need to take care to avoid Wardale, who was no doubt itching to go over any details he had uncovered during the ball last night. But Rafe was in no state to temper that man's disappointment.

He was so damn tired of it all. Tired of the subterfuge, of the lies, of constantly having to keep straight who knew what, of which version of himself he could be. The thrill of the game had fed him for years, kept him moving, always moving, but now all he wanted was to stop.

Get ahold of yourself. Remember what is at stake. This is no time to lose your head.

Rafe had always obeyed the no-nonsense voice in his head. The voice that told him to work harder, aim higher, and ignore emotional entanglements.

It was the voice of every person who had ever doubted him. Who had ever insinuated he was less than nothing. Not even worth acknowledging.

It was the voice of Gerard.

Rafe came to an abrupt halt in the middle of the hallway. He stood frozen in place as the realization echoed throughout his skull. The ticking of a clock on a nearby credenza slowly brought him back to himself. Rafe inhaled rapidly as decades of pent-up frustration, of pain, of rejection barreled through his veins. He couldn't even escape judgment in his own mind. There was only one way to end this for good. Rafe's hands clenched into fists by his sides as he turned on his heel and stalked down the hallway. He would prove once and for all what he was made of and who was truly worthless.

When Rafe reached the hallway that led to Wardale's study, he had regained some of his reasoning. But his purpose remained the same. For days he had ignored the nagging doubt at the back of his mind. The instinct that screamed something about this entire mission wasn't right. Instead, he had given Gerard and Wardale too much credit, blinded by the prize they dangled before him. But Rafe was no man's lackey. And he would not leave this castle without uncovering some truth. As he grew closer, a soft rustling sound came from the sitting room that led to the study. Rafe slowed his steps. It could be a maid cleaning the grate, though it was a bit late for that. He pressed himself against the wall and crept closer to the open door. The rustling grew louder, along with the grumbling of a very annoyed person. Rafe's curiosity won out, and he peered around the doorframe. He then immediately leaned back before they could notice and let out a soft curse. After allowing himself a moment to collect his racing thoughts, Rafe stepped into the doorway and placed his hands on his hips.

"Just what the *hell* do you think you're doing?"

Sylvia let out a yelp and dropped the pocketknife she had been using on the lock to Wardale's study.

Whatever benefit of the doubt Rafe had given Sylvia before now vanished entirely. He had caught her red-handed, attempting to break into their host's study. There could not be an innocent explanation for this. His feelings would not cloud his judgment again. There was simply too much at stake.

But instead of admitting her guilt, Sylvia had the gall to cross her arms. "I might ask *you* the same question," she said suspiciously.

Rafe stormed into the room and picked up the pocketknife. "Are you serious? I caught you trying to pick a damned *lock*." He waved the object in her face. "Which won't work, by the way. Unless your goal is to cover it in scratches."

Sylvia tried to grab the knife. "How on earth would *you* know?" she scoffed. "When have you ever had a door closed to you?"

Rafe could hear her voice beginning to break, could see the desperation flashing behind the anger in her eyes, but just once in his life he needed to be seen for who he truly was. He needed to be seen by her. He dropped the knife and crowded Sylvia against the wall, bracketing her in with his forearms.

"More than you could ever know, my dear," he growled.

Sylvia lifted her chin, refusing to be cowed by him. And as angry as he was, Rafe couldn't deny that he bloody loved that about her.

"Now tell me what you were doing."

Sylvia gave him her cheek. "I think you've already deduced that."

Rafe dragged his nails against the patterned wallpaper. "Please don't mistake me for a patient man, Sylvia. I'll have the truth from you one way or another."

That seemed to reach her. Sylvia faced him again, but she

looked at him with new eyes. And Rafe didn't particularly like whatever it was she saw. "You're working for Wardale, aren't you?" He was momentarily stunned and stepped back. It was technically true, of course, but there was no possible way she could know that. "That was all this ever was, wasn't it? A way to keep track of me," she added, so softly he nearly missed it over the pounding of his blood in his ears.

Rafe swallowed hard. "No. I've been harboring suspicions of our host for some time now. I came here to find answers. I had no idea you would be here."

There. That was close enough to the truth.

Sylvia stared at him for an endless moment. "Prove it."

"As you noted last night, I haven't exactly been discreet when it came to my interest in you, have I? And if my objective was to simply watch your movements, I could do that without us ever having to speak." Let alone make love. Her frown deepened as she considered this. "Please, Sylvia," he added, rather more desperately than he would have liked.

Her eyes softened. "I suppose that's true," she acknowledged.

"Of course it is," he said, ignoring the guilt that thundered through him over all he hadn't said. But he must remain silent. "Now tell me why you're here."

Sylvia let out a sigh. "I'm being blackmailed." The shock Rafe felt must have been clear on his face, for her caginess faded. "That was why I was in the woods yesterday. I was delivering something, but now I think...I think Mr. Wardale has been behind it all."

An icy pit formed in the bottom of his stomach. *The envelope.* But why would Wardale want to blackmail an innocent lady's companion?

Or perhaps she is not so innocent after all.

202

Rafe ignored the voice and took her by the shoulders. "Sylvia, you must tell me *exactly* what happened from the very beginning. So I can help you."

"First I need to get into that study," she burst out. "Then I can know for certain."

"All right. I'll do it," he grumbled. "But *only* if you promise to answer every question I ask afterward."

She reached down and gripped his hand. "Promise me the same."

He stared into her eyes, but the earlier fear had been replaced by a familiar determination that centered him. Hadn't he wanted this? To be unmasked before her?

Rafe ran the back of his finger against her cheek, where the skin was impossibly soft. "Just know that no matter what happens after this, every moment I spent with you was real."

He then bent down to pick the lock, unable to watch the tangle of emotions playing across her face at his cryptic words, but Sylvia squeezed his shoulder.

"Someone's coming," she hissed just as Rafe noted the heavy footfalls coming down the hallway. There wasn't enough time to close the sitting room's door without drawing notice. And if it was Wardale, there would be no explaining this.

A surge of adrenaline pumped through his veins. *This* was the bit he had conveniently forgotten about. The absolute thrill of the game. The part that reminded him he was alive. And gave him a sense of purpose he hadn't found elsewhere.

Rafe retrieved the pocketknife from the floor and strained to listen more closely. Whoever was approaching kept stumbling every few steps, as if they were foxed. There were several bedrooms nearby, so it was entirely possible that they were on their way to bed. He leaned closer to Sylvia, and her soft inhalation shot straight to his groin. "I think it's another guest," he whispered by her ear as her scent filled the scant air between them. "But they can't have any idea why we're really here."

There was only one thing Rafe could think of, but he wouldn't voice it. Not first, anyhow.

Sylvia slowly tilted her head up to meet his gaze. "Well, then," she murmured as her eyes warmed. "I suppose we'll need to create a distraction."

Rafe's hands immediately went to her waist as he pressed her firmly against the wall. It was the height of madness, but they didn't have many choices, and his cock was already straining toward her. "I believe I can manage that." Before she could say another word, he took her mouth in a hungry kiss, and her hands plunged into his hair. Then Rafe was utterly lost, reveling in the feel of her curves pressed against him, the now familiar taste of her lips, and the low sounds of pleasure she made.

Everything he had ever learned over the course of his career warned that she shouldn't be trusted, that he was making a dangerous mistake, but his instincts screamed louder.

This is right. This is real.

After a few moments someone cleared their throat behind them. Loudly. As if they had done it several times already. Rafe slowly pulled away, and Sylvia blinked up at him, dazed. He flashed her a smile, then tucked her head to his chest and glanced back. "Oh. I didn't see you there, Templeton."

The gentleman raised an eyebrow at his nonchalance. "Yes. You seemed to have your hands full."

Sylvia let out a muffled laugh, and Rafe patted the back of her neck. "Something like that."

Templeton continued to stand in the doorway, though he couldn't manage to stop swaying.

"I trust you have found a *willing* participant?"

"About as willing as they come." Rafe then let out a soft yelp as Sylvia pinched his side.

"All right, then." Templeton sounded amused as he moved away. "Carry on."

Good. He bought it.

Rafe turned back to Sylvia, who was giving him an arch look. "What?" he whispered. "Shall I tell him you're not?"

She rolled her eyes and moved to push him away, but Rafe held up a hand.

He hadn't heard the man's departing footsteps. "I think he's still in the hall."

Sylvia frowned. "But why?"

"Maybe he wants to listen." *Or watch.*

Templeton would hardly be the first person with such proclivities.

He could see her cheeks flush even in the dim room. "What are we going to do?"

Rafe nuzzled her neck, his blood still buzzing. "The same thing we were doing before, if you'd like."

Her breath caught. She had to feel the same rush of excitement as he did, knowing how very close they had come to danger only to escape by their own force of will.

"You aren't going to get shy on me now," he teased, shamelessly baiting her.

The corner of her mouth turned up. Before he could say more, she pulled his mouth down to hers, kissing him with a renewed enthusiasm that set him on fire.

"My God," he panted, breaking the kiss as he rolled his

hips against her. "I wish you were wearing those delectable trousers again."

"Me too. Then I might be able to feel something."

Rafe snorted and leaned closer. "Is that a challenge, Miss Sparrow?"

She answered with a wicked little smile, and Rafe began to push up handfuls of her sturdy wool skirt. "You know, much as I enjoy the utility of your wardrobe, I'd love to see you in something lighter, say, silk."

She laughed. "Mrs. Crawford is a generous employer, but she doesn't pay me quite *that* much."

That won't matter anymore.

For whatever else happened tonight, this would not be goodbye. He would protect her with everything he had. No matter the cost.

Rafe pressed his hard length between her thighs, driven by a sudden desire that felt alarmingly close to possession. He wanted to take care of her. To wrap her in the finest silks. To ensure she could spend her days doing whatever she wished, not painstakingly recording the bygone pastimes of an old woman. But he kept these thoughts to himself. Sylvia hitched her leg against his hip. "Again." Rafe repeated the motion, the friction already fraying his self-control.

"Rafe," she breathed. The word was barely louder than a whisper. But it tore through him. It was the sound of aching need. Of surrender. "I want you." Her hand had already drifted toward his waist.

Based on the way Rafe strained toward her, maybe he wasn't the possessor after all. "Christ, Sylvia," he groaned. "You're going to kill me."

She lifted an eyebrow. "Not a bad way to go, I imagine."

And like hell would he miss a chance to be with her.

Rafe found the will to tear himself away long enough to walk over to the doorway and check the hall. It was empty. Templeton had toddled off to bed. And they were alone. He drew the door shut behind him and began unbuttoning the front of his pants as he stalked toward her. In one swift motion he hooked her legs around his waist, then found the slit in her drawers and buried his cock between her plump thighs. His forehead fell against the wall behind her as he gasped with relief.

Yes, this was certainly what possession felt like.

Chapter Seventeen

❧

Sylvia clung to Rafe's solid shoulders, already trembling on the edge of release. The angles created by this position were like taking a matchstick to dry kindling. As he began to slowly pump his hips, she quietly moaned against his neck. This was absolute madness, she knew, but the physical pull between them was too much to resist. She couldn't even consider the sizable tug on her heartstrings that had reverberated through her when he offered to help.

"That good, eh?" he quipped though even he couldn't entirely mask the ragged tones in his voice.

Sylvia squeezed her thighs, and he let out a very satisfying grunt. "Tolerable."

After that, no more intelligible words were uttered until Rafe slipped his hand behind the crook of her knee and pressed it toward her chest. This only heightened the pulsing sensations inside her.

Sylvia tilted her head back. "Oh *God*," she panted. When she lowered her eyes, he was looking at her with such raw intensity, such naked longing, that she nearly had to turn away again.

"The next time we make love, I'm doing it in the middle of the day, in a room filled with light," he promised, his voice rough and urgent. "So I can watch your lips form every single cry you make. Every quiver from even the slightest of my touches. Every tensing muscle as you desperately seek more and more friction. I want to stare at you until I go sun blind."

Next time. His brazen words burned through her, and all too quickly her entire body began to shudder toward her release. But as she moved to bury her face against his shoulder to muffle her cries, Rafe wrapped his other hand around her neck and took her mouth in a hard, all-consuming kiss, demanding everything from her. When he pulled away, she was still gasping with pleasure.

He stared back at her with wild eyes, his chest heaving from unspent desire. "Dammit, Sylvia," Rafe bit off, wrenching himself from her. Sylvia managed to pull a handkerchief from her sleeve and watched in fascination as he groaned with relief. It was the only time when he seemed to let his guard down entirely. The only time when his mask truly fell.

Rafe began placing soft kisses against her cheek, her lips, her neck, while murmuring words of promise as he gently set her down. Sylvia closed her eyes and allowed herself to imagine for a moment what their future might look like, but nothing came.

"No," she said briskly before pushing him away. "We don't have time for this."

Hurt flashed briefly across his face before he resumed control once again. "Of course."

Rafe turned away to button his pants and then knelt before the door. He pulled something from the inside of his jacket and set about working on the lock.

Sylvia raised an eyebrow. "Do you always carry lock picks on you?"

He kept his gaze fixed on his task. "When I'm traveling, yes. I've found they come in remarkably handy from time to time."

Sylvia tensed and swallowed the urge to pry deeper into exactly what kinds of situations he found himself in that necessitated lock picks.

After another minute the lock clicked, and Rafe flashed her a self-satisfied smile. "There. We're in."

Sylvia stepped away to make sure the hallway was still empty. When she returned, Rafe was already inside the study and had lit a desk lamp. The interior was decorated in dark colors and sumptuous fabrics, while the scent of leather and wood soap filled the air. There was a large stuffed pheasant on display behind the desk, and his beady black eyes seemed to be staring directly at her. Sylvia shuddered and Rafe cleared his throat, drawing her attention back to him.

"Now will you tell me about the blackmail?"

"I received a letter before I came here instructing me to take an envelope from Mr. Wardale's room."

Rafe was silent for a long moment. "And if you didn't?"

Sylvia swallowed and looked away. "They would reveal my past to the viscount."

"You mean about Bernard."

"Yes," she said roughly. Among other things.

"What did you do with the envelope?"

She glanced up at his forbidding tone. "Nothing. A few days later a note was slipped under my door telling me where to deliver it."

"In the woods." She nodded. "Did you open it?"

"No. I was warned not to."

Rafe held her eyes. "Good." For a moment he looked nothing like the charming rogue she had come to know and instead exuded a stark graveness that sent a chill down her spine. She wouldn't want to evoke the ire of this man. "Did it say anything else?"

Sylvia came around the desk and began looking through the piles of papers. Mr. Wardale may be many things, but organized wasn't one of them. "They indicated that they would want information on the viscount once I returned to London." She pushed a stack of papers aside as her anger bubbled to the surface. "I, stupidly, thought this would all be over with once I delivered the envelope. But of course it's not. Of course I have to continue to pay for my mistakes again and again and again." Just as she slammed another stack down, Rafe gently seized her hand.

"Careful," he said. "We need to put everything back just as it was."

"But *look* at this mess." She shook her head in frustration. "How could he possibly tell?"

"Don't be so certain," Rafe cautioned, keeping his voice calm. "Never assume that someone won't notice when their things have been rifled through."

Sylvia took a deep breath and waited for her heartbeat to settle. He was right. She would have to take her anger out on something else. Rafe retrieved his glasses from his jacket pocket and put them on. They really were horribly unfashionable, and yet he managed to look adorable.

"Yes?" he asked, with a raised eyebrow.

Sylvia had been staring. "You don't wear your glasses often."

He grimaced. "Only when absolutely necessary."

"I like them."

Rafe gave her a quizzical look, as though he was waiting for her to make a joke. But Sylvia merely held his gaze. The corner of his mouth turned up, and he began looking through the papers she had disturbed before carefully replacing them. Sylvia followed suit. Most of the materials on the desk made up the typical paper trail of a wealthy man—receipts for items so expensive Sylvia's eyes nearly watered, old dinner menus, deeds to various properties, lists of actions to take or dates to remember. In short, nothing that signaled their host was up to anything nefarious.

Sylvia pressed her hands to her hips and shook her head. She could feel Rafe's eyes on her. But she couldn't give up. Not yet. Sylvia knelt down and began to check the desk drawers. The first two easily opened, revealing nothing more titillating than blank paper, envelopes, and hundreds of embossed business cards for Wardale Enterprises. But the last one held fast. Sylvia rattled the handle, but it refused to budge. Her heartbeat quickened as certainty suddenly filled her and she tugged even harder.

"Stop that." Rafe covered her hand with his own. "I'll open it."

He brushed Sylvia aside and retrieved his lock picks once again, but this one proved more challenging than the door. Rafe cursed under his breath and shifted his position. Sylvia's certainty only increased, though she hadn't yet a clue how she would prove her suspicions. After another few minutes, the lock finally turned.

Rafe stood and wiped his brow. "I've never seen a lock on a drawer like that," he said ominously.

Sylvia knelt down and pulled the drawer open. It contained

several leather-bound folders. She pulled out the first one and placed it on the desk, then looked at Rafe.

"Well? Open it."

Sylvia held her breath as she opened the folder, but as her eyes scanned the document, her heart began to sink. She quickly moved on to the next letter, then the next, but they were all the same. Nothing more than standard business letters to various tradespeople asking for payments. That was not unusual, seeing as how Mr. Wardale owned properties all over London.

Sylvia's shoulders slumped. No doubt the other folders would hold more of the same. But as she continued to diligently flip through the letters, something began to stand out. A pattern. Something familiar. She stopped on a letter and leaned forward, dragging her finger across the text.

Rafe immediately took notice. "What is it?"

"I can't be sure, but see here?" She pointed to the word "evening." "See how the 'e' is slightly faded? And here again each time the letter is used? It was the same in all the notes I received. I might not have noticed if it hadn't occurred so frequently." Or if she hadn't stared at them so often they had been imprinted on the backs of her eyelids.

She turned eagerly to Rafe, but he looked skeptical. "That could be a manufacturing error. Every typewriter of that model could have the same issue."

"Yes, but—"

"It's not that I don't believe you, Sylvia. But it isn't enough. We need to prove intent." Her mouth went dry at the word. "If you're right and Wardale is the one blackmailing you," Rafe continued, "then that is *illegal*."

Sylvia knew this, of course, but hearing someone else say it was sobering. And terrifying.

"I don't want the law involved."

Then her past would come to light and she would still be forced to leave her position. Everything she had tried to protect would be ruined anyway.

Rafe watched her carefully, but she kept her expression blank. He could not know what this would do to her. "I can only agree to that if we don't find anything. It is likely you aren't the only person he is blackmailing."

Sylvia turned away. "Fine. Do as you wish." It wasn't the answer she wanted, but that didn't mean she needed to keep helping him.

* * *

Rafe stared at Sylvia's profile. He could see the fear behind her frustration. For whatever reason, she didn't want the authorities involved. But Rafe would have to reassure her later. He couldn't quite explain it, but something else about these letters was off. Rafe frowned and began going through them again one by one. Sylvia was right about the "e" key, but that wasn't what was sticking out to him. It was something else. Something that was just out of reach. He had to close his eyes for a moment to keep them from crossing, then moved on to the next letter. It was addressed to a Mr. Drummond, apparently the owner of a drapery shop, and appeared to ask for the monthly rent payment. But something caught his eye in the top corner. The property was listed at a tony Mayfair address, and Rafe happened to know there was no drapery shop there.

Because it was his brother's town house.

He then went back and checked the previous letters. One was for an address in Belgravia. Another for Portman Square.

A third for a home he happened to know belonged to a cabinet minister.

"My God," he swore. "He's blackmailing the lot of them." Rafe would have been tempted to be impressed by Wardale's audacity if he weren't caught in the middle.

"What? What is it?" Sylvia tugged on his arm, but Rafe immediately bent down and pulled out the remaining folders. Most contained similar documents, but at the very end of the last folder he found what he was looking for.

"You were better staying disorganized, you wily bastard," he muttered.

Sylvia took the document and scanned it. "I don't understand. Why does he need a list of lords and politicians?"

Rafe tapped the far column. "For that." It listed the alias used for every man, in every letter. "See this?" He pointed to a letter. "I believe Mr. Drummond is actually my brother." He then ran his finger under Gerard's name and the corresponding columns that listed his alias and an amount of money that made Rafe choke a little.

Sylvia's eyes widened. "He's given Wardale *that* much? For what?"

"I have no idea. Truly. Gerard is meticulous about his public image. He never even goes outside without so much as a hair out of place. Whatever Wardale has on him must be...earth-shattering."

Rafe immediately began replacing the papers in the corresponding folders.

"Wait," Sylvia protested. "That's more than enough evidence."

Rafe shook his head and continued to put the folders away, working through the panic slowly brewing in his stomach.

"No. You don't know what this means. Even I don't fully understand. Some of the most powerful men in the country are on this list, Sylvia. They are *all* paying Wardale a king's ransom." And at the moment he was complicit. Just thinking the words made him break out in a cold sweat. Only Gerard knew he was here, and the provided reason was likely a load of horse shit. Henry had been right all along. There were no Scottish separatists, just Rafe rifling through his guests' personal belongings to provide more fodder for blackmail. Nearly every man he could think to approach with this information was mentioned here. He could claim he had been lured here under false pretenses, but would anyone believe him?

He closed the drawer and fastened the lock as best he could, then rose to face Sylvia. She had gone as white as a sheet. "We need to leave. Immediately."

"What?" she sputtered, but Rafe was already pulling her toward the door. "But what about the authorities?"

"I'm not sure who can help us at the moment. I need more time."

"But I can't just leave. What about Georgiana? And Mrs. Crawford?"

Rafe halted and gripped her by the shoulders. "Do they know anything? Anything at all?"

"Of course not, but—"

"Good. Then they shouldn't be in any danger." It also meant Rafe wouldn't have to find a way to spirit away a viscountess and a septuagenarian to Glasgow under the cover of darkness. He needed to speak to Henry first.

Sylvia's mouth dropped open. "You—you think *we're* in danger?"

"Yes. We've uncovered a very powerful secret, and I don't know how far Wardale will go to keep us silent. Or what he might demand from both of us if he realizes what we know. Blackmail could be the least of what he is capable of. And he clearly has the connections to make any number of things possible." Sylvia blanched.

"He warned me to stay away from you, you know," Rafe continued. "At the time I thought he was simply concerned for your reputation, but I think he wanted to make sure we didn't grow close and compare stories." Sylvia looked away and gave a single nod in agreement. There was more she wasn't telling him. And when they were far from here, he planned to get some damned answers from her.

"If you're still worried about the viscountess, we can smooth things over with her later, but for now I think it's best if we leave." He brushed his hand along her jaw and tilted her chin up to meet his eyes. "Agreed?"

As Sylvia held his gaze, those wide gray eyes filled with curiosity. And suspicion. "You aren't really a rake at all, are you?" she murmured.

The relief in her voice made him smile. "I most assuredly *am*," he said as he pulled back and took her arm in his. "And much, much more."

Rafe locked the study door and guided Sylvia down the hallway, which was thankfully still empty. The other guests should be mingling over after-dinner drinks and card games. Rafe prayed that gave them enough time to slip away. He waited as Sylvia grabbed a coat and quickly packed a small bag; then they slipped into his rooms, where he retrieved his long coat, hat, and checkbook.

Rafe then knocked on Tully's door before he entered. His valet was seated by the fire with an open book on his lap.

"I have to leave. No, don't get up. Here." Rafe dashed off Henry's address on a slip of paper. "If you need to contact me, use this address. Don't give this to anyone. If you are asked, I was never here. Understand?"

Tully nodded. "Perfectly."

"Good man. I suggest you leave the castle no earlier than a day after my departure to avoid suspicion. Return to London and wait for my word."

"Yes, sir."

Rafe ducked his head to his chin and left the room. He then took Sylvia's arm. She was still worryingly pale. "Everything will be all right. I promise." Then, without thinking, he pressed a soft kiss to her mouth. She relaxed a little, and Rafe pulled her to his side. "We're going to leave through the servants' staircase and go out the back. The train station is about two miles from here." Sylvia nodded, but she still looked dazed. "Take a breath," Rafe instructed and breathed along with her. "There. Now we go."

He needed to focus on their escape, but the feel of Sylvia tucked against him, the sound of her soft inhalations, and the tight squeeze of her hand was a welcome comfort. The servants' staircase was cool and quiet, as by this time most of them had gone to bed. They crept down the darkened stairs as quietly as possible, but Sylvia tensed at every creak. When they finally stepped out into the night, Rafe took in a gasping lungful of crisp air. He hadn't even realized he had been holding his breath.

Sylvia began to sag beside him, but Rafe propped her up. "We can't stop yet, my little bird," he whispered. Then he pointed up ahead. "We'll cut through the back garden and head toward the main road."

"But what if someone sees us?"

"They won't. Come along." He took her hand and strode down the path. If he acted confident, Sylvia wouldn't know how bloody terrified he was. Rafe had been in tighter spots before, but he had either been alone or with another agent. Putting Sylvia in any kind of danger was maddening, but it was a risk he had to take. There simply was no other choice. The moon was even bigger tonight, and though he was grateful for the light, it also increased the chance that someone would see them. As they darted across the lawn, Rafe glanced back at the castle. The drawing room was toward the front of the property, and only a few rooms on the upper floors emitted faint light. Hopefully no one happened to look out their window at this precise moment.

Up ahead, the labyrinth rustled softly in the breeze, making it look particularly Gothic and menacing in the moonlight. Sylvia paused just a moment, distracted by the sound.

And then Rafe heard the click of the gun.

CHAPTER EIGHTEEN

❧

"All right, Davies. You know how this goes. Put your hands up and turn around. Slowly."

Rafe squeezed his eyes shut for just a moment, then raised his hands and nodded at Sylvia to do the same. "It's fine," he murmured, trying his best to reassure her. She didn't look very convinced but complied all the same.

"Wardale," Rafe began once they faced their pursuers. "Not exactly surprised to see you here, but using the dastardly gardener as your lackey is an inspired touch."

Brodie frowned and rolled his substantial shoulders back. Apparently he didn't like being described in such terms.

Wardale's lip curled into something resembling a smile. "Don't listen to him, Brodie. Davies never knows when to keep his mouth shut." He took a few steps forward, eyeing the pair of them.

Rafe exhaled loudly. "Can we get this over with? Sylvia and I have a train to catch. We're eloping."

Don't let him see your fear. He will use anything he can against you.

Wardale's half smile turned into a grin. "Oh, is that what this is? My mistake. I'd have thought you were stealing away in the dark of night because of the incriminating papers you found."

Rafe bit the inside of his cheek. He would have to play this straight and hope it worked. "There never were any threats, were there?"

"Correct. Brodie helped me with those letters. Though I think he took real pleasure in calling me a rat, didn't you?" The gardener grunted his response, and Wardale laughed.

"I was only here to help you spy on your guests. Gather more material for blackmail."

"You're smarter than you look, Davies. Too bad it took you so long to catch on."

"And my brother knew all of this the entire time," Rafe ground out.

Wardale nodded. "He failed to gain support for a bill I was very invested in seeing passed, so he dangled you before me to make amends. Even I couldn't resist having someone like you in my pocket."

"Careful there. I don't belong to you."

"Yet." He drew out the word, enunciating it perfectly. "You know, part of surviving on the street means watching what a man does and finding his weakness before he can find yours. Then doing whatever it takes to beat him. The Crown would do well to consider recruiting urchins like me rather than fancy lads like you."

Rafe saw Sylvia turned toward him out of the corner of his eye. He needed to change the subject away from himself. "What do you have on Gerard?"

Wardale could barely hide his glee. "He's been keeping an actress as his mistress. Sound familiar? Like father, like son. Blathering on about the importance of conservative values in parliament and then sneaking off to Covent Garden at night." He chuckled, then glanced at Rafe. "My goodness, you really didn't have any idea, did you? And you look positively *scandalized*. Aren't you supposed to have elevated debauchery to an art form?"

Rafe clenched his hands into tight fists but said nothing.

"I suppose it's the part about following in your father's footsteps that grates the most, isn't it? And after all that fuss Gerard made about your mother." Wardale clicked his tongue. "Despite your pretenses otherwise, it was you who took the more noble path." He shook his head. "I didn't expect you to have such an ingrained sense of justice. It's really quite irritating. You could be so much more if you'd simply let it go."

Rafe managed to lift his chin. "What? A damned blackmailer, like you?"

Wardale shrugged. "It works. I learned long ago that scruples are useless. No one with any real power bothers with them. And certainly not the upper class. Why should I hold myself to a higher standard? If you work for me, I'll see that the prime minister accepts your little proposal. You'll be able to create an elite group of agents and have a legacy of your own." He then addressed Sylvia. "Yes, our friend here does a bit of gentlemanly spying. Quite tied up in Crown business, aren't you, Davies? That's what makes you so valuable to someone like me. I can't resist having a man on the inside."

Sylvia tensed, but Rafe kept his focus on Wardale. "If you are on such good terms with the PM, why do you need me at all?"

"Because his time in that position is limited," he snapped. "And there is information even I am not granted access to. That is where you come in."

"I will never agree to that."

Wardale tilted his head in consideration. "What on earth are you trying to prove, and to whom? Men like your brother? They all think your mother was nothing but a common whore who swindled your idiot father into marriage. No matter what you do, your blood will never be as blue as theirs. That's why I didn't even bother trying to impress those people in the first place. They only react to threats, and the greatest threat of all is their social standing. As you no doubt saw earlier, they will pay nearly *anything* to keep it."

"I understand what you're getting at," Rafe began through gritted teeth. "But that hardly makes it right. You shouldn't have more power simply because you'll stoop to any level necessary. We live in a society. We have laws. And there are certain lines that should never be crossed."

Wardale turned to Sylvia, amused. "I imagine you have much to say about that, don't you?"

"Don't talk to her," Rafe growled.

"If you'd like. And no, I don't agree about not crossing certain lines. I think the worst thing a man can do is allow someone else to hold power over him. I learned that lesson very young. A pity you never did."

"Say it plainly, Wardale."

"When your brother told me you would do anything to gain his favor, I didn't quite believe him. What sort of man still cares what his *brother* thinks? I certainly never gave a damn about any of my siblings."

"That isn't true," Rafe protested hotly, wincing even as he said the words.

"Poor little rich boy. It must have been a lonely childhood. Waiting for visits that never came. Big, joyous family

Christmases. Birthdays where everyone fawned over their baby brother. Just how often do you think your father regretted marrying your mother? Gerard claims to have several letters on the very subject."

Rafe took a heavy step forward, and Brodie immediately raised the gun higher. "I swear to God, if you—" But Sylvia grabbed his arm and pulled him back before he could go any further.

"Stop," she hissed in his ear. "Don't listen. He's only trying to upset you."

Rafe blinked, dazed by the force of his own anger.

Wardale gave him an apologetic smile. "Sorry. I've always wanted to break a spy, but I didn't think it would be quite so easy. You're much softer than I imagined." He then gestured to Sylvia. "Which I suppose explains this. I'll admit, even I couldn't foresee it. I thought for certain you were bedding Lady Taylor-Smyth. Not this plain little thing. Though I'm told she has her charms."

Rafe inhaled slowly, this time forcing himself to control his anger before he dared to speak. "Say that again and see what happens to you."

"Still, I wonder what on earth has drawn you to each other," Wardale continued, entirely unconcerned. "The anarchist and the queen's agent. Oh, did Miss Sparrow not tell you about her little flirtation with anarchy?" he asked as Rafe whipped his head toward Sylvia. She dropped his arm. Now it was her turn to avoid his gaze. An *anarchist*?

"Seems like the kind of thing one would mention before getting married, especially when any association with a woman who believes the monarchy should be blown to bits wouldn't exactly help your cause. But then, every sacrifice you have ever made for queen and country is worth less than *dirt* to people like her."

Did she truly think that? Rafe's jaw tightened at Sylvia's silence. His career would be ruined. No one in government would ever trust him again. A hollow sliver began to open in his chest.

"Yes," Wardale continued. "She wrote quite eloquently on the subject. Lots of railing against the hallowed institutions that you hold dear. But the most amusing bits by far were her thoughts on women's labor. How the domestic sphere should be considered equally important as men's work." He paused to chuckle before addressing Sylvia directly. "It was your inability to compromise on this particular aspect that drove your lover away, wasn't it? Dear Mr. Hughes told me all about it. How you actually expected him to participate in *domestic activities*." He laughed again, louder. "No wonder he wouldn't marry you. Imagine it, Davies. Darning socks and changing nappies. A world where cooking breakfast is as invaluable a service as enlisting in the Royal Navy or running a factory. Out of all your outrageous ideas that was the most implausible to him. Well, that and giving all women the vote," Wardale added.

"So, it was Bernard who told you about me," she muttered. The betrayal in her voice sank under Rafe's skin, but again, she made no move to correct any of Wardale's accusations.

The man nodded. "You will be flattered to know that he's never forgotten you. I believe he even had you followed when you returned to London."

Sylvia made a choking sound, as if the very idea repulsed her. "And I suppose you're blackmailing *him*, too?"

"Oh, naturally." Wardale waved a hand. "He couldn't pay

my fee, and he doesn't have enough power in government yet to make up for it. But that will no doubt change. Exceedingly average men like him always seem to succeed in spite of themselves. And, as I'm sure you know, the man can't budget to save his life. But he mentioned he knew someone who had access to Lord Arlington's household. I've been looking for evidence on the viscount for years, so we made a trade of sorts. He spoke very highly of your passionate nature, but the trouble is, my dear, that at the end of it all, a man may enjoy a revolutionary in his bed, but he wants a wife in his home." Even in the moonlight, Sylvia looked ashen. "Though I don't agree that you should have been arrested," Wardale added. "That must have been an ugly business for you."

Despite all Rafe had just heard, he still managed to be stunned. *"What?"*

"Ah, yet another stone unturned. Yes, our Miss Sparrow— though it's actually Wilcox—was arrested during a raid on a bawdy house. Isn't that right? Bernard said you were trying to unionize the tarts." He laughed again. "That was what really did you in, wasn't it? You had ruffled one too many feathers by that point, and not even Bernard could save you from that scandal, though he could have at least tried. If only he wasn't so dependent on Daddy's purse strings. As I recall, the newspapers had quite a time with that story. I believe my favorite headline was *Lady Anarchist Lures Innocent Men to Her Cause.*" He snorted. "Innocent indeed."

As Sylvia looked around at all three of them, her eyes grew even wider. Rafe knew he should say something comforting, but he couldn't find the words.

She wasn't simply an independent woman who had been jilted by a selfish lover.

Sylvia was an anarchist. Living under a false name. Who had been *arrested*. And her ruination had been a part of public record.

"So you see," Wardale continued. "I think you will do exactly as I ask of you, Davies. Otherwise, I'll shoot you and frame your beloved Sylvia. And with her past, no one will question it. You'll be given a nice long sentence this time, my dear. That is, if they don't hang you first." Then he turned to Rafe. "Unless, of course, you've no more use for her and we can dispose of her now. Tie up those loose ends?"

Rafe gaped at him, and at that moment Sylvia turned on her heel and raced toward the labyrinth, disappearing into the darkness.

Wardale let out an irritated huff. "Damn. I suppose I pushed her a little too hard there, didn't I? Go after her, Brodie. No. Give me the gun first." The man took off in pursuit. "He'll find her in no time. Brodie has been walking that labyrinth since he was a boy here." The little spring of hope that had opened in Rafe dried up, and his shoulders sagged. "Don't worry. I have no intention of hurting her, as long as you both cooperate. That girl will supply me with plenty of valuable information on Arlington. I've been giving her little tasks ever since she arrived. A most enterprising creature, when given the right motivation."

"There wasn't ever anything in that envelope, was there?"

Wardale grinned. "Just blank paper. I wanted to see how motivated she was to keep her past quiet and how resourceful she could be."

"You enjoy toying with people."

"Oh yes. So many things lose their allure once you become as wealthy as I am. It gets harder and harder to find things that bring one pleasure."

"What a conundrum."

Wardale frowned. "I don't care for sarcasm, Davies. If we're going to work together, you'd better smarten up. You have too many weak spots for a spy. And don't think I won't exploit every single one. Beginning with that delightful mother of yours. Have I told you we met in Monte Carlo last winter?" Rafe swallowed hard. "See?" Wardale's eyes practically glowed. "You're telling me even more already."

Just then a piercing scream tore through the air. Wardale looked toward the labyrinth, but Rafe never lost his focus. He lunged at Wardale and knocked the gun to the ground, then quickly punched him in the stomach. Wardale groaned and fell to his knees. Rafe came up behind him and locked his arms around the man's neck.

"I may not have been brought up on the streets," he said harshly against Wardale's ear as he slowly cut off his oxygen supply. "But I also made my own way in the world. Made my own choices, same as you." Wardale grabbed at his arms, trying in vain to pull out of his hold, but Rafe only pressed harder. "I'll *die* before I let anyone say otherwise. And take you with me, if I have to."

Wardale wilted against his chest, now out cold, and Rafe dropped him to the ground. He then raced toward the labyrinth. Branches whipped against his face as he frantically searched for the opening. At the sound of Sylvia's soft cries, he tore down the path like a madman.

Just let her be safe. Please, God. That's all I ask.

After the third turn he found her kneeling on the ground next to the motionless body of Brodie. The pocketknife protruded from his side, where she had stuck it between his ribs. Sylvia turned at his approach, and the terror in her eyes gutted him. No matter what she may believe, in this moment she needed comfort. Even from him. Rafe collapsed beside her and wrapped her in his arms. She let out panicked gasps against his shoulder, her entire body trembling. Rafe rocked her gently against him and stroked her hair.

"There, now. It's all right. You're safe."

"Is...is he dead?"

Rafe glanced toward the body. It looked as though she had pierced an artery. The man would have died instantly. "I think so."

"I took the knife out while I was running." Her voice began to shake as her body trembled even harder. "And when he grabbed my arm, I—I—"

Rafe's heart twisted as she broke into a sob. "You were defending yourself. You didn't know what he would do to you."

"I know, but—"

"No. I would have killed him myself if I saw him with his hands on you," he admitted. "But it's over. I'll take care of everything now."

Sylvia gripped him even tighter but didn't respond. Rafe couldn't say how much time passed while he stroked her back and whispered soothing words. It could have been minutes or hours. Eventually, her trembling subsided, and she pulled back. A fresh wave of anger broke over him at the sight of her stricken expression. She would be haunted by this. Possibly for the rest of her life.

"Come," he said as he rose to his feet. "I'm afraid this night is far from over."

CHAPTER NINETEEN

❧

The moment Brodie fell to the ground, a suffocating numbness came over Sylvia. She hadn't wanted to harm him, but there was no trace of the kind gardener she'd met only days ago who so admired her. Instead, the man who relentlessly hounded Sylvia as she tore through the labyrinth's twists and turns let out a string of foul curses the closer he came.

"There will be no more running when I'm done with ye," he had growled just as he grabbed her arm. She had blindly thrust the knife toward him on impulse, and with all her might.

Jab at the soft parts, he had once told her. So that was what she did.

His sharp, surprised breath cut through the air, followed by a low gurgling noise impossible to forget. Then he fell to his knees and gazed up at Sylvia, his beautiful green eyes wide with surprise, before he crumpled heavily to the ground.

Sylvia knew Rafe was holding her now, knew he was murmuring words of comfort as he stroked her hair, but she could barely feel anything. As he led her out of the labyrinth, she moved in clumsy steps, like a newborn colt. Rafe had to stop every other step just so she could keep up, but he said nothing. And when she dared to look at him, she found only pity there.

Though Sylvia had long suspected there was more to Rafe than the face he showed the world, it had still been a shock to learn he was a spy. But so many of his behaviors, his contradictions, now made sense. And created a number of complications for them both. Complications that likely meant the end of anything between them. When Rafe had told Wardale they were eloping, a thrill had rushed through her, though she knew it was only a lie. But a part of her so desperately wanted it to be true, even while it seemed impossible.

What must he think of you now?

And what would you *say if you knew all he had done?*

As they exited the labyrinth, Sylvia cried out again when she saw Mr. Wardale's body lying motionless in the grass, but Rafe was quick to reassure her that he was only unconscious. He took the gun that had fallen from his hands and then led her inside.

"W-we can't just leave him there," she stuttered.

"He'll be like that for some time. I'll come back for him later." Rafe's jaw hardened. "Which is more than he deserves."

He then guided her down to the empty kitchens and instructed her to sit in a chair by the hearth. The cold from the damp stone floor seemed to seep into her bones. Sylvia watched in a daze as he moved around the room, opening and closing cabinets, and pulling out various jars. It proved rather soothing. Eventually she realized he was trying to make her a cup of tea.

"Here," he said some minutes later, as he thrust out the steaming beverage. "Drink this."

Sylvia took the warm earthenware mug and clutched it in her shaking hands. At some point Rafe had wrapped his coat around her. She felt nothing. Neither warm nor cold. Yet her teeth chattered uncontrollably.

He knelt down before her and gestured to his own cheek. "You've a scratch there."

Sylvia lightly brushed the spot. "It must be from the branches." She had turned to look back at Mr. Brodie and stumbled against the labyrinth's wall of brambles.

"It should be seen to," Rafe said stiffly, but he made no move to touch her. Still, this excruciating formality was preferable to the horror that had flashed in his eyes when Mr. Wardale called her an anarchist and relayed that vile newspaper headline. "Say something."

Sylvia took a tiny sip of the tea. It tasted warm and herbal. "Thank you," she whispered hoarsely. Rafe watched her for another agonizing moment before he got up and left the room. He didn't look back.

Sylvia stared into the mug. Now she could feel the steam kissing her face and smell the delicate scent. But she could only bring herself to drink it in small sips.

Every sacrifice you have ever made for queen and country is worth less than dirt *to people like her.*

Mr. Wardale had gotten some things wrong, but the fact remained that, in one way or another, she had fought against many of the things Rafe had dedicated his life to upholding. She could try to explain her beliefs to him, but she certainly wouldn't renounce them.

I'd like to know more about your opinions.

Sylvia wasn't so sure he would make that claim anymore.

The tea had gone cold by the time she heard footsteps

approaching, but they were too quick and light to be Rafe's. Just as she looked toward the doorway, Georgiana rushed in, clad in a night robe, her hair in wild disarray.

She ran over and threw her arms around Sylvia. "Thank God you're all right."

"Yes," she replied, though Georgiana's significant bosom smothered the response.

After a moment Georgiana released her and stepped back. "I've just heard what happened. You must have been terrified!"

Sylvia wasn't exactly sure what Rafe had shared with her friend, so she simply nodded.

"To think, this whole time I was encouraging you to spend time with that man!"

Sylvia frowned. She must still be dazed from shock. Georgiana wasn't making any sense.

"And the poor gardener. Oh, it's all so *awful*," the viscountess continued, unaware of the sense of horror slowly dawning on Sylvia. "But don't worry. Mr. Davies won't be getting away. That murderer is locked in Mr. Wardale's study, and the authorities should be arriving soon. They will take care of everything."

The viscountess moved to pat her hand, but Sylvia gripped her wrist. "Mr. Davies didn't kill the gardener, Georgiana." Her throat began to go dry, but she pushed ahead. "*I* did."

Georgiana stared in shocked silence for what felt like an eternity. "But...Mr. Wardale said—"

"He is a *liar*," Sylvia bit off. The numbness that had cloaked her for the last hour had finally begun to dissipate. "Don't listen to anything he says. He has been blackmailing me for weeks to get information about your husband.

Rafe—Mr. Davies and I uncovered the evidence earlier this evening."

Georgiana shook her head, marveling at the revelation. "But he's made the same accusation of Mr. Davies. The guests are nearly ready to take up arms over it."

Sylvia's blood went cold. "Tell me."

"He claims that Mr. Davies has been collecting information to blackmail the guests since he arrived and that the gardener found Mr. Davies accosting you in the labyrinth. The man was killed in the struggle."

Sylvia stubbornly shook her head. "No. No, that isn't true at all!"

But it would be much too easy for everything to be pinned on Rafe. Hadn't he warned her about this very scenario mere hours ago? Wardale was giving her the chance to maintain the alias she had given up so much to create. To remain nothing more than quiet little Sylvia Sparrow, an unassuming lady's companion. At the cost of Rafe's life.

"Mr. Davies must be protesting this."

Georgiana shrugged. "As far as I know, he's refused to say anything until the authorities arrive."

Sylvia pressed her palms against her face. Two weeks ago it would have been unthinkable that she would even consider destroying the meticulously crafted life she had constructed. And all over an *earl's* son. But she sensed Rafe wouldn't say anything that would implicate her, even if it meant saving himself.

So Sylvia would simply have to do it.

She shot up from her seat so quickly that she startled Georgiana.

"Where are you going?" she called after her.

"To save Mr. Davies. And make sure that Wardale gets what he deserves."

Georgiana gave her a puzzled frown. "How are you going to do that?"

Sylvia paused by the doorway and looked back at her friend. "By telling the truth."

"No, Sylvia. Don't get involved," Georgiana called after her. "You have so much more to lose. Mr. Davies can take care of himself!" But all her reasonable points faded in the darkness as Sylvia marched up the staircase toward the study, prepared to defend the man she loved.

* * *

For the second time in as many days, Rafe found himself tied to a chair but under much more unpleasant circumstances. He hadn't even bothered trying to convince the men who surrounded him of his innocence. Each one looked prepared to tear him limb from limb—not that Rafe could blame them. Wardale had made a fine show of dragging himself back into the castle just as Rafe had emerged from the kitchen. A group of guests had found their host dirt-covered and bedraggled and throwing all kinds of accusations at Rafe, ranging from assault, to blackmail, to murder. The men had hustled the both of them upstairs into Wardale's study, where he immediately produced the notes Rafe had given him detailing unsavory details of nearly every person in the room.

"I had my suspicions about him for days now and found these in his room," Wardale had explained. "When I confronted him, he tried to escape. But poor Mr. Brodie went after him.

What a brave man." He then let out a theatrical sigh and cast his eyes downward.

It was an incredibly damning performance.

Wardale was now talking in a low voice to Lord Caldwell, who had proved to be the most levelheaded man in the room so far, as his only skeleton was a rather expensive penchant for betting on the ponies. But then Wardale glanced over and caught Rafe's eye. His lips curved in the subtlest smirk, and a new wave of anger thundered through Rafe.

He inhaled slowly to calm himself.

His best chance was to remain silent in the face of Wardale's accusations and wait until he could speak to someone who might actually *listen* to him.

That is, if he even made it out of this room.

He tried to shake away the dark thought, but it stubbornly remained. Wardale had evidence that could support his claims. Unless Gerard decided to speak out in support of Rafe and implicate himself, it was his word against theirs.

Not bloody likely.

Just as hope began to seep from him, the sound of racing footsteps came from the other side of the study door, followed by furious knocking. Someone opened the door and Sylvia burst in.

Rafe's entire body tensed. Dammit, she shouldn't be here. He glanced over at Wardale, who looked only slightly perturbed. Some of his claims against Rafe depended upon Sylvia's silence, but if she decided not to cooperate, he could just as easily destroy her.

"Miss Sparrow," Lord Caldwell began. "We are all grieved to learn of what you endured at the hands of this brute, but you should be resting now. This is no place for innocent young ladies."

Sylvia stepped calmly into the center of the room and raised an arm to point at their host.

"The only brute in this room is Mr. Wardale. He has been blackmailing me for weeks. I told Mr. Davies, and he helped me uncover the truth. When we tried to leave, Mr. Wardale stopped us. Then Mr. Brodie—"

"*Sylvia.*" Her name burst from him. Rafe couldn't let her do this. Exposing herself to these men would only complicate things for her. Things Rafe couldn't fix.

She approached him, and he felt a vicious tug on his heart at the pleading look in her eyes. "Tell them. Tell them it's true."

"If I do, it will *ruin* you," he hissed as desperation bubbled through him. With every second that passed, another crack appeared in the careful facade she had created. Soon it would shatter completely.

"I don't care." She shook her head. "I don't care anymore."

Before Rafe could respond to that inane statement, Wardale roared from across the room, "You cannot listen to a word this woman says. She is obviously lying in a desperate attempt to protect her *lover*."

Some of the men voiced their outrage, while others grumbled that it was patently absurd until Lord Templeton, who had been silent this entire time, chose that moment to clear his throat and step forward. "It's true. I saw them together earlier."

Rafe muttered a curse. This was growing worse by the second.

Sylvia turned to face her accusers. "I am *not* lying. Mr. Wardale wanted someone to spy on Viscount Arlington. So he used information he had about my past to force my hand."

Lord Caldwell frowned. "Exactly what kind of information?"

Rafe's breath caught, but Sylvia didn't even hesitate. "That I was once arrested and publicly accused of harboring anarchistic sympathies. Then in order to gain my position with Mrs. Crawford, I lied about my identity." She looked back at Rafe. "Which is true."

The room exploded in an uproar as the men all began talking at once, arguing over what to do with the pair of them.

Rafe closed his eyes as regret tore through him. He sensed someone move behind him to loosen his bindings and turned around. It was Sylvia.

"You shouldn't have done that. You've destroyed your credibility for nothing. Now Wardale will simply accuse us both. And this mob will believe him."

"It wasn't for nothing." She kept her eyes fixed on untying his wrists. "I couldn't stand back and let you sacrifice yourself."

"That is what I *do*," he bit off. Christ, did she really think her little confession was enough to save him?

She looked up at him, and their gazes locked together for an agonizing moment. The room suddenly went quiet as someone else entered.

It was the viscountess. "I was coming down the hall and heard everything," she explained unprompted.

"Then you know what this vile woman—this *harlot* has done," Wardale said, still trying to maintain control of the situation.

But the viscountess narrowed her eyes and stood even straighter. "That is my dear friend you speak so ill of, Mr.

Wardale. I am here to defend Miss Sparrow's character. And to take full responsibility for her deception, which, frankly, is a family matter and not any of your concern," she added, now addressing the entire room.

Sylvia went still behind Rafe. "Oh God," she whispered.

"Miss Sparrow was slandered years ago, thanks to a cowardly man and the newspapers' insatiable thirst for gossip. When she asked for my help to find a position, I knew she would be the perfect companion for my aunt, but the viscount would be incapable of looking past her tarnished reputation. So together we created a fake name and credentials in order to deceive my husband. I don't know how Mr. Wardale learned of our actions, but I have my suspicions, and they paint an ugly picture," she said as she slanted him a scowl. "In any case, Miss Sparrow is telling the truth. And though you may not want to believe her, you can hardly say the same of me. Isn't that correct, gentlemen?"

The room was so silent, one could have heard a pin drop. Then Lord Caldwell stepped forward.

"Of course, my lady." The other men immediately mumbled their agreements.

Georgiana gave a single nod. "Then we will wait for the authorities to arrive, and we will stop treating Mr. Davies like a convicted criminal."

Rafe pulled his hands loose and rose. No one moved to stop him, and for the first time that evening, Wardale looked worried.

Sylvia rushed over to the viscountess. She had just admitted to a room full of peers that she had conspired to deceive her husband, who was not known for his forgiving nature. Though her declaration had swayed the other men against Wardale for the time being, Rafe was concerned for what lay ahead. But Lady Arlington was practically glowing. It was as if an invisible chain had been removed from her person. As if the truth really had set her free. Just as a kind of envy began to trickle through him, someone announced that the police were coming up the drive. It was the first time in hours Rafe felt anything close to relief. There was still no guarantee that these men would listen, but they would be a hell of a lot easier to convince than Wardale's friends.

And Rafe needed any chance he could get.

* * *

Sylvia stood with Georgiana in watchful silence as a group of Glaswegian policemen headed by a stern-looking constable swarmed through the study. No one bothered to approach them at first, as it was assumed the two ladies were too overcome to provide any useful information. Through all of this Mr. Wardale remained seated behind his desk, his eyes never leaving Rafe. It turned out the police had already been tipped off by an associate of Rafe's—Sylvia didn't know the particulars— so he was treated as a colleague, not a suspect. Eventually, the guests were told to head back to their rooms. More extensive interviews would be conducted in the morning. For now it was best to get some sleep. Georgiana moved to leave, but Sylvia hung back a little, waiting for Rafe to at least acknowledge her presence.

"Come, dear," Georgiana murmured. "We aren't needed." She hooked her arm through Sylvia's and tugged her into the hallway. The viscountess was still talking, but Sylvia didn't hear a word as Rafe finally looked over at her through the open doorway. His arms were crossed, his necktie was loosened, and his handsome face was twisted in a frown. She had never seen him look so intimidating. Commanding. And dangerous.

Even at this distance, his gaze pinned her to the spot, and she shivered a little. Rafe then took a few steps forward, and Sylvia's breath caught, until he slowly closed the door, his eyes never leaving hers. The decided click of the lock sank through her.

"Are you listening?" Georgiana asked.

Sylvia forced herself to turn away from the door. "Sorry, what?"

"Lord Caldwell thinks Mr. Davies is acting on behalf of the Crown. That is why he is staying behind."

"Oh?" Sylvia hoped that came off slightly more convincing than it sounded to her ears.

Georgiana's eyes softened. "You look exhausted. We need to get you to bed."

Lord Caldwell offered to escort them, but Georgiana waved him away, and within minutes they were in her room.

"If you need anything, come to me straightaway," the viscountess insisted.

Sylvia nodded and sank back against the pillows. Her eyes had already begun to close. "Georgiana?"

"Hmm?"

"What will you do when the viscount finds out what we've done?"

They both knew it was only a matter of time before he learned of their deception.

"Let me worry about that."

Her gentle tone only increased Sylvia's guilt. She hadn't

considered the consequences revealing the truth could have for Georgiana.

"I'm sorry. About everything. You deserve a better friend than me."

Sylvia planned to make a much more thorough apology in the morning, but she couldn't go to sleep without at least saying something. After a moment, she cracked one eye open.

Georgiana was giving her a tender smile. "Already forgiven, dear one. Now go to sleep."

Sylvia closed her eyes. "Yes," she mumbled before drifting off.

CHAPTER TWENTY

❧

"S o, then, do you still intend to marry your little revolution-ary, or was that just a story?"

Rafe tried to ignore Wardale as he packed up the last of the incriminating files in a box. The man's time would have been better spent burning the evidence rather than chasing after him and Sylvia. His confidence would be his undoing. "Take this downstairs," he instructed a young police officer.

"Yes, sir," the lad said eagerly and left.

Rafe immediately began to rifle through a stack of papers to keep from engaging with Wardale. Thank God Henry had had the foresight to contact the authorities regarding his suspicions. The constable in charge had deferred to Rafe and treated Wardale as a suspect, but the trace of worry he had briefly displayed was gone now. Even after the blackmail files had been recovered, Wardale appeared entirely unconcerned. He had grown cocky once again. Rafe had seen it before in other powerful men. They spent so long at the top that they forgot how far they had to fall.

"You must know what being associated with her will mean for your career," Wardale continued, unaffected by Rafe's blatant attempt to ignore him. "She may not have been formally charged with a crime, but the papers won't care. They'll be relentless. I can see the headlines now: 'Notorious Rake Ensnared by Disgraced Rebel.' No one in government will take you seriously. Not with her taint upon you. Then again, perhaps you aren't as ambitious as your brother thought…"

Rafe slammed the papers down. "Shut up," he growled. "I suppose it's been ages since anyone told you that."

Wardale merely laughed. "You are correct. I'd nearly forgotten what it was like having someone else tell me what to do."

"Well, I suggest you get used to it. I foresee your future being full of taking orders from other people."

Prison guards, mostly.

Wardale frowned and opened his mouth to respond, but the door opened and the head constable entered.

"All right. That's the last of it. You've been incredibly helpful, Mr. Davies." He stuck out his hand.

"Of course," Rafe said, shaking it. "What will you do with him?"

"Mr. Wardale can spend the night in his own bed. Then we'll transport him to Glasgow tomorrow and await word from Scotland Yard. My guess is they will send their own officers to escort him back to London."

Rafe could only imagine the number of men who were itching to finally have Wardale at their mercy. But if he didn't plead guilty to his crimes, a long, ugly court battle lay ahead. He glanced over and noticed that Wardale had gone a little pale. Perhaps the reality of what lay ahead had finally begun to sink in.

"Gentlemen, will you grant your prisoner one last request?"

Wardale asked. "This may well be my last chance to enjoy a whiskey alone in my study."

Rafe shot Wardale a glare. "Absolutely not."

But to his surprise, the constable touched his arm. "We already have what we need from him, and all the entrances are being watched. What's the harm?"

Rafe furrowed his brow as Wardale's eyes glinted. It *was* a simple request. And he couldn't directly challenge the constable without appearing bitter and unreasonable. No doubt just what Wardale wanted.

"Fine. Do as you wish."

He strode from the room and was followed by the constable a few moments later, who closed the door behind him.

"Thank you, Mr. Davies. I know he's been baiting you all evening. Get some rest. Your day has been longer than most."

Rafe dragged a hand over his face. The man was right. The adrenaline that had been powering him for hours was finally beginning to subside. God only knew what fresh hell tomorrow would bring. He could still see Sylvia's hurt expression when he closed the door on her earlier. But he needed time. Time to sort through everything she had revealed, and what it meant for them. Though he was loath to admit it, Wardale had a point. "Very well. See you in the morning, then."

He'd taken only a few steps before the sound of a gunshot from the other side of the study's door brought him to a halt.

* * *

Sylvia woke to late-morning sunshine and a tea tray filled with still-warm scones on the bedside table. After a quick washing up, she availed herself of the tender pastry. She was partway through her second when Georgiana poked her head in.

"Oh! You're up," she said as she breezed into the room, dressed in a gauzy sage morning gown. "How are you feeling?"

Sylvia swallowed her mouthful and nodded. "Much better, thank you. I never sleep this late."

Georgiana took the seat across from her. "Yes, but you aren't usually involved in violent altercations with beastly gardeners and devious millionaires, either."

Sylvia shifted in her chair. She had spent so long determined to hide the truth from Georgiana that it felt a little strange to have no secrets between them any longer. Well, except for her involvement with Rafe.

"You look as if you barely slept," she said, noting the shadows under the viscountess's eyes.

Georgiana hesitated, and in that brief moment Sylvia aged a decade. "Something's happened to Mr. Davies."

"No," Georgiana said quickly. "But...Mr. Wardale is dead. He shot himself."

Despite everything she had uncovered, everything she had witnessed last night, Sylvia was still shocked. "I suppose it was either that or go to prison," she finally said.

"Yes, I suspect so," Georgiana agreed. "Most of the guests are planning on leaving today, after they speak with the police."

Sylvia's hands instinctively tightened on her lap, and Georgiana patted her hand. She knew how harrowing Sylvia's last encounter with the law had been. "Do you want me to be with you when you do?"

"No, that's all right. I just...I need to see Mr. Davies first."

Georgiana watched her carefully. "I can send him a note, if you'd like."

Sylvia shook her head. "I'm sure that won't be necessary."

He would find her when the time came.

They talked for a few more minutes about their travel plans before Sylvia excused herself to dress for the day. As she put on another one of her utilitarian skirts, Rafe's words from last night floated through her mind. But if his behavior yesterday was anything to go on, it seemed increasingly unlikely there would be silk gowns and daylight lovemaking in her future. No. She just needed to speak to him. To finally explain how she felt. Then he would understand.

He *must*.

Sylvia added a white blouse and matching vest, then fixed her hair in a simple chignon. She looked at her reflection in the suite's floor-length mirror. From the outside, she appeared just as she had when she first arrived here: tidy and professional. Things would be so much simpler if that was all she was, an innocent lady's companion. Sylvia's shoulders slumped from the weight of all she had accumulated these last few days. Weight she would have to learn to bear, just like the rest of it.

When she emerged from her room, the castle was buzzing with activity. Downstairs, several police officers stood talking with guests, while members of staff and personal servants rushed around, trying to prepare for early departures. Stacks of trunks and other pieces of luggage were already piled near the entryway.

But there was no sign of Rafe.

Sylvia let out a sigh and headed toward the library, but an achingly young officer blocked the way.

"Sorry, miss. You can't go in there. That's where we're interviewing guests."

Sylvia backed away. "Oh, I see."

The door then opened, and Rafe stuck his head out.

"Mackenzie, is it?" he asked the officer. "Can you call for another pot of tea? Lady Delacorte is feeling parched. *Again.*" Rafe looked incredibly annoyed to be delivering the request. Then he noticed Sylvia. His eyes widened for just a moment before he mastered himself. "Oh. Hello, Miss Sparrow." He hesitated slightly before speaking her false name.

Sylvia lowered her head. "I was just leaving."

But as she turned around, Rafe called out to her. "Would you mind waiting a few minutes while I finish up here?"

Sylvia looked over her shoulder. Rafe's scowl indicated that this was more of a command than a question. He didn't wait for her response. "You can sit there," he said, gesturing to a chair by the wall. Sylvia nodded and walked toward it. She could feel his gaze on her, but when she took her seat, he had already gone back into the room.

Sylvia tried to master her racing heart. Would she still be questioned regarding Brodie's death, or did none of that matter because of Mr. Wardale's confession? Yesterday, Rafe had promised that he would take care of everything, and he knew she had acted in self-defense when she plunged the knife into the gardener. But that was before she had laid her past bare to a room full of men. Before she had watched the light seep out of his eyes while Wardale revealed her deepest secrets.

Eventually, a maid delivered the requested tea, and a few minutes later, Lady Delacorte bustled out of the room and huffed, "Why, I've never been treated so *rudely* in all my life," she complained to Sylvia. "Don't let them bully you, my dear."

"Yes, madam."

Then the grand lady flounced off. If she felt any grief over Mr. Wardale's demise, she certainly didn't show it. Sylvia couldn't imagine that she was under suspicion, but it was likely that her very public attachment to their host had been a source of great interest.

Another few minutes passed before another man emerged from the room. He was middle-aged, with hair graying at the temples.

"Miss Sparrow?"

Sylvia rose stiffly and approached.

"I'm Chief Inspector Bagby." The man gave her a kind smile that did little to settle her nerves and extended his arm, letting her pass first into the library.

Her heart pounded furiously in her chest as she entered the room, and her hands tightened into fists. She couldn't do this. Couldn't face both Rafe *and* a member of the law. The detective who had interrogated her after her arrest in London had lobbed increasingly personal questions at her for hours and even tried forcing her to sign a confession. It had been an exhausting, demoralizing experience. And as much as she disliked her brother, she knew that without Lionel's interference she might not have left the jail at all. After a few steps, Sylvia glanced back, but the inspector hadn't followed.

"See you later, Davies," he called out before shutting the door behind her.

The echo resounded through the silent room. Sylvia stared at the closed door for several moments before it registered that he was truly gone. The tightness in her chest began to loosen with relief, and she cast a hopeful glance toward Rafe. He stood by the massive stone fireplace looking far more imposing than she had ever seen him. How strange to think this room had been the setting for their first glorious kiss only days ago. He still wore the same suit from last night, now slightly rumpled, and the faint circles under his eyes betrayed his lack of sleep. No doubt he had been dealing with Mr. Wardale's death for hours. She clasped her hands in front of her and buried the instinct that longed to press a soothing palm to his troubled brow.

"I heard about Mr. Wardale. How are you?" Sylvia asked as she walked toward him.

Rafe leaned his back against the mantel, ignoring the question. "I told Inspector Bagby I needed a few minutes alone with you."

"And that was allowed?"

Rafe gestured to a high-backed chair before him. "It wasn't his choice."

She swallowed hard at his dark tone. "He knows who you are, then?" she asked, taking a seat.

Rafe remained standing. She didn't like this, how he loomed over her, but that was probably by design. "More or less. And that this is an extremely delicate matter based on the nature of the documents we uncovered."

"Does...does he know about me?" Sylvia realized that could mean all sorts of things. "And what I did?" she added.

A muscle twitched by his jaw. "He knows that you were accosted by the gardener and acted in self-defense. But I did have to explain your presence in the garden. With me."

Sylvia's cheeks heated at the inference. But then, that was the kind of woman she was, wasn't she? As she opened her mouth to begin her explanation, Rafe let out a frustrated sigh and narrowed his eyes.

"You've put me in a hell of a position after your confession, Sylvia. And frankly, I don't know how to fix it."

She bowed her head. "I know. But I couldn't stand by while Wardale filled those men's heads with nonsense."

Rafe didn't respond to this. He was staring off, thinking through something. "I've spoken with everyone who was in the study and made it very clear that it is in their best interests to keep their mouths shut, but it's hardly a guarantee. Some of those men are so broke they would sell their own mother's secrets if they could. The best I can come up with is we both go abroad for a while until this business with Wardale is out of the papers, though God knows how long that could take."

Sylvia felt a weight lift as relief began to sweep through her. He wanted to make things work between them. There would be hurdles, no doubt, but if they supported one another, they had a chance. "Yes, I agree."

"I know how you feel about marriage, but my name can protect you."

It wasn't a remotely romantic proposal, yet Sylvia's heart still warmed as if he had released a hundred doves into the air and gotten down on both knees. But then Rafe continued:

"And as long as the press doesn't catch wind of your involvement in this mess, your past shouldn't affect my career."

She froze as his words slowly penetrated her woolly brain. Granted, she had slept terribly, but still. She must have misunderstood. She *must*. "You...you actually plan to continue to work for the Crown despite all you uncovered?"

Rafe's broad shoulders tensed. The movement was slight, but she didn't miss it. "I'm not sure what you mean. Of course I do."

She shook her head in disbelief. She had been prepared for

him to be upset over her deception, to even end things with her because of it. But it truly hadn't occurred to her that he would actually continue his work under any circumstance. That he would even *want* to. Sylvia stared into his dark eyes, eyes that betrayed nothing. There was no trace of the man who had spent the past two weeks flirting with her, teasing her, making love to her. A man she ached to have once again. He now stood before her as hard as the stone walls that surrounded them.

Sylvia took a moment to compose her thoughts as outrage welled inside her. "While I appreciate your willingness to go to such great lengths to suppress any knowledge of my past," she began tartly, "if it is all in the name of preserving your sodding *career*, then you needn't bother. I will make this easier for you: I am not interested in any kind of future together as long as you spy for the Empire. And I urge you to reconsider, not for me but for your own sense of self-respect. Or did you give *that* away to the Crown too?" Rafe shot her a glare and opened his mouth, but before he could respond, Sylvia talked over him. "As it stands, I fail to see how those men aren't just as corrupt as Mr. Wardale. I saw that list. I recognized many of those names. Lords, politicians, industrialists. All men who have long abused their power and social standing for personal gain. Mr. Wardale beat them at their own game. I certainly don't condone blackmail, but you don't need to protect them either."

"Sylvia," he warned, but she wouldn't stop. She couldn't. Not until he heard every last thing she had to say.

"How can you do this? How can you continue to support a government run by those men? What right do they have to govern over the rest of us? These are the same people who deny countless citizens the vote. Who claim it is patriotic to invade other countries and then force the inhabitants to work for our benefit, while refusing to recognize their basic humanity."

"That's enough," Rafe snapped.

"Is that the kind of man you want to be?" she pressed. "Is your ego so *insatiable* that you need to help destroy the world in order to feel important? If you do, then I feel so sorry for you. I may be a liar, but at least I know what I've lied to protect. Can you say the same?"

"Enough." He banged his fist on the mantel.

Sylvia stood, undeterred. "Wardale was right. You're still seeking their approval. You think you need it. That you're following the nobler path this way. But they'll never truly accept you. You're only a tool to them, and they will never see you as anything other than something to use."

At that, all of Rafe's cool control evaporated. "What do you suggest I do, then? I am trying to bring the guilty parties to justice here, but I can't do it from the outside. This is the *only* way I can make a difference."

Sylvia merely lifted her chin in the face of his indignation. "It certainly is not. Dedicating your life to supporting the actions of a corrupt government only does more harm. And makes you complicit. How can you not see that? How can you live with yourself?"

He stared like she was a wild thing poised to strike at any moment. "You don't have a damned clue what I have given up," he finally said. "The *years* I have spent working toward this. And if I walk away now, it will all be for nothing. *All of it.*"

He exhaled a harsh breath and turned away. As Sylvia stared at his heaving shoulders, the anger that had fueled her only moments ago began to fade. She stood by what she said about the Empire, but perhaps...perhaps there were things about him she hadn't considered. Things she didn't fully understand. "Rafe," she began.

His neck flexed at the sound of his name. "You can go now," he murmured, and the softened tone pierced far deeper than his anger. It was the sound of defeat. Of hurt.

"Doesn't the inspector want to speak to me?" She could hear the desperate note in her voice.

Rafe shook his head as he faced her once again. "That won't be necessary," he said coolly. "You've said quite enough." Any trace of vulnerability had vanished so completely Sylvia wondered if she had imagined it. "Tell Bagby to send in the next guest. I'll be leaving this afternoon," he added and turned away, as if she were simply another guest. Not the woman he had just offered to marry.

His dismissal resounded throughout the quiet room. Sylvia resisted the urge to apologize, but she didn't know how to fix this either. Didn't know how to stop him from slipping through her fingers like grains of sand. She headed to the exit in a daze, then paused and glanced back as she grasped the doorknob. Rafe watched the unlit hearth with his hands clasped behind his back.

Know that every moment I spent with you was real.

And now they had both made their choice.

Sylvia left without another word, her heart pounding with the certainty that she would never see him again.

CHAPTER TWENTY-ONE

❧

Once Rafe heard the door shut, he collapsed into the near-est chair. But he was hardly alone. Sylvia's damned scent still hung in the air, along with the many accusations she had so freely lobbed at him.

You're only a tool to them.

Something to use.

Rafe's fingers dug into the fabric of the armchair. What the hell did she know about his work? About *him*?

He let out an exhausted sigh, poured a cup of the now tepid tea Lady Delacorte hadn't even touched, and brought it to his lips. And to think, he had actually believed they were falling in love. That Sylvia saw past the image he displayed for the world to the truth that lay beneath and could love him even more for it. But she hadn't at all liked what she found there.

Is your ego so insatiable that you need to help destroy the world in order to feel important?

Christ. He would never forget the disgust that had flashed in her eyes as she said those words. How little she must think of him now.

Just as he felt a hot flush creeping up his neck, Rafe

shook his head and rolled his shoulders. Enough. The pressure of the mission had clearly gotten to him. That was the only explanation for the avalanche of mistakes he had made since the moment he set foot in this damned castle.

No. Since the moment your eyes entangled with Sylvia Sparrow's.

Correction: Sylvia Bloody Wilcox.

"Dammit."

Rafe practically threw the teacup down. He needed something much stronger. So what if it wasn't even noon? He hadn't yet gone to sleep. Surely certain allowances could be made under the circumstances...

"You look like hell."

Rafe startled to attention and noticed Henry standing before him, clean-shaven and much more clear-eyed than he had been at his sister's. "When did you get here?"

"A few minutes ago. You were busy staring daggers at a tea set and muttering to yourself when I came in. Didn't even hear me knock."

Rafe dragged a hand over his face. "I take it you got my message?" He had cabled Henry last night.

"Yes." Henry took the seat opposite him and set his cane aside. "Though I would be remiss if I didn't mention that *you* never responded to *my* message yesterday." Then his brow furrowed with concern. "I was worried."

"My apologies. I was occupied."

"I gathered," Henry drawled. "I don't suppose the young lady I just met fleeing this room was somehow involved?"

"That's the woman I told you about."

"I see. And is there a reason you both look utterly devastated, or is that merely a coincidence?"

Rafe shot him a scowl. "I don't want to talk about it."

"That usually means you absolutely should."

"That's rich, coming from you."

To Rafe's surprise, Henry let out a laugh. "Quite right. But on this particular occasion we are discussing *your* romantic foibles."

"I don't have time for this," he grumbled. "There is the body of a man who held the entire government in his palm locked in the larder and a mountain of evidence to go through."

"This is where I point out that if you had bothered to read my message yesterday, you would be several steps ahead by now."

Rafe narrowed his eyes. "What do you know?"

"Well, after your visit the other day, I did some investigating and found that most of the servants left Castle Blackwood after Wardale took over. That in itself isn't unusual, especially if the staff were older. But one name kept coming up: James Brodie, the unfortunate gardener in your message."

"Yes. He grew up here."

"He also had a fairly extensive arrest record and a reputation as a strong body. None of the locals like him, since he had a nasty habit of not paying his debts. But they were all paid in full once he was hired on by Wardale. A few people assumed he was acting as Wardale's personal lackey, even though his official position was gardener, something I'm told he wasn't really qualified for. It caused lots of talk in the village. But I suspect Wardale valued loyalty above all else, even his landscaping."

Rafe's eyes widened. "How did you uncover all of this so quickly?"

Henry shrugged. "Hero status does have its benefits,

especially around the local pub. Everyone wants to slap you on the back and buy you a drink. Once they start talking, it's rather easy to bend the conversation as you wish."

"And I gather no one said anything about threats or separatists."

"Not a word. There were a few people who grumbled about an Englishman buying the castle, but nothing unusual. It was Brodie they focused on. Some thought Wardale didn't know about Brodie's past. A few others assumed he knew exactly what he was getting, and that made me suspicious. So I did some digging into the king of the castle. Did you know that for the last several years most of his building permits were blocked either by the local council or for violating some government ordinance? Sometimes the courts got involved, but in the end Wardale always got what he wanted. And quickly." Henry gave him a pointed look. "It wasn't surprising to me that a man of his stature would grease the wheels, but he never lost. Ever. Even when there was a clear case against him. That signaled that something else beyond mere bribery was afoot. I wasn't terribly surprised when you mentioned the blackmail in your message."

Rafe shook his head. "But the sheer scale of it, Henry. And the people involved. It's...it's a disgrace."

"Yes, but it isn't your mess to clean up," he said gently.

"I can't ignore it, either," Rafe shot back. His chest had started to tighten again, just as it had while Sylvia was berating him. Why didn't either of them understand?

"Of course not. But I don't think that's your only motivation here." Henry paused and took a breath. "I think you're protecting Gerard." He held up a hand as Rafe began to speak. "I understand, in a way. Despite everything, he's still your brother. But he sent you up here completely in the dark, knowing what Wardale was."

"He was desperate," Rafe protested. "Wardale intended to ruin him."

"And why is that *your* concern? If the tables were turned, Gerard wouldn't lift his pinkie finger to help you."

"Because I'm better than him," Rafe growled.

"Yes," Henry agreed. "And you don't need to keep proving it."

Rafe inhaled slowly until the tightness in his chest released. Henry was his friend. He'd had a hellish year. And Rafe valued his help. But he didn't have to explain himself to him. To anyone.

"You've made your point. Can we move on?"

Henry watched him for a moment, but there was a flicker of disappointment in his eyes. "Of course. Tell me what I can do."

* * *

As Sylvia fled the library, she nearly knocked down a gentleman.

"I'm so sorry." She reached out to help him, but the man's hand wrapped around her arm to steady her instead.

"Careful, now. If you topple over, I'm afraid I won't be much help," he said with a wink and gestured to his cane.

Sylvia blushed and finally got a proper look at him. The man wasn't much older than her, with a rangy build, dark blond hair, and a pair of arresting brown eyes. He wasn't exactly handsome, but his angular features were striking, nonetheless.

After a moment Sylvia realized she had been staring and blushed again.

"Thank you. I won't keep you from Mr. Davies." Her voice grew hoarse as she spoke his name, and the man's eyebrows rose, clearly noticing her distress. He opened his mouth, but before he could speak Sylvia gave him a brief nod and continued on her way. That was enough embarrassment for a first meeting.

As she continued down the hallway, she met Georgiana, who shot her an accusatory look.

"I was just coming to meet you. Why didn't you tell me you were going to speak to Mr. Davies?"

Sylvia shook her head, still distracted by her argument with Rafe. "It wasn't planned. I didn't know he was in the library. Then he came out and saw me standing there."

Georgiana glanced past her shoulder toward the library. "Is it true? Is Captain Harris here?" That got Sylvia's full attention. "The naval hero?" She'd never before seen the strange mix of apprehension and interest on her friend's face. "I think I just met him now. You know him?"

"No," Georgiana immediately burst out, then bit her lip. "Well, yes. But it was years ago. In London."

That sounded awfully suspicious. But before Sylvia could say more, Georgiana tugged her into a nearby alcove. "Never mind about that. Tell me what happened with Mr. Davies. And Mr. Wardale. I assume there's far more to the story than what I heard last night."

Sylvia's natural instinct to evade surfaced, but she pushed past it. She was so tired of hiding everything. She had done that for far too long. Sylvia explained most of what had occurred since she had received the first blackmail letter, but she couldn't yet speak about Rafe. Not while her heart was still breaking.

By the time she had finished, Georgiana's eyebrows had nearly reached her hairline.

"Oh my God," she murmured. "You should have come to me as soon as you got that letter! I would have helped you."

"I know. I know I should have." Sylvia turned away from the hurt in Georgiana's eyes. "But I thought I could take care of this. I *wanted* to. I've had to rely on other people for so long. Ever since Bernard. I've felt so useless. And now...now everything I touch seems to go to ruin," she said miserably.

She had deceived people she cared about because she was too ashamed to ask for help. Of course that hurt them. Why had she ever thought it would be otherwise?

A gentle hand gripped her shoulder. "Don't be so hard on yourself, Sylvia. If not for your own sake, then do it for mine. It pains me to see you like this. You've had so much to deal with. Let me help. Please."

Sylvia's throat tightened with emotion as she marveled at the viscountess. She had just confessed to lying to her for weeks. To keeping secrets that could bring irreparable harm to her family's reputation, to say nothing of the personal cost to herself. And though Georgiana had every right to demand Sylvia leave this instant, she only asked to help.

She placed her hand over Georgiana's and faced her. "Thank you."

If only her conversation with Rafe had gone so easily, but they had caused each other different wounds, and both hid their hurt behind a stubborn desire to be right. She could not make him want to understand her any more than he could do the same with her, and her chest ached with this knowledge.

That despite the many ways in which they seemed to find a unique kind of acceptance in the other, it still wasn't enough in the end.

Georgiana's eyes filled with relief. "Good. Now let's discuss—"

But before she could continue, a footman came running over to them. "Lady Arlington! I've been searching all over for you," the man panted. "An urgent message from London has come." He held out the missive.

Georgiana shot Sylvia a bewildered look as she took the envelope. But a feeling of dread began to kindle in Sylvia's belly. Had the viscount already learned of their deception?

"Odd," Georgiana began as she unfolded the paper. "I can't imagine what's so important that—"

But the rest of the words remained unspoken as she gasped and brought a hand to her mouth.

Sylvia gripped her arm. "Georgiana? What is it?"

Instead of answering, the viscountess held out the telegram. Sylvia took it from her trembling hand.

It contained just three short lines announcing the viscount's death.

"Oh, Georgiana."

The words seemed to penetrate Georgiana's shock, and she let out a cry as she crumpled to the floor. The footman, thinking she had given in to a swoon, called out for help. Sylvia knelt down and wrapped her arms around Georgiana, who pressed her head heavily to Sylvia's shoulder and sobbed against the fabric of her dress. Rafe and Captain Harris came rushing out of the library and were joined by a few officers and guests. Sylvia caught the tormented look that briefly flashed across the captain's face before his mouth settled in a grim line, as though he was disturbed by the scene before him, but she did not look at Rafe at all and returned her attention to Georgiana.

To anyone else it must have looked like she was in the throes of wrenching despair.

Only Sylvia knew the truth.

They were tears of relief.

CHAPTER TWENTY-TWO

❧

Rafe's footsteps echoed off Whitehall's spotless floors. He hated coming here. It was an unwelcome reminder of his minuscule place within the vast inner workings of the Empire. Though he had been born to a life of privilege, his personal power was worth very little within these walls. But today he was on a mission of justice. He gripped the leather folder he carried even closer to his chest. After weeks of delays, Rafe would finally have a chance to discuss all he had uncovered in Scotland. Representatives from the Home Office and the office of the prime minister would be present, along with his brother.

They hadn't spoken since Rafe's return to London. Once Gerard learned he was back in town and that Wardale was dead, he'd sent a note asking to meet so he could explain and had even attempted an apology, but Rafe had thrown it away before he'd finished reading it and had ignored the others that followed.

The assistant Rafe had been following led him to a large office. "Have a seat here, Mr. Davies. Someone will be with you shortly."

"Thank you."

The assistant then dipped his head and left. The office itself was remarkably devoid of personality. It contained the customary polished mahogany desk, a barely used leather chair, and shelves of reference books that likely had never been opened.

It could belong to anyone.

Rafe placed the folder on the desk and walked over to the room's lone window, which looked out onto a small courtyard. Empty at midmorning. He had already submitted a report to the Home Office detailing everything he had uncovered and sent along the files from Wardale's desk, save for the one on Sylvia. There was no question that the man had been involved in an elaborate blackmail scheme targeting prominent members of government and business. They didn't need clippings of her old newspaper columns to prove that. And yet, instead of burning them on the spot like he should have, he had tucked the file safely away at the back of his desk drawer unopened.

As for now, Rafe planned to discuss his experience and answer any questions the panel had. Then the government would proceed with a formal investigation to ensure that any criminal wrongdoing was prosecuted. Justice would be served. And it would have been worth it.

All of it.

Rafe turned his head at the sound of the door opening and immediately scowled.

"Try not to look so happy to see me, Rafe." Gerard entered the room and closed the door behind him. They had both inherited their father's strong jaw and dark hair, but only Rafe got the impressive Davies height, which he lorded over Gerard every chance he got. "People might actually think we like each other."

Rafe's frown deepened in response. He hadn't agreed to this. Just as he opened his mouth to say so, Gerard held up a hand. "I need to speak with you. In private."

"Then this is your office, I take it?"

"Yes. Though I rarely work here."

"It certainly looks that way."

Gerard winced slightly but didn't respond to the dig. "You've been ignoring my messages."

"Because I have nothing to say to you."

"Perhaps, but I have some things I'd like to say."

Rafe crossed his arms and turned to face him fully. "All right. Where would you like to start, Gerard? Would you like to apologize for lying to me about this entire mission? For knowingly sending me into a trap? Or for risking my life to protect your precious reputation? Take your pick."

The earl went paler with each accusation. "I never thought about it like that. I swear to you," he insisted. "I only wanted to appease Wardale so that I could have more time. That's all. I didn't think for one moment that you'd uncover... well, *everything*." He flapped his hands before him. Rafe had never seen Gerard this rattled before. If he wasn't so damned angry, he might've enjoyed it.

Instead, he raised an eyebrow and cocked his head. "You do understand what spying involves, don't you?"

"Yes," Gerard said through gritted teeth. "I underestimated you. Obviously. It won't happen again."

No. It won't.

Because Rafe didn't intend to give him the chance.

"I know you're furious with me. And you have every right

to be, but there's something else." Gerard hesitated and shot him a sheepish look. "It has been decided that there won't be a formal investigation."

"What? That's absurd!"

"Keep your voice down," he hissed. "Come now, you knew this was a possibility. Luckily, we have been able to suppress knowledge of the sheer scale of the blackmail. Just imagine the scandal that would result if word got out. My God, the press alone..."

They would be merciless. But Rafe was unrepentant. "I fail to see the issue."

"Well, unfortunately your approval isn't required. Wardale confessed and took his own life. As far as the Crown is concerned, justice has been served."

"He is hardly the only operative here. What of the officials he blackmailed and the people who were wronged by their actions? Will there be no justice for them?"

"This is as close to it as they will get." Gerard sighed and passed a hand through his hair. Rafe hated himself for recognizing the movement as one of his own. "I know this isn't what you wanted. And I sympathize. *Believe* me. But dragging this debacle out into the open will only create unrest. We can't have people losing confidence in their government."

"Then perhaps the lot of you shouldn't have made yourselves such easy targets," Rafe spat. "I suppose simply *not* engaging in corruption was never an option?"

"That isn't fair, Rafe. I can't speak to Wardale's other targets, but all I did was fall in love. That isn't a crime."

"No, but adultery is."

God, he sounded like a pompous twat, but Rafe couldn't let this go so easily.

"And how would you know anything about that?" Gerard snapped. "You're a bachelor. Beholden to no one. Whereas I have spent my whole *life* doing my duty. This is the one time I've had something just to myself. Something that is entirely my own."

"You don't even see it, do you?" Rafe marveled. "How this makes you a bloody hypocrite."

Gerard's brow furrowed. "I've no idea what you're talking about."

His utter lack of self-awareness only made Rafe angrier. "You've treated me and my mother like pariahs for as long as I can remember. Yet you've gone and done nearly the same thing as our dear old papa. How can you not have realized that? Even Wardale knew. *Like father, like son*, he said."

Gerard stared in silence as his face slowly flushed. When he did manage to speak, it was only in short, barely intelligible bursts. "That isn't—I didn't—It wasn't—"

Rafe almost felt sorry for Gerard as he watched his brother wrestle with this dawning realization.

"This isn't the same!" he finally finished.

"Yes, hence the 'nearly.' Because Father wasn't still married when he met his actress. And I hope you haven't gotten this woman with child. If so, I pity her."

For years Rafe had dreamed of the moment when he would finally gain the upper hand over Gerard. Then he would experience how Rafe had so often felt: small and stupid and unwanted. The satisfaction would be incomparable. And he would soak up every single second of it.

But the satisfaction didn't come. Instead, Gerard looked exhausted. And troubled. And so very much like their father. Rafe's jaw hardened against the sympathy trying to brew inside him. Why should he give this man any more than he had ever received?

Gerard rubbed a hand over his face. "Christ," he muttered. "Christ. You're right. I've been so consumed with the black-mail, I never really thought about it. These last few months have been hell, if I'm honest—not that you care."

Rafe ignored the prickle of guilt in his belly. "Then why become involved with her in the first place? You knew the risk," he countered.

Gerard glanced at him. "You make it sound like it was a choice." Then he let out a heavy sigh. "The countess and I married young. We both knew it wasn't a love match, but neither of us cared. She got a title and I got my heirs. We have a good partnership. And for many years that was enough. Why, I didn't even believe romantic love existed. I thought it was just drivel poets made up to sell books," he said with a dark laugh. "When I met Eloise, I simply wasn't prepared. It was immediate. And horribly trite. Like a damned lightning bolt. I had no idea I could ever feel this way."

Rafe swallowed hard against the nagging familiarity of his words, and the flash of gray eyes that accompanied it.

"You know, I'm nearly the same age Father was when he remarried." Gerard shook his head. "I never...I never tried to imagine what it must have been like for him. I was so *angry* after Mother died. And my sisters were shattered. I simply couldn't understand how he could go on living as if nothing had even happened. It seemed obscene to me."

"He did mourn her."

"I know," Gerard acknowledged. "I know he did. But his loss was different from ours. I didn't understand it then. I couldn't." He turned to Rafe. "I really hated you for the longest time, even though I knew it wasn't fair or logical. But I didn't care. You and your mother made him happy in a way the rest of us never could. He got to start a new life. A new career. A whole new adventure. While we were left behind."

"But you weren't a child anymore, Gerard. You could have visited. You could have made a damned *effort*." Rafe hated how upset he sounded. How wildly his heart now beat in his chest. This wasn't the reckoning he had imagined at all.

"I was thirteen when you were born. Not exactly a time when one is known to face life's difficulties head-on. As I recall, you ran away from home at about that age."

"Fair point," he grudgingly admitted. "But what about later?"

"By then I had a life of my own. As well as my own regrets," Gerard added softly and hung his head.

The movement suddenly brought to mind Father's funeral. It had been a bitterly cold day. Mama had insisted on attending and then sobbed hysterically the entire time. Rafe, then eighteen, was so busy tending to her that most of the ceremony passed by in a blur, and by the end he was hardly able to say a proper goodbye himself. After he had packed her into the carriage, he'd raced back to the gravesite. But there was someone else standing there. They had met only once, briefly, years before, but Rafe immediately recognized Gerard. He was on his knees before their father's headstone, his shoulders shaking violently from his tears. Rafe sensed he was witnessing something deeply personal. But just before he turned away, Gerard reached out and stroked their father's name carved in stone with surprising tenderness. That brief moment had stayed buried within him all this time. His only evidence that Gerard did have a heart after all.

"I can understand that," Rafe murmured.

Gerard's head jerked up in surprise, but his gaze was wary. "I don't suppose your understanding will extend to this situation as well?"

"No. Not yet, anyway," Rafe amended, and Gerard actually smiled a little. As they stared at each other, Rafe didn't feel the usual tightness in his chest and shoulders. As if his every move was being judged. His illustrious brother was infallible, just as he was—if not more.

"Back to the business at hand." Rafe cleared his throat. "Since no charges will be brought, why was I asked to come down here?"

"To discuss your proposal, of course. Your actions these last few months have been watched with a great deal of interest. The PM is particularly impressed with how you handled this situation. When I told him about your idea, he was elated."

Rafe couldn't hide his surprise. "But you were so against it before."

Gerard looked a little chastened. "I was at first. But I can see now that I should have listened to you."

Dedicating your life to supporting the actions of a corrupt government only does more harm.

At the time Rafe had thought Sylvia was overreacting, but he couldn't dismiss her words so easily anymore.

"I don't know." He shook his head. "I don't know if helping this government attain more power is something I can have on my conscience."

Gerard looked genuinely confused. "Your *conscience*? I thought this was what you wanted?"

"I did." Rafe shrugged. "But that was before I understood what I was asking for."

271

Gerard's gaze turned suspicious. "Does this have something to do with that woman you were found with?"

"Keep her out of this." The vehemence in his voice surprised him, and even Gerard raised an eyebrow at his sudden growl.

"You needn't worry. Bernard Hughes has already spoken on her behalf."

"What?" Rafe practically shouted, irrationally irate at the very idea of anyone else speaking for Sylvia, let alone the former lover who had so coldly deserted her. He had already taken steps to minimize her involvement as much as possible and had been prepared to do more, if needed.

"He's an MP," Gerard explained, unaware that Rafe already knew exactly who the cad was. "A member of the opposition, but he comes from a respectable family. Married one of the Holloway girls." Based on Gerard's impressed tone, they were aristocrats, or close enough. "I can't imagine why he is so taken with a self-righteous little harridan. She sounds absolutely exhausting. But I suppose we all have our quirks."

Rafe's breath caught. He had no right to feel so jealous that her former lover had come to her aid. Gerard watched him carefully, no doubt cataloging his reaction, but Rafe couldn't speak. Not about this.

"In any case," he continued, "you don't need to make a decision now. Talk to them. See what they have to say."

There was little harm in that.

"And if I decline their offer?"

"I know you probably don't give a damn, but you'll have my blessing." Gerard held out his hand. "Whatever you decide."

Rafe stared at his outstretched palm for a moment before taking it in his. "I plan to hold you to that," he grumbled.

Gerard cracked a smile. "I certainly hope so."

* * *

Sylvia exited a nondescript building in Bloomsbury, having just attended her first meeting of the newly formed Union for the Advancement of Women. When she had arrived earlier, she'd hesitated for a moment before signing the ledger as Sylvia Wilcox. But the young Indian woman manning the desk hadn't screamed in horror, hadn't called her a harlot or demanded she leave. She simply smiled and said, "Welcome."

Welcome.

Sylvia had forgotten how one little word could hold so much power.

She had then taken a seat in the back, intending to spend this first meeting silently observing. But as she listened to the other speakers, ideas began to form in her head. By the time the meeting ended, she had spoken up three times, to both offer her support to others' suggestions and to make her own. The moderator seemed impressed and sought Sylvia out afterward.

"Where have you been hiding all this time?" she had teased, after introducing herself as Mrs. Henrietta Wakefield, the union's vice president and a well-known advocate for social reform and universal suffrage.

Sylvia gave her a smile. "In plain sight. But I won't hide any longer."

Mrs. Wakefield nodded. "We need more women, especially those of us in the middle and upper classes, who are willing to make their voices heard. Our silence helps no one."

"I agree."

They talked for a few more minutes, and when Sylvia

admitted her past involvement with the Aurelias Society, Mrs. Wakefield didn't even blink.

"We have a few members who used to belong to that group, but they became disillusioned by the leadership."

"Yes, so did I."

"I hope you'll find us more welcoming. We try to operate as a collective and encourage people from all classes, creeds, and races to join. Here everyone has a vote and a voice. We encourage dissent and spirited debate on all issues brought forward, but any kind of abusive rhetoric is not tolerated."

Sylvia nodded gravely. "Of course. I understand."

"Excellent. I look forward to seeing you at our next meeting."

As Sylvia walked down the street, she buttoned her coat against the chill November air and tilted her face up to feel the fading afternoon sun on her face.

This was the closest she had come to feeling happy in weeks.

After their return to London, Georgiana had dutifully entered her mourning period for the viscount. Mrs. Crawford insisted they stay with her to provide support, and Georgiana and Sylvia decided it was time to reveal her true identity. Remarkably, the old woman took their duplicitousness in stride.

"An anarchist, you say?"

"That's how the papers put it, madam," Sylvia explained. "But they were more interested in creating salacious headlines than printing the truth. I advocated for universal suffrage and more aid for working women. And I don't believe the current government has any interest in meaningful reform."

"So you think the whole system should be blown to bits, then?"

"Only in a metaphorical sense," she pointed out. "I've never called for violence."

Mrs. Crawford eyed her for a moment. "You remind me of a woman I knew who was part of the Paris Commune. Only *she* demanded blood. Frequently. Different generations, I suppose." Then she shrugged. "Did you really go to all this trouble just to hide your opinions from me?"

Sylvia and Georgiana exchanged looks of surprise.

"Well, yes," Georgiana replied. "It was a terrible scandal, Aunt. Sylvia's name was dragged through the mud. The viscount never would have allowed her to work for you if he knew the truth, but it was still wrong of us to deceive you so."

"And I understand if you no longer wish to use my services," Sylvia added.

Mrs. Crawford blinked. "Why on earth would I do that? You're the best secretary I've ever had!" Then she turned to Georgiana. "I know it's uncouth to speak ill of the dead, and he was my dear sister's only child, but your husband was a brute and a fool. I never understood how you put up with him all these years. And with such grace. I only wish you girls had told me the truth much sooner. I would have kept your secret."

"Thank you, madam. I wish we had," Sylvia answered truthfully. "I've been slow to trust anyone these last few years. I've let fear rule so much of my life. And my choices. But not anymore."

"Good. I'm glad to hear it." Mrs. Crawford nodded. "Now, then, about chapter four..."

Sylvia had never been so grateful to work on those memoirs. They had kept her blessedly occupied these last weeks. For her mind wandered whenever it was given the slightest opportunity. Always to the same few memories. Always of Rafe: his wicked smile, teasing words, and the moments of unexpected tenderness she had found in his gaze.

Mrs. Crawford was still planning their trip to Egypt, and Sylvia had eagerly begun to count the days. She needed new memories to fill her mind. And space. Thousands and thousands of miles' worth. Then she might begin to forget.

Sylvia was so lost in thought that it was several minutes before she realized someone was calling after her. She turned around, expecting to see one of the people she had just met at the meeting, but then her heart plummeted to the pavement.

Bernard was practically hanging out the window of a very fine carriage. He looked mostly the same, apart from the addition of a patchy beard that did not suit him.

"What do you want?" she hissed as the carriage pulled alongside her.

He seemed taken aback by the cold greeting. "Come inside. I will take you home."

She shot him a scowl. "I suppose you've been spying on me again?"

Bernard grimaced, which meant it was true. "I need to speak with you. Sylvia, please," he murmured.

Sylvia let out a huff and looked around. For the moment the street was nearly empty. "Fine," she said tightly, praying none of the people from the meeting came around the corner as she was climbing in.

She didn't look at Bernard as he gave the driver Georgiana's address. But as she settled herself in the seat across from him, she could feel his gaze on her. It made her skin crawl.

"What a lovely carriage," she said as she glanced around before finally meeting his eyes. "I see you've put your wife's dowry to good use."

He at least had the decency to look guilty. Now that his

eyes were lowered, Sylvia allowed herself to look at him more closely. Bernard wasn't unattractive, but he had never been particularly handsome, either. His defining features were perfectly regular. Unassuming. With light brown hair and eyes to match. He wasn't short or tall, and his body was a bit soft around the middle. All in all, he was the kind of man she might have overlooked until he spoke. He had always seemed so confident, so determined, that it had been hard not to be flattered by the respect she thought she found in his gaze. But now Sylvia was struck by just how very average he was. And always had been.

Bernard folded his hands on his lap and looked up. "So then, how are you?"

Sylvia laughed. This situation was veering dangerously into the absurd. "I think that question is two years too late, don't you?"

Bernard bit his lip. An admirable show of contrition, but it was far from enough.

Nothing would be.

"I did want to see you. Afterward."

A convenient excuse. And no admission that he had even once considered coming to the jail for her. Why, he couldn't even bring himself to say the words.

"After my *arrest*, you mean?"

"Yes. That." Bernard wrinkled his nose in disapproval, as if she were being terribly vulgar by simply stating the facts. "But your brother wouldn't allow it."

"Lionel wasn't my keeper. Nothing was stopping you from taking the train to Hawthorne Cottage. Or writing to me."

Instead, he had let his silence speak for him. Loudly.

Bernard shifted in his seat. "No. I suppose there wasn't.

But you can understand why I couldn't be associated with you anymore. Not after all those stories in the papers."

Even after all this time, those words still stung, especially since they echoed Rafe's. "Stories *your father* had planted."

"You don't know that," he insisted. "Not for certain."

She scoffed and turned toward the window. It was useless trying to make him see.

You threatened some part of him. Some part that he won't let go of.

Rafe had certainly been right about that.

"And yet you couldn't leave me well enough alone, could you?"

Bernard was silent for a long moment. "I never intended to involve you in Wardale's schemes. But I was desperate. Jennie's family has certain expectations of me. Demands, really, and...and it got to be more than I could manage."

Sylvia gave him a withering look. "You're in debt. Just say it plainly."

He frowned. "I've *overspent*. I needed to take out a mortgage on the house, and Wardale's company offered twice what anyone else did. But he wanted a meeting first."

"Oh, Bernard." She sighed.

He shot her an aggravated look. "You don't know what parliament is like, Sylvia. It's impossible to get anything passed unless you have the right connections. Make the right deals. See the right people. It's nothing like we imagined. I *do* want to make a difference, but I couldn't until I had more influence."

"And Wardale provided that."

He nodded. "As long as I signed with his company. The effect was immediate."

"But it came at a price."

He met her eyes. "Yes. When I fell behind in payments, he threatened to take the house. To make my debt public. My wife's family would have been outraged. Please. I swear I never meant to hurt you. But I didn't have a choice."

She crossed her arms. "Shall I apply those words to now or two years ago?"

Bernard paled. "You can't know how often I've thought of you. I started so many letters."

"And yet you never sent a single one. Because you are a coward, Bernard. You were *always* a coward. You only talk of reform, but you will never do what it takes. Nothing that would sully your reputation or anger your family." She paused to catch her breath. She shouldn't let this man make her so upset anymore. "Why are you even *here*?"

"I want to help you, Sylvia. To make things right, like I should have."

She hated hearing her name on his lips. He had forfeited the privilege long ago.

"It's far too late for you to make things right, and I won't help you ease your conscience. You'll just have to learn to live with your regret. Like everyone else."

Sylvia glanced out the window. Thank God they had turned onto Georgiana's street. She couldn't take any more of this.

Bernard's mouth hung open for a moment. "Is that all you have to say? I thought we—"

"No," she snapped. "I also want you to *leave me alone*. That means no more spying. And I'll know if you do. I have connections of my own now."

He narrowed his eyes. "You mean that mysterious Crown agent you were mixed up with? Yes, I saw the report," he said in response to her look of surprise. "Rumor is it's Rafe Davies, of all people. You can't really be expecting any kind of commitment from a man like *that*."

Sylvia's hands tightened at his derisive tone. Even now she couldn't help feeling defensive on Rafe's behalf. "Who I associate with is none of your concern."

Bernard's expression darkened. "I wasn't going to mention this, but you should also know I made a point of speaking on your behalf so that no one questioned your loyalties once they learned who you really are. That could have made things very difficult for you."

Despite their parting, Sylvia believed Rafe when he said he would take care of everything. How dare Bernard take credit. How dare he act as if he had done her some kind of *favor*. Obviously, he had expected to find her in a vulnerable state. Grateful for whatever piddling assistance he planned to offer. But no matter what happened, she would never go to him again.

Sylvia had to take a few deep breaths before she could respond without screaming. "That was hardly a noble sacrifice on your part, considering it was *you* who brought me into that mess in the first place," she pointed out.

He cleared his throat. "I know you're incredibly angry with me, and you have every right to be. But that doesn't erase what we had together. I only wish you knew how much I still feel for you."

At her lowest point, Sylvia would have done anything to hear those words from him. Now it was all she could do to keep from retching. He hadn't listened to her at all.

The carriage came to a halt, and a footman promptly descended the front steps. Sylvia turned back to Bernard, who had begun to affect a pout. "I'm afraid that is your problem. Not mine. Good day."

Sylvia then held her head high as she climbed down from the carriage and entered the town house without a backward glance. It was as if a millstone had been removed from her neck. She wasn't just walking away from Bernard but from a part of her past she had held on to for far too long. And she had never felt so free.

CHAPTER TWENTY-THREE

After enduring a thoroughly dispiriting, mind-numbingly long meeting at Whitehall, Rafe made his way to his club, where Henry was waiting for him, having taken the train down from Glasgow. Rafe had no idea what had brought him to London, as Henry tended to avoid the city like the plague.

"I take it the meeting didn't go well?" Henry asked as soon as Rafe found him tucked away inconspicuously in a corner.

He sat down heavily in a club chair and immediately waved the waiter over to order a very large whiskey. "No, it did not." He then relayed that morning's activities, including the revelation that Wardale's blackmail scheme would be quietly swept under the rug.

"Well, that can't have been much of a surprise," Henry said with a shrug.

Rafe scowled at his nonchalance. "Actually, it was, rather."

Henry chuckled. "Sometimes I forget you're still an idealist."

"I most certainly am not."

Henry gave him a gentle smile. "You must be. Otherwise I can't imagine why you've continued to do this work for so long. I know you aren't a damn imperialist."

Rafe sighed and took a sip of whiskey. "About that...I resigned at the meeting."

Now Henry looked suitably shocked. "Really?"

"They accepted my proposal to form an elite group of agents, but not without my conditions. So I refused."

Among them was the appointment of an independent inspector to oversee the new department, as Rafe argued that more oversight was needed to prevent corruption. The panel disagreed. "I thought we could usher England into a new age of intelligence, but I can't live with myself if it only creates more opportunities for malfeasance."

"See? Idealism at work."

Rafe took another, larger sip. "Fine," he grumbled into his glass. "If that's what you want to call it."

"It sounds like the stalwart Miss Sparrow had quite an impact on you."

Rafe longed to disagree, but Henry had the right of it. Before he met her, he might have felt uncomfortable or even a tad guilty about his work, but he seriously doubted he would have taken such drastic actions. Instead, Rafe would have continued to delude himself into thinking that he alone could fix the Empire.

"Wilcox," he muttered.

Henry leaned forward. "What's that?"

"Her name. Her real name is Sylvia Wilcox. She lied about that. Among other things," he couldn't help adding.

Rafe had already related the broader points of Sylvia's deception back in Scotland, but not the extent of the pain and humiliation it had caused him. Both of which he was now determined to forget, with mixed results.

"Ah. I don't suppose she's related to Lionel Wilcox?"

Rafe shrugged. "I've no idea."

Henry glanced past Rafe. "Hmm. Well, I'm not sorry to hear you've left. You've given enough of your life to the Crown."

"I appreciate the support," Rafe said dryly.

"How did Gerard take the news?"

"He said that though he didn't agree with my decision, he respected it."

Henry raised an eyebrow. "Yet another surprise. I didn't think the old boy had it in him."

"We had words before the meeting. We both said some things that were...long overdue."

"I'm happy for you. Perhaps this will be the start of a more amicable relationship with the rest of the Davies clan."

"That's a little premature," Rafe said, though privately he harbored the same hope. Then he narrowed his eyes. "You're in rather high spirits today."

Henry came dangerously close to a smile. "Yes, I am. I suppose you're wondering what brought me to town."

"It did cross my mind."

"I've decided to go into business for myself. As a private investigator."

Rafe, who had been midsip, began coughing. "You're joking," he managed to choke out.

"Not in the least," Henry said brightly as he slapped Rafe on the back. "I've been toying with the idea for years, and now that Agatha's properly settled, it seems like the right time. Especially since she's informed me she's with child," he added with a slight grimace.

"Ah. You aren't interested in doting on a little niece or nephew?"

"I've no objection to children. I just don't want to *live* with them. Besides, I was getting tired of her constant hovering. Now she'll have an actual babe to care for."

"Will you be based in Glasgow, then?"

Henry shook his head. "I thought I'd return to London," he said hesitantly. "It seems like the best place to set up business. And I still have connections here."

"A sound idea."

Rafe wanted to ask if a certain recently widowed viscountess was involved in this decision. He hadn't missed the intensity that flashed in Henry's eyes when he saw Lady Arlington at the castle. But he sensed that such a question would quickly bring Henry's rare good mood to an end.

"I could use a partner, if you're interested."

Rafe sat back in his chair, considering the offer. It certainly would make good use of the skills he had spent years refining. But that would also mean staying in London. And the city had grown even more stifling since his return. To say nothing of his desire to avoid any chance meeting with Sylvia. The thought alone made his stomach turn with shame.

"I am honored you would even ask me, but I must decline."

Henry gave him an understanding nod. "You've never been able to stay in one place for very long, as I recall. I suppose I still hoped you were preparing to settle down."

Rafe shot him an irritated look. "That's all over with."

"Are you sure of that?"

"Considering Miss Wilcox thinks me nothing more than a *tool of destruction*, I'd say yes," he snapped. "Emphatically."

"What on earth brought that about?"

Rafe sighed. Did they *really* have to discuss this? But Henry gave him an expectant look. "She assumed I would leave my post after the business with Wardale was uncovered."

"Which you now have," Henry pointed out.

"It's too late," Rafe said tightly as his frustration mounted. "I am not the kind of man she wants. It would go against her principles."

He didn't add that watching her speak about her convictions had been electrifying. Even when she was tearing him to shreds.

"They didn't seem to stop her from associating with a useless aristocrat such as yourself in the first place," Henry teased.

"We had a connection," he murmured. "Or so I thought."

You make it sound like a choice.

His brother's words rang in his ears. They had sounded like sentimental drivel only hours ago. But now...now Rafe couldn't strike them from his mind.

"Thought or did?"

"I don't know," he said petulantly. "It was hard to distinguish the truth from the lies."

"Bit hypocritical to get upset over her lying to you. She certainly had no idea you were a spy, did she?"

"Well, obviously I couldn't tell her about *that*. At least not at first." Henry shot him a skeptical look. "I did intend to," Rafe protested, but he knew how he sounded. Like a self-righteous ass. Like a man looking for any available excuse to dismiss her.

"If you were actually considering a future with her, you absolutely could have. Rather owed it to her, in my opinion."

"It wouldn't have changed anything anyway," he groused. The waiter returned with his drink, and he took a long, considering sip. Despite his words, image after image of Sylvia flashed in his mind: her smiling, her laughing, her patiently listening to stories from his miserable school days. Could he really dismiss *all* of that, even when he had held the evidence in his very arms? Felt her writhe beneath him, felt her slick with desire for him, and swallowed her cries of pleasure with his own lips.

"You are far more than your work, you know."

Every muscle in Rafe's body tensed at Henry's gentle tone.

He uttered a dark laugh and stared into his glass. "And what is that? The disgraced second son of a scandalous earl? Yes, how irresistible."

"Is that truly how you see yourself?" Rafe refused to look at Henry. Refused to see the pity he knew he would find there. When he didn't answer, Henry sighed. "What will you do instead?"

Rafe tried to picture his future. The years seemed to stretch endlessly before him, devoid of color. Alone.

"I'm due to visit my mother in Monaco. Perhaps I'll spend some time at the tables in Monte Carlo and live up to this damned reputation I've created."

"You'll be bored in a week."

"I know," he muttered.

Henry then looked past Rafe again and narrowed his eyes. "Seeing as how according to you there is no hope of any future whatsoever with Miss *Wilcox*, I suppose you wouldn't have any interest in meeting the man who just might be her brother."

"What?"

Henry gestured behind him with his chin. "See that fellow over there? That's Lionel Wilcox. I met him during my ill-fated London Season. Bit of an ass, as I recall."

Rafe turned and immediately spotted the man in question, who shared Sylvia's coloring and a likeness about the eyes. He had to be her brother. Rafe's shoulders tensed as he watched

Wilcox share a laugh with another man. He seemed entirely at ease with himself, wearing a suit cut in the newest style.

He turned back to Henry, who was studying him like a hawk. "She said he turned her out of their childhood home because he needed the money."

"Well, I'd say that appears to be no longer a problem."

The club fees here were eye-watering.

Rafe was on his feet in an instant and headed directly toward the swine. He stopped just before the two men. "Are you Lionel Wilcox?"

The man raised an eyebrow at the blunt question. "Yes."

"Brother of Sylvia?"

Wilcox's expression darkened for a moment before he smiled at his companion. "Please, do excuse me." Then he rose and led Rafe a few steps away. "What is this about?" He lowered his voice and glanced around the room. "I gather she's your mistress. Have you got her with child? I'm not interested in raising any bastards, so you'll have to take care of it yourself." Rafe was rendered speechless by the man's assumptions about his *sister*. Even if that were the truth, how could he be so callous? Was this the treatment Sylvia had learned to expect from her own family? "Or is it money you're after? Well?" Lionel prompted at his continued silence. "Listen. I'm a reasonable man, but you'll need to explain."

"I don't want your *money*," Rafe said as a cold fury gripped him.

"Oh." The man seemed genuinely perplexed. "Then what do you want?"

Rafe's hands tightened into fists. "I want you to give Sylvia what is owed to her," he growled.

"I'm not sure I follow."

"The house."

Lionel had the audacity to laugh and shook his head. "I've no idea what she's told you, but you must not know my sister very well. She forfeited all rights to her inheritance when she tarnished the family reputation."

"Actually, I do. And it doesn't work that way. You had an agreement, which you reneged on. You claimed to be desperate for funds, but it doesn't appear that way to me."

Lionel's face fell, and any pretense of friendliness disappeared. "Who *are* you?"

Rafe ignored the question. "Someone needs to look out for her, as her own flesh and blood has failed miserably."

"Well, I don't give a damn—"

Rafe grabbed his shirtfront and pulled him closer. "Unfortunately, I do. Give her what she is owed."

Fear flashed in the man's eyes, but he still attempted to lift his chin. "And if I don't?"

Rafe leaned in even closer. "Whatever ruination you think she caused will be nothing compared to what I will do to you," he whispered calmly by his ear. "And with great pleasure." Then he unceremoniously released Lionel, who stumbled backward. "You have twenty-four hours."

Rafe then spun on his heel and walked over to Henry as every pair of eyes in the room followed him. "We should leave."

Henry nodded and stood up. "You always did know how to cause a scene."

Rafe picked up his glass and swallowed the remnants. "I learned from the best," he said with a wink.

CHAPTER TWENTY-FOUR

❧

"Sylvia, what do you think of this?" Georgiana asked from her corner of the library. "Installing a classroom on-site for the children of the garment workers. They would have their own teachers and two meals a day."

Sylvia glanced up from her notebook. "It's marvelous. But can the business afford it?"

Georgiana *tsk*ed. "It can if the board takes a comparatively minor cut in profit shares. And as I now own a majority, that won't be an issue." Her eyes glinted with purpose.

Sylvia smiled at her friend's zeal for progress. Though Georgiana was publicly adhering to the strictest rituals of mourning, in private she had blossomed. Away from the prying eyes of society, she was even more relaxed than she had been in Scotland and was rarely without a smile on her face. She also had ambitious plans for the garment factories that had once been part of her dowry, which she now owned outright.

Between watching Georgiana come into her own and speaking her mind to Bernard yesterday, Sylvia was beginning to feel more optimistic about the future. She might have even been happy, if Rafe still wasn't invading her thoughts on a regular basis.

Someone lightly scratched at the door before entering the room. It was Mossdown, Georgiana's faithful butler, who had left her father's house when she married.

"My lady, Mrs. Fernsby is here to pay her respects. Shall I tell her you are at home?"

As a widow still in deep mourning, Georgiana was supposed to remain housebound and receive visits only from intimate family members. But after nearly a month, she was starved for company.

"Aunt Violet wouldn't exactly approve, but she's still out with Mrs. Barnes. Please, show her in." Once Mossdown left, Georgiana tossed her pen down and moved to the sofa. "Bertha Fernsby *always* had the best gossip. How do I look?"

"Like a very respectable widow."

Georgiana smoothed the skirt of her black cashmere gown. "Excellent."

A few moments later, Mrs. Fernsby breezed into the room. "Georgiana, darling!" she cried out and moved to embrace her. "Oh, I've been so worried for you."

"I'm perfectly well, Bertha. All things considered."

"Yes, of course. Of course. I was *so* sorry to hear about Albert, though. Poor man. Such a dear."

Sylvia covered her snort with a cough and turned back to her work, but not before Georgiana cast her an arch glance over Bertha's shoulder.

The women sat down on the sofa, and Georgiana rang for tea. She also introduced Sylvia as her aunt's secretary. Bertha gave her a dismissive nod before turning back to Georgiana.

As the two ladies began catching up, Sylvia returned to her work. She was making excellent progress on the sample chapters and planned to spend the evening typing up this latest batch of notes. But her pen came to an abrupt halt at the mention of the name "Wilcox."

"Do you know the family?" Bertha asked casually.

Georgiana paused to take a sip of tea and likely collect her thoughts. "Yes."

"There was some sort of scandal there. I can't remember the particulars." Bertha frowned as she tried to recall the details of Sylvia's ruination, but Georgiana remained silent. "Well, it doesn't matter," she said with an airy wave of her hand. "As I was saying, my dear Harold was at his club yesterday afternoon when all of a sudden a *man* came charging up to Lionel Wilcox. They had some words, and then he grabbed Mr. Wilcox by his shirt and nearly lifted him off the ground. Right there! In front of everyone!"

Sylvia's heart began to race, and she leaned forward, now desperate to catch every word.

"Who was he?" Georgiana asked with studied disinterest.

Bertha's eyes practically glowed. She was truly in her element. "That's the most intriguing part. Harold *swore* it was Rafe Davies. You know, the Earl of Fairfield's wastrel brother?"

Georgiana set down her teacup and clasped her hands, but her gaze remained cool, controlled. "Yes. I've just met him. We were both guests at Castle Blackwood."

Bertha nearly squirmed with delight at this news. "Really? What's he like? I've heard such stories—" She then shot a glance at Sylvia and tried to compose herself.

"I found him to be a perfect gentleman," Georgiana said

in the lofty tone of a powerful society matron. "He was the picture of politeness to both my aunt and myself. I can't imagine what he would want with Mr. Wilcox."

"Quite right." Bertha nodded furiously in an attempt to align herself with Georgiana. "I can't imagine either. Harold hadn't a clue. He doesn't really know Mr. Wilcox. I'm not even sure how that man even became a member."

Georgiana didn't deign to answer. She merely sipped her tea. But she had made her point. Bertha, now positively desperate to regain her favor, changed the subject.

Sylvia tried to return her attention to her notes, but the words swam before her.

Rafe had confronted her brother. Publicly. She couldn't think of any reason why he would do such a thing and draw such attention to himself if not for her.

Bertha stayed for a few more agonizing minutes, but as soon as the door shut behind her, Georgiana rushed over to Sylvia.

"Tell me you heard that."

Sylvia couldn't look up from her desk. "Every word."

"Did you tell him about Lionel?"

She managed a nod.

"Oh, Sylvia. Can't you see what this means?"

Sylvia bit her lip, still unable to give voice to her greatest wish. But for the first time in weeks, a dangerous hope sparked in her chest, and she simply didn't have the will to snuff it out.

When she finally looked up, her friend's eyes were filled with concern. "Yes," she answered softly as her throat tightened. "Yes."

Georgiana wanted to review everything Bertha had

mentioned, but Sylvia shook her head. It was too much, too soon. Everything felt so fragile at the moment.

"You still doubt his intentions, even now?" Georgiana asked. Though she understood why Sylvia had been both hurt and disappointed by Rafe's decision to continue to work for the Crown, she had also made no secret of her desire to see them reconciled.

"I have to."

"Then I'll hope for the both of us." Georgiana reached out and grasped her hand. "You deserve someone who will fight for you."

Sylvia turned away as her longing raged against her desire for self-protection and threatened to overwhelm her entirely. But it came to a head later that evening when a large envelope arrived for her with the last post of the day.

Sylvia's hands began to tremble as she opened it, recalling the last time she had received a mysterious letter. But when she removed the sheaf of papers inside, her apprehensions were replaced by shock. Complete, utter shock. Sylvia brought a hand to her mouth as she stared at the documents, while Georgiana quickly grew impatient.

"Well? What is it?"

Sylvia opened and closed her mouth a few times before she was able to answer. "It's the deed to Hawthorne Cottage."

Georgiana came over to see for herself. "Oh my goodness."

"This...this can't be right," she said weakly as she stared at the documents before her. There was no note, but the intent was clear. Under "Owner" was her full legal name: Sylvia Marie Wilcox.

"This must have been what Mr. Davies was arguing with your brother about. Sylvia?"

But she couldn't speak. She could only shake her head.
Sylvia could finally go home.

* * *

Rafe rolled over onto his side and squinted against the brilliant
light that had just flooded his bedroom. "Dammit, Tully! Close
the curtains. It's barely morning."

The valet paid him no mind as he tied the drapes back.
"Actually, it's well near one o'clock. *Sir*."

Rafe grumbled and dragged the pillow over his head. It had
been a week since he'd publicly threatened Lionel Wilcox. He
had gone out every night since, living up to the reputation he
had so meticulously crafted over the years. Tully hadn't even
tried to hide his disapproval. Rafe supposed that's what he got
for hiring an impertinent ex-seaman.

"And I wouldn't have disturbed you," Tully added cavalierly,
"except you have a visitor."

Rafe pulled the pillow away and cracked one eye open.
"Who the devil is it?"

"Captain Harris. I tried to tell him you were indisposed,
but he wouldn't hear of it. Told me to come and get you
anyway."

Rafe pushed up on his elbows. "And you listened to him?"

"Of course." Tully looked at him like he was mad, which
wasn't too far off at the moment. "The man's a national
hero!"

Rafe did not have the energy to argue with the both of them.
Not when his head felt like the site of a mining operation.
"Fine. Go and tell him I'll be ready in ten minutes," he said
as he sat up. Tully glanced at him and mumbled something

as he left the room that sounded an awful lot like *It'll take longer than that.* "And make me one of those vile drinks you claim cure hangovers," Rafe called after him. Tully grumbled in response.

Rafe dragged a hand over his face. Last night he had gotten extremely drunk at his club and then had the excellent idea to visit one of the city's most exclusive brothels. He never visited such establishments, but Rafe reasoned that if he engaged someone's services, then he most *definitely* couldn't be in love with Sylvia anymore. Instead, he'd sat in the corner of the elegant parlor nursing brandy after brandy while the increasingly irritated madam brought him every woman in the entire house. But he dismissed each one. The dark-haired ones reminded him too much of Sylvia, and the rest didn't interest him in the slightest. Finally, when dawn had just begun to show her face, Rafe gave the ladies all a generous tip and left.

He walked over to the washstand and looked in the mirror. Tully was right. It would take a hell of a lot longer than ten minutes before he was anything close to presentable. Luckily, it was only Henry. Rafe splashed water on his face and did his best to clean himself up. Then he changed into a fresh shirt and trousers that hadn't been slept in. His eyes were still rimmed with red, and his heavy stubble would remain until Tully could give him a proper shave, but it would have to do.

Rafe found Henry in the parlor comfortably seated in his favorite chair by the fire with a pot of tea and a tray laden with Tully's freshly baked buns.

"Well, don't you look cozy?"

"Hard not to in here. I've never seen a man own so many decorative pillows."

Rafe rolled his eyes. "I'm a bachelor, Henry. Not a

barbarian," he said, collapsing in the chair across from him. "Let me guess. You sleep on a cramped cot that can barely fit you with a scratchy blanket and a single flat pillow."

Henry's lips quirked. "Two, actually."

Rafe narrowed his eyes. "And is all that self-denial working?"

"Well, now you're just being mean." Henry finally looked up from the opened folder that had so engrossed him and raised an eyebrow at his appearance. "Late night?"

Rafe glanced away. "I went to the club."

"That's interesting," Henry began as he set down the folder, "because Tully said you came back reeking of cheap perfume."

Damn his meddling valet. And damn Madam Fleur's potent potpourri mix.

"Then I stopped at Madam Fleur's." Rafe sighed. "Don't give me that look."

Henry raised his hands. "I didn't take you for that sort of fellow."

"What, a live one?" Rafe's half-hearted attempt at a joke completely failed as hurt flashed across Henry's face. "Sorry, I didn't mean that. It's just that you've come at a terrible time."

Henry leaned over and placed a hand on his shoulder. "Those are the times when you need friends the most. You showed me that."

Rafe's throat tightened. "Thank you."

"Here, have a bun," Henry prompted. "They're extraordinary. Tully refuses to give up the recipe."

Rafe took one from the proffered plate and couldn't hold back his smile. "We're all allowed a few secrets."

"Easy for you to say when you have access to a never-ending supply."

"Actually, Tully only makes them when the spirit moves him."

And that always seemed to coincide with times when Rafe was feeling down or had to do something difficult. Perhaps his surly valet deserved a raise.

Henry gave a thoughtful nod as he took another bun for himself. They both ate in satisfied silence for a few moments.

"Now, then," Rafe prompted. "I know you didn't just come here to have my valet harangue me and share a pot of tea."

Henry set down his half-eaten bun. "No. I didn't." He then handed Rafe the folder he had been reading. "That is everything I could find on your Sylvia Wilcox."

Rafe's eyes widened. "I didn't ask you to do that," he snapped. "And she isn't *my* anything." But he took it without another word and began leafing through the papers. He squinted and drew a page closer. He needed to find his damned glasses. "How on earth did you manage to get her university exam scores?"

"Took the train up to Oxford. Not bad for my first case, eh? Do you know, if Oxford actually bothered to bestow their female students with degrees, she would have gotten a first in the English tripos? A rather impressive woman. But I suppose that's not entirely surprising, given her parents."

Rafe looked up from the documents. "What do you mean?"

"Her father, Richard Wilcox, was an economist and moral philosopher. Rather well known in his day. Of course, he published so rarely after his wife died that whispers grew that she was the real brains behind him."

"Sylvia mentioned her once. Something about how she had always wanted to go to university."

"Yes, she was the daughter of a wealthy Bristol merchant. He hired a young man just down from Oxford to tutor her." He then arched a brow.

"The aforementioned Richard Wilcox," Rafe guessed.

"Correct. They married and she bore him a son shortly afterward. Never did make it to university."

Henry didn't need to say the rest. The implication was clear. Apparently the study of morality stopped at his own behavior.

"Well, perhaps she was happy," Rafe said weakly. "Perhaps...that was what she wanted."

"A possibility, certainly, or *perhaps* she had regrets of her own. So she encouraged her daughter from a young age to prioritize her education. To make bolder choices. Choices that had been lost to her."

Rafe looked back at the documents before him. "You can't possibly know all that from this."

Henry chuckled. "If only. No, I spoke to some of Professor Wilcox's old colleagues at Oxford. And the wife of one of his oldest friends who lives in a neighboring village, a Mrs. DeLacey. She had quite a lot to say about the family." Rafe found himself leaning forward, rapt. "Nothing good about the son, or old Wilcox himself. But she adored the late Mrs. Wilcox and said Sylvia took her mother's death very hard."

"After Sylvia came back from London, there were some who shunned her, but others approved of the way she took on the household management and cared for her father until he died, especially given Lionel's absence and the rumors of money troubles. Mrs. DeLacey expressed surprise when she learned the house had been let after Richard Wilcox passed. She had assumed Sylvia would continue to live there."

Rafe had discovered that Lionel had been letting it to a retired bachelor professor for a handsome price these last few months.

"Well, at least justice has been done in that case," Rafe muttered.

Henry watched him for a long moment. "Will you really let that be the end of it? One anonymous grand gesture?"

"It was what she was owed."

"I think you owe her something as well. The truth."

"She already knows I was a spy," Rafe grumbled.

"I'm referring to the fact that you've spent the last few weeks pining for this woman, and she has absolutely no idea."

"For God's sake," Rafe said tartly. "I do not *pine*."

Henry did not do a very good job of suppressing a smile. "Well, you had me fooled."

Rafe was silent for a long moment. Obviously, he couldn't go on like this, for then Tully would leave him, and he would truly be lost. But the thought of facing Sylvia again filled him with an unfamiliar kind of longing. Both dreadful and desired.

"I don't...I don't know how to go about it."

"Why, you have any number of options before you," Henry marveled, ignoring his true meaning. "You can take a carriage, the underground, or even walk yourself on over to Lady Arlington's." Even in his state, Rafe didn't miss the slight waver in the captain's voice when he spoke the viscountess's name. "It shouldn't take that long from here," he continued. "And it's rather lovely out."

Now it was Rafe who failed to suppress the smile tugging at his lips. "I liked you better when you were a horrid grump."

"So did I." Henry sighed a little. "But we can't both of us be misanthropes. It throws off our dynamic."

Rafe turned back to the folder. Henry had found more newspaper clippings detailing Sylvia's arrest. Each one was more awful than the last. "They really went after her, didn't they?"

Henry hummed his agreement. "I can't imagine the humiliation she must have suffered. None of it was anywhere close to the truth, you know."

"Yes," Rafe agreed. "It appears that Bernard Hughes's family invested a great deal of time and money in ruining a young lady from Oxfordshire."

"They most certainly did. For the young lady from Oxfordshire was spouting a lot of dangerous ideas to their son."

"And yet he gave her up so easily. So readily."

Henry shrugged. "Not everyone wants to fight. Most of us choose to lumber along with the status quo, keeping our heads down, never questioning anything. Not her though."

It was an admirable quality, but Rafe's shoulders still tensed. "I know. But I'm the man women use for a little distraction. I'm not the one they pour their hearts out to...or even *give* them to."

"That's just for show," Henry said. "It was part of your cover."

"Perhaps. At first. But at some point it got away from me. I spent so much time being *him* that I stopped being myself. Then I met Sylvia, who saw past all this." He waved a hand at his face. "And liked it. Or so I thought. I hoped," he added softly.

"Don't second-guess yourself," Henry said. "I know you had a quarrel in Scotland, but you have incredible instincts. Always have. Listen to them. Listen to what your heart is telling you."

Rafe closed his eyes. The doubts that had been his constant companion these last weeks still echoed in his head, telling him that she was disgusted by him, that he had disappointed her unforgivably, that he deserved to be alone. But gradually each one fell silent. Until only one voice was left.

Go.

Go to her.

Say what's in your heart. Just this once.

Rafe let the voice grow louder until it echoed just as strongly as the others had. When he finally opened his eyes, Henry was looking at him expectantly.

"Well?"

"You'd better go. I've somewhere to be, and I'm in desperate need of a shave."

Henry grinned. "That's just what I wanted to hear."

CHAPTER TWENTY-FIVE

❧

For the first time in months, Sylvia woke up in her old room. She had come to Hawthorne Cottage yesterday on Georgiana's orders after the sample chapters for Mrs. Crawford's memoirs had been sent off to the publisher.

"Take some time for yourself," the viscountess had suggested.

Sylvia tried to protest, but even Mrs. Crawford insisted. "We'll be waiting for you whenever you decide to return, my dear."

None of them needed to voice the obvious: that she might decide not to return at all. The income generated from her small inheritance was just enough for Hawthorne Cottage's up-keep if Sylvia economized, which wouldn't be an issue. That had been her plan anyway until Lionel had ripped it away from her. But now so many things had changed.

Sylvia had changed.

Though working for Mrs. Crawford had its challenges, she no longer felt the need to stay hidden away for the rest of her life. And without the constant threat of exposure hanging over her, she was learning how to be Sylvia Wilcox again.

After washing and dressing, she headed downstairs to the

kitchen, where Mrs. Thomasin, their old cook, was just pulling a fresh tray of golden biscuits out of the oven.

"Good morning, Miss Sylvia," she said with her usual cheerfulness.

For the last few months Lionel had let Hawthorne Cottage to a retired professor who had absolutely no appreciation for Mrs. Thomasin's talents in the kitchen and insisted on very bland food. When she learned that Sylvia was returning, she had pulled out all the stops and cooked a feast for her last night.

"Those smell wonderful, Mrs. Thomasin." Sylvia moved to help, but the cook shooed her away.

"I remembered how much you loved them," she said with a broad smile. "Now go sit yourself down in the dining room. I'll bring them right in."

Sylvia did as she was told and entered the sun-filled room. She was used to eating by herself here. Father had taken most of his meals in his study until he was too ill to leave his bedroom, and Lionel had rarely bothered to visit. But when her mother was alive, they always ate together. Sylvia took her usual seat and stared at the empty chair at the foot of the table, where Mama had once sat.

You've done well for yourself, my sparrow. But you still have miles to go.

Just as her eyes began to prickle, Mrs. Thomasin bustled into the room carrying a tray bearing the fruits of her morning's labors, along with a fresh pot of tea, butter, and the honeypot. Sylvia immediately began taking plates off the tray.

The cook gave her an arch look, but Sylvia flashed her a smile. "You must let me help a little, Mrs. Thomasin. I'm a working woman, you know."

Mrs. Thomasin clucked her tongue. "Pardon my impertinence, but it is a disgrace what your brother did. Turning you out of your home just so he could earn a little rent money. The whole village was horrified. And after all you did for your poor father." She shook her head. "It wasn't right. Thank the good Lord he came to his senses."

Sylvia's hand tensed on the handle of the teapot. "Yes. Thanks indeed."

The hope that had briefly filled her last week had waned a little more as each day passed and Rafe didn't appear. The role he had played in facilitating Lionel's abrupt change of heart had ended. It seemed that Hawthorne Cottage was to be a parting gift, not a sign of things to come. Sylvia still planned to thank him for his generosity — it would be unthinkable not to — but it would have to be through the post. Not in person.

She thought she had already experienced the depths of her disappointment after they parted in Scotland, but this was much worse because it had followed on the heels of such hope. Mrs. Thomasin hurried back into the kitchen, already planning an elaborate lunch Sylvia would barely touch. She let out a sigh and turned toward the window that looked out onto the back garden. The remnants of an early-morning frost framed the panes. The leaves had long turned shades of brilliant red and gold. Now most had fallen away. She certainly could not spend winter here, alone with her thoughts and Mrs. Thomasin's hearty cooking. No, she would tell Mrs. Crawford that she still wished to stay on and take their trip. Perhaps Georgiana would come with them now. That lifted her spirits slightly. Then she could decide what to do with Hawthorne Cottage. It was a house meant for a family, after all. Not an aging spinster.

Her chest ached at the thought. She had been honest with

Rafe before. Sylvia had never dreamed of becoming someone's wife. Never imagined having a gaggle of children to care for. Once she knew what her mother had sacrificed, it seemed important to take advantage of all the opportunities that had been closed to her. And for years her studies and her writing and her work had been enough. More than enough. But as Sylvia sat at a table built to accommodate eight, sipping her tea and eating her crumbling biscuit, the loneliness that had once been only a whisper in her heart grew louder and louder until it seemed to fill every corner and crevice of the room.

Sylvia abruptly stood up, splashing tea onto her mother's favorite tablecloth and her lap. She let out a curse, reached for a small pitcher of water, and began dabbing furiously at the stain. Mrs. Thomasin must have heard her because she rushed into the dining room.

"I'm afraid I upset the tea, Mrs. Thomasin. But I think I've saved the tablecloth," Sylvia explained as she looked up.

But the cook didn't seem to notice. "I was just outside speaking to Mr. Meyer next door, and he says there's a man in the village looking for you."

Sylvia stilled her hand. "What?"

Mrs. Thomasin came closer, her brown eyes wide with interest. "Mr. Meyer went to the post office to see if a package from his sister in Portsmouth had arrived, and there was a fancy gentleman down from London asking which way to Hawthorne Cottage. Mr. Meyer assumed the fellow was looking for the old tenant and told him the man was gone. But the gentleman said he had come to see you."

Sylvia straightened. "Oh."

"And you *know* how suspicious Mr. Meyer can be when it comes to strangers, so he came straight here rather than help the gentleman find the place. In case you weren't wanting to see him," she added.

"Yes. Of course. How thoughtful," Sylvia murmured. She dropped the damp napkin she had been twisting into a ball.

You don't know it's him.

It could be anyone.

But as she walked to the front parlor and looked out the picture window, a figure was already coming up the short drive. One who moved with an unmistakable air of grace and confidence.

Sylvia pressed her palms against her stomach to calm herself, then looked down. In her rush to save the tablecloth, she had forgotten about her dress, which now boasted a rather large tea stain across the front. She muttered another curse and immediately ducked out of view. He would be here in a matter of moments.

"Mrs. Thomasin?" Sylvia cried out as she raced toward the kitchen.

The cook met her at the door. "Is he here?" Sylvia nodded, still barely able to believe it herself. "You know him, then?"

"Yes, from London."

"And do you want to see him?"

Sylvia hesitated before nodding again.

Mrs. Thomasin's gaze grew suspicious as she began to ask something else—something Sylvia probably didn't want to answer—but then she noticed the stain. "Goodness! What happened to your dress?" Just as Sylvia opened her mouth, a loud knock echoed through the house, and they exchanged looks of terror. "I'll answer it. You go get changed."

Sylvia shook her head. "There isn't time."

Mrs. Thomasin arched one blond brow. "If this man came on the early train all the way from London, I think he can wait a few more minutes while you put on a clean gown. I'll put him in the parlor with some biscuits. He won't even notice the time."

Rafe knocked again, louder, and Sylvia was spurred into motion.

"Thank you, Mrs. Thomasin!" she called out as she headed up the back staircase to her room.

"Don't thank me just yet, my dear. Not until we learn what he's come for."

* * *

Rafe's fist had been poised to knock on the door of Hawthorne Cottage for a third time when it swung open and revealed a pleasingly plump blond woman around middle age. Based on the faint smear of flour on her left cheek, Rafe guessed she was Mrs. Thomasin, the cook the postman had told him about. If he had any hope of crossing the threshold, he needed to win her over.

"Good morning," he said, flashing her his widest smile. "I'm Mr. Davies. I've come to see Miss Wilcox. Is she in?"

The cook slowly eyed him up and down, not looking even a little charmed. "You're the fellow from London?"

"Yes," Rafe answered, resisting the urge to tug on his collar. "I see my reputation has preceded me?"

The cook snorted. "You could say that. Now, before I let you in, would you mind telling me what business you have with the lady of the house?"

It had been years since Rafe lived in a household that

employed a full-time cook, but this seemed rather overfamiliar. Then again, perhaps things were different in the country...

He cleared his throat. "Ah, it's a personal call. I am a friend of Miss Wilcox."

The cook raised an eyebrow, imperious as a duchess. "A *friend*, is it?"

Rafe blinked. "Yes." Mrs. Thomasin said nothing in return, and in the face of the woman's commanding stare, Rafe did something unforgivably stupid. He broke. "But I hope to be more," he sputtered.

After another moment of excruciating silence, the woman's stern expression dissolved into a knowing smile. "All right, then. Come in, Mr. Davies, 'the friend who would like to be more,'" she teased. "Miss Sylvia will be down shortly. You're to wait in the parlor for her."

Rafe paused in the doorway for a moment. He had just been interrogated. By a country cook. And it had *worked*. While he pondered this, he took in his surroundings. Hawthorne Cottage was a handsome two-story redbrick home with a thatched roof and loads of ivy. The kind of house one read about in children's books. A similar aesthetic was on display inside. The furniture, while not new, was well kept and well loved. Everywhere he looked were soft velvet and brocade coverings in rich jewel tones, freshly polished wood, tastefully patterned draperies, and plenty of small pillows. Rafe heartily approved.

"What a lovely home," he called out to Mrs. Thomasin.

"Isn't it? My late mistress had a wonderful eye for decorating. She made this place what it is."

Rafe followed her into the sun-filled parlor, where a fire burned in the hearth. "You've worked for the family for a long time, then?"

"Since Miss Sylvia was born," Mrs. Thomasin said proudly as she showed him to an overstuffed pale pink sofa. "I was a scullery maid in the house Mrs. Wilcox grew up in until I came here to work as the cook. So kind and intelligent. I've never met a lady like her, not before nor since. But Miss Sylvia inherited many of her best qualities."

So that explained her behavior. She was a fiercely loyal servant. Rafe had come here today with no expectations, only hope, but he already felt better just knowing Sylvia had someone like Mrs. Thomasin in her life.

"She sounded like a gifted woman. I'm sorry I won't get the chance to meet her myself."

That answer seemed to please Mrs. Thomasin. She took his coat, hat, and gloves, then excused herself to fetch some tea. No doubt she would continue her inquisition upon her return. And Rafe would gladly endure it if it meant seeing Sylvia. Even if all she did was call him a coward and throw him out. He would suffer any number of insults and humiliations just to bask in her presence once again, however briefly.

When he had arrived at Lady Arlington's town house yesterday afternoon, the viscountess had conducted an interrogation of her own before finally admitting that Sylvia wasn't in London at all, but had gone to the cottage that morning.

"I must protect her, you see," Lady Georgiana explained once she revealed the truth. By then it was too late to catch the last train north. "And I needed to know what your intentions were first."

Rafe had been both highly irritated and reluctantly impressed. "I won't hurt her again. You have my word."

The viscountess shook her head. "You'll have to prove it.

But that will take years. Years I hope we will spend together, as friends," she added with a sly smile.

Rafe had been so overjoyed to win even her tacit approval that he leaped to his feet and grabbed her hands. "Then you think she'll have me?"

The viscountess's eyes widened at his desperate tone. "I won't speak for her, Mr. Davies," she said gently. "And given her past disappointment, she is already slow to trust. But you should go to her. Make your case. That is all I can say."

And that was enough for Rafe.

The sound of the door opening roused him from his thoughts, but it was only Mrs. Thomasin returning with the tea tray.

"She'll be down in a moment, Mr. Davies." The cook then gave him a conspiratorial wink before she swept out of the room. Rafe had passed the inquisition after all.

As he moved to pour a cup of tea, he heard urgent whispering coming from the other side of the door. He immediately set the pot down and strained to listen. It had to be Sylvia talking to Mrs. Thomasin, but he couldn't make out any of the words. Rafe was seconds away from pressing his ear to the door when it swung open and Sylvia marched in. She was wearing a fetching day gown in buttercup yellow. As Rafe rose, his gaze immediately slid down her form. Gone were the serviceable tweed skirts, plain blouses, and navy ties—though he rather liked those. But then, here at Hawthorne Cottage she was the lady of the house, not a secretary. And she certainly dressed the part.

It wasn't until Sylvia cleared her throat that Rafe realized his gaze had lingered on her exposed décolletage.

He immediately looked up and met her eyes. "You look beautiful," he blurted out.

Well, then. So much for subtlety.

Sylvia glanced away as a blush colored her cheeks. "Thank you," she murmured as she sat down in a chair across from him.

Rafe followed suit and immediately began tapping his foot. Christ. His nerves were at it again. He could stare down the barrel of a gun without issue but sitting in her eyeline had him thoroughly rattled.

Because there is more at risk here.

"Thank you for seeing me," he began as Sylvia moved to pour tea for them both. "I know you hardly expected to find *me* on your doorstep this morning."

Sylvia looked up from the teacups, and that familiar steel gaze shot through him like hot iron. "Correct. Would you be so kind as to enlighten me to the purpose of your visit?"

Rafe's throat suddenly felt as dry as the Sahara, while his tongue was too big for his mouth. "I—I wanted to see you."

Good God, what had happened to him?

Sylvia raised an eyebrow at the silence that followed. "I seem to remember you being much more charming in Scotland."

He huffed a laugh. "Yes, well, that was because I was not being myself. Entirely."

Sylvia set down the teapot and sat back in her chair. "What do you mean?"

Her gaze was one of calm assessment, as if she were trying to decide which path to take or bouquet to buy. It wasn't exactly encouraging.

Rafe took a deep breath. He had never tried to explain himself to anyone before. It felt like he was standing before her stripped naked. And not in a pleasant way. "Years ago I created a public version of myself—a sort of carefree reprobate. So no one would ever suspect what I was really up to."

Sylvia's face remained perfectly blank. "The spying?"

Rafe nodded and dragged a hand through his hair. This was so much harder than he had ever suspected. He wanted to throttle Henry for suggesting otherwise. "I emphasized certain traits and played up certain behaviors depending on the company I was in."

Sylvia gave a solemn nod and steepled her fingers. "So, when you're around other aristocrats, you act like a pompous twat. Have I got that right?"

Rafe smiled. "The Honorable Rafe Davies would object to that description, but yes."

Sylvia briefly pressed her lips into a firm line. "Doesn't that get tiring?"

He sighed with relief. She understood. "I didn't realize just how sick of it I was until I...until I met you."

Surprise flashed in her eyes. Then she frowned. "But you were still acting a part when we met. Playing this role you created."

Rafe's smile fell, and he fiddled with the handle of his teacup for a moment, unable to bear the disappointment in her gaze. "I told you before. Everything between us was real."

Sylvia shook her head slightly. "But how can I know that? And how can I know what's real now?"

He could hear the fear behind her words. "Well, I suppose you can't. Not entirely anyway." Rafe leaned forward, wishing so desperately to push the damned tea tray out of the way and hold her, but he needed to go slowly. At her speed. "You'll just have to take a leap of faith. The same as me."

She turned away again. "And then what? You said yourself that an association with me could threaten your *career*."

The betrayal in her voice tore at his heart. "I was embarrassed and hurt to learn you had kept so much from me, and I handled it badly. For that I will always be sorry." She glanced back at him, and seeing the moisture in her eyes was agony. "Please. Let me show you who I can be."

"I don't understand. This doesn't change my past," she said thickly. "And you were right. I *am* a threat to your career—"

To hell with decorum. Rafe knelt at her feet. He grasped her trembling hands in his. "Sylvia, I resigned last week. I should have listened to you back in Scotland. I tried to ensure justice was served, but I was overruled. They didn't care about investigating the extent of the blackmail or any resultant corruption. They only wanted to protect themselves. And I was helping them do it."

"So, you left?"

Rafe nodded, praying he hadn't imagined the hope in her voice. "I should have done it years ago, but I didn't think I was enough on my own."

Sylvia's brow furrowed. "How could you have ever thought that?"

Rafe reached out and tucked a loose curl behind her ear. "It was hard not to at times. People have been looking down on me my entire life, so I decided to use it. I found I enjoyed having another side of myself. Of subverting peoples' expectations right in front of their eyes. And, frankly, I was damned good at it. I fooled most of them. Except you."

Sylvia's eyelids fluttered closed, and she leaned into his touch. "Oh, Rafe."

"But I can't go back to being that man now, even if I wanted to. Any chance of that was gone when we met. Because knowing you has changed me. If nothing else, I wanted you to know that. I wanted you to know how powerful you are."

Sylvia stared at him in stunned silence. He took an unsteady breath, as his heart practically beat out of his chest. "I think— I think I've been falling in love with you since that first afternoon at the castle, when you looked at me with barely veiled contempt."

Her eyes widened. "No, I didn't!"

"It's all right." He chuckled. "I deserved it."

Sylvia turned her head and pressed a kiss to his palm. Then she met his gaze. "You were the handsomest man I had ever seen. And I thought for certain I knew exactly who you were and what you were after. But I was so wrong. I don't think I've ever met anyone as surprising as you."

Rafe felt his cheeks heat at her kind words. "You saw me for who I really was," he explained. "You were the only person who ever wanted to. And I shouldn't have dismissed you so readily in Scotland. Especially after what you went through with Brodie."

Sylvia shook her head. "You knew I had Georgiana. I wasn't alone. And I said some ugly things too. You were in a difficult position because of your brother and your history with your family, but I didn't try to understand you, either."

It felt as though Rafe's heart was breaking from happiness. "You are much too generous, my little bird."

Sylvia inhaled softly as he continued to stroke her cheek. "Says the man who bought me a house."

Rafe's hand stilled. "Who told you that?"

The corner of her mouth tugged up. "You aren't the only one who can do a bit of spying. When I came back to the village, I paid a visit to our family lawyer, and he told me what you did. Well, actually, he said a 'fine gentleman from London' bought out the lease and negotiated an outrageously low price for Hawthorne Cottage. It could only be you."

Rafe's hand fell away, and he sat back. "I tried to get Lionel to give it to you outright. I nearly thrashed him at our club. But he refused. Not without the promise of money. You weren't supposed to know," he added.

"Why ever not? Rafe, what you did for me—"

"Was only what your brother should have done," he insisted, then looked down. "I know how important this house is to you, but I don't want you to feel obligated to me in any way. Truly."

Sylvia slid off the chair and joined him on the floor. She pressed her palms against the sides of his face and forced him to look at her. "Is that what you think? That I would only want to be with you if I felt obliged?"

Christ, he sounded pathetic. "I don't know," he whispered. "I don't know what to think. I'm still working out how to be just myself. No false identities. No secret missions. Just plain old Rafe Davies."

Sylvia broke into a watery smile. "That makes two of us, then." She gently dragged her fingers through his hair and let out a thoughtful sigh. "You said earlier that everything that happened between us was real. Well, I have a confession of my own to make."

Rafe swallowed. "Oh?"

Sylvia leaned in close, until their noses touched. "It was real for me, too."

He squeezed his eyes shut for a moment to savor the feeling of his heart setting on fire. "All of it?"

"I'm afraid so." Sylvia wound her arms around his neck, and Rafe slid his hands up her back.

"Even the bit where you said I was perfect?"

"Oh, *especially* that." Sylvia then placed a soft kiss on the underside of his jaw, followed by another and another. "Though I wouldn't let that go to your head. Too much."

Rafe let out a soft groan as the scent and heat of her skin and the feel of her curves overwhelmed his senses. "Sylvia," he murmured as he glanced toward the closed door. "Where is your cook?"

"She left to buy provisions for supper. Tell me you'll stay?"

"Of course." Rafe then bit his lip. They were alone. "How long do you think she'll be gone for?"

"Oh, at least an hour. I told her to take her time," she purred by his ear.

Rafe immediately buried his hands in her hair and pulled her mouth against his in a rough, urgent kiss. He had absolutely no finesse around her. She reduced him to nothing but raw need. Sylvia matched his intensity, pressing into him with an eagerness that threatened his threadbare control. And his sanity. He tore his lips from hers.

"Not here?"

She shook his head, already focused on untying his necktie. "This is *my* house, and I can do whatever I like wherever I like." Then she looked up and arched a brow. "Will you deny the lady of Hawthorne Cottage?"

That impertinent tone of hers never failed to inflame him. "Heavens no. I would never." He pulled off his jacket, tossed it on the sofa, and then laid Sylvia down on the plush carpet in a sun-dappled spot. "But I wanted to go slow. Savor every breath. Taste every inch of your skin."

"Well, you can't," she sighed, already impatiently tugging

open the buttons of his waistcoat. "You'll just have to save that for next time."

Next time.

He couldn't stop grinning.

Sylvia paused and raised an eyebrow. "What's wrong? You look a bit deranged."

Rafe only grinned wider. "No. I'm just happy." He placed a kiss on her nose. "Deliriously, dementedly happy." He then began to gently nibble her earlobe before moving to suck the sensitive spot of skin just below it and Sylvia inhaled sharply. Rafe's cock strained against the fabric of his trousers as she pushed his waistcoat off his shoulders before dragging her hands down his suspenders. He pulled away just as she reached his waistband and sat back on his heels.

"Not yet. I have other plans for you," he murmured as he pushed up her skirt to her waist. He skated his palms up her legs and pressed her thighs wider.

Sylvia let out a startled gasp, but when Rafe met her gaze, she gave him an encouraging nod. Rafe smiled and leaned down, his fingers searching for the slit in her lacy drawers. "God, you're so lovely, Sylvia. Everywhere." She gave a little laugh of disbelief, which quickly turned into a surprised sigh as Rafe lightly stroked through her silky curls. "Do you not believe me?" he teased.

"No. I—I don't know," Sylvia breathed, disoriented by his touch.

Rafe continued until he found that sensitive bundle of nerves, and Sylvia cried out, arching her hips against his hand. He loved how responsive she was. "Do you like that, my little bird?"

"Yes," she gasped and pressed harder against him.

Rafe began to rub the spot in slow, torturous circles, and Sylvia squeezed her eyes shut, her hips chasing to meet his touch. He let out a dark laugh. "So impatient. As always." He then pressed a finger to her entrance. She was already so wet. Wet for *him*. He forced himself to go slow as he pressed one finger inside her, reveling in the soft moans she made, before he added another.

Sylvia cried out and grasped at his shoulders, but he swiftly pulled out of her. She made a noise of protest and opened her eyes in time to see Rafe bring his fingers to his lips and suck her essence from them. Her eyes widened in shock.

Good. Then no one had ever done that for her before.

"I'm afraid that isn't enough. I need more of your taste."

Sylvia watched in silence as Rafe leaned down and pressed her thighs even wider. "Open for me, my love." She obeyed immediately, and Rafe pressed his lips to her core. His little bird was as delightfully sensitive as ever, arching and twisting against his mouth. Rafe clamped his hands on her waist to hold her in place as he began to lick her delicate folds, and Sylvia practically sobbed his name. Then he gently raked his teeth across the nub of her sex before he began to suck on it, and she arched her back as her release thundered through her. He immediately pushed two fingers into her, reveling in her throbbing sex, and gently worked her until she came again. By then Sylvia's hands were fisted in his hair.

When he pulled away, she gazed up at him, flushed and spent. She then opened her thighs wider and tugged at his shirt. "Please. I need you," she panted.

It was just what he longed to hear.

Rafe tore open his trousers and fit his aching cock to her opening. She was already so wet. So ready for him. As he leaned over her, Sylvia's hands slid up under his shirt, stroking the muscles of his back and shoulders. She then hitched one leg up against his waist. Rafe reached down and took hold of himself, pressing slowly but relentlessly into her inviting warmth. Sylvia's light gasp set him on fire anew. Within moments he was fully sheathed inside her, but that wasn't enough. Rafe then hooked one hand under her knee to open her even more.

Sylvia's hands dragged down his back, and she grasped his bottom firmly, urging him even deeper. He muttered a curse. She gripped him as tight as a vise. With his other hand Rafe dug his nails into the fine pile of the carpet so hard he swore he would scrape the wood beneath. When he began to thrust, she looked him directly in the eyes, her rosebud mouth parted in pleasure.

"Yes," she gasped. "Just like that."

"I love it when you order me about," he said raggedly. "If you told me to go to hell, I'd do it just to please you."

Sylvia let out a soft laugh. "Let's hope it never comes to that."

Rafe thrust again and again, watching as her eyes fluttered shut and she tilted her head back. He wrapped his hand around the back of her slender neck and took her lips in a fierce kiss that nearly wrenched everything from him. Everything he had to give was now hers. Forever.

He suddenly tore his mouth away. "Say you're mine," he barked against the release barreling down on him.

Sylvia opened her eyes and looked deeply into his as she slowly pulled a hand through his hair. "I'm yours, Rafe," she murmured gently. "And you're mine."

That was all it took. Rafe groaned as he pulled out while the hardest release of his life washed over him. "Dammit,

Sylvia," he panted into her hair as he crushed her against him. "Goddammit." Rafe rolled onto his back beside her and stared blankly at the ceiling as the sparks from his release slowly faded. "I hope you weren't planning to rid yourself of me anytime soon," he began after he caught his breath and fixed his trousers. "I'd put up a hell of a fuss now." He glanced over, hoping his cavalier tone successfully hid his desperation.

Sylvia laughed and met his gaze. "No. I'm afraid we're stuck with each other."

Relief flooded through him. "Excellent." He smoothed her gown down and pulled her to his chest, where she readily nestled against him. It felt like the most natural thing in the world. Like they had been already doing this for years.

Rafe broke the pleasurable silence after a few minutes. There was more he still needed to say. "I read some of your columns. The ones I could find anyway."

She lifted her head. "You did?"

"They gave me much to think about. Things I had never really questioned before. I didn't agree with everything you wrote, but I appreciate your perspective."

"Well, then, I'll just have to do more to convince you," she said with a cheeky grin.

"I'm open to suggestions, especially if provided with the right incentive." Rafe waggled an eyebrow before he turned serious. "Have you thought about writing a column again?"

"Lord, no." Sylvia shook her head.

"You should. You've a powerful voice."

She relaxed back against him and was quiet for a long moment. "Do you really think so?"

Rafe smiled and kissed the top of her head. "I do. You have my full support, whatever you decide."

Sylvia tilted her face up to his and stroked his jaw. The wonder in her eyes nourished him more than ten banquets ever could. "Thank you. That means a great deal."

Rafe grasped her hand and kissed her knuckles. "Good. You'll soon get used to being adored by me."

Sylvia laughed again and ran a finger along his jaw. "No, Rafe," she began as she pulled him toward her for a kiss. "I don't think I ever will."

EPILOGUE

~

December 22nd, 1897
Monaco
Hotel Luna

O h my. You were a *chubby* baby!" Sylvia squealed with delight as she picked up the framed photo from the table.

Rafe shot her an unamused look as a faint flush crested his cheeks.

The Dowager Countess of Fairfield glided beside her to admire the photograph, a fond smile on her lips. She was a strikingly attractive woman—intimidating, really—with hair as dark as her son's and a pair of luminous blue eyes. It was easy to see how she had once commanded the stage. But she had warmly welcomed Sylvia when they arrived earlier at her suite to spend the holidays together. Sylvia had been a bundle of nerves from the moment they boarded the train in London, but Rafe had assured her that his mother was eager to meet her.

"She's been begging me to bring you over for *months* now."

Sylvia frowned in confusion. "Really? But we haven't even been together for that long." It had been only five weeks since their enthusiastic reunion on the floor of Hawthorne Cottage.

Rafe turned away shyly. "I may have mentioned you in

one of my letters from Castle Blackwood, long before I should have."

Sylvia had been unexpectedly moved by this admission and hadn't been able to put it out of her mind their entire trip.

Now the countess touched the frame with a perfectly manicured finger. "Oh, he was such a darling baby. And so sweet. *Everyone* adored him." Then she let out a mournful sigh. "I wish I had a whole gaggle of them."

"No, you don't," Rafe insisted. "Then you never would have played Aida. Or Cordelia. You would have been stuck at home with us and absolutely miserable."

The countess sighed again. "I suppose you're right." Then she turned to her son. "Did you ever resent me for not giving up my career? I've wondered..."

Rafe shook his head soundly. "Never. You were the best mother a boy could want." Then he grabbed her hand and gave it an affectionate squeeze before turning serious. "But promise me you won't show Sylvia any more pictures."

The countess pressed her hands to her chest. "But she must see the ones of you in your short pants with your pony."

Sylvia raised an eyebrow. "You had a *pony*?"

Rafe blushed again. "Only for a little while. When we lived in Greece."

"Named Baklava," the countess added. "His favorite food back then. Though the poor dear could barely say the word, so half the time he just called her Baki." Sylvia shared Lady Fairfield's delighted laugh. "Oh, it all passes by so quickly. Now look at you. I'm so glad you've come. The both of you."

"Yes, she's been planning activities for weeks now," Mahmood Previn, the owner of the spectacular Hotel Luna and the

Lady Fairfield's long-standing partner, said. "You'll have to stay at least a month."

"Oh, at *least*," the countess happily agreed as she slid her arm around Mahmood's, who gave her an indulgent smile. The French-Moroccan hotel magnate was about a decade older than the countess and tall and lean with a head of thick silver hair. Together they made an impossibly elegant pair.

On the journey over, Rafe explained that they had met a few years after his father's death.

"Was that difficult for you?" Sylvia had asked, but Rafe shook his head.

"Given my work at the time, it was a comfort to know she was well taken care of," he admitted.

Now Sylvia could see that for herself. The countess lived in a luxurious light-filled suite decorated in soothing hues of cream and lavender at the very top of Mr. Previn's finest hotel, which was nestled on a cliff overlooking the bustle of Monte Carlo. Guests flocked to the Hotel Luna for its breathtaking views of the Mediterranean, relaxing atmosphere, and unparalleled luxury, all while being just a short carriage ride away from the excitements of the city.

"I've an idea," the countess began, addressing Mr. Previn. "Why don't you take my son to see the new electric light system you've just had installed while Sylvia and I have tea on the terrace. It's so lovely out right now."

Rafe raised an eyebrow. "Trying to get rid of me already, Mama?"

"Of course not!" The countess waved a hand. "But Mahmood won't stop talking about it, and I reached my limit days and days ago. Perhaps you'll find it interesting."

"The man who developed it worked under Mr. Tesla," Mr. Previn added.

Rafe looked intrigued. "Oh, that does sound interesting. Lead the way."

Once they left, the countess turned to Sylvia and gave her a conspiratorial smile. "Whenever Rafe visits I always like to have them spend a little time alone together. I think it's good for them."

"Certainly."

The countess then rang for tea and led Sylvia out onto the terrace. Despite the season, the weather was much milder here than in London. The brilliant midday sun sparkled off the turquoise water, while the air was lightly scented with sea salt and citrus from the lemon trees that dotted the hotel's grounds.

"How marvelous," Sylvia breathed. "I can't imagine waking up to this view every morning."

"Yes. I've lived here for nearly ten years now, and it still takes my breath away," the countess agreed as she gracefully took her seat on a cushioned lavender chair.

Sylvia took the seat across from her, and the two made idle chitchat while they waited for tea. The countess asked about their journey and Sylvia's writing. Over the last month she had been helping the women's union launch a magazine and planned to pen a monthly column. Mrs. Crawford's publisher had also been impressed with her work, and she was considering several offers to assist other prominent people writing their memoirs.

"Perhaps you could help me!" the countess said excitedly.

Sylvia smiled. "That is tempting, my lady."

"Oh, please call me Cecily. I stopped with all that titled

nonsense when my husband passed. He never cared much for it either."

"He sounded like a wonderful man. Rafe speaks of him often."

"That's good," Cecily said softly. "My son was a young man when he died. It was a difficult age to lose his father. And I know he felt guilty because he was away at the time. And you lost your mother even younger?"

Sylvia nodded. "I was fourteen."

The countess gave her an understanding smile and patted her hand. "I was about that age when my own mother died."

Sylvia's throat began to tighten with emotion, but before she could respond, a very serious butler appeared with the tea cart. He removed several domed platters loaded with mouth-watering pastries each more beautiful than the last and poured them both a cup of tea. The countess then thanked him in French, and he gave a low bow before disappearing.

The countess selected a dainty chocolate Napoleon for herself while Sylvia chose a brightly colored framboise tart.

"Excellent choice," the countess said with a wink before sinking back into her chair with her dessert. "So then," she began without preamble. "Rafe says you don't believe in marriage." Sylvia nearly choked on her tart, but there was no censure in the countess's tone or gaze. "I'm not judging you," she added quickly. "Mahmood has proposed half a dozen times. But at our age, I don't see the point."

Sylvia took a long sip of tea to buy herself time to formulate an answer.

In truth, she and Rafe had yet to discuss the particulars of their relationship or the future.

She had been busy these last few weeks finishing Mrs.

Crawford's memoirs before she left for Egypt, Georgiana having decided to accompany her in Sylvia's place. And though the newspapers had been full of stories about Mr. Wardale's death, none had mentioned either of them.

Rafe had still suggested going abroad a few times for their own enjoyment, but nothing had been decided, and there was Hawthorne Cottage to consider. The only thing they both knew for certain was that they wanted to be together.

That hadn't changed, but Sylvia also hadn't realized it could be like this. Hadn't understood that another person could possess such a capacity to love her while also giving her the space to be herself. Over these last few weeks, Sylvia recognized that she needed Rafe in a way that would have once terrified her. Because she hadn't known that with such a need also came strength. Rebirth. She had come to reimagine everything about her life. A life she now shared with Rafe. And together they had chosen one another again and again. Every day since that afternoon at Hawthorne Cottage. But it no longer felt like enough.

She met the countess's eyes. "Women have to give up so much to their husbands in marriage. I've always believed they should approach the institution with great caution."

The countess nodded. "You're smart to think that way. Frankly, I got lucky in marrying Rafe's father. He was so different from every other man I had met. He appreciated having a partner." She then hesitated for a moment. "I'd like to think we instilled those same values in our son."

Sylvia ducked her head. "You have."

When she looked up, the countess was giving her a knowing smile as if she could read her thoughts. "Good." She then smoothly changed the subject. When the gentlemen rejoined them an hour later, they were laughing together like old friends.

Rafe smiled widely as he sat beside Sylvia. "Having fun?" he asked as he reached for an apple tart.

"Yes, we were enjoying getting to know one another."

"*And* talking of the future," the countess added, making no attempt to minimize her innuendo.

Rafe cleared his throat and seemed uncharacteristically nervous for a moment. He avoided Sylvia's questioning gaze and instead took a large bite of tart.

The countess then turned to Mahmood. "Why don't we give these two time to relax while we check on their rooms. I want to make sure everything is perfect."

They would be staying in another suite in the hotel. As eccentric as the countess was, she had still insisted that Rafe and Sylvia maintain separate rooms, though they shared a connecting door.

"Splendid idea, *ma chéri*," Mahmood agreed. They then said their goodbyes, and within a few moments Sylvia and Rafe were alone on the terrace.

He still wasn't looking at her, having now taken great interest in his teacup.

"Rafe," she began as she smoothed a hand on his sleeve. He finally glanced up, and she nearly lost her nerve at the wariness in his gaze, but then she took a breath and plowed ahead. "After talking with your mother, there's something I want to say to you."

He frowned, his confusion replacing whatever else he was feeling. "Oh?"

Sylvia nodded. "I know in the past I said I wasn't interested in marriage. And for a long time that was the truth. But I had only been thinking of what I stood to lose. Now, though, I see that I've much to gain as well. And I want that. With you." She said this all while looking just past his shoulder, at the glittering sea. When she finally found the nerve to meet his eyes, he looked pained. It was not exactly the reaction she had hoped for. A hot flush spread across her chest, and her nose began to sting. She had misread this entirely.

Rafe noticed her disappointment and moved closer to cup her cheek. "My love, you honor me."

"Then why do you look like someone has just killed your pony?" she managed to ask.

Rafe chuckled. "It's not what you think. I promise. But first I want you to know that I heard from Gerard before we left. I've been offered the chance to work in the German ambassador's office. In Berlin."

Sylvia's mouth went dry. "What will you do?"

Rafe's gaze turned thoughtful. "I think this could be a good opportunity. I saw the kind of work my father was able to do. The changes he could enact through his influence."

Sylvia bit her lip. Though Rafe claimed he had no regrets over his decision to resign from his post, even she could see that he had been rudderless ever since. As his cover was no longer needed, he had removed himself from the social whirl of London. But a man with his energy would not be content to spend *every* evening by the fire. Rafe needed a purpose.

"I know how you feel about this government," he continued. "And I share your concerns. I can't promise that there won't be times of trouble, but I'd like to think that with you there beside me, I can make a meaningful difference—we can do it together. And I don't see why you couldn't continue your writing. It could make for an interesting subject, the fight for women's rights abroad."

"You...you told Gerard you wanted *me* with you?"

Rafe nodded. "I said I couldn't make my decision until I asked you something. And if I got the answer I wanted, you would be coming with me. That was nonnegotiable. But it's really up to you." He then reached into his vest pocket and pulled out a small velvet box. Sylvia's breath caught. "I've been carrying it around for days, trying to work up the nerve. I should have known you'd beat me to it," he added proudly.

Sylvia reached out and ran her fingers over the velvet surface. "Can I see it?"

Rafe laughed again. "I hope you'll do far more than that." He opened the box, and Sylvia gasped at the large diamond cluster nestled inside. "It was my mother's engagement ring. You don't mind, do you?"

"Of course not," Sylvia heard herself say, as she was still rather gobsmacked by the sight of the impressive bauble.

"Can I take your dazed reaction as a yes?"

She met Rafe's eyes and managed a smirk. "Excuse me, but you still haven't responded to *my* proposal."

"Terribly sorry. My deepest apologies," he said as he removed the ring from the box. "Of course I will marry you, my little bird. A thousand times over." Rafe then moved to place it on her finger and paused, raising an eyebrow. "Well, what do you say? Are you ready for a new adventure?"

"Always." Sylvia grinned as he slid it on her finger. "Especially with you," she added before pulling Rafe toward her to seal it with a kiss.

AUTHOR'S NOTE

As *The Rebel and the Rake* is set in 1897, I thought it might be interesting to include some background to provide more context to this fascinating time period:

Early on in the novel Rafe refers to Sylvia as a "New Woman." This term originated in the early 1890s and was used to refer to the growing population of independent, educated women who challenged ideas of Victorian femininity. Uninterested in the traditional paths of marriage and motherhood, these women found meaning outside the sphere of domesticity. They came to London to work while also engaging in artistic pursuits and social or political activism. Though many saw the wisdom in women being able to earn a living and an education, the New Woman was also a target of ridicule for adopting so-called "masculine" behaviors like smoking or cycling. One can find many examples in contemporary literature of the time both commending and condemning this movement.

This growing acceptance of female independence also coincided with a loosening of sexual mores, and the last decade of the 19th century is sometimes referred to as the "naughty nineties." However, toeing the line between the public and private self could be dangerous for many women and men.

Even those who frequented Bohemian circles could still find themselves the subject of scandal if their affairs were made public. And with few protections for workers, let alone female workers, they could be dismissed from their jobs and turned out of their homes with little recourse.

The Aurelias Society is based on the Fabian Society, a socialist political group that was founded in 1884 and popular with London intellectuals. George Bernard Shaw, H. G. Wells, Emmeline Pankhurst, E. Nesbit, and Charlotte Wilson—a self-described anarchist and one of the models for Sylvia— were all members at various times. However, much like Sylvia, many female members were frustrated by the group's reluctance to engage meaningfully with women's suffrage and their role in a swiftly changing society, referred to as the "Women's Question." This led to the formation of the Fabian Women's Group in 1908, but even then, little headway was made and some female members left the group entirely. Notably, Emmeline Pankhurst went on to found the Women's Social and Political Union (WSPU) in 1903, which famously adopted more militant tactics to win the vote. Even still, it took until 1928 for the United Kingdom to grant all women twenty-one and over the right to vote.

Don't miss Henry and Georgiana's love story in the next thrilling League of Scoundrels story

Available summer 2022

ABOUT THE AUTHOR

EMILY SULLIVAN is an award-winning author of historical fiction set in the late Victorian period. She lives in New England with her adorable baby and slightly less adorable husband. She enjoys taking long drives, and short walks, and always orders dessert.

You can learn more at:
Website: https://www.emilysullivanbooks.com
Twitter: @paperbacklady
Instagram: Paperbacklady

*Get swept off your feet by charming dukes,
sharp-witted ladies, and scandalous balls in
Forever's historical romances!*

THE PERKS OF LOVING A WALLFLOWER
by Erica Ridley

As a master of disguise, Thomasina Wynchester can be a polite young lady—or a bawdy old man. Anything to solve the case—which this time requires masquerading as a charming baron. Her latest assignment unveils a top-secret military cipher covering up an enigma that goes back centuries. But Tommy's beautiful new client turns out to be the reserved, high-born bluestocking Miss Philippa York, with whom she's secretly smitten. As they decode clues and begin to fall for each other in the process, the mission—as well as their hearts—will be at stake...

Discover bonus content and more on read-forever.com

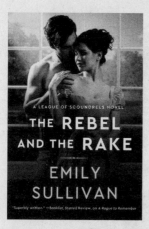

THE REBEL AND THE RAKE
by Emily Sullivan

Though most women would be thrilled to catch the eye of a tall, dark, and dangerously handsome rake like Rafe Davies, Miss Sylvia Sparrow trusted the wrong man once and paid for it dearly. The fiery bluestocking is resolved to avoid Rafe, until a chance encounter reveals the man's unexpected depths—and an attraction impossible to ignore. But once Sylvia suspects she isn't the only one harboring secrets, she realizes that Rafe may pose a risk to far more than her heart…

WEST END EARL
by Bethany Bennett

While most young ladies attend balls and hunt for husbands, Ophelia Hardwick has spent the past ten years masquerading as a man. As the land steward for the Earl of Carlyle, she's found safety from the uncle determined to kill her and the freedoms of which a lady could only dream. Ophelia's situation would be perfect—if she wasn't hopelessly attracted to her employer…

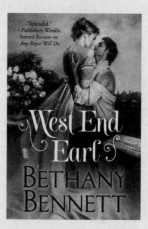

A LADY'S GUIDE TO MISCHIEF AND MAYHEM
by Manda Collins

The widowed Lady Katherine eschews society's "good" opinion to write about crimes against women. But when her reporting jeopardizes an investigation, attractive Detective Inspector Andrew Eversham criticizes her interference. Before Kate can make amends, she stumbles upon another victim—in the same case. With their focus on the killer, neither is prepared for the other risk the case poses—to their hearts.

A DUKE WORTH FIGHTING FOR
by Christina Britton

Margery Kitteridge has been mourning her husband for years, and while she's not ready to consider marriage again, she does miss intimacy with a partner. When Daniel asks for help navigating the Isle of Synne's social scene and they accidentally kiss, she realizes he's the perfect person with whom to have an affair. As they begin to confide in each other, Daniel discovers that he's unexpectedly connected to Margery's late husband, and she will have to decide if she can let her old love go for the promise of a new one.

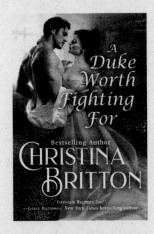

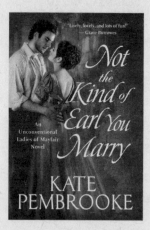

NOT THE KIND OF EARL YOU MARRY
by Kate Pembrooke

When William Atherton, Earl of Norwood, learns of his betrothal in the morning paper, he's furious that the shrewd marriage trap could affect his political campaign. Until he realizes that a fake engagement might help rather than harm...Miss Charlotte Hurst may be a wallflower, but she's no shrinking violet. She would never attempt such an underhanded scheme, especially not with a man as haughty or sought-after as Norwood. And yet...the longer they pretend, the more undeniably real their feelings become.

A NIGHT WITH A ROGUE
(2-in-1 Edition)
by Julie Anne Long

Enjoy these two stunning, sensual historical romances! In *Beauty and the Spy*, when odd accidents endanger London darling Susannah Makepeace, who better than Viscount Kit Whitelaw, the best spy in His Majesty's secret service, to unravel the secrets threatening her? In *Ways to Be Wicked*, a chance to find her lost family sends Parisian ballerina Sylvie Lamoureux fleeing across the English Channel—and into the arms of the notorious Tom Shaughnessy. Can she trust this wicked man with her heart?

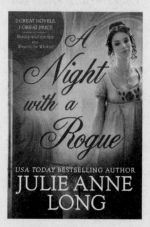